"PREPARE TO BE SPELLBOUND."
—#1 *New York Times* Bestselling Author
Sherrilyn Kenyon

PRAISE FOR THE EDGE NOVELS

"Full of action-packed adventure, secrets, betrayal, and powerful love refusing to be denied. Pure genius!"
—Fresh Fiction

"A page-turner." —Night Owl Reviews

"An exciting new series. . . . By delivering a dynamic thriller that only peels back the first layer in a mystery, Butcher ensures that fans will be desperate to get their hands on the next installment. Terrific!" —*RT Book Reviews*

"An emotional roller-coaster ride." —The Reading Cafe

PRAISE FOR
THE SENTINEL WARS NOVELS

"Amazing and dramatic . . . heart pounding [and] heartbreaking." —The Reading Cafe

"A wonderful paranormal debut. . . . Shannon K. Butcher's talent shines."
—*New York Times* bestselling author Nalini Singh

"You'll be thrilled, entertained, enamored, and when it's all done, you'll be begging . . . for more." —Fresh Fiction

"There's only one way to describe this book to me: fabulous!" —Night Owl Reviews

"You are always guaranteed generous portions of pulse-pounding action and romance in a Butcher tale!"
—Romantic Times

"Keeps you hooked till the end." —Smexy Books

"An entertaining and thrilling series." —Fresh Fiction

ROUGH EDGES

AN EDGE NOVEL

SHANNON K. BUTCHER

A SIGNET ECLIPSE BOOK

SIGNET ECLIPSE
Published by New American Library,
an imprint of Penguin Random House LLC
375 Hudson Street, New York, New York 10014
This book is an original publication of New American Library.

First Printing, August 2015

For more information about Penguin Random House, visit penguinrandomhouse.com.

ISBN 978-0-451-46617-4

Printed in the United States of America
10 9 8 7 6 5 4 3 2 1

Penguin
Random
House

For Jayne, the best cheerleader ever.

Chapter One

Dallas, Texas, April 28

After two weeks of sleepless nights, little food and end-less hours spent working beside a man who lit her li-bido up like the surface of the sun, Bella Bayne wanted nothing more than a little quality time with her vibrator and a solid eight hours of shut-eye. In that order. Instead, what she got was the man of her fantasies—highly inappro-priate ones at that—standing on her front porch, making her mouth water far more than the fragrant bags of Indian food he was toting.

"Thought you might be too tired to cook," said Victor Temple, the most perfectly formed male of any species ever created.

He stood a few inches over her five-foot-ten-inch frame, blocking out the streetlight behind him. He had aristo-cratic features that were made more interesting by the three scars decorating his face. They were small, but broke up the sea of masculine beauty enough that she could look at him without sunglasses to mask the glare of perfection. His dark blond hair was cut with military precision, falling in line exactly as he pleased. After sev-eral missions with this man, she'd learned he defied the laws of helmet hair in a way she still couldn't understand. Blood pact with dark forces, no doubt.

His clothes were casual, but neat and extremely high-end. Victor came from money. Old, refined, nose-in-the-air money, yet she'd never once seen him flaunt it. No diamond cuff links, flashy cars, or pricey watches for this man. No, Victor Temple had way more substance than that, which was another reason she wished he was anywhere else than standing on her front porch. It was his substance combined with those stunning good looks that made him dangerous to her professional ethics.

"Hungry?" he asked.

Bella was hungry, but not for what was in those sacks. If not for the fact that she was Victor's boss, she would have feasted on him weeks ago. But her strict no-fraternization policy meant she had to keep her hands and mouth off. Way off.

"You should be at home asleep," she said, forcing censure into her tone. "If you think I'm giving you the day off tomorrow so a pretty boy like you can get his beauty rest, you're wrong."

"I slept more than you did while we were away. And when one comes bearing gifts, Bella, it's customary for the receiver to at least pretend to be gracious."

"Sweetheart, I don't like pretending. And I'm not gracious."

He smiled as if he found her amusing. "Only because you're hungry, which I have learned over the past few weeks makes you cranky. Now step aside, Bella. I'm coming in to feed you. Then we have to talk."

Talk? At this hour? That couldn't mean good news.

He didn't give her time to move. Instead, he stepped forward, and she had no choice but to step back or feel his body collide with hers. As nice as his body was, as off-limits as it was, she wasn't sure she'd survive the crash without tossing him to the carpet and riding him until she got off. At least twice. Maybe then she wouldn't be so cranky.

"Talk about what?" she asked as he strode past her like he owned her home, heading unerringly to a kitchen he'd never before even seen, much less navigated.

"It can wait until after food."

His clean scent lingered on the air around him, crossing her path and making her drag in a deep breath to capture it. For a moment, the urge to bury her nose against his chest took over and she forgot all about why she didn't want him here. She had to shake herself to get her brain working again. "You're *my* employee in *my* home, honey. If I tell you to talk now, then that's what you'll do."

He glanced over his shoulder at her, daring to give her a grin. "I'm off the clock. You can't order me around. Deal with it."

Fury struck her for a second before it turned to lust. She had no idea what it was about this man. She was the owner of a private security firm. She worked with badass men all day long, every day. None of them had ever held her interest for longer than it took her to flatten them in the sparring ring.

But Victor Temple was different. He got under her skin and made it burn. It didn't matter that he was her subordinate, or that he was on loan from the US government to help her deal with a situation of nightmarish proportions. She couldn't seem to be near him without wishing they were both naked, panting and sweating.

Maybe it had something to do with the one and only time she'd taken him on in hand-to-hand combat practice. They'd both been panting and sweating then, and while they hadn't been naked, she was acutely aware of just how skilled he was. How perfectly built he was. Not overblown or bulging with showy bulk, his big frame was instead wrapped with sleek, functional muscles that rippled with power. She'd fought bigger men than him and won, but only Victor had been able to pin her to the mat.

She was a strong, independent, kick-ass woman, but even she had to admit she liked that in a man.

"I was half hoping you wouldn't answer the door—that you'd be asleep," he said.

"I needed to unwind a bit first."

He lifted a wayward lock of damp hair that had escaped her haphazard ponytail. Only then did she realize just how close he was standing. Too close.

"Shower didn't do the trick?" he asked.

No, but her vibrator would have if he hadn't shown up. After all the time she'd spent with him recently, she wondered if she'd still be able to keep his face out of her fantasies. "There's a heavy bag in the garage. A little time with that would have worn me out."

He stepped away, leaving her feeling adrift for a second before she caught up with reality. She could not be drawn to Victor. She had to lead by example, and fucking her employee on the kitchen floor whether or not he wanted it was not the kind of tone she wanted to set for her workplace.

"You're worried about Gage, aren't you?" He glanced over his shoulder as he washed his hands. Muscles shifted beneath his tight T-shirt, adding fuel to the naughty fantasies she already had of this man.

Her gaze slid past him to the window over the sink. She didn't want him to see how appealing he was to her. Even more than that, she didn't want him to see her fear for Gage, who had willingly walked into the hands of a monster in the hopes of taking her down for good. No one had heard from him since. Bella had to stay tough, appear confident and provide leadership to her men. That included Victor.

She straightened her spine. "Gage has been gone for

weeks. He was ordered to make contact with me as soon as he could. The fact that he hasn't is more than a little concerning. Sweetheart, any sane person would be worried."

Victor turned back around to her as he dried his hands. A flicker of sympathy crossed his features, making him even harder to resist. "He's smart. And tough. I'm sure his silence is a sign that he's working an angle with Stynger, not that he's in trouble."

"Easy for you to say. You weren't the one who sent him into that crazy bitch's hands."

"He volunteered for the job. He knew exactly what he was doing when he let her men take him into custody."

"He did it to save Adam from taking his place. I know Gage. The second he learned that Adam was his brother, his decision was made."

"Are you saying that he wouldn't have volunteered if it wasn't to save Adam?" asked Victor.

"No, he was on board the whole time, but now that he knows he has a brother, there's no telling what kind of sacrifice he's making to keep Adam safe."

Victor stepped closer, easing into her personal space like he belonged there. "There's more at stake here than one man. Gage knows that. He's smart enough to realize that the only true way to keep Adam safe is to take Stynger down for good."

"That's part of what worries me. It's personal for Gage. If he gets the chance to kill Stynger, he'll do it. Even if it means sacrificing himself." Maybe he already had, and that was why no one had heard from him.

Victor must have read her mind. "He's still alive, Bella. You have to believe that." He came toward her, compassion shining in his bright eyes. One lean, hard hand was extended. She knew he meant to offer comfort, but she was too fragile for that right now. She had to stay strong, stay tough. As tired as she was, as worried as she was, it would be too easy for her to crack under the strain and let her emotions run free. One touch from him might be all it took to shatter her self-control.

She hadn't cried in years—not since the night she killed her husband in a blind rage—she wasn't about to start now.

Bella moved away before he could reach her. "I'm sure he's alive," she lied. "I'm also sure we'll find him soon. I just have to keep looking and stay vigilant for even the smallest signs of his whereabouts. We've been on enough missions together that I know how he thinks."

Victor's hand fell to his side. "You'll be a lot more vigilant after you get some food and sleep. You know him better than any of us. If we're going to see some obscure sign he left behind, you're the one most likely to spot it. But only if you're not exhausted."

She gave him a pointed stare. "I'd sleep better without one of my men in my kitchen, honey."

"When was the last time you ate?"

She couldn't remember, but that didn't make him right. "If it's that important to you, then feed me already so we can get to whatever it is you need to talk about. I'm wrung out."

"Maybe the talk should wait until tomorrow."

"I'm busy tomorrow. Talk now."

"I don't think so. Your blood sugar is too low for my peace of mind. It'll only take a minute to warm up the food."

She watched him move around her kitchen, opening cabinets and finding what he was looking for. The smell of curry filled the room, making her stomach rumble.

He set a plate of food in the microwave, pushed some buttons. Nothing happened. He frowned as he checked to make sure it was plugged in. "It's not working."

Bella went to his side and tried to make the appliance

go with no luck. "Sorry. It's one of the few kitchen tools I know how to use. I must have worn it out."

"No worries. We have other options." He opened her oven door and pulled out her box of business receipts, staring at them as if they might bite. "You keep paperwork in your oven?"

"It's a handy spot. Nothing blows away when I open the windows."

"What about when you cook?"

She laughed. "Honey, I work eighty-hour weeks, minimum. I spend more than half of my time out of the country, run a reputable business where lives are on the line every day, and you think I have time to cook? You're adorable."

A blush brightened his cheeks and made his glacier blue eyes stand out. She knew he was a poster boy for the military, all upright and honorable, but there was something about the clarity of his eyes that really sold the whole look. She swore she could see right through him, like he had nothing to hide.

No one was that honorable. Especially not her.

"Does your oven even work?" he asked.

Bella shrugged. "Who knows? Never tried it."

He turned a knob to get the gas-fueled contraption working. She probably should have been paying attention to how he operated it, but all she could concentrate on was the way his fingers gently gripped the knob, giving it the slightest twist.

Her nipples puckered in response.

After a few seconds, his brow scrunched up as he turned the knob again. "Your pilot light's out."

"I didn't want to set my receipts on fire. The IRS frowns on excuses like that during an audit."

"Got any matches?"

She pulled a lighter from her junk drawer and handed

it to him. He knelt down, making his jeans go tight over a manly ass that looked like it was carved by God himself. She was so busy admiring him, she barely heard his question.

"Did you move the oven out recently?"

Bella shook her head to get it set on straight again. "Why on earth would I do that?"

"To clean under it."

She grinned. "So adorable. I just want to pinch your cheeks." His ass cheeks, if she had her choice.

"Right. Got it. You don't clean, either."

"I have a housekeeper who comes in once a month to keep the place livable."

"When was she here last?"

"I don't know. While we were gone sometime. Why?"

He pointed to some crumbs on her floor next to a rusty brown smudge line, his face taut with concern. "Scuff marks. Someone's moved your oven."

Before she had time to follow why he was upset by her oven's position, he turned on a flashlight app on his phone and shone it back behind the oven.

"Bella," he said, his tone that same eerie calm he got during a firefight. "Turn around and walk out the way I came in. Don't touch anything."

Serious worry settled in between her arousal and fatigue. "What's going on?"

He took her arm and forced her to start walking. "Someone tied what looks like an explosive device into your gas line. Time to go and call the bomb squad from outside."

Chapter Two

Randolph eyed Dr. Norma Stynger with caution as he entered her stark white office. She was dressed in a clinging black sheath dress and a white lab coat that did little to hide the bony lines of her aging body. She sat behind her white desk with a backdrop of white walls and a white tile floor surrounding her. The only color in the room was a worn, singed, brown leather journal and the bright red lipstick that made her mouth look like a bloody gash in her face.

She looked up at him, and the cold emptiness of her eyes hit him like a brick launched from a cannon. He let out a whoosh of air and struggled for his next breath.

"You're late," she snapped, her tone waspish.

Randolph knew better than to show fear. Dr. Stynger was dangerous in a way that was hard to predict, much less understand. His instincts had started shrieking the second he'd laid eyes on her, and over the past few weeks he'd come to realize that even that shrill warning hadn't been loud enough.

He was always only one mistake away from having a hole drilled in his skull and electrodes shoved into his brain. It didn't matter that he was tough as hell, deadly with just about any weapon ever built, and ruthless in combat. One snap of the freaky doctor's bony fingers and he'd wake up a puppet, like all of the other tough guys here.

Randolph forced out a nonchalant shrug, keeping his expression flat. "Traffic."

Her eyes narrowed, and even that tiny movement was enough to make his blood run cold.

"Is the job done?" she asked.

"It is. I put the drug in her hot water tank, just like you wanted."

"And the explosives?"

"A woman like that doesn't bake brownies. You should have let me rig the device to something she was going to use."

"Adrenaline is necessary to initiate the chemical reaction of the drug. The threat needed to be real enough to create fear and paranoia, but not deadly. If she's blown into a thousand pieces, not only do I lose an opportunity to see if the new drug works, it's going to be much harder to autopsy her brain once I'm done with her."

"You'd be better off taking her out. I used to work at the Edge. She keeps that place running. Without her, the whole structure crumbles and all the people searching for you go find new jobs."

Stynger stood, and it was all Randolph could do not to back away. "I only need a little more time. Once the island facility is finished, they'll never find me. If Ms. Bayne is killed, her men will never stop looking for the person responsible for her death. It's possible they could assume it was me, even after you parted company with Ms. Bayne on such unfriendly terms."

He'd been fired. One little mistake and she'd cut him loose. No one was even going to miss the kid he'd accidentally killed. She'd been a street rat, worthless. Certainly not worth losing his job over. Considering the dusty, poverty-stricken hole she'd lived in, he'd probably been doing her a favor by putting her out of her misery.

Bella had seen things differently. With the clout she had in the industry, Randolph hadn't been able to find work since. At least not until Stynger's job offer came along.

Then it had hit him. Stynger had hired him *because* of his unhappy ties to Bella. The good doctor had set him up to take the fall if things went wrong, and it was only now that he realized how she'd set him up. *He'd* drugged Bella's water supply. *He'd* rigged an explosive device in her house. Even as careful as he'd been there could still be some piece of evidence tracing him back to the job. Some camera that recorded him near her home. If anything happened to her, her people would find it. And then they'd find him.

"You knew they'd come after me, didn't you?" he asked, barely keeping his anger in check.

"I have no doubt that I'll be blamed eventually, but by then I'll be out of reach, hidden and protected by my gracious benefactors. And their army."

Randolph had been played. The money she'd offered him was too good to be true. He should have known not to make a deal with the devil. There was no love lost between him and Bella, but he'd been an idiot to let his fury for the woman who fired him drown out his better judgment.

Too late now. His only hope was to move forward and do whatever it took to keep Stynger from eating him alive. Because as deadly as the men and women who worked for the Edge were, not one of them was anywhere near as soulless and evil as the woman standing in front of him. All that would happen to him if Bella's men found him was he'd be killed. If Stynger turned her wrath on him, he'd pray for death.

"What do you want me to do now?" he asked.

The red slash of her lips curved up in a smile. "Just a little errand. It's nothing, really."

Chapter Three

Bella didn't call the authorities as Victor had hoped. Instead, she called in one of her employees who knew his way around explosives. Within thirty minutes, the device was disarmed and her house was being searched for other unpleasant surprises by a crew of people skilled enough to ease some of the tension radiating down through Victor's limbs.

If he hadn't seen the device, there was no way to know how long it would have stayed there, ready to blow. The fact that it hadn't detonated when he tried to turn on the oven was a small miracle. Just the idea of it happening while Bella was home was enough to make him sweat.

Then again, Victor had spent the past several weeks sweating, constantly worried about a woman who would likely rather break his nose than welcome his concern. She took too many risks with herself while proactively guarding her employees. She was impatient. Impulsive. Sometimes even a bit reckless. And sexy as hell.

He knew better than to stare, but he couldn't help himself once her back was turned. She had the body of an Amazonian princess—tall, lean, with just the right balance of softness to round out the rough edges that made her the tough, kick-ass chick she needed to be to do her job.

Tonight her black hair was damp from her recent shower, pulled up in a messy ponytail that made a man think about how it might have gotten into such tangled disarray. Friction from rubbing against bed sheets? Or a wall? A man's fingers gripping her hair while he pulled her head back, taking her from behind? In every scenario he imagined, he was the one mussing his boss, and that was way out of line.

Not that his body gave a damn that she was his boss. No, his body wanted him to take her, claim her. Make her his in the most primal, uncivilized way possible. Over and over.

Victor's very civilized, cultured parents would have been scandalized by the thoughts going through their son's head. They had dreams for him that involved political office, exclusive charity galas and buildings named in his honor. His respect for them ran so deep, he'd never once thought about not following the path they had laid out before him.

Until Bella.

She wasn't at all the kind of woman a man like him dated. No connections. No vast wealth. No pedigree.

No hidden agendas.

Mom and Dad would hate her on sight. Maybe that was part of what made her so appealing—a youthful rebellion arriving twenty years too late.

The clingy black yoga pants and thin gray T-shirt she wore highlighted her curves, rather than hiding them. In the glow of her front porch light, he could see that her feet were bare, her toes tipped in a glossy hot pink polish that seemed completely out of place next to the weapon strapped to her hip. Her gun was the only thing she'd insisted on taking out with her that wasn't already attached to her body. Not her purse, cash, keys or ID. Just her Glock.

He kept a close eye on her, making sure she didn't do

something stupid like run back inside to disarm the bomb
herself. Instead, she sat on the hood of her truck, her hot
pink toes propped on the front bumper. Tension radiated
through her sleek body, and the promise of retribution
was in her gaze as she stared at her front door.

"Any idea who did it?" he asked, taking up a position
next to her knee. If she jumped down, it wouldn't take
much for him to grab her around the waist and restrain her.

He guessed that letting go, however, would have
taken considerably more effort.

A large part of him hoped she would stay true to her
impulsive nature and charge into the house just so he
could have an excuse to manhandle her.

The one time he'd had his hands on her for sparring
practice, it had been all he could do not to kiss her once
he'd had her pinned beneath him. To this day he still
wondered how she would have reacted. Would she have
thrashed his ass and aimed a gun at his head for daring
to take advantage? Or would she have welcomed his ad-
vance, melting beneath him in a way that had his balls
tightening just imagining it? Sadly, his opportunity to
find out was gone now. Lost.

"There is a long list of people who want me dead," she
said, answering his question with a shrug. "Once we analyze the tech, we'll be able to shorten that list."

"How long is long?"

"I've pissed off a lot of powerful, spiteful people over
the years. Good thing they were too stupid to know I
couldn't cook or I'd be charcoal by now."

The thought made some dark, feral part of him raise
its head. "You knew you were in danger and didn't have
your house swept for devices before you came home?"

"I did. Either the crew missed it, or the bad guy did
the job this afternoon, after the crew left."

"How much time did the intruder have between the
sweep and when you got home?"

She swung her foot, distracting him with the shiny polish and her pretty toes. "A few hours. The crew doing the sweeps had the rest of the team's homes to do. Including yours."

"Why not have them do your place last?" he asked. "You're the biggest target, being the head of the company."

Her tone was distracted, and her gaze held on the front door with absolute focus, as if she could will the cleanup team to come out faster. "I don't have family since I disowned Payton. Not as many people would miss me as would miss the rest of the team. The bigger window of time is a calculated risk I'm willing to take to protect my people."

Victor's body tensed at her casual dismissal of her safety. He tried not to let his anger at her recklessness invade his tone, but failed. "Next time I'm checking your place out myself before you step so much as one pink toenail inside your front door."

She slid from the truck in a single, controlled move. Feminine muscles rippled under her skin, and the scent of ripe berries flowed around her damp hair. She faced him, hands on her hips as she got right up in his personal space.

It took all his willpower to not grab her hips and drag her body up against his. Only the look of hostility on her beautiful face helped him hold his position. "If you think I need you to protect little ol' me, baby cakes, then I'm going to have to fire you."

"Why?"

"Because I don't work with stupid people, honey. I may be a lot of things, but weak and helpless aren't anywhere on the list. Or haven't you heard about my past?"

Victor had heard rumors. And ignored them. "Office gossip doesn't interest me. Your safety, however, does."

"You were raised with genteel manners, so I'll forgive

you the slipup, but you'll be happier if you don't question my capability again. Especially not where my men can hear you."

"Your men are inside your house. They can't hear a thing."

"Franklin," she called without raising her voice.

A second later, a young man with wing-nut ears, a crooked nose and an eager-to-please vibe poked his head out of her front door. "Yes, ma'am."

Bella gave Victor a look that screamed *I told you so*. "How's progress?"

"The device is disarmed and removed. We're packing it up now for analysis."

"And the rest of the house?" she asked.

"Clean, ma'am. And I fixed your microwave."

Franklin went back inside. Bella grinned, obviously pleased with herself for showing up Victor. "Kid's got good ears. Handy as hell with tech, too."

"So what now?" he asked.

"I go back inside and go to bed. You do the same."

His eyebrows went up at the idea of going to bed with her. A thrill of excitement surged through him, settling in his cock, and it began to swell with eagerness.

"Your own bed," she hurried to say.

"What about dinner? And our conversation?"

"The conversation you can have, at least for as long as it takes the team to clear out. After that, you'll have to make an appointment with Lila to meet with me some-time this week."

Victor had been with Bella every day for two weeks, searching for signs of Gage or the hidden lab of a crazy scientist who needed to be put down like the rabid ani-mal she was. Sure, there had been other people on the team with them, making the task less intimate, but he'd still felt like they'd grown closer—close enough that he didn't need an appointment to see her.

Apparently he'd been wrong.

Victor covered his irritation and disappointment. She was his boss. He had a job to do, both for her, and for General Norwood, to whom he owed his life half a dozen times over. Whatever it took to complete this assignment of taking down Dr. Norma Stynger, he'd do. Even if it meant controlling his inappropriate feelings for the woman of his dreams.

"Payton asked me to speak to you," he said. "You have to stop ignoring him."

"Like hell." Bella held up her hand. There was a small cut along her palm. Victor wanted to pull her hand to his mouth and kiss away her hurt so badly he had to clench his fists to keep from reaching for her.

"You have to deal with him. He's part of this whole mess."

Fury burned in her gray eyes, turning them the color of cold steel and hot ash. "He *caused* this whole mess, sweetheart. He was there from the beginning, helping drag kids in for those experiments. He covered his tracks. Hid the truth. From all of us. Don't sit there and tell me I have to deal with him. He's lucky I don't simply put a bullet in his skull for the betterment of mankind in general."

She lurched forward, toward the house with the bomb still inside. Victor grabbed her wrist and pulled hard enough to make her turn to face him. "He's trying to make up for what he did."

Anger was a living, breathing thing inside her. He could see it coursing just under her skin, tinting it a dark, furious red. "There is no making up for mistakes that big. What he did was intentional. He hurt *children*. Took them from their families. He used them."

She was hurting, and the wild feelings of anger and ferocity that evoked in him were barely controlled by his sympathy for the woman who stood before him now. He kept his voice calm and quiet, stayed as far away from pity as he could. Bella wasn't the kind of woman who would react well to pity, no matter how well placed it might be. The children of the Threshold Project had been used as lab rats, subjected to experimental drugs and brainwashing protocols that were designed to alter them in fundamental ways. Permanently. Bella loved people who'd been part of that, and that made her as dangerous as those who had hurt those kids. "Who did you lose, Bella?"

She swallowed hard. Cleared her throat. "No one important."

"That's not the whole truth. Tell me."

"It's all the truth you're going to get. And don't bother searching the file, either. I've made sure everything was removed from the data we recovered. My life is my business. Only mine. Keep your nose out, Vic."

"Victor," he automatically corrected.

"I mean it, *Victor*. You stay out of my business or you're fired."

"You can't fire me. Not if you want to keep your juicy government contract. You're going to have to find a bigger stick if you want me to be a good dog."

"I may not be able to fire you, but I can make you beg to quit."

"If you think that, then you don't know me at all. I don't have an ounce of quit in me anywhere. Why do you think Norwood asked me to take this job? His daughter works for you, for heaven's sake. The man isn't going to put some wet-behind-the-ears kid on this assignment. He wants results."

She closed the distance between them, dropping the anger from her expression until all that remained was a relaxed, almost wanton look. Her lips were parted. Her pupils dilated. Her gaze fixed on his mouth.

Victor didn't know what the hell to think. If he wasn't certain that she had no interest in him as a man, he would have been convinced she was about to kiss him. Instead, her voice dropped to a slow, sexy Texas drawl. "Honey, there are an awful lot of things a girl like me can do to a man like you that would make him beg for mercy. And only half of them would actually hurt. The rest would feel oh so very nice."

She was right. She had much more power here than he'd first suspected. She might not be able to make him quit, but she sure as hell could make this assignment one he would regret for a long, long time.

Victor closed his eyes to block out the sight of her lovely face, and took a deep breath. "Do what you want, Bella. I'm here until the job is done, and right now that job means getting you to talk to Payton. Someone has to be in charge when you're out looking for Gage, but none of the men will take orders from him anymore."

"Because I told them not to."

"But he's the one with the most intel. You can't just shut him out."

"I can. I have. End of conversation."

A grizzled old man came out of the house carrying a cooler. Victor recognized him but couldn't place his name. He moved slowly, taking each step with measured care. No doubt the device was inside.

"We're done," said the older man in a voice as rough as crushed gravel. "We had to cut the gas line, so you won't have any hot water. You need to find another place to stay tonight. We'll do another sweep tomorrow in the daylight and fix your gas line."

"I'd rather sleep in my own bed," Bella said.

"Yeah, and I'd rather not be mopping up squishy pieces of you come morning."

She straightened and squared her shoulders. "That one didn't go off. There aren't that many incompetent bombers with enough fingers left to do a job, but apparently, our guy was one of them."

"Wrong," said the man. "The work was solid. Set on a timer so the boom wouldn't happen until the room had time to fill with a small cloud of gas. Whoever did this wanted to make sure you were *in* the blast, not just next to it. If you'd taken more than a few seconds to realize there was a problem and turn off the gas, you would have been one crispy critter." He strapped the cooler into the back of his truck, inside a custom-built steel container.

Bella's jaw tightened in anger, but the rest of her body was loose and relaxed—just like she always was before a fight. "I didn't see the problem. Uncle Sam's poster boy here did." She hooked a thumb toward Victor.

The man's bushy eyebrows lifted in a show of surprise. "Good eye. Bella assign you to a team yet? We could always use a man with a brain."

"He's spoken for," she said before Victor could say a word.

The older man nodded in acceptance. "Fair enough. I'm taking the device to my place out in the country to dispose of it."

"Have you gotten all the information from it you can?" she asked. "I'd really like to find the person who's trying to kill me before they succeed."

"I'll do what I can before destroying it, but it's not the kind of thing we can have sitting around while the egg-heads do their thing. That's a really good way to lose eggheads."

"I understand," she said. "I don't want you to risk your fingers doing anything unsafe. You're my man and I want you in one piece."

"Yes, ma'am. We're of a mind there. I'll call you when I know more." He got into his truck and pulled away slowly.

A minute later, Franklin and two other men came out of Bella's place, carrying the gear they'd toted in.

"We'll come back after the sun is up and do another sweep. Do you want me to stay here tonight and keep watch?" Franklin asked Bella.

"No. I got it."

The young man's face turned red and he shifted uncomfortably from one foot to the other. "You know I can't let you back in the house until the boss gives the all clear, right?"

She crossed her arms over her chest, pressing her breasts upward in a mouthwatering display that made Victor squirm.

"*I'm* the boss, Franklin," she reminded him.

"Yes, ma'am. You're my boss's boss and I respect that. But he promised me that he'd beat the everlovin' hell out of me if I let you go back in there. I'd really rather not have that happen."

"Sugar, don't you think I'd do the same thing if you tried to keep me out of my own home?" she asked, almost sweetly.

Franklin's eyes widened. His ruddy skin went splotchy. He looked to the man next to him for support, but found none. He opened his mouth to say something, then clamped his lips shut.

Victor took pity on the poor kid and spoke up. "I'm sure she's just teasing," he said. "Bella has no need to resort to violence. She knows you're only doing your job."

She fixed Victor with a death ray stare. Her gray eyes narrowed, and he swore he could feel the heat of her anger blasting through his clothes. "I try to always reprimand in private, so you all should leave now. Victor and I need to talk."

The men scurried off. She didn't spare them so much as a glance. As soon as they were on their way down the street, she got right into his face. "Don't you dare speak for me again. Ever."

"You were scaring that poor kid half to death."

"Good. Proves he has half a brain. You'd be smarter if you were a little scared, too."

Victor tried not to scoff. Sure she was tough as nails and deadly in a fight, but he never once imagined she'd inflict violence that wasn't deserved.

Perhaps that was his mistake.

"You want to hurt me?" he asked, refusing to so much as blink under the force of her furious stare. "Go ahead and try. I dare you."

"Tough talk."

"We both know how it will end. You'll be on your back under me, pinned and panting, unable to move until I let you go."

Her pupils flared so wide he was sure it had to have hurt. "You got lucky once. Doesn't mean it will happen again."

"Anytime you want a rematch, I'm ready to go."

She pulled in a deep breath. "I don't have time to waste on your petty pissing matches. I have a company to run." She turned and headed for her truck only to realize it was locked and the keys were inside her house. "Shit."

She looked at her front door as if she was actually considering going back in there.

No way was Victor going to let that happen.

"Come home with me so you can get some sleep. I know you're exhausted."

She stared at him for a full ten seconds. He wasn't sure if she was deciding whether to accept his offer, or calming herself down enough to speak. Either way, he stood there, taking the heat of her gaze for as long as she needed to give it.

Finally, she said, "Take me to work."

"You won't sleep at work."

"I might. We have on-call rooms I could use."

"I know you better than that. If you go to the office,

you'll work. And if you don't get some sleep soon, you're going to start making bad decisions. We both know you can't afford to do that."

"I know my limits. I haven't reached them yet."

"And if a new lead comes up tomorrow, sending you on another two-week chase after Stynger or Gage with no time to sleep? What then? Will that be past your limit?"

She closed her eyes for a split second, but it was long enough for Victor to see the dark stain that fatigue had left beneath her eyes, as well as the slight wilting of her slender frame. "I don't suppose you'd front me the cash for a hotel room, would you? My purse is inside."

He wanted her in his space, in his home. He knew that having her in his domain would change nothing between them, but the urge to drag her to his lair by her hair was clearly still encoded somewhere in his DNA. "When I have a perfectly good guest room available? Are you that afraid of me, Bella?"

She snorted. "Afraid of you? Hardly."

"Then what's the problem? We've slept in close quarters for weeks now and I haven't groped you in your sleep. I'm not about to start now, considering how exhausted I am."

Her gray eyes darkened to a deep slate color. Her nostrils flared as she breathed in, and the tip of her tongue grazed across her bottom lip, leaving a wet trail he ached to taste.

"If exhaustion is the only thing making you mind your manners, then we have a problem," she said. "I think I should get that hotel room."

"I'll be good. My mother trained me to be completely civilized." Or at least give one hell of a good performance. Not that Bella needed to know that part. Better she think he was a good lapdog, rather than the rabid pit bull straining at his chain in an effort to reach her.

Bella wasn't his type. He had to remember that, despite the fact that his body disagreed. She came from a different world than he did. She wasn't the kind of woman who fit into his carefully planned future. There was nothing refined or genteel about her.

Which only made him want her more.

"Fine," she finally said in utter exhaustion. "Take me home. But if you so much as step one foot inside your guest room while I'm there, honey, I'll break your knee-caps."

For some reason Victor couldn't fathom, his cock twitched in excitement at her threat of violence.

He grinned. "I'd like to see you try."

Chapter Four

Bella hated to admit it, but she liked Victor's home.

It was in a nice part of town. Safe, but not showy. The house was beautifully built, but not huge. She knew he could afford way more, but apparently felt no need to do so.

Everything was done in calming neutral tones. The furnishings were of high quality, but didn't have the ostentatiousness she'd come to expect from the ridiculously wealthy.

There was no clutter or dust. No dishes in his sink. Everything about the place was appealing, all the way down to the large gun safe he'd installed where a wine cellar had previously been.

"Your room is in here," he said, opening a door on the opposite side of the house from the master suite. "The bathroom is stocked with all the basics. If you need anything else, just ask."

The guest room was done in soothing greens and blues. One step onto the soft carpet made her worry that she might sink in all the way to the foundation. A giant bed sat in the center of the space, its covers turned down on one corner in welcome. She wanted to sink into its pillowy depths so bad, she nearly groaned in need.

"This is beautiful. Thank you." She turned in time to catch him staring at her. "What?"

"Just adjusting to the idea of you being in my home."

Now she felt like a charity case. "I really don't want to intrude. I'll just call a cab to take me to work." She was in the act of dialing her cell phone when he covered her hand with his.

"I didn't mean that in a bad way. I'm glad you're here."

"Why in the world does an inconvenience make you glad?"

"I like knowing you're safe. When you're under my roof, I can be certain that's the case."

She didn't know what to say to that. She wasn't used to men worrying about her—not even the ones who knew and understood what she did for a living. They all knew she could take care of herself, which made her wonder if Victor thought less of her abilities, or if he simply cared more.

"You know I can take care of myself," she reminded him.

"Better than almost anyone I know," he agreed. "But someone is out to hurt you, and no one is invulnerable to a bullet from a well-trained sniper. Not even you."

The idea gave her pause, and sent a trail of apprehension snaking up her spine. She felt the need to hide, like she used to do when Dan came at her and the fear set in. It took an effort of will to shrug off the need to pull her hands away from Victor's.

"Is your house sniper-proof?" she asked, half teasing.

"Metal shutters over bulletproof glass. Reinforced cement walls. Strategically designed landscaping that gives every advantage to us inside, and enough guns and ammo to wage a small war."

"Wow," she breathed. "Now I know what a guy like you does with all that money." And it was damn hot, too.

Victor grinned. "Get some sleep, Bella. I'm nearby if

you need me." Something about the way he said it made her think he was hoping she would need him.

She clenched her thighs together to ward off the most pressing need she had for a man like him.

He shut the door to her room, leaving her alone.

Normally she enjoyed time to herself. She spent so much of her life working with clients and employees that she could go for days without any time alone. But now, standing on the plush carpet of Victor's guest room, surrounded by beautiful things, all she wanted was to trail after him so she wouldn't feel so damn lonely.

Not going to happen, so time to suck it up.

She turned and surveyed her surroundings. The space was too big. As safe as his house might be, there were too many places where a bad guy could hide.

The cozier bathroom on the far side of the room beckoned. She headed for it, closing the door behind herself.

The room was bigger than she'd first thought, with both a giant tub and a separate walk-in shower. There were two sprawling counters with sinks, and another at a lower height that she presumed was for putting on makeup.

All the surfaces in here were hard stone, glossy tile, or gleaming metal. The only softness she found were the thick rugs and fluffy towels waiting for use.

There was a closet on the other side of the bath. She went over, hoping for a smaller space she could burrow into and hide.

As soon as she realized what she was doing, she stopped dead in her tracks.

Bella didn't hide anymore. She didn't need to. Her husband was dead. She was strong. Deadly. No one could hurt her now.

She had no idea why the need to hide had come on so suddenly or was so strong, but she fought back, refusing to give in to the compulsion.

She was safe. Her only problem was her worry for Gage and not enough sleep or food for too many days.

That, and a raging case of lust for a man she couldn't let herself have.

Bella made use of the toothbrush and toiletries set out for her. Then she stripped down to her panties so her clothes wouldn't be a wrinkled mess when she went to work tomorrow morning. She slid into sheets so soft they had to have been woven from angelic spider silk. The cool brush of fabric against her skin made her shiver with delight, lighting up nerve endings everywhere. The sensation added to her lust, as did the knowledge that Victor lay only a few yards from where she did.

As need crawled through her system, she ran her hands over her skin, pretending that the hands that touched her were bigger and rougher. Victor's face formed in her mind as clear as if he'd been lying beside her.

The thought gave her a naughty thrill as she drew her fingers over her abdomen and lower to glide beneath her panties.

She was wet. Hot. She needed relief so bad it made every muscle in her body tense.

There was no sleeping with this kind of lust clawing at her, so she did the only practical thing she could do and began working herself toward orgasm. Even one would be enough to ease her.

Victor's image was with her the whole time. It was his hand that stroked her, his fingers that toyed with her nipples. When her climax washed over her, it was his name she cried out.

Finally, her body relaxed and let go of all the tension it had been hoarding. As she drifted off to sleep, she was almost certain that she could smell his scent filling the air.

*   *   *

Victor knew the sound of a woman's orgasm when he heard it. But he'd never expected to hear that lovely noise come out of Bella Bayne.

Especially not calling out his name.

He let his hand fall from where he'd been about to knock on her door. He still hadn't fed her yet, and in all the excitement, he hadn't realized it until his own stomach reminded him.

There was no way he was knocking now. His cock was hard enough to rip his fly open if he so much as breathed too deeply.

It was better to leave now, before he saw the flush of her arousal staining her cheeks, and forgot he couldn't fuck his boss. He didn't know how long he'd last before he gave in to his need to come, but he knew that when he did, he'd be remembering the sound of Bella calling his name.

Chapter Five

Bella had woken up in Victor's guest closet, shivering with both cold and fear. She couldn't remember the dream that had driven her to cower and hide, but that didn't make it any less humiliating. Or any less frightening.

She was furious for reasons she refused to acknowledge—reasons too big for her to allow them to distract her now, while so much was at stake. She used that anger now, channeling it into a tightly controlled bundle of energy she burned to fuel her muscles.

Sweat dripped from her chin as she faced her opponent in the sparring ring, but she didn't dare stop to wipe it away. If she did, Adam Brink would pounce.

Now that she knew Adam was Gage's brother, she could see the similarities in them. They were both tall and lean, with sharp, angular features and keen minds. She'd once thought of Adam as her enemy, but he had since proved himself a formidable ally. Not only had he saved the life of more than one of Bella's employees, he'd also made her friend and tech goddess Mira a very happy, very satisfied woman. So much so that Bella ignored the fact that Adam and Mira were breaking several company rules with their engagement and frequent bouts of monkey sex in the server room.

If only Bella could ignore those rules herself long enough to see if Victor was as tasty as he appeared. Maybe then she'd be able to get some decent sleep.

A sigh of longing slipped past her lips.

Adam moved so fast Bella hardly saw it coming. She was too slow to stop his attack, which earned her a position with her face pinned against the sparring mat.

"You're distracted today," Adam said with complete calm. None of the heat of their practice battle seemed to touch him.

Her elbow and shoulder begged for him to release her arm, which was currently twisted behind her back with great force. Talking with her cheek smooshed against the mat was hard, but she managed. "I let you pin me."

He immediately let her go, lifting her back to her feet with one graceful tug. Behind him, not twenty feet away, stood Victor, watching her.

He was shirtless, showing off a body meant for a woman's hands. And her tongue.

Lean, functional muscles gleamed with sweat under the gym's lights. His shorts gave her a clear view of his long, strong legs. Even as tall as she was, as ripped as she forced herself to stay for her own safety, she knew without a doubt that there was more than enough room on his thighs for her to snuggle up in his lap.

The fact that the word *snuggle* even entered her vocabulary was proof of just how sleep-deprived she was. Women like her didn't snuggle. They trained and worked and issued orders. They strategized and did paperwork and kicked ass when the need arose. Which was often.

The sharp sting of Adam's hand against her shoulder refocused her attention.

"Does someone need a nap?" he asked.

This time Bella kept her gaze where it belonged—on her opponent—and made her move. Adam let her think she had the upper hand right up to the point where she landed flat on her back, her body completely immobilized beneath his.

The smell of his sweat invaded her nose. A sick swell of nausea clogged her throat. This wasn't the way it was supposed to go. She was supposed to slip away. Stay on her feet.

Run.

Something dark and terrifying spewed out of the dark recesses of her memory. She'd been helpless like this too many times before. Trapped.

The memory of being strapped to a hospital bed flooded her mind. She was small. Weak. Something hot and biting was being pumped into her veins. It set the back of her skull on fire and made every muscle in her thin body strain and clench. It didn't matter how hard she fought or how much she pulled on her restraints, there was no escape.

That memory melded into another, more recent one. This time she was older, bigger. Still, she was powerless to stop the violence coming toward her. Her husband's hard hands bit into her skin, bruising as they tightened and pinned her arms down. His snarl of anger was proof of what would happen next—a precursor to the pain that was speeding her way. First the physical pain, then the emotional aftermath.

She had to fight back. Run away. But her body refused to cooperate. Instead, she went limp and weak, accepting her fate. This fear and violence was her home—where she'd been created to live. All the fight had been stripped from her, leaving behind only a weak, spineless shell. There was no avoiding the inevitable.

Adam's weight shifted atop her, flinging her mind back to the here and now. Helpless terror still clung to her, fogging and jumbling her thoughts.

The need to fight, to flee, rose up, taking over her limbs. The victim in her retreated back into her cage, leaving the need to survive shining bright like a beacon of strength.

There was no technique to her efforts now—just pure instinct and rage. She didn't care if she hurt him or herself. All that mattered was freedom.

She thrashed around, clawing and kicking at her captor. She couldn't let him win. Couldn't let him hold her down. Hurt her. Kill her.

Bella was not a victim. Not ever again.

The keen blade of panic cut through her, shearing away all reason. She heard her blood pound in her ears and saw her vision dim. The rough edges of her own screams barely penetrated the fog of her fear. Beyond that were the startled grunts of an opponent expecting her attack.

"Get off her!" A man's hard order. She knew the voice, but couldn't place it.

Friend or foe? She couldn't remember. Better to run from him, too.

Her fingernails bit into sweaty skin. Her toes met dense flesh, hitting hard enough to shove a grunt from her captor and send a streak of pain up her shin.

Then he was gone. His weight evaporated as if it had never been. Her panic dissipated and vision cleared in time to see Victor's arms extend as he bodily threw Adam to the far side of the sparring ring.

He landed well, coming up on the other side of a graceful roll. Apology was clear on his face, along with a dizzying dose of confusion.

Victor crouched beside her, blocking out the sight of all else. A look of concern creased his aristocratic brow. He didn't touch her, but his hand hovered only inches away from her shoulder, as if he was thinking about it.

In that crazy, emotional moment, she desperately wanted his touch—something to ground her in reality, not that insane place she'd been inhabiting a second ago. A place she'd lived for too many years.

"Are you okay?" he asked.

The normal noises of the gym had gone silent. No one spoke. There were about half a dozen people present, and most of them were staring at Bella with varying looks of shock and worry. A couple were grinning, like they were certain her freak-out had been a joke.

Nothing could be further from the truth.

Her face burned with embarrassment. Her whole body trembled. She wanted to stand and tell them all to mind their own damn business, but her throat was still constricted from her strangled screams of panic. She swore she could still hear them echoing in her ears.

Victor's voice quieted so no one else could hear, but his tone was no less insistent. "Tell me you're okay or I'm picking you up and taking you to a hospital."

"Fine," she managed to squeak out, though the weak sound was almost as embarrassing as her episode.

His lips flattened in acceptance, and she saw his expression change to the one he wore when he was getting ready to plow through an impossible task. He stood, and his voice filled the gym. "She just got the wind knocked out of her. Clear the room. She says employee meeting in fifteen minutes in the conference room."

The gathered people looked at her as if expecting her to issue a different order.

Victor's voice took on the boom of a drill instructor. "Move!"

Everyone scurried to obey except Adam, who gave her a long, scrutinizing look. "I'm sorry if I hurt you," he said.

She waved him away, hoping her hand wasn't shaking too hard to reassure him.

He nodded. "I'm going back out to look for Gage again," he said, and then left the room.

While Bella appreciated the privacy Victor's lie had

afforded her, she knew better than to believe it herself. She'd had more than the wind knocked out of her. Somewhere between Adam's hold and her abrupt landing on the mat, she'd lost part of her mind.

You're never going to escape the person you were. You'll carry her with you for the rest of your days. Acceptance is your only option. Payton's voice wriggled in the back of Bella's memory, taunting her with failure.

She would not be that person again. Weak. Spineless. A victim. She was too strong for that now. Dan had tried to break her, but she'd survived. Unbreakable.

At least until today. Whatever Adam had done to her had thrown her back into her old self, where panic and fear ruled her every action.

She couldn't go back there. Never again.

The gym doors clicked shut as the last person filed into the locker room. Victor stayed behind, though she couldn't understand why.

"Go with them," she ordered. "Get dressed. I have to figure out what I'm going to talk about at our employee meeting. Nice cover, by the way."

"Best I could do on short notice. You scared the hell out of me."

Why, she had no idea, but his concern was as touching as it was irritating. "I'm fine. Just got the wind knocked out of me."

"Like hell. You were screaming. Care to tell me what happened?"

Shame tightened her skin until she wanted to crawl out of it and go hide. "I'm not used to being pinned. Got a little claustrophobic," she lied.

"You didn't panic when I had you pinned."

Even the memory of that moment had the power to soften her muscles and ease a bit of the harsh tension radiating through her. "It's no big deal. Won't happen again."

She hoped.

"Are you sure?" he asked. "I know this job is a lot of stress. You never sleep; you don't eat right. If it's getting to be too much for you, I need to know."

She pushed herself upright, but didn't dare risk trying to stand. Her wobbly legs weren't going to hold her up yet.

She put as much force as she could behind her words. "Stop right there. I'm not some fragile flower you have to protect. I handle the stress just fine. And you need to pay less attention to my eating and sleeping habits and more to using your government contacts to find Gage and Stynger. I'm a big girl. I can take care of myself. I'm fine."

His brows went up. "Oh really? Is that what you call your little panic attack? Fine?"

"Leave it alone, Victor."

"That's not going to happen. Lives depend on you being at the top of your game. If the stress is getting to you, then you owe it to your team to take some time off and relax. Go lounge on a beach or enter a mixed martial arts tournament or skydive naked into shark-infested waters—whatever de-stresses you. We'll all be here when you get back."

"Gage is still missing. Stynger is still out there hurting people. Every lead we get on her goes cold fast, and all that's left is the string of dead bodies and destroyed lives in her wake. If you think I'm going to sit on a beach, sipping fruity drinks out of coconut shells while that's going on, you're insane."

"And if you think I'm going to work with a woman who's half a step away from breaking down, you're an idiot."

Frustration and anger fueled her limbs, giving her the strength to stand. Her knees shook, but she pretended not to notice. Through gritted teeth, she said, "I'm fine. Back off."

With slow, deliberate care, Victor used one finger to push against her shoulder.

The slight pressure unbalanced her. Her unstable knees gave out on her and she stumbled backward. She would have landed on her ass if he hadn't reached out and grabbed her arms before she fell.

He pulled her upright, supporting her weight against his hard, sweaty frame. After a good workout, most men reeked, but not Victor Temple. The scent of his skin was an intoxicating mix that distracted her from her anger for a split second. She breathed him in, trying to remember that she was pissed at him, that he'd overstepped his bounds.

His grip on her arms shifted, reminding her that she still hadn't found her footing. If not for his hold, she would have crumpled to the mat like some kind of fainting maiden.

Those clear blue eyes of his were fixed on her with absolute calm. No accusation, no anger, only casual acceptance for what he obviously believed was the truth. "You're not fine. But you will be, because everyone here needs you to be. We all need you to take better care of yourself. And if you don't, I *will* make you."

The statement should have made her furious, but the way he said it with absolute authority short-circuited her brain, tricking her into thinking she should accept his statement as wholeheartedly as he did.

It took her a few seconds to realize she'd been manipulated, and when she did, the fire of anger sparked back to life. "You have no right to make me do anything."

"Actually I do. You signed the contract. I'm your liaison. You gave me the authority to interfere if I didn't like the way you were handling the mission to find Dr. Stynger and destroy her research. And I really don't like the way you're handling things."

"So, what?" she asked, finally finding her balance

enough to step out of his grasp. "You're going to run off and tattle to the US government that I'm not taking enough naps?"

"No, I'm going to act in accordance with our contract and take over the mission myself. Remove you from your position of leadership, and finish the job without you." He crossed his arms over his chest, making the muscles in his chest ripple beneath a gleaming layer of sweat. "Or, you can play nice and you can continue to be in charge."

"I can always rip up the contract and fire your ass."

He shrugged as if he didn't care. "You can, but the instant you do, there will be no more funding. You'll be forced to cut back your efforts to find and help the people hurt by Stynger's research. And to find Gage. This isn't exactly the kind of work that pays well, unlike your usual wealthy clientele."

"You would do that? You'd really pull funding when you know how much we need it to help those poor people?"

"If it means keeping your team alive to fight another day, I'd do it in an instant. I've come to care for the people that work here."

She could see that he wasn't bluffing. The man hid nothing inside his clear eyes.

As much as Bella hated it, she was bent over, ass up, with no choice left but to take her punishment. The contract she'd signed was her only means of funding the efforts to help those who needed it. No one else was going to do the job. It was too dangerous. Only her team of badass private soldiers was capable of dealing with the crazy, violent people Stynger controlled.

Defeat rode Bella hard, but she squared her shoulders under the weight. She would take whatever she had to take to do the job. If that meant bending her will to a man she'd given way too much power, then that was what she'd do.

After all, she'd been a victim of Stynger's research, too. She knew what it was like to have her life destroyed by the whims of a madwoman, even if she had been too young and hadn't known what was happening at the time.

Bella pulled in a long breath to steady her nerves and quell the angry words burning her lips. "What do you want me to do?"

"Three simple things. Get some rest. Have a decent meal. And talk to Payton."

She shook her head before he was even done speaking. "No way am I speaking to that man ever again."

"It's not an option, Bella. The man knows things we don't. We need him and his knowledge."

"He lied to me. Used me. Who's to say he's not still using me?"

"It can't possibly be that bad. You're just being stubborn."

Fury lashed in her gut, sending acid churning into her throat. "Stubborn? Is that what you think? That I'm just throwing some kind of petulant fit?"

"You were speaking to him only a few weeks ago. What could he have done in that time that's so terrible? All I've seen is a man who is desperate to help."

At that moment, the gym doors opened and Payton walked in. His expensive suit was in perfect order, without a wrinkle. His hair was still thick and full, even though he was nearing sixty. Despite his age, he had the bearing of a man who knew his way around a fight. She'd never seen him in action, but now that she knew what he really was—a highly trained one-man fighting force with enough experience and political pull to be spooky—she could see the subtle signs of his skill flicker through his movements now and then.

He stared at her as he approached with caution, the way a man would an angry rattlesnake. "I heard about your mishap. Are you okay?"

Bella refused to acknowledge his question. Unfortunately, that gave Victor an opening to respond for her. "She's not, but she will be. Nothing a nap and a good meal can't solve. She didn't sleep worth a damn last night."

"How do you know?" she demanded.

"Because I heard you moving around."

Shame flamed in her cheeks. She only hoped that he didn't realize she'd been cowering in the closet like a frightened child.

Payton's gaze remained fixed on her, unmoving. "Is that true? Someone said you didn't seem like yourself. You were afraid. If that's the case, then we may have a bigger problem on our hands."

Victor frowned in confusion, glancing between them. "So what if she was afraid?"

Payton's pale eyes stayed on her. His expression was grim, his stance determined. "Do you want to tell him? Or shall I?"

Bella didn't want her team knowing anything about her past, and she didn't trust Payton not to spill his guts if she didn't stop him. "It's none of his business."

"I disagree. You signed the contract with Norwood. That put Victor in the field with you, by your side. He needs to know if there's a risk."

Victor held up his hands. "Whoa. What risk? What the hell are you two talking about?"

"If you don't tell him, I will." Payton's expression was one of pure warning. There was no love between them now as there once had been. The man who'd been like a father to her since her own had died was nothing to her now. He'd lied to her for years. Hidden what had been done to her. How was she supposed to forgive not only the horrible things he'd done, but also years of hiding those things from her?

The only way Bella could mitigate the damage was to suck it up and tell Victor the ugly truth. Better he hear it from her lips than have Payton twist the story to suit himself.

She clasped her shaking hands together and stared at the wall just beyond Victor's shoulder. She couldn't look him in the face when she admitted her shame. "I didn't know it until recently, but I was one of the kids Stynger experimented on years ago. And like all of them, I'm fucked in the head. There's a chance I could crack the way they do."

Victor went still. "How much of a chance? Is that what happened with Adam a minute ago? You started to crack?"

She swallowed down her anger at Payton for his hand in getting her to this place. "No, I don't think so."

Victor's mouth hardened. "You don't think so? This is the kind of thing you need to be sure about, Bella."

"I'm fine. You don't need to worry."

"Yes, you do, son," said Payton to Victor, though his gaze was fixed firmly on Bella. "You've seen what can happen with the people who were part of the project. You close your eyes to that, and you're asking to become a victim."

Bella's voice vibrated with anger. "I'm not like them. I've got things under control."

"For now," Payton said. "But you didn't always. You've let your anger get the best of you before. Or have you forgotten Dan?"

"That was different. I was defending myself."

"Sixty-seven stab wounds is a bit more than self-defense. It's rage."

"That's not the way the jury saw it."

"Wait a minute," Victor said. "What are you two talking about? What jury?"

Bella was a little surprised that he didn't already know. Some folks in the office loved to gossip about her. If Victor hadn't heard the rumors, it was only because he'd chosen not to listen.

For some reason she liked that he didn't know about her past. She wasn't ashamed of what she'd done—it had been absolutely necessary. But she was ashamed of the person she'd been before she'd killed Dan. Weak. Helpless. A total victim.

"It's none of your business," she snapped, hoping to stop the conversation right here before it changed how Victor saw her.

"He needs to know the level of violence of which you are capable," Payton said.

"Oh, I know all about her skill with violence," Victor said. "I've been working with her for weeks. If violence were an art form, she'd have a display at the Smithsonian. What I need to know is whether or not there's a risk she'll become unstable and inflict that violence on the wrong person."

It grated against her nerves that Victor would ask Payton instead of her, but she hid her irritation so she wouldn't appear unstable when Victor was already questioning her mental health. "I'm completely steady. That little incident with Adam was just a fluke—a product of too many hours of sleep deprivation."

"If that's the case," Payton said, "then you won't mind if I keep an eye on you. You have nothing to hide."

"I mind," she said. "I know you're looking for a way to make things like they used to be, but it's never going to happen. Not now that I know the kind of man you really are."

"I'm the man I've always been—one trying to make up for past mistakes."

The slow, hot burn of anger and betrayal she'd felt for weeks flared to life. Ever since she'd learned that Payton had been a part of the Threshold Project, she'd struggled with knowing that the man she used to trust was actually one of the bad guys.

How could she not have seen the kind of man he really was? How could she have misread him so completely? He'd come into her life when she was young and vulnerable. He'd helped her get her life back together. Gotten her a good lawyer when she'd been charged with murder, paid all her legal fees so she could walk out of court a free woman, helped her start her company.

Those kindnesses had all been done out of guilt, and she hadn't been smart enough to see through his lies. He'd told her it was all about money, that she was a good investment. It was enough to make her question her judgment about people in general. Who else in her life wasn't what they seemed?

"Your words don't mean a thing to me anymore, Payton. If not for your fancy lawyers and the way they worded our partnership agreement, I wouldn't even let you set foot inside my office."

"Our office."

"For now," she agreed. "I will buy you out. I will cut you from my life at the first possible opportunity."

He flinched, but covered it fast. "Perhaps, but for now you're stuck with me. Just as the employees here are stuck with you. They all deserve to know if there's any threat of you breaking down the way so many of Stynger's victims have."

Her words hissed out from between her clenched teeth. "I told you I'm fine."

"You weren't fine when you killed your husband and left him lying in a pool of his own blood. I just want to make sure that doesn't happen again with Victor or one of the others."

Victor's gaze hit her, filled with suspicion. Whatever trust he'd had in her, whatever respect he'd had for her as his employer—it was all gone. He watched her as he would a wild animal, unsure of what she might do next.

In one single stroke, Payton had completely usurped her authority. Rage sizzled just below her scalp, scalding her brain. She knew if she didn't turn and leave now, she was going to do something to Payton she'd regret as soon as she got finished enjoying it.

In an uncharacteristically jerky move, she turned on her heel and left. Let these two men say whatever they wanted about her. It didn't matter. She knew that her little freak-out was nothing—certainly not something that would get in the way of her finding Stynger and taking her down for good.

And anyone who tried to stop her would find out just how clear her mind really was.

Chapter Six

Victor didn't dare try to stop Bella from stalking away. It was obvious she was on the verge of violence, and he wasn't sure he'd be able to stop her from hurting Payton without hurting *her* in the process. And he really didn't want to have to hurt her.

The second she was behind the locker room doors, Victor turned to Payton. "That was completely uncalled-for. I thought you were trying to make amends with her, not push her farther away."

"I can't baby her anymore, though God knows I wish I could." Payton ran his manicured fingers through his perfect hair, mussing it. The look of distress on the man's face was almost enough to make Victor feel a pang of sympathy.

"There's a long way between babying her and airing her secrets in front of me."

"I thought you needed to know. You two are spending a lot of time together."

"No more than anyone else."

"You're wrong about that," Payton said. "I've been keeping a close eye on her. She still works with the others, but not like she used to. She loves them too much to put them at risk, which makes me worry that something has changed."

"Like what?"

"Like what happened with Adam."

"It wasn't that big of a deal."

"If you knew her history, you wouldn't say that."

"So enlighten me." Snooping was generally a disgusting habit, but Victor forgave himself because lives were on the line. If there was something he needed to know, it was best to find out now while there was still time to make preparations to deal with it.

Payton shook his head. "No. That's too much a breach of trust even for me. She already hates me enough. No sense in throwing fuel on the fire."

"If I need to know—"

"You don't. All you need to know is that she's not as tough as she would like us all to believe. I used to step in and help her shoulder the burden of running this place, but she's shut me out. I can't help anymore. I can barely get in the front door." Payton gave Victor a hard stare. "You have to be there for her now."

"Why me?"

"Because she has no choice but to let you in. I cut her off from my money, so she was forced to accept the contract that compels her to keep you on staff."

"I'm not here to babysit one woman. My orders are to help locate Stynger and take her and her work down. I'm not paid to do your dirty work."

"If Bella cracks, this whole place will go down with her. No more front for you or Norwood to do what the powers that be so desperately want you to do. If he was here, he'd order you to keep an eye on her. If you don't believe me, ask him. I've known the man for more years than you've been alive. I'm sure about this one."

Victor didn't doubt it. And as much as he hated the

idea that Bella might be in a mentally precarious situation, he knew he could help. She was strong. She could get through this. All she needed was a man with the balls to make her do the right thing.

Right now, that man was him.

Chapter Seven

Bella stumbled through her impromptu employee meeting as fast as she could, then headed back to her office, where she could hide for a few minutes and calm down.

Was Payton right? Could the response she'd had to Adam be a sign she was cracking? Or was it just a random throwback to a time when she was her old self, completely incapable of fighting back against a bigger, stronger opponent?

She wasn't sure which she preferred. Both were enough to mess with a woman's head, and right now she needed her wits about her.

Gage was still missing. She'd thrown him to the wolves and she couldn't help but wonder if he hadn't been eaten alive. Even the thought was enough to make her blood go cold and sluggish in her veins.

She *had* to find him. Fast. Something deep in her gut told her that his time was running out. Assuming it hadn't already.

She rounded the corner to her office. Her secretary, Lila, sat at her desk, her standard uniform of oversize drab brown clothing in place. Bella had no idea why the woman felt the need to continue hiding from an ex who was dead, but she'd remained timid and mousy long after she should have been bouncing back from her abusive relationship.

At least there were no tearstains on her ugly shirt today. Bella didn't think she could handle witnessing sweet Lila's pain on top of everything else.

She stood as Bella passed, handing her a chilled bottle of water. There were signs of nervousness in Lila's stance. Her hand shook slightly around the water bottle, making the surface ripple under the bright office lights. "There's a man in your office. He's here about a new contract for his employer."

"I didn't know I had an appointment this morning."

"It was on your calendar."

"I don't remember seeing it."

Lila's nervousness increased until her whole body was shaking. If Bella kept pushing Lila, the girl was going to be in tears before lunch. Again.

"Never mind. Just tell me it's going to be quick."

"No more than an hour or so, I'm sure."

Bella stifled a groan of agony. She knew bringing in new clients was important, but she just didn't have it in her today to play nice, give the tour, pretend to be interested and generally suck up. That was Payton's strong suit, but she'd been refusing to let him meet prospective clients since she'd learned about his betrayal.

Which meant she had to shove her need for alone time down for at least another hour.

She plastered what she hoped was a reasonable facsimile of a smile on her face as she pushed through her office door.

Sitting at her glass desk was a man in his forties. He'd moved her guest chair so that it was turned sideways, presumably to watch for her. He had a muscular build and was wearing a suit so expertly tailored she could barely see the concealed weapons he carried. Chances were the camera peering through her open office doorway couldn't pick them up at all.

He rose as she came in, holding a steaming mug of coffee in his huge hand. He set it down and smiled as he gave her a professional once-over. No doubt checking for concealed weapons on her as well as sizing her up. A small part of her wished she'd taken the time to change out of her clinging workout clothes so her weapons were all back in place again. As it was, the only thing she was armed with was a layer of dried sweat.

"Bella Bayne," she offered as she shook his hand.

"Charles O'Dell, head of security for a man who is interested in acquiring your services."

"No name?" she asked.

He had pockmarked skin and eyes set too deep beneath a ridged brow. He wasn't exactly ugly, but he was far from handsome. Those deeply set eyes did, however, track her every move as she went behind her desk. There was nothing at all wrong with his attention span or his vigilance.

"No names yet," he said. "If you make it past this interview, there are two more you'll have to undergo before we sign you on and disclose details."

That was a little paranoid, but whatever. People with a lot of money often thought they were far more important than they really were. Nothing new there.

"So, what can I do for you, Mr. O'Dell?"

"Chuck," he offered. "My employer has a trip to the Middle East coming up and would like a team to escort him there and back. You come highly recommended."

Bella didn't let his praise throw her off her game. She stayed focused, determined to find out what this job was before she went putting the lives of her employees on the line. "You're his head of security. Why don't you do the job?"

"He needs more men than we have on staff. It's a temporary job—one that will last about a week."

"What's the threat?"

"He's going home to visit his family. Some of them want him dead."

She let out a low whistle. "Bet that makes for an interesting family reunion."

Chuck flashed her a charming smile. "Please tell me you're interested in the job."

"When?"

"The day after tomorrow."

"That's fast."

"His father is gravely ill. It came up suddenly."

"I understand. But the short notice will cost extra. How many men are we talking?"

"Three. Plus you, of course."

"I'm sorry, but I'm not personally available. I have other commitments."

"My employer insisted that you be part of the team. One of his business associates sings your praises, and my employer finds you intriguing."

Bella shook her head. There was no way she could leave the country while Gage was still missing. She had to stay here, where she could jump if there was any sign of him popping up, especially if he was in need of a rescue.

"I'd like to help you," she said, "but I'm afraid that my services are booked for the next several weeks. If he'd like to postpone his trip, I could try to schedule something."

"If you can't come, then I'll have to look elsewhere."

"My involvement is not negotiable, Chuck. I'm sorry. I have commitments."

Something about the way the man moved triggered her instincts. The relaxed, friendly look on his face fell away, leaving behind something blank and cold. His chest expanded with a deep breath, parting the lapels of his suit enough that they weren't in the way when he reached for the gun riding his ribs.

By the time his fingers wrapped around the butt of his weapon, before her sense of *what the fuck?* even had time to register, Bella was already flying into motion.

She stood, using the full force of her body to fling her glass desk, and the hot coffee sitting atop it, into his lap.

Chuck didn't even flinch as his crotch was soaked with scalding-hot liquid and his legs were pinned between the edge of the heavy glass desktop and the chair.

His hand came up in a fluid move. Through the glass she could see the barrel of his gun aimed right at her chest.

Bella dove to the side as his weapon fired. Glass shattered and fell over her legs.

She ignored the sting she felt and rolled toward the filing cabinet.

Her workout clothes gave her freedom of movement, but her 9mm was still in her gym locker, right where she'd left it. She'd never thought that someone would come after her in her own office while she was surrounded by a bunch of armed employees.

Apparently, she'd been wrong. The trick now was to stay alive long enough for one of those employees to come running to her aid before Chuck blew her brains out.

He fired again, and this time, she could feel the heat of the bullet slide past her cheek. Too close.

There was no way she was getting past him to the door. At least not without a few extra holes.

Bella looked around for some kind of weapon. The cup with her pens and letter opener had toppled to the floor about two feet from Chuck's left boot. She didn't even have her purse with her to swing around like a sling. It was still in her house, which had yet to be officially cleared of explosive devices.

The only thing she could think to use was a heavy shard of glass.

She pulled her sleeves down over her hands and

grabbed a thick triangle of glass. The tip was pointed enough to pass as a dagger, but she was going to have to get close for it to do any good.

Really close.

Bella regained her feet as the third shot went off. Through the open door she could see Lila standing there, shaking and doing a great impersonation of an easy target.

"Run!" yelled Bella.

The man turned just enough to give her an opening. She rushed through the shattered pile of glass that had once been her desk and kicked the man's weapon hand.

A bone broke hard enough she heard it snap, but he didn't let go of the gun. Instead, he jerked his head back around and leveled the barrel right at her chest.

Bella slammed the glass shard into his forearm. She hadn't felt it cut her, but the blood slickening her grip proved that it had.

The shard stuck in between the bones in his forearm. She tried to pull it back out for another strike, but it was too slippery to dislodge.

The hand not holding his gun slammed against the side of her head, knocking her stupid. She stumbled under the blow, struggling to figure out which way was up for a second.

It was long enough for him to rip the glass from his arm and move his gun to his unbroken hand. He leveled it to fire.

There was nowhere for Bella to go. She was pinned in the corner with only a flimsy bit of fake ficus tree to shield her. Chuck stood between her and the door, and she didn't think she had time to cross the space and engage in hand-to-hand combat before he could pull the trigger.

Still, a slim chance was better than none at all.

She charged on a bellow, going low to sweep his legs

out from under him while making herself as small a target as possible. Before she'd made contact, a heavy boom exploded in the small space, followed by two more.

Chuck stiffened and flailed as he spun around. His legs seemed to give out, and he slowly twisted as he toppled, landing on what had once been her desk.

Standing in the doorway was Victor, gun trained on Chuck's immobile body. Behind him, a crowd of armed men was forming in the hallway.

"Bella?" Victor asked, his voice tight with worry.

"I'm good," she said between labored breaths. "Pissed as hell, but still alive."

Chuck didn't move. He'd taken three bullets at close range, delivered by a man who knew how to kill. She was certain Chuck was never getting up again.

Adrenaline began trickling from her system, leaving her shaking and dizzy, with the oddest urge to break into a sobbing fit.

She never cried—at least not in the last decade. And yet she knew that hot prickling in the corners of her eyes was a sure sign she was about to do just that.

"Clear the area," ordered Victor. "This is a crime scene now."

Her office a crime scene? Even the thought was enough to send a giggle worming up her throat.

Victor stepped inside the office and checked Chuck for a pulse. The grim look on his face told her there wasn't one.

His eyes met hers. Some hot, fierce emotion was shining just beneath that clear blue surface, but she was too wigged out to spend any time deciphering it. His voice was calm and quiet, but the words were clipped with anger. "You're bleeding."

She looked at her hands. They were sticky and red, with shallow cuts left behind by the glass.

She'd never before been squeamish, but the sight of

her blood and the smell of gunpowder turned her stomach.

Bella swallowed a couple of times to keep her breakfast where it belonged. "I need to go wash up."

Victor shifted slightly, blocking her path. "I can't let you do that. Not until the police arrive and see the damage."

"I'll get a first aid kit," said someone from the hallway. She wasn't sure who. Didn't care.

"Show me your hands," Victor said.

She held them out for inspection without even considering that she had an option to refuse him. Somewhere in the back of her mind she knew that wasn't like her, but she wrote it off as a bit of scrambled brain matter from Chuck's fist hitting her cheekbone.

"Stay here," he ordered.

She did. He went only as far as the door, where he exchanged a few quiet words with someone in the hall. When Victor came back, he had some gauze pads in his hand, along with a roll of paper tape.

"The cuts aren't too deep. You might need a couple of stitches in one spot." His voice was quiet and soothing. "Your pants are bloody, too. I think it's your blood, honey."

She thought about telling him that he didn't need to treat her so gently, that she'd been hurt far worse than this and survived, but she liked the sound of his voice too much.

"Is she okay?" asked Payton from the doorway.

It wasn't until she heard his voice that she realized that he'd been standing there. How long? She wasn't sure, but if he'd been there for more than a second, she was worse off than she thought. She should have been aware of what was going on around her, especially with so much adrenaline running through her system. High stress situations were nothing new to her, and yet she felt . . . off. Not at all like herself.

"She's going to be fine," Victor said, carefully taping the gauze pads over her palms and fingers. He looked down at her, tipping her chin up so she looked him in the eye. "Aren't you?"

"I'm fine," came out automatically.

It was then that she realized she wasn't fine. She was barely inside her own skin. Most of her had retreated to that safe place she used to go when Dad would lay into her. And later, Dan. Nothing could hurt her there.

She hadn't been to this place for years, but she recognized the soft, warm walls now. How much time had she spent curled up here? How many years had this been her home?

A burst of hot rage sliced through the fog, burning some of it off.

Fuck that place. She didn't need it anymore. She was strong. Solid. Safe.

Because she'd *made* herself safe.

Bella forced herself to look at Chuck's body. There were three holes in the back of his shirt. Now that he was facedown, she could see a puckered scar at the base of his skull—the mark left behind by the experimental implants Stynger had surgically inserted in too many men in an effort to control them. And if they couldn't be controlled, the poison housed inside the implants would kill them so they couldn't rat her out.

A team of scientists and engineers had been working on stopping and reversing the effects, but so far hadn't had any luck.

"He's one of Stynger's," she said.

Victor nodded and shared a look with Payton she couldn't translate. All she knew was that it was full of concern. "We saw that. Do you not remember us talking about it a second ago?"

She didn't, but years of spinning lies had given her the

skills she needed to do so now. "I remember. I'm just a bit distracted by the dead man in my office."

"One of the lawyers will be here soon," Payton said. "Bella, you should limit your statement to the police until you're feeling like yourself again."

"I know what I'm doing," she said. "I don't need your advice."

"Then take mine," Victor said. "Play the scared-victim card until the lawyer arrives. I'd really rather not spend more time in jail than I need to."

Victor in jail? That didn't seem right. All he'd done was stop a man from killing her.

Sirens grew louder outside. A couple of minutes later, police and paramedics arrived on the scene. She and Victor both gave their statements. When they came back for another round of questioning, she grudgingly took Payton's advice and told them she was too rattled to talk about it more—they could speak to her lawyer.

"You're going to need some stitches," said one of the paramedics. He was crouched at her feet. He'd cut away the bottom half of her yoga pants and she hadn't even realized it had happened.

She looked down and saw the cuts across her calves. As if her acknowledgment of the wound triggered something in her brain, she finally felt the sting of the injury. Strangely, she wasn't sure what she was supposed to do about the problem, though she knew she *should* know.

Payton must have seen her distress. He stepped forward and addressed the paramedic. "Dr. Vaughn is on her way. If there are no serious injuries, she can handle things from here."

"She should go to the hospital," said the young man at her feet.

"No," Bella said, too fast and loud. Her denial sounded desperate even to her own ears. "No hospitals."

She'd spent enough time in them already. A few little cuts weren't going to send her back.

"You'll have to sign some paperwork if you're refusing to let us take you in."

Bella held out her hand. "Give me a pen."

As she finished scrawling her name and looked up, she saw one of the officers handcuff Victor and escort him out.

Fury exploded in her gut, clearing her foggy head for a second. "You can't arrest him," she said. "He saved my life."

The lawyer shot her a harsh glare and shook his head. "Stay quiet. All you're going to do is make things worse."

Bella clamped her lips shut and swallowed down the string of vile curses she wanted to fling at both the lawyer and the cops. How dare they handcuff Victor like he was a criminal? He was a good, honorable man. He'd risked his life to serve his country and keep all of them safe. And this was how they repaid him?

She grabbed the lawyer's thousand-dollar suit jacket in her bloody fist. "You get him out, understand?"

"I'll do my best."

"Your best had better have him back at his place before dinnertime. Or we're finding a new law firm to represent the Edge."

Payton shifted his stance. She wasn't sure if it was to block her view of Victor being hauled away in handcuffs or to get close enough to stop her from inflicting violence on the suit. Whatever the case, the lawyer left, bringing up the tail end of the police parade.

Payton gave her a paternal frown. "No need for threats, Bella. I'm sure Victor will be free soon. He did nothing wrong. He's a highly decorated soldier with a lot of powerful friends."

She unleashed some of her anger on Payton, not even caring that they had an audience. "This is all your fault.

If you'd taken Stynger down years ago, rather than helping her, that man they just wheeled out of here would
still be alive. He never would have attacked me, and Victor never would have had to shoot him. You don't get to
pretend like it's all going to work out fine, like it isn't a
fucking tragedy that someone lost a son, a brother, or a
father today. That man's blood is on your hands, just like
mine is." She thrust her bloody palms in his face.

Payton flinched and closed his eyes for a split second
before facing her again. "I'm fully aware of my role in all
of this. I accept responsibility for my actions and lack
thereof. If you want to punish me, so be it, but your energy is better spent on finding Stynger and stopping her."

"You think I don't know that? I've worked myself
sick trying to clean up your mess. She's in the wind—
vanished—and she's taken Gage with her. If he doesn't
come back in one piece, if she put one of those damn
implants in his head, I'm holding you personally responsible."

Payton bowed his head. "That makes two of us."

Chapter Eight

Jordyn Stynger pulled up the video feed connected to Gage Dallas's cell. She'd been watching him for weeks now and still couldn't figure out why he was here.

Mother always began altering her test subjects within a few days of acquiring them. What was so special about this one?

Maybe it was because he'd come of his own free will, knowing what awaited him. His brother Adam had been the one who was supposed to come, but Gage had taken his place.

Was it possible that Mother was growing a conscience? Jordyn had hoped to channel her mother's abilities into something less destructive for a long time—ever since she'd learned that the work they did was less about saving the world and more about money and power. There was no impending threat as Jordyn had always been taught. The world wasn't coming to an end. Mother's cash was.

Jordyn had had more than one opportunity to leave, but if she did, who would mitigate the damage Mother did? Who would dare go against a woman who had an army of men willing to do whatever she ordered, no matter how horrible or dangerous?

The only saving grace Jordyn had was that she was

Norma Stynger's daughter—her only genetic link to the future. There was power in that, but as time went on, Jordyn began to wonder if even that was enough to protect her from Mother's wrath.

The video screen blinked to life, showing the newcomer in his cell. He was shirtless as he exercised, using what little furniture was in the small space as his gym. Sweat trickled down his spine. His muscles quivered with effort as he pulled himself up inside the frame of the door. There was only the thinnest strip of material to cling to, but his strong fingers held tight as he slid up and down along the locked door.

He was never let out of his room, and the deep tan of his skin had begun to fade from lack of sunlight. Other than that, he showed no signs of deterioration as some of the men who came here did.

Then again, the records showed that none of Mother's protocols had been inflicted on him.

Yet.

The only entries Jordyn found after hacking into the encrypted files on him listed a series of blood draws, sedatives to keep him asleep at night, and one other procedure she'd never seen before: DNA extraction.

There were no more details listed that she could find, and there was no way something as simple as a mouth swab could hurt a man as strong as Gage.

He went on with his exercises, winding down with a series of slow poses that looked vaguely like yoga. There was more violence than relaxation in the moves, but each one put a new set of muscles on display for Jordyn's enjoyment.

She often spied on the men who were brought here, but not one of them had compelled her the way Gage had. Not even Jake Staite. And she'd nearly died helping him escape.

She still wasn't sure if he'd survived, or if her efforts

to help the kind soldier had failed utterly. Perhaps even killed him.

The question was, could she risk that all over again for Gage? Could she help free him knowing it would cost her who knew how many days in the White Room?

A wave of nausea overcame her at the mere thought. She rushed to the bathroom with just enough time to empty her stomach into the toilet. After the retching stopped, she sat back on her heels and breathed.

She couldn't face the White Room again. She'd barely survived last time. It had taken her weeks to recover, and she often had nightmares that she was trapped in there again, strapped down and unable to escape the pain.

She could only hope that her punishment hadn't been in vain, that the package she'd delivered to Jake's best friend had made it to him and done some good. Assuming he was even still alive.

She kept telling herself that she had no other choice. She couldn't sleep at night knowing there was something else she could do to save the one man who'd bothered to give her the truth about Mother and her work.

Still, the threat of the White Room hung heavy over Jordyn's head. No matter how compelling Gage was, reaching out to him was dangerous. Perhaps even deadly.

Unless she was out of Mother's reach. That had been her mistake with Jake. She should have let him take her along with him when he escaped. Surely whatever she faced in the outside world was better than her life here.

Jordyn rinsed the bile from her mouth and went back to her computer. Gage's chest was heaving from whatever he'd been doing a second ago. He stood in front of the camera, staring at it as sweat slid down his muscular frame. His skin was flushed, and his faded blue eyes seemed to glow as he looked at her through the lens.

Not that he could see her. The video feed was one-way. There was no way he could even know she was watching him.

Still, he watched the camera, his face showing no hint of emotion. No fear. No anger. Just endless patience.

For what, she had no idea. All she knew was that she couldn't look away. He was a real man, living and breathing, with hopes and dreams. Mother hadn't destroyed that for him yet. But she would. Soon.

Jordyn knew in that moment that she had to help him escape. He deserved a life, and unlike the other men she'd seen pass through the labs, Gage could actually still have one.

The only question was whether or not she'd survive to have one, too.

Randolph dialed his contact inside enemy lines. Lila, Bella's secretary, answered in a voice soggy with tears. "Hello?"

"Where are you?"

"At home. How's my baby?"

"He's fine. Stynger has kept him safe, just like she promised." It was mostly true. The toddler was still alive, but there was no guarantee how long he'd stay that way if Stynger got bored and decided to use him as a lab rat.

"I want to see him."

"You will. Soon." That was a lie, but a necessary one. If Lila freaked out, she'd be no good to anyone. And Randolph really needed her to stay sharp for just a while longer. "But for now you have work to do."

"I've done everything you said. I even let that man into the office without running a background check. If Bella finds out, I'll be fired."

"Would you rather have a job or a son?"

She stifled a sob. "Please don't hurt my baby."

"Then do your real job and focus. How was Bella after the attack?"

"Shaken. Angry. The police were at the office for hours. There's still a mess to clean up. Papers everywhere, broken glass. Blood."

"Where is she now?"

"I don't know. I don't track her after hours."

"Then start. I want to know where she is all the time."

"What's going on? Is something about to happen?" asked Lila.

The woman was too smart for Randolph's peace of mind. It was best if he changed the subject before she asked any questions that would make him need to kill her. She was far more useful alive. At least for now.

"What's on Bella's schedule for the next few days?"

"She told me to stop booking appointments for her. She wants to spend all her time looking for Gage."

Interesting. One man was that important to her? Randolph had worked for her long enough to know that she was possessive and territorial, but she'd never been quite so concerned about his well-being when he'd worked for her. Then again, she'd always had it in for him.

"Do you know her plans? Where she's going to look?"

"She doesn't share that kind of thing with me. Especially not since the incident a few weeks ago when I was forced to leave a secured door open and drug an innocent girl so one of your men could abduct her. The whole office is still nervous about that."

"Do they suspect you?"

"Not that I can tell. Bella keeps telling me to be careful and never walk to my car alone at night. If she thought it was me, she wouldn't worry so much, would she?"

Bella was smart enough to pretend not to suspect her, but he didn't think that the emotionally precarious Lila needed to know that. He needed her too much to unsettle her nerves.

"I'm going to send you a listening device," Randolph said. "I want you to plant it in her office once the mess is cleared away."

"No. I can't. I've already done too much for you. Bella is a good woman. I know you want to hurt her. I can't help you do that."

"I have no desire to hurt her or anyone else," he lied.

"Then why did you send that man?"

"We just wanted to scare her a little, rattle her so she'll start making mistakes."

"Mistakes that could get her killed."

"I'm not going to debate this with you. Plant the device, Lila. Unless you don't care what happens to your baby boy."

"No," Lila rushed to say, tears roughening her tone. "I'll do it. Just don't hurt him."

"I'll have someone drop it off at your home tonight. It's small. You shouldn't have any trouble hiding it."

"There's a team that sweeps for bugs every couple of days. They're going to find it."

"Do you know the sweep schedule?"

"No."

"Then I suggest you find it. If you get caught there will be nothing I can do to help you."

"This is the last job, Randolph. Once I do this, I want my son back."

He laughed. "If you really think you can make demands, then you just do that and see how well it ends up. For both you and your boy."

She was crying now, not even bothering to hide the tears in her voice. "If I get caught, what will happen to him?"

"There's no telling what Stynger might do. I suggest you don't get caught."

"Will you keep him safe from her?"

The thought of Randolph being any kid's caretaker

was laughable. But rather than push Lila further, he played along. "I'll do what I can. You need to do the same. Between us, I'm sure we can have your boy home soon."

She sniffed. "Thank you."

"Don't thank me. Just do your job." He hung up.

With any luck at all, this would all be over in a few more days. Stynger would be safely ensconced in her new home, out of reach. Keeping Lila calm would no longer be necessary. And Bella would learn that tossing aside a man with his skills was the biggest mistake of her life.

Randolph dialed another contact. He gave the man careful instructions, outlining every step of the prisoner transport he wanted to happen. If Bella wanted to find Gage, then that was the bait Randolph would dangle.

Chapter Nine

It was nearly midnight when Victor finally pulled into his driveway after a long day of interrogation and bad coffee.

Bella was waiting for him. He recognized her shiny red truck instantly, and some of the grinding fatigue of the day faded away under a sudden burst of excitement.

He'd missed her, and until now, he hadn't realized just how much. Perhaps it was ridiculous of him to do so, but he couldn't deny that's how he felt. They'd been together for so many days in a row, he'd gotten used to her company. Spending the day at the police station, undergoing a nonstop string of questions while Payton and a team of lawyers pulled strings to earn Victor's freedom, had done nothing to change that.

A heavy pile of tension slid from his shoulders as he opened his garage door and pulled inside. One long, curvy leg exited Bella's truck, followed by the rest of her. The sinuous glide of her body as she walked into his garage filled his rearview mirror and his attention.

What was it about this woman that got under his skin? He'd had plenty of beautiful women in his life. Family money made sure of that. There was always another pretty face hoping to help him spend his wealth.

None of them had ever captured his attention so completely. None of them made him ache with the need to be near her.

Whatever his odd feelings, he wished like hell they'd just go away. Wanting a woman whom he worked with—whom he worked *for*—was both inconvenient and uncomfortable.

When it wasn't completely thrilling.

By the time he turned off his engine and got out of his car, Bella was standing beside him. "Rough day?" she asked.

He nodded to her bandaged hands and the bulges of more bandages under her soft, clingy pants. "No worse than yours."

"Payton told me they let you go."

"I'm sure I'll have a few more people to convince, but the lawyer is confident that this will all go away."

"The company will cover the legal expenses, of course."

There were a few small bruises on her cheek from where she'd been hit. Victor wanted to kiss them away so badly he had to plant his feet to keep from taking a step toward her to do just that.

"That's not necessary," he said.

She looked down at her shoes. "It is. The least the company can do is cover your expenses. You saved my life." Her chin lifted and her striking gray eyes met his gaze. "Thank you, Victor. I really didn't want to die today."

He saw his fingers settle lightly on her cheek. Only then did he realize he'd let himself touch her.

The feel of her warm, smooth skin under his hand streaked through his nervous system, setting it on fire. Part of him that had been tense all day began unclenching, while the rest of him was waking up and preparing to wage whatever battle he had to face to make her his.

Her eyes fluttered for a second before she refocused on him. She wet her lips. He didn't know if she was nervous or sensed his intense desire to kiss her. Either way, his animal brain saw the action as a green light.

His feet shifted closer to hers. He could feel her body heat now, sense how well she would fit his frame if he ever got lucky enough to have her pressed against him. He wouldn't have to strain his neck to kiss her. She was just the right height for him to really take his time with her mouth and coax her body to soften for him.

Victor struggled to pick up the conversational thread she'd laid down. "Anyone would have done the same thing."

Her long fingers settled on his chest, causing a roar of victory to course through him. She'd touched him. She wouldn't have done that if she didn't see him as more than her employee, would she?

"You're wrong," she said, though her gentle tone eased the sting of her words. "I'd like to think that most of the men I've hired wouldn't hesitate, but there were several of them nearby. You were the one who got there first. You were the one who risked his freedom by pulling the trigger. I won't forget that."

If he didn't ease back, he was going to kiss her. And as much as he wanted his mouth covering hers, he didn't want her to think that he was demanding payback in the form of sex. She was too important to him for him to screw up things between them with such a stupid, rookie move.

It felt like ripping off his own fingers one at a time, but he managed to take his hands from her skin and shove them in his pocket, right next to his growing erection.

"Does that mean I get a raise?" he teased.

"Not even close, honey." She grinned and pushed against his shoulder. The slight wince tightening the skin around her eyes reminded him that she was injured. Whatever things he might want to do with her, however willing she might momentarily be because of his actions today, there was no way in hell he was going to fuck an injured woman and risk hurting her more.

His libido screamed as he shoved it back in its cage and forced himself to pretend he didn't want her.

"I'm starving," he said. "Want to come in for a really late lunch?"

"It's almost midnight."

"Both me and my empty stomach are well aware. Join me?"

She hesitated so long he was almost sure she was going to turn him down. "Okay, but just for a minute. Franklin is house-sitting for me. They spent so many hours going through my place with a fine-tooth comb, they didn't want to leave the house unattended."

"I like this plan. It'll keep you safe." He led the way inside, looking at his empty house with fresh eyes. Everything was new and in good repair, but he hadn't lived here long enough to make it feel like home. There were no pictures on the walls. The furniture was of high quality, but in bland neutral colors. His kitchen was stocked with only the bare necessities. As they entered it, he heard his footsteps echo against the empty walls.

"I guess you didn't want to eat police station food?" she asked.

"They didn't offer a meal. I think they were trying to make me crack." He opened the fridge, hoping there was something fast and easy to fill his growling stomach.

Bella laughed, and the sound stroked along his spine, making his toes curl like he was some kind of lovesick schoolboy. "Guess they didn't know how tough you were."

He knew he was tough, but it made him proud that she thought so, too. Not that she would have hired anyone who wasn't tough. "They figured it out relatively fast. Once General Norwood started calling in favors, people started paying attention."

"Did you get any uncomfortable questions?"

"You mean about what we do at the Edge?"

She nodded, and her glossy hair slipped over her shoulder to caress her breast. Victor's mouth began to water in a way that had nothing to do with food.

He cleared his throat and peered into the refrigerator, seeing nothing half as appealing as the woman standing ten feet away. "I'm trained in how to deal with interrogations. They didn't learn any secrets from me."

"That's good." Her voice was closer now. He hadn't heard her approach, but she was right behind him, staring over his shoulder. "Bachelor fridge. Looks like mine, only yours has less fuzzy stuff in it."

He grabbed a block of cheese and a couple of apples. "Can't get your housekeeper to clean out the fridge?"

"Nope. She says it's a biohazard."

"She's probably right." He sliced the cheese into cubes and arranged it on a plate.

Bella moved around his kitchen, opening cabinets and snooping without apology. "Was it horrible?"

"The interrogation? Nah. I can take it."

"No," she said. "Killing a man."

The knife stilled in the middle of cutting an apple. He hadn't expected the question, nor was he sure why she was asking. "He's not the first man I've killed, Bella."

"I know, but that doesn't make it easy, does it?"

"I didn't enjoy it, but there was no choice. He was going to shoot you. I couldn't let that happen."

"He had no choice, either." Her voice wavered for a second before she continued. "Stynger made him attack me. He was as much a victim in this as I was."

"Are you saying you wished I hadn't killed him?"

Her long fingers curled around the handle of his silverware drawer. Her back was to him, but he could see some kind of tension vibrating along her spine. Anger? Fear? Stress? He couldn't tell, but whatever it was, he wanted to soothe it away until she was calm and relaxed.

"No," she said. "He had to die before he hurt some-one else. The men Stynger controls are like rabid ani-mals, even after the implants are removed. Razor's friend Jake had his removed and he's still being held for his own safety as well as hers. If that ever happened to me, I'd rather eat a bullet than be held in Payton's secret prison for the rest of my life." She turned to face him. "Wouldn't you?"

"I haven't thought about it."

"We've spent weeks hunting down a woman who can crawl inside your brain and make even a strong man like you do whatever she wants. How can you *not* have thought about it?"

"I think about how to find her, how to stop her. I think about what her next move might be and how I can prevent it from happening." He also spent a fair amount of time thinking about Bella and how she might sound, taste and feel if he ever got her in his bed. Not that he was going to admit that.

"If you'd seen the videos of Jake since his imprison-ment, you'd have the same nightmares I do. I had to stop watching them."

"I have seen them. All of them. Norwood required it of me before I took this job."

"How can you not have thought about what you'd do if it happened to you, then?"

"Because it doesn't matter. If Stynger gets her hands on me, what I want will no longer matter. She'll make sure of that. Our only option is to keep it from happening."

Her hands shook so hard he could see it from across the room. She shoved them into her pockets and swal-lowed hard. "She has Gage. I've known him for years. He's unstoppable. Incorruptible. I honestly thought that his volunteering to go inside the belly of the beast was a good idea." Her gray eyes brightened, but he couldn't tell if it was from tears or anger. "Letting him go was a mistake. He hasn't made contact as ordered because he's no longer the man I knew."

"You don't know that. You can't let yourself think like that. He probably just hasn't had a chance to make contact. You have to give him more time."

"As if I have any other choice. We still have no clue where she is. With all the cameras and satellites we have access to, how is that even possible?"

"She moves her operation around a lot. She uses multiple locations. She hides underground and keeps her reach small enough that we have trouble seeing it."

"She's destroyed dozens of lives. We should have been able to find her by now."

Victor wiped his hands and went to Bella. He couldn't stand seeing her suffer without trying to ease her pain. It wasn't his place, but he didn't care. She looked like she needed to be held, so that's what he was going to do.

He didn't give her time to protest his hug. He simply wrapped his arms around her and pulled her close.

She flinched and tensed for a second, but then her body melted, giving in to his hug.

Every sweet curve and sleek hollow of her body fit against him with an almost palpable click of completion. He felt like the parts of him that had been missing all his life were finally back where they belonged. The feeling was so strong, so keen, it nearly scared him. If not for his original goal of offering comfort to a woman who so desperately needed it, he would have backed away and fled.

Instead, he tightened his hold, squeezing a nearly silent groan of contentment from her chest. She laid her cheek on his shoulder and pulled in a long, deep breath. As she let it out, her hands settled tentatively on his back, returning the hug.

"What the hell are you doing, Temple?" she asked, her voice far too faint and weak to sound like the authoritative woman he knew.

"Reminding you that you're not alone. Seemed like the kind of reminder you needed."

"If I'd wanted a hug, I would have ordered you to give me one." The words were delivered with no bite. If anything, she tightened her hold on him.

"No one's watching. You don't have to be in boss mode."

She pushed away so suddenly, he knew it had been the wrong thing to say.

"Being boss isn't a mode, sweetheart," she snapped. "I *am* boss. Twenty-four, seven. Next time you need to hug something, find a teddy bear." She dug in her pocket for her keys and headed for the door.

He put his fingers on her shoulder, but even the light touch was enough to stop her in her tracks. "Bella, don't go. I didn't mean to question your authority."

She didn't turn around. Her shoulders straightened and went rigid. "My authority is strong enough to handle a little questioning, but it was clearly a mistake coming here. You're more than capable of dealing with your legal issues. I shouldn't have worried. I should have known you'd have a team of lawyers on retainer, not to mention Norwood backing you."

"I'm glad you came. It was nice knowing that you care." He wanted her to turn around. Look him in the eye.

She didn't.

"I care about all of my employees. Don't think this is some kind of special treatment. Good night, Victor. See you bright and early tomorrow morning. Don't be late."

Chapter Ten

Gage had no access to a clock, but he could tell it was getting close to the time the lab tech would come in and take his vitals. The big-boned, beady-eyed nerd in a lab coat came in at the same time every day. At first he'd been accompanied by an armed guard who was clearly annoyed by the distraction.

Gage offered no resistance, showed no sign of aggression. After a couple of weeks, the guard disappeared. The nerd was skittish at first, but Gage was careful with his body language, keeping it open and nonthreatening.

After a couple more weeks, the nerd seemed more at ease. He even smiled back at Gage once.

That was the sign he'd been waiting for. The nerd in a lab coat large enough to fit Gage trusted him. It was time to escape and find some way of making contact with Bella.

Sitting around this place locked in a cell for weeks was doing nothing but driving him crazy. He'd seen nothing of importance. He'd been knocked out before coming here, so he didn't even have any idea how far away Stynger's current lab might be from home. For all he knew, he was on another continent entirely.

The only way to find out was to get out of here and discover where he was.

Gage was careful not to alter his routine in any way. He'd set it up for exactly this purpose—to make whoever was watching him on that camera feel safe that all was well. Nothing had changed. Nothing to see. He was still the same docile, caged animal he'd been all along. They were completely in control.

He washed away the sweat from his workout and put on a pair of drawstring pants provided for him. He didn't know if the string threaded through his waistband was an oversight or a test. Either way, the improvised garrote was coming out tonight. He'd cut off the flow of blood to the nerd's brain, steal his clothes, and make his escape.

His skin prickled an instant before he saw the shadow of feet beneath his door.

It was time.

The door opened, but instead of the beady-eyed nerd, there was a young woman wheeling the instrument cart into his room.

She was dressed in jeans and a sweater the color of a forest in spring. The white overcoat she wore identified her as one of the lab techs or doctors. Her long dark hair spilled down over her breasts, falling in a silky wave that made his fingertips twitch against the need to touch.

She was pretty. Distractingly so. Her skin was so pale from lack of sun he could see a delicate network of veins just below the surface. There was a slight pink flush in her cheeks that warmed her complexion, but it was her eyes that held his attention. Light gray-green, fringed with long black lashes and filled with the kind of compassion he never thought he'd see here.

She closed the door behind herself and pushed the cart into the center of the room. "Peter wasn't feeling well, so I'm here to take your vitals."

It was a lie. He could see it in the way she couldn't hold his gaze, in the minute shift of muscles around her eyes and mouth.

"He's sick?" asked Gage, hoping to trip her up in her lie so he could figure out what her game was.

Had they realized he was making his move tonight? Had something he'd done given away his intentions? If so, he couldn't think of what it might be. He'd been careful in the way only a man whose life is on the line could be.

"Something he ate," she said. Another lie.

She opened a case and took out a stethoscope. Her hands were shaking.

Fear? Nerves? Did she know something he didn't?

"What's your name?" he asked.

"Jordyn. Have a seat, please."

He did as she asked, wondering if he was going to have to lull another lab tech into a false sense of confidence. If so, that could take weeks, though he had to admit that the scenery this time would be a whole lot nicer.

She wrapped a blood pressure cuff around his arm. It took her a couple of tries to get it right, telling him that either this was not her normal job, or he was making her nervous.

Her light, feminine scent drifted to his nose, sparking something in the deepest, most primal part of his brain. He wasn't sure what had happened, but she no longer felt like a complete stranger to him. For reasons he couldn't name, he felt like he *knew* her.

Maybe she was a walking form of chemical warfare, laced with something to throw him off guard.

If so, he was half convinced she'd just won a damn big battle.

"Will you tell Peter I hope he feels better soon?" asked Gage.

Jordyn went still with the stethoscope halfway to her ears. "I will. Thank you."

"For what?"

"Caring. There's not enough of that down here."

Ah, so they were underground. That was a little piece of information that would no doubt prove useful at some point.

Gage wondered what else he could get her to tell him. He wasn't normally much for conversation, but he'd make an exception if it meant accomplishing his mission.

"No one will tell me why I'm here," he said, hoping she'd take the bait.

She remained silent while she took his blood pressure and recorded it. He played along, refusing to push. This kind of interrogation was more about enticing and coaxing than it was about force.

She pressed two fingers against his wrist to take his pulse. They were icy cold, and his protective male instincts hot-wired his brain for a second as he took her hands in his to warm them.

Her lips parted in surprise. She even let out a little gasp, but she didn't pull away.

Gage let the small victory course through him. Perhaps he was better off listening to his instincts with this woman. His brain had served him well, but he was still locked up down here, and the only piece of information he'd been able to collect had been from Jordyn's lovely mouth.

He pressed her hands flat against his chest and covered them, pinning them against his warmth.

A flicker of something passed through her eyes, but they closed before he could tell what it was. She stood there for a moment, eyes closed, completely vulnerable, letting him warm her hands.

Didn't she know how dangerous it was to be this close to him? Had no one warned her to keep her distance?

The idea that she wasn't protecting herself set his teeth on edge. He didn't like her putting herself in danger, though he had no idea why he cared. She worked for Stynger. That made her suspect at best and enemy at worst.

Didn't it?

After a few seconds, she opened her eyes again and looked at him. Even though the room was brightly lit, her pupils were large enough to drive a truck through them.

Either she was drugged, or really liked what she saw.

Gage wished it was the latter for several reasons, most of which he had no business considering. The rest of them would make this job so much easier. If she was attracted to him, he could use that to his advantage. All he had to do was play along. Let her think he was interested.

That wasn't going to be hard at all. She was lovely in a rare, unattainable kind of way, like an orchid growing from a sheer cliff. Only she smelled far better than any flower ever could.

Her voice had a bit of roughness to it, like she didn't speak very often. "Rumor is you came here of your own free will. Shouldn't you know why you're here?"

"I know why I came, not why I'm *still* here. Alive, I mean." He looked straight into her eyes and asked, "Do you?"

She glanced nervously at the camera and pulled her chilly fingers out of his reach, turning her back to him. "No, and if I did, I wouldn't tell you. It's not my place."

When she turned back around, she had a needle and several empty vials in her hands. Her face was empty of the feminine interest he'd glimpsed earlier.

So much for winning her over.

He extended his arm to let her do what she'd come to do. They'd taken blood from him every few days. He had no idea why they wanted it, but was afraid that if he asked her, she'd clam up even more.

His job was to learn what he could, escape, and contact Bella so she could take this whole place down. The idea wasn't nearly as compelling as it had been before Jordyn had walked into his room. He wasn't sure what it was about her, but he didn't want her to be here when the shit hit the fan.

Which was a ridiculous notion.

Maybe they had drugged him with something more than the sedative they pumped into his room every night. Maybe whatever they'd given him had already started screwing with his good judgment. Maybe *she* was doing the screwing.

She finished taking his blood and set everything on the cart. She would leave now, and his opportunity to escape would go right along with her.

His fingers grazed the drawstring at his waist. It wouldn't take much to rip that free and wrap it around her slender throat. He wouldn't even have to kill her. He'd just knock her out, take her key card and find the exit.

Of course, part of his plan had been stealing the nerd's lab coat to help him blend in, and there was no way the one Jordyn wore would stretch across his shoulders.

She turned to face him. Her back was to the camera. He didn't know if it was monitored or not, but he needed only a few seconds to knock her out and clear the door.

"Is there anything you need?" she asked. Her voice dropped to a faint whisper. "A book to read, maybe?"

Reading would alter his schedule, but if she was offering gifts, he didn't want to turn them down and shove a wedge between them. Better to accept what she wanted to give him and show his gratitude. "Yes. Thank you."

She reached into her lab coat pocket and pulled out a small leather-bound book of poetry. He'd just as soon gouge his own eyes out one at a time with flimsy sporks as read it, but smiled anyway as he took it from her hands.

His fingertips grazed hers, and he felt the connection wing down his spine like an electric current.

Her eyes met his and he watched as her pupils expanded to eat up the pretty gray-green ring.

Again she spoke in a whisper. "My favorite one is on page thirty-two. You should read it and tell me what you think."

"I will."

"I'll try to come back tomorrow so we can discuss it."

Great. Now he had to actually read the thing or offend her. "I look forward to it."

"You're not allowed to have the book, so you should tuck it away somewhere safe."

He realized now that she'd been using her body to hide what they were doing from the camera. Her whispers were probably hard to pick up with most microphones, confirming his suspicion that he was being monitored that way, too.

Gage leaned forward so she could hear his quiet words. "I won't rat you out. Promise."

Her slender shoulders sagged in relief. He didn't think she was faking her reaction, which meant that she wasn't just planting the book to get him in trouble or to see where he might hide it, leading them to find other things he might have hidden.

He hadn't. Not that there'd been anything to hide. Every contact that had been made with him had been carefully controlled.

Until this one.

So what had changed? Why send her now? If she was meant to rattle him, why not send her before?

He had no idea what to make of it, and until he did, it was best if he kept up with his normal routine and pretended like nothing had changed.

"I have to go now," she said.

"I hope to see you again," he said, and interestingly, it wasn't a lie. He did want to see her again.

She left. Gage sat on his bed for several minutes while her scent dissipated. He was almost convinced that as soon as it did, his mind would start running smoothly again. If she was a walking chemical weapon, surely her power over him would fade as soon as she was gone.

It didn't. Instead, his thoughts stayed fixed on her, trying to piece together the puzzle she created. When nothing came to him, he angled his body so that the camera couldn't see and opened the book to page thirty-two.

Inside was a stick of chewing gum acting as a bookmark. The poem on the page was titled "On Your Side." He opened the foil wrapper carefully, wondering if it might contain some kind of poison. What he found was far more intriguing. She'd written on the inside of the wrapper, *Use the gum to plug the tube under the bed. Pretend to sleep.*

Gage didn't know what the note meant, but there was only one way to find out. He popped the gum in his mouth and flushed the wrapper down the toilet. If Jordyn was truly on his side, there was no way he was going to let her get caught helping him. And if she wasn't on his side, he'd overpower her and escape without the benefit of a lab coat that fit or the hindrance of guilt over hurting an unarmed woman.

Randolph answered his phone out of fear, rather than any sense of duty to the woman he worked for. "Yes?"

"It's been hours. Has the second dose been administered yet?" asked Norma Stynger.

He briefly thought about lying, but decided that was too high of a risk. "She hasn't been home yet. She only left the office a few minutes ago."

"Your job was to ensure she was subjected to the drug once a day for several days. Are you telling me you failed?"

"She has to go home and shower sometime."

"And if she doesn't? If she leaves town again or spends the night at work?"

"Security at the Edge is too high for me to sneak in, especially after I took care of that other thing you wanted."

"I wanted you to frighten her, to increase her output of adrenaline to trigger the serum."

"That's what I did."

"No, you killed one of my men and gave the enemy another device to reverse engineer."

"But Bella was scared. My contact at the Edge confirmed that." Lila wasn't of much use, but there were a few things she was good at. Reporting about her boss's emotional state after the attack at the office had been one of them.

"You're careless," Stynger said. "Perhaps you should come in and we'll work on that flaw."

Panic flowed through Randolph's system. He knew what she meant—that she would fuck with his head until he did whatever she asked of him. Even if it meant drilling a hole in his skull and shoving one of her precious devices inside.

"I've got this," he hurried to reassure her. "I'll make sure she gets the next dose soon."

"You'd better. If she goes without it for too long, we'll have to start the process all over again. My test results will be skewed, and I'll be very displeased."

"You just worry about the relocation. I'll handle Bella."

"See that you do," Stynger said. "Or I *will* make you."

Chapter Eleven

Bella was still shaking by the time she pulled into her driveway at home.

What the hell was she thinking letting Victor pull her in like that? And hugging her? That was so far out of line, she didn't even know what to call it. Insubordination seemed a tad extreme, especially considering how good it felt. Disrespectful was closer to the mark, but even that left a bad taste in her mouth. His intent seemed pure, if a bit misguided.

The real problem was that she'd liked the hug far too much. Between the shitty day she'd had, which had caused a basic human need for comfort, and the way he lit her body up with physical need, being in his arms had been pretty fucking awesome.

If only he hadn't talked and screwed things up like that, they would have gone a lot further than just hugging. If she was smart, she'd thank him for opening his mouth and stopping her from making what would undoubtedly have been a huge mistake.

Exhaustion bore down on her. She hadn't slept well last night, and had spent the entire day knotted with nerves. Attackers with lethal intent had a way of taking the energy out of a woman like nothing else could. Sure, the adrenaline rush kept her high for a while, but the crash was brutal, and Bella was definitely crashing.

She took several deep breaths and forced herself to get out of her truck and go inside. Her legs were heavy. Her feet felt like they weighed ten tons each. The stairs leading to her door seemed more like scaling a mountain than a quick climb.

The lights were on, reminding her that Franklin was in there, waiting for her return. All she had left to do before falling into bed was to smile and thank him for his efforts.

Even that seemed like almost too much work.

She unlocked her front door and stepped inside. The smell of lemon cleaner filled her nose, telling her the team had taken a bit of extra time in their efforts to make sure her house was free of danger.

Franklin came out of the kitchen wearing yellow rubber gloves. His gray T-shirt was stained with bleach spots, and there were smudges of dirt on his face and forearms. The knees of his jeans looked like they'd been used to clean an engine.

As soon as he saw it was her, all the color drained from his face. He looked genuinely afraid, and he wasn't a man who scared easily. "I know you're going to be pissed, but please understand I had no choice."

She wasn't going to be pissed that he cleaned. Saved her the trouble of caring enough to do the job herself. "Let your neat freak flag fly at my house all you like, sweetheart. I don't mind."

He looked at the gloves as if just realizing he wore them. "It's not that. It's . . . the other thing."

Bella stifled a growl. "I'm tired. It's been a long day. Whatever the other thing is, we'll talk about it in the morning."

She headed for the kitchen to grab a glass of water, but Franklin stepped in her path. His voice was a mix of fear and apology. "Payton's in there."

"Oh, *hell*, no." She shoved past the young man, and sure enough, Payton was sitting at her kitchen table, sipping hot tea. "Get the fuck out," she ordered.

"I tried to call. Apparently you've blocked my number."

"You think? Perhaps because I didn't want to talk to you."

"That's enough, Bella. Your childish tantrums aren't going to help Gage."

She opened her mouth to show him what a real childish tantrum looked like when his words finally registered through the fog of her exhaustion. "What about Gage?"

"We have reason to believe he'll be moved soon."

"Moved? From where? How do you know this? And who the hell is *we*?"

"Norwood contacted me an hour ago. He's been working his own angles."

"And you hid this from me?"

"No. I swear I didn't. He didn't tell me anything until tonight. He knew I might share with you, and he wasn't ready for that."

Bella turned to Franklin just long enough to say, "Thank you for watching the house. Now go home."

"Are you sure you don't want me to stay?" he asked. "Play referee?"

She lifted her eyebrows and stared at him. That was enough to send him scurrying away.

"Were you worried about what he might hear?" asked Payton. "Or about having a witness to your impending violence?"

"Don't flatter yourself. As much as I want to punch you in the face, you're not worth even a single night in jail for assault. Now spill. Where is Gage?"

"We don't know. All Norwood got was a bit of chatter between two people we know work for Stynger."

"What *do* you know?"

"Only that there's some kind of important cargo being moved tonight."

"And you think it's Gage?"

"One of them slipped and said *he* instead of *it*. We're assuming the cargo is human rather than a lab animal."

She shoved away her exhaustion and forced herself to start putting together a plan. "Where?"

"As soon as I tell you that, you'll fly out of here to go after him."

"He's my friend—a concept with which you're doubtlessly unfamiliar."

"Bella," he said, in that paternal tone that set her teeth on edge.

"Don't. Just don't. There's no time for one of your lectures. Where is Gage?"

"I'll tell you under one condition."

She didn't want to bargain with the devil, but this was not the time to be stubborn. Gage needed her. "What?"

"When this is all said and done, when Gage is home safely, you and I are going to sit down and hash things out. We've spent too many years together to let our relationship fall apart the way it has."

The need to scream at him surged up her throat. She had to grit her teeth and swallow hard to hold it in. "Fine. You want to talk, we'll talk. Just know that it's not going to be some polite chat. You were part of the project that ruined my life. You hid that from me for years. Lied to me. That's the kind of thing that deserves some raised voices. Possibly broken bones. You're going to sign a waiver stating you're okay with that."

"I understand. You can yell at me all you like so long as we work through our differences. I love you, Bella. You're the only family I have left."

"I'm not your family. Never have been. Family doesn't do the things you did to me. But if you want to pretend like a few nice words are going to clear the air, then fine. Whatever you have to tell yourself. I don't care anymore. All I want is to find Gage and kill Stynger."

His face fell with disappointment, but he hid it fast. "I want that, too. I've already called in a team to meet us at the Edge. A helicopter is waiting for us."

As soon as Victor arrived at the Edge to board the chopper heading out on some secret assignment and saw Bella, he knew why Payton had insisted he come along. She was out of control, and not a single one of her employees had the guts to stand up to her when she got like this. Except him.

She was pacing like a caged beast on the building's rooftop, her black hair flying around in the wash of the helicopter's blades. It was dark, but the roof was bathed in more than enough light to see her clearly. She was dressed in clinging black. A small arsenal of weapons and armor was strapped to her lean body, disguising the sleek curves he knew lay beneath. Each step she took vibrated with the need for violence, but it was her eyes that pulled him in.

She looked up as he approached, and the fear he saw on her face—the worry and pain—broke his heart. She covered her emotions as he neared, pulling on that mask of badass indifference she frequently wore, but he knew the truth.

Bella was hurting. Afraid. Gage was still missing, and it was tearing her up inside.

Victor was drawn to her, wishing he could pull her into his arms and offer her some kind of comfort. But with the pilot looking on and Payton lurking nearby, Victor knew his efforts would be both unwanted and futile.

He'd already pissed her off once tonight. He really had no desire to do so again.

"Took you long enough," she yelled over the sound of the chopper.

He didn't bother wasting his breath with excuses. He'd grabbed his gear the instant Payton had called. The only way he could have arrived faster was if someone had invented teleporters.

"Is this about Gage?" He couldn't imagine anything else that would have caused such an emotional reaction in her. Unless someone else she loved had been hurt.

She nodded, but said nothing. She got on board and strapped in. He followed her lead. Once their headsets were in place, the chopper took off.

"Fill me in," he said.

Payton was the one who spoke first. "We're intercepting a transport."

"Is Gage on it?"

"We don't know," Bella said. "I sure as hell hope so."

"Do we have more men en route?" asked Victor.

"No," Bella said, eyeing Payton with suspicion. "We still don't know who is behind our recent breach in security. The fewer people who know about this, the better. This may be our only shot at rescuing him."

Payton rolled his eyes. "I was the one who told you about the chatter, remember? I'm the one who set up the flight so we could reach the transport before it's too late."

Her lip curled with mistrust. "For all I know, you're sending us right into a trap."

"If that had been the case, I wouldn't have insisted on coming along. Or that we wait for Victor to arrive before takeoff. You're the one who wanted to rush in alone without any details."

"Maybe if you'd shared them with me, rather than keeping secrets like you always do, I could have made a more informed decision."

Victor needed to stop this argument before it esca-
lated and someone got thrown out of the chopper door.
"Can we focus on what we know? What are we walking
into?"

"Norwood has electronic eyes on the truck—a twenty-
six-foot trailer," Payton said. "My hope is that Gage is inside, but the truck could be on the receiving end, picking
him up. We'll wait until it stops, then make our move.
Chatter says the rendezvous is at oh four hundred."

Victor glanced at his watch. "Location?"

"We're not entirely clear on that. That's why Norwood is playing eyes in the sky with a satellite feed."

"How long until we intercept the truck?" asked Bella
as she began checking her weapons.

The pilot chimed in. "Forty minutes. Sit back and relax."

No way was that happening. Each second stretched
out, the tension so high it vibrated the air between Payton and Bella. Victor waited until the man was distracted
with the pilot, then reached over and put his hand on her
knee.

He knew it was inappropriate. He knew he was risking pulling back a stump where his hand used to be. He
just didn't care. All he could think about was how stiff
she was beside him, how worried and afraid she looked.

As tough as Bella wanted the world to think she
was—as tough as she had made herself—she was still
breakable. Everyone had a breaking point, and he didn't
want to see her reach hers. A little bit of comfort could
go a long way. Assuming she took it as such.

She looked at his hand for a few seconds, then up at
him. He had expected to see anger on her face, but instead, he saw something else. Lines of strain and fatigue
fanned out from her eyes. Their usual bright gray color
was a bit dull. There was a weariness about her that lasted
for the space of three heartbeats before dissipating.

She covered his hand with hers, gave him one tight

squeeze, then lifted his hand away. As soon as she did, the cracks in her usual facade closed up and that invulnerable badass he knew so well returned.

The dark landscape flew by. Victor had been on many a flight like this one before, headed into an unknown situation. He wasn't nervous, but there was a faint hum of excitement just below his skin.

His senses were running hot, taking in every detail. He could smell Bella's skin, along with leather, a metallic hint of rust and the damp nighttime air.

She stared out the window, giving him the opportunity to look at the side of her face. He loved the curve of her cheek and the little swirl of her dainty ears—not that he'd ever call them dainty to her face. Her glossy hair was tied back in a ponytail, the ends dangling down her back in a complete windblown mess. He wanted to run his fingers through it and undo the damage the chopper's blades had done, feeling the cool strands slide along his skin. They'd be warm near her scalp, and he wondered how she'd react if he grabbed a fistful of her hair and held her head in place while he kissed her.

No doubt his balls would be relocated into his throat by her knee, but it was almost worth the risk on the off chance that she wouldn't try to unman him when he touched her.

He didn't know how long he stared at her, but the sight was intriguing enough that time slid by faster than it usually did on the way to a mission.

"The truck is up ahead," said the pilot.

"Veer north so we're not noticed," Payton said.

"No," Bella said. "If Gage is on that truck, then I want to stop it in its tracks before it reaches reinforcements."

"What are you going to do?" asked Payton. "Jump on top of it?"

"Why the hell not? We brought rappelling gear for a reason. Seems a shame not to use it."

"You're injured and not in any shape for that kind of maneuver," Payton said.

"I am," Victor said. "What do we have to breach the trailer's shell?"

Payton shook his head. "Doesn't matter. It's not going to happen. We head north."

The chopper turned north.

Bella leaned forward in her seat to address the pilot. "If you don't turn this chopper back around, you're fired."

"Sorry, ma'am," said the pilot. "I work for Norwood, not you. He specifically said to follow Mr. Bainbridge's orders."

Bella reached for the latch on her harness. Victor grabbed her hands before she could do something stupid like parachute out of the chopper over farm country with no idea where she was or where she was going.

"The truck is too far away already," Victor said. "You can't reach it on foot. We stay put until we can do some good."

"Don't tell me what to do," she snarled.

"Then don't be an idiot. This is Gage we're after. He needs us. We do this the right way."

"*Right* would have been keeping that truck in sight." She glared at the back of Payton's head. "I swear that if we lose that transport, I will make you pay."

"We won't lose it. Norwood has it on satellite. It's not going anywhere we can't find it."

She took a deep breath. Then another. After two more, Victor felt like she was steady enough to face their next move. "What's the plan?"

Payton turned in his seat enough to look at them. "We wait to see where they stop, then we move in."

"Why not act now?" Victor asked. "We could get ahead of it. Set up a roadblock."

"No. This is bigger than Gage. If there are more of

Stynger's men at the rendezvous, then we owe it to them to find them, too. The more people we save, the better."

Bella let out a long breath. "He's right. Someone loves those men the way I love Gage. We go after all of them, but once we hit the ground, it's my show. Agreed?"

Victor was too busy wincing at her mention of loving Gage to follow the rest of what she said. He didn't know why it should bother him that she felt that deeply for a man who was as good as they come, but it did.

Payton nodded. "Agreed."

"And when we're done and Gage is safe," Bella said, "you're going to turn in your resignation. Norwood can work with me or Victor directly from now on. Or he can fuck off."

"We're old friends, Bella. He trusts me."

"He also trusts Victor or he wouldn't have put him in this position. Your resignation isn't optional. I can't work with you. Not after what you've done."

Payton nodded slowly. "Fine. Once Gage is home safe, I'll give you what you want."

"Promise. I don't know if you're the man of your word I always believed you to be, but if you are, then prove it. Promise me."

Payton bowed his head in defeat and regret. "I promise. Once Gage is safe I'll resign."

The pilot waved to the left. "Satellite shows the truck turning off onto a gravel road. It leads to only one structure. A house. No heat signatures inside. Looks like the truck is early."

"That's the meeting point," Payton said. "Head that way, but stay low."

Bella was planning something. He could see it in the way she began to look around the chopper with that calm, determined expression she wore right before going into a dangerous situation.

"What are you up to?" he asked.

She grabbed a rappelling harness and began strapping it on. "Getting a closer look."

No way was anyone stopping her now, and he sure as hell wasn't letting her go down there alone.

Victor grabbed a second harness. He attached the line onto the helicopter's frame and slid his gear on his back.

"There's the house," Payton said.

"Don't get too close," warned Bella. "We'll go in on foot and radio you when we're in position."

Payton saw she was ready to jump. And if he saw her determination the way Victor did, it was clear that no one was going to stop her short of knocking her out.

"Take us down," Payton ordered the pilot. "Be ready to take off once they're on the ground."

"You're going to have to get close," Victor said. "We can't risk you getting injured further."

"I'll be fine," she said.

The chopper was still several yards too far off ground when Bella slid the door open and stepped out into the night sky.

Chapter Twelve

Bella moved over the ground as fast as she dared. Tall grass and weeds parted under her feet, leaving a clear path. She was still at least a mile from the house and Gage, but pushed herself to go faster, despite the cuts on her legs. Victor was right behind her, keeping up with her brutal pace the way he always did.

She admired the hell out of him for that. And truth be told, she was so very grateful that he had her back. He'd proven himself capable over and over again, and of all the badass men she'd worked with, his ass was the baddest. And the firmest and most lickable.

She was nearly to the top of a rise when he grabbed her around the middle and pulled her to the ground in a soft tackle. Rather than question his motives, she trusted him to have one and stayed put where she landed on the ground, waiting for an explanation.

While she waited, she couldn't help but notice how good his weight felt on top of her. He didn't crush her, but there was no doubt that she had a solid piece of prime male flesh pinning her down.

Her body reacted with a hot wave of want that started in her womb and slid down all the way to her toes. As it passed, it took with it all the lingering pain of her injuries.

Thank God for those lovely endorphins.

Victor put his gloved finger to his mouth, indicating the need for silence. Then he pointed over the hill and began crawling on his belly to the top of the rise.

Bella did the same, ignoring the tickle of weeds and grass on her face the same way she ignored how much she missed having his body atop hers.

The moon was bright overhead, giving her plenty of light to see by. As soon as her path was clear, she saw why Victor had gone all linebacker on her.

In the valley below sat the small farmhouse. Its roof was sagging under the weight of years of neglect and exposure to the elements. The columns holding up the front porch had rotted out and now lay toppled against the warped boards leading to the front door. Weeds grew up all around, without even a path of tire tracks to show someone had been here recently.

In the distance was a barn that had given up and collapsed completely. The gravel driveway had been all but reclaimed by nature, giving the incoming truck only the narrowest path to follow.

The truck stopped. The back opened. A metal ramp was shoved out the back. Down it came two men holding a third, who had a heavy pair of metal restraints around both his wrists and ankles. There was a hood over his head. He was built like Gage, and was wearing the same clothes and worn cowboy boots he'd had on the day he'd let Stynger take him.

It was Gage. He was safe, but those fuckers had him.

Not for long.

Bella's hand was on her tranq gun before she had time to think. Victor's hand settled on the small of her back, silently telling her to hold. Wait. Be patient.

None of those were her forte. All she wanted to do

was rush in, kill the bad guys and take back her friend—the one she'd let walk into the belly of the beast, hoping to give it a fatal case of indigestion.

Victor's voice brushed past her ear in a soft tickle. "He's alive. That's enough for now. We need to plan our next move so he stays that way."

She knew he was right. Forced herself to take several deep breaths rather than attack the men escorting Gage.

He was alive, and until this very moment, she hadn't realized just how worried she'd been that she'd never see him that way again.

Tears of relief stung her eyes, but she swallowed them down and cleared her vision.

Victor's hand swept over her shoulder, an offering of comfort. She soaked it in, pretending like she couldn't feel it through her armored vest and gear.

She activated her mic. "We have eyes on him. Two guards."

Payton's voice came through her headset after a pause. "We have four on thermals. Three in the house. One in the truck. Another vehicle is closing in on your position. ETA three minutes."

She started to push to her feet to close in and rescue Gage before reinforcements arrived, but Victor's hand held her down.

He kept his voice low. "That's not enough time to get there and free him."

"It is if we hurry."

"He'll get caught in the cross fire. And while most of our ammo is nonlethal, theirs isn't. He's not wearing a vest."

Bella cursed under her breath and stopped trying to squirm out from under Victor's hand. No matter what she did, she couldn't risk getting Gage shot. They were nowhere near a medical facility, and she'd seen more than one man bleed out before they could reach aid.

That wasn't going to happen to Gage, no matter how much she wanted to rush down there.

"What do you suggest?" she asked.

"We wait until the handoff is complete. Once we're down to only one set of guards, we move in."

"What if we lose him?"

"We won't. Norwood's got our back. I trust him with my life."

"What about helping as many of Stynger's victims as we can?"

"We will. We'll keep eyes on the second set of guards and take them as soon as Gage is secured."

She heard the rumble of another truck crunching gravel, and moved in to investigate. There was a driver in the first truck, still sitting behind the wheel with the engine running. The second truck's trailer doors opened and two more men jumped out. They were both heavily armed and carried themselves like they knew how to use the firepower they were toting around.

One stopped and peered across the landscape, his gaze sweeping by Bella and Victor's location. She froze, praying the grass obscured her face enough to keep her hidden. He kept looking back in their direction, like he thought he saw something, but didn't make any kind of move.

A few seconds later, he spoke to the second guard, who was standing on the run-down porch. She couldn't hear what they said, but the second guard nodded and went inside.

She waited until both guards had moved into the run-down farmhouse before she holstered her tranq gun and brought her rifle around to get a better look through the scope.

Victor pulled out binoculars and scooted lower to help obscure them from sight.

Through the broken windows, Bella could see a faint glow, like someone had turned on a lantern. Shadows moved across the opening, giving her a clear view of Gage being shoved into a chair. He was secured in place with several layers of duct tape, struggling the whole time to free himself.

His back was to her. They ripped off his hood, revealing several bloody gashes and bruises across the back of his head and neck. His shirt was torn at the collar, and blood soaked through in several places.

Bella had gotten his name in the secret Santa gift exchange at work last Christmas. She'd bought him that shirt knowing it would match his faded denim blue eyes perfectly. He'd worn it enough times for her to know he really did like it.

She couldn't see his face, which was probably a small blessing. There was no telling how battered he'd be by now. They'd had him for so long. She only hoped that whatever had been done to him was something that would heal.

One of the guards slugged him in the gut.

Bella's stomach did a swooping dive. She had to look away and take a couple of deep breaths before she could face seeing more abuse.

"Easy, honey. He's tough," said Victor. "And he's almost home."

She called people honey all the time, yet on his lips it sounded different. More intimate. "I really want to go down there and bash in a few heads."

"So do I, but that's not going to do him any good if he gets shot. Every one of those men is armed. Even the drivers."

She'd been so focused on Gage she hadn't even bothered to look at the drivers. When she did, she saw the unmistakable outline of automatic rifles visible through the windows.

Her attention went back to Gage. He was slumped over, his shoulders heaving with pain from another blow.

"It looks like they're interrogating him. Why would they do that now?" she asked. "Why not do that when he's safely behind locked doors?"

"Something's not right here," said Victor. He began scanning the area.

Bella couldn't take her eyes off of Gage. She needed to get down there and free him. He was tough, but he looked like he had already been through hell. Each blow those men struck seemed to weaken him.

"We need to move in," she said. "He can't take much more of this."

"Don't you dare go down there," said Victor in a tone of absolute command. "I think that's what they're hoping for."

"What?" She had no idea what he meant.

"I think they know we're here."

Before she could so much as open her mouth to question him, a twig snapped behind them.

Bella spun around to deal with the threat, but the barrel of her rifle caught on the long weeds, slowing her down. An armed man was right behind them, his rifle aimed at her head. She couldn't bring her own weapon around in time to stop him.

She saw his finger tighten on the trigger and knew there wasn't a thing she could do to stop it.

Chapter Thirteen

Fear flooded Bella's system. In a fraction of a second she sorted through all her options and discarded each of them as useless. Even if she dropped her rifle and went for her nonlethal sidearm, she'd never get a shot off in time. Rolling aside in an effort to dodge a bullet was also a futile effort.

All she could do was hope the man hit her body armor and not her skull.

She was vaguely aware of Victor beside her, moving too fast for her to track. He had rolled onto his back, lifting his weapon as he went.

Gunfire exploded, ringing in her ears. She jerked, certain that she'd been hit. There was no way she couldn't have been at this close range.

A dark spot bloomed between the man's eyes. It was the only skin showing beneath the matte black fabric covering his body. He went still, blinked once, then fell backward.

Victor had killed him and no doubt saved her life. Again.

Payton's voice was a frantic buzz in her ear. She stopped questioning what was going on and reacted to the events happening around her. They weren't out of the woods yet.

There was movement on her left. She abandoned her rifle and pulled her tranq gun from the holster on her thigh. By the time she had the weapon aimed, the movement had solidified into the shape of a man in a skintight suit. Only his eyes were visible beneath the matte black fabric he wore, and they were camouflaged with dark greasepaint.

Bella fired her gun at the same time the man did. She felt his bullet graze her calf, adding to the pain of the wounds she'd already sustained. He grunted and flinched back under the force of her hit to his shoulder. The dart stuck, but he didn't go down.

She fired again, and this time, Victor added his own tranq dart.

The man fell back. Transparent yellow fluid spewed from the skintight suit, arching up to catch the moonlight. He landed on his ass. His gun fell from his limp grip to clatter on the rocky ground as he finally passed out.

"What the hell is going on down there?" barked Payton over the headset.

Bella responded. "We were ambushed. It's a trap."

"Get out of there!"

She scanned the area, searching for more signs of movement. A quick glance at the pool of liquid forming under one of the men told her it wasn't blood.

"Coolant," said Victor. "Their suits are filled with coolant so we can't see them on thermals."

"Hold on," said Payton. He came back on the line a second later. "Norwood switched the satellite feed. It's too dark for a clear picture, but there's nothing visible from our end."

"Watch my back," ordered Bella. "I'm checking on Gage."

She rolled back into position, taking up her rifle in her hands again. There was no way the men below hadn't heard all the gunfire. She just hoped that they hadn't managed to haul Gage off before she could stop them.

Through the scope she saw two men exit the house and take up covered positions. They were armed with automatic rifles. There was still one man left inside guarding Gage.

One of the trucks backed up toward the farmhouse. The rear doors were still open.

The men were going to get away. With Gage.

"Like hell," she spat as she leveled her rifle and took aim. This time the ammo was one hundred percent lethal.

Her shot tore through one of the truck's tires. A volley of automatic gunfire erupted from the porch as the men defended their means of escape. Bits of grass and weeds rained down on her, tickling her cheek.

She ignored the sensation in order to take out another tire. Just as she was about to pull the trigger, a strong hand closed around her ankle and dragged her down the hill.

She realized it was Victor right before she did something stupid, like shoot him.

"I almost had the shot," she said.

"You certainly did." He pointed to the shredded weeds that had been mowed down by the men at the house. She'd been in that exact spot only a second before.

Her armor might have held at this distance. Then again, it might not have.

"Your muzzle flash gave you away," said Victor. "We have to move."

She nodded and pushed to her feet, keeping below the ridgeline. They skirted around the hill and took up position several yards away. The house was a bit farther away, but she had a clear shot. Assuming they didn't locate her again quite so fast.

"Can you hit tires from here?" she asked Victor.

"I can."

"Start at the front. I'll start at the back. We'll only get one shot before we have to move again."

He nodded and they both crawled up the slope to take their shots.

She found the window again to check on Gage. He was still tied to that chair, facing away. Part of her was glad she couldn't see his face. He wasn't the kind of man who showed fear, but if she saw he was afraid now, it would have made it only harder for her to focus.

"They're on the move," said Victor. "Two men heading for the truck."

As he said the words, the man in the house lifted his pistol and fired a round into Gage's head at point-blank range. He slumped in the chair where he was bound. The chair tipped over in slow motion, but he didn't so much as twitch to stop his fall.

Gage was dead.

Bella screamed in denial. Her friend of more years than she could count—the man who'd saved her life over and over—was dead.

It couldn't be real. He was too good a man to die like that.

Her roar of grief and rage exploded out of her chest. She shot to her feet and charged the man who'd taken her friend's life. She was going to kill that bastard, even if it was the last thing she ever did.

Chapter Fourteen

Victor realized what had happened the second he heard the single shot below followed immediately by Bella's tormented scream.

Gage was dead.

She burst from their covered position. He wasn't quite fast enough to let go of his rifle and grab her before she could bolt. His only option now was to keep her alive long enough to yell at her for being so reckless.

He laid down a steady stream of cover fire while she raced to the farmhouse. The men below stayed pinned down, but there were too many of them. One of them was going to take her out, even if it was with a lucky shot.

He was almost out of ammo. She was almost out of time.

Bella emptied her rifle as she ran. Her shots tore through a rotting support post, hitting the man hiding behind it. He fell and didn't get back up.

Another man darted from cover toward the back of the open truck. Victor didn't want to kill the man, but at this range, he had no choice. His tranq gun wouldn't work at this distance, and once that man reached the truck, he'd be in the perfect position to kill Bella.

Victor aimed for the man's right arm. His hit was

good, but the man didn't stop. He snarled as he turned, tossing his gun to his left hand in a move worthy of Hollywood. The look of hatred on his face as he spotted Bella was more than enough proof that he thought she'd fired the shot.

The man raised his weapon. Victor shifted his aim and fired.

The man fell where he stood, dead.

So much for saving the lives of the people Stynger had hurt.

Before Victor had time to think about what he'd been forced to do, another man flung the farmhouse door open and started firing at Bella.

She fired back, but her rifle was empty. As she ran, she pulled a pair of tranq guns from her holsters and fired.

Another man popped up from his concealed position, taking aim at her.

Victor's gun clicked. Empty. He was useless from here now. He had to get closer.

He broke through the weeds, running as fast as he could to close the distance between him and the men below.

Shots rang out from everyone. Bella must have finally realized the danger she faced and dove behind a low stone wall around what had once been a decorative planting. The men who remained started retreating for the truck at the same time, playing a deadly game of leapfrog as they covered one another.

One of them spotted Victor in the dark. He called out a warning to his buddies, who turned to face the incoming threat.

There was nowhere for Victor to hide. The best he could do was hit the ground and hope that the shallow depression in the earth and his body armor would keep him from being injured, or worse.

As he dove for the dirt, one of the bad guys fell. Bella

rose from her hiding place, wielding a pistol in each hand.

"You will not kill another one of my men!" she screamed as she fired.

There was no calm in her anywhere. He could see the frantic flurry of emotion rioting through her shaking frame, hear it in her wavering voice. Still, her guns were steady as she fired, felling another man.

The last one dove headfirst into the truck and yelled, "Go, go, go!"

The truck took off, gaining speed as it went.

Bella kept firing into the back. The man inside returned fire, and based on the dirt flying up around her feet, it was only a matter of seconds before she took a hit.

Victor sprang up and tackled her to the ground, covering her body with his as the truck and its occupants fled.

She fought against his hold, but he kept her pinned down safely until the sound of the engine was too faint to be heard.

By the time it was safe to let go, her body was shaking with sobs of grief.

Victor turned her over, and the emotional devastation lining her face was enough to break even a strong man's heart.

"They killed him," she said between hard, heavy breaths. "Shot him in the head at close range."

He didn't ask if she was sure. Every tear that fell told him she was. And he sure as hell wasn't eager to let her go in that house and see the damage that had been done to their friend's body up close.

"Confirm what you just said," Payton said.

"Gage is dead," she said, then shoved off her headset.

"We're coming for you now," Payton said, but only Victor heard it.

All he could do was hold her while the emotional storm raged through her, so that's what he did. He wrapped his arms around her and held on tight. Their weapons and armor made the hug awkward, but no less potent. He would have rather felt her body's softness against him, but even this—with the tough plates of armor blocking the feel of her—was good. It struck some chord deep inside of him, creating a kind of harmony he'd never before experienced.

He hated her pain, but felt like he'd been born for this very moment—born to hold and comfort her when no one else could.

Victor kept his senses open, making sure none of the enemy was left behind. He stroked her hair and face, giving her every bit of solace he knew how to offer.

After a few minutes, her tears dried up and she began closing herself off from him. He could feel the process happen in the way she went tense, in the way she began peeling herself away from his embrace.

He let her go grudgingly, wondering if he'd ever again have the chance to hold her while simultaneously hoping he'd never have a reason quite so gruesome. Suffering was the last thing he wanted for her.

She got to her feet and scrubbed the wetness from her face. She put fresh magazines in her weapons and dusted the dirt and weeds from her clothes. By the time she looked at him again, she was wearing her game face.

"I'm going in there to get him," she said.

"Let me do it," Victor offered.

"He's *my* man. My *friend*. I'll do it."

"I'm not letting you go alone. I don't care if you scream at me or hit me or draw a weapon. I'm going in there with you."

She swallowed hard and nodded.

Victor walked beside her to the house, letting her set the pace. He kept his body between her and the dead men lying nearby. They hadn't been her friends, but that didn't mean she couldn't be hurt by their deaths, too. As tough as she was, she still had a heart—one he was just now learning was vulnerable to pain and grief like everyone else.

For some reason, that made him like her even more. It also made him want to protect her, which for a woman like Bella, was practically a sin.

She paused in the doorway. There was a battery-operated lantern still glowing inside. They couldn't yet see Gage's body, but even knowing it was there was enough to give the house the feel of a tomb.

Victor put his hand at the small of her back, offering what support he could. He didn't push or hold her back. He simply waited beside her until she was ready.

Bella stepped inside the threshold and stopped. Blood lay splattered across the dusty wood floor in a pattern that reminded him of fireworks. The body lay slumped, still tied to the chair. The back of his head was a pulpy crater where the bullet had exited his skull.

The sound of her breathing through her mouth was loud in the quiet house. She let out a faint whimper that Victor studiously ignored.

He couldn't let her see more. It wasn't fair to let the sight of Gage with a gunshot wound to his head be the last memory she had of him.

"Stay here," he said, using the same tone he did to order men under his command.

He stripped out of his armor and shirt. The armor went back on, but the shirt was going over Gage's head to hide it from sight.

Victor stepped around the body to cover his face and stopped dead in midmotion. He tilted his head to get a better view.

"It's not Gage," he said.

Bella blinked twice and frowned, confused. "What?"

Victor looked again to be sure. He didn't want to get

her hopes up, but there was no way he was wrong. This man's nose was too large, his face too wide. "It's not him."

"But I was so sure. The build, the clothes . . ."

He lifted his gaze, hating that he had to ask her to do this. "I was sure, too. But come see for yourself."

She stepped around the body, giving it a wide margin. The dead man stared lifelessly at her boots. "His eyes are brown. Gage has blue eyes. It's not him." The sound of relief in her voice was palpable.

She covered her mouth with her fist and raced out of the house.

Victor blanketed the man's head with his shirt and followed after her. He found her crouched at the bottom of the next hill, several yards from the house, hugging her middle. She sucked in huge gulps of air and rocked slightly as she sobbed with relief.

"Are you okay?" he asked.

"Not even close. But I will be. Gimme a minute."

Victor hovered at her side as relief washed through him. He looked for some way to help but found none, so he simply stroked her hair, hoping it would calm her as it had before.

After a few minutes, she gathered herself and stood. Her pale gray eyes seemed too bright under the moon, blazing with a kind of warning he didn't understand.

"I'm okay now. But if you ever tell anyone that I broke down like his, I'll cut off your balls and wear them as earrings. Understood?"

He let his hand fall from her hair and took a step back. He hated it that she had the power to hurt him with just a few words. "You think that's the kind of man I am? That I'd mock your grief or think you less of a woman because you care about your friend enough to show emotion when you thought he was dead? We've been working together for months now. If that's the type of man you think I am, then you haven't been paying attention."

"I know you're worried that I'm going to crack like the others. I know you're watching me. Judging me."

"I'm not doing anything that I wouldn't do with any other man whom I was with in the field. It's our job to watch out for each other. If you have a problem with that, then you're not fit to step foot outside of your office. The stakes are too high."

"I'm not too weak to be in the field. I'm sorry if that threatens your manliness, honey."

Victor laughed, though the sound was empty of all humor. "My manliness is completely intact, *honey*. And if you don't believe me, I'll be happy to prove it."

He grabbed her hips and pulled them so tightly against his body it made the armored vest bite into his skin. He knew holding her, provoking her, was a mistake, but he couldn't seem to stop himself. She tested him at every turn, pushing him away when all he wanted to offer her was a little comfort and compassion.

The second he felt her body heat against his groin, he got hard in a nearly painful rush. She was tall enough that their bodies lined up a little too well. He knew without a doubt that she felt his erection grow.

The way her pupils flared and her cheeks flushed proved it.

He should have let her go at that point. But he couldn't. He needed this contact. And after what she'd been through, so did she. Maybe it wasn't soft and gentle, but it was definitely the kind of thing that reminded a woman she was alive.

Victor was definitely feeling alive now. The adrenaline rush of battle was singing through his veins, heating his blood and bringing out all kinds of barbaric instincts. If she even knew half of the things he wanted to do to her right now—with or without her consent—she'd have pressed her gun against his head.

But she didn't know what he wanted. What he needed. And he wasn't about to let go and allow his instincts free rein. He would stay in control long enough to deal with what they had to face.

After he found the strength to pull his body away from hers.

It felt too good to have her pressed hard against him. His hands controlled her hips completely, pinning her in place. His fingers clenched against her compulsively as he tried to convince himself to let go.

Maybe it was the heat of battle, but he'd never before wanted a woman as fast and hard as he wanted Bella right now.

She licked her lips, leaving behind a moist sheen that glistened in the moonlight. He saw the instant she shifted from shocked to something else. Something hot and filled with acute feminine awareness.

Her muscles relaxed, surrendering to his hold. She went soft in his arms—something he wasn't sure a woman as hard as Bella even knew how to do.

She stared at his mouth for a moment too long, telling him she was thinking about kissing him—something he'd been trying to avoid for too many weeks now.

They were too far away from the house to even see its light. Darkness enclosed them. The night air swirled around them, humid and scented with wild, growing things. It cooled the sweat of combat and the heat of his growing desire that clung to his skin.

Her lips parted, and he realized that he'd been staring at her mouth too. Had she noticed?

A quick glance at her eyes told him she had. There was a knowing quality shining in those pale gray eyes. That, and a whole lot of interest.

That was all Victor needed to know. If she wanted his

kiss half as much as he did hers, she wasn't going to shoot him for what he was about to do.

He let his hands slide up her body, skimming over weapons and armor until he reached her slender neck. His fingers trailed along her hot skin, sliding through her hair until her head was in his grip.

As his boss, she controlled a lot of things between them, but she wasn't going to control this.

Victor gripped her hair just tight enough to elicit a gasp from her lips so they would open, then dove in to take what he'd been wanting for far too long.

The second his mouth covered hers, he knew he was in trouble. This wasn't just a meeting of skin — a quick thrill of the flesh or a postcombat stress relief. This was coming home. It was something he'd been searching for all his life with no success. Until now.

She tasted sweet, hot and wild. The soft sound of her voice lifted in a quiet moan went to his head. He thrust his tongue between her lips, giving her no time to deny him.

The slick skin just inside her mouth contrasted by the sharp little edges of her teeth was a tactile treat. The way she gripped his arms like he was the only thing keeping her upright fueled his need for more of her. He'd wanted to savor this moment and ease her into the idea of having his mouth on hers, but all the plans he'd ever made had dissipated like a puff of smoke in the wind. All he could think about was claiming this space as his own. Leaving a mark on her she'd never be able to erase.

Anytime for the rest of her life that another man kissed her, he wanted her to think of this moment.

Some violent, territorial part of him rose up, taking over where his brain should have been. He'd kill another man for even thinking about kissing her. She was his now. He was keeping her.

Something about that line of thinking seemed wrong,

but he didn't care what it was. Let the rest of the world sort itself out later. Right now, in this moment, there wasn't anything else he needed.

Her hips shifted against his, rubbing his erection. A low growl of approval rumbled in his chest. She shivered in reaction, telling him without words that she could handle a man who wasn't entirely civilized. Which was good, because right now, he felt feral and wild.

In a move that surprised even him, he swept her legs out from under her and controlled her fall to the ground. His body came over hers, pinning her in place while he feasted on her mouth.

She uttered some faint protest and pushed against his shoulders. His response was to tighten his hold on her and force her to take more of his weight. He wasn't done kissing her yet. Not even close.

After a couple of seconds, she abandoned her efforts to slow him down and simply gave in.

The uncivilized part of him approved and tipped her chin up so he could kiss her deeper. That seemed to set her off, sucking a sweet sigh of pleasure from her. She gave back as good as she got, thrusting her tongue against his, tasting him and teasing him with the sinuous glide of her wet mouth over his own.

He needed to devour her. Strip her bare. Fuck her right here on the hard ground.

He'd wanted her for too long to control the feelings that were flooding him in a wave too powerful to resist.

His hand tried to find her breast, but all he could reach were the hard edges of her tactical vest. He abandoned the search and moved south, needing to feel more of her skin under his palm.

He pushed her thighs apart wide enough that he could cup her mound. His fingertips met hot, damp fabric.

That was enough to send him past the edge of reason,

all the way to the point where he felt he had the right to unfasten her pants and work his long fingers right up into her sweet pussy.

The second he reached under her vest to tug at the button of her waistband, she went stiff. Her hand circled around his wrist and squeezed. Hard.

Pain shot up his arm, clearing away some of the lust fogging his brain.

This was Bella. His boss. He couldn't fuck her here on the ground. Hell, he couldn't fuck her anywhere.

Victor rolled onto his back and breathed out his sexual frustration. His cock was throbbing, wetting the front of his pants with precome. He'd never been turned on like this before from just a single kiss, but that was Bella—a force of nature, tearing down walls and blowing up every defense he had without even trying.

He risked a glance in her direction. She was on her feet, weaving slightly from side to side. Her face was flushed, and her mouth was a dark, wet red.

It took every ounce of restraint he had not to charge her and tackle her right back to the ground where he could kiss her until she changed her mind about stripping out of those pants.

Just the idea of getting his mouth between her thighs was enough to make his cock lurch toward her in protest. He needed to taste her like he needed to breathe. And once he got his mouth on her, he knew there'd be no stopping him until he was balls deep inside her, driving them both toward sexual oblivion.

"I can't believe you did that," she said, her voice too faint to be recognizable. If she hadn't been standing right there, if he hadn't been watching her mouth move, he never would have believed that shaky sound had come from a powerhouse like her.

The idea that he could do that to her made his head swell. Both of them.

"It was just a kiss," he said, knowing every word was a lie. It had been a hell of a lot more than that. There was no way she couldn't know it, too.

"You don't kiss your boss." The way she said it made it sound almost like a question, as if she wasn't completely sure of her statement.

"Apparently, *I* do. Are you going to fire me?"

"You know I can't, not when there's all that money attached to your continued employment." She came to stand over him, her combat boots only inches from his head. "But if you ever do that again . . ."

"What, Bella?" He rose to his feet, trying to ignore the way his knees shook. "What will you do?"

She stared at his mouth. Swallowed hard. There was want in her gray eyes—the kind of want a man might see only once in his lifetime. If he was a lucky son of a bitch.

Her lips parted for her to speak, but nothing came out but the tip of her pink tongue. It wet the smooth surface he'd just explored, making him wish he could spend another year claiming the territory as his own.

She was not the kind of woman he would end up with. He knew that. She wasn't refined or well-bred or pedigreed. She didn't have any wealth to speak of, nor did her name carry any political clout. His parents would never approve. Victor was on the path that had been set out for him at birth. He was nearly done serving his time in the armed forces. After that, he'd begin his political career. Whether or not he ended up in the White House was anyone's guess, but he was almost sure to win a senate seat. His parents were expecting no less.

Bella would never make a good politician's wife. Not only did she have too many skeletons in her closet, she was as likely to stab a foreign dignitary in the eye as she was to offer him a drink. Her violent streak was far too wide for her to hide it under a cocktail dress and a string of pearls.

But even though Victor knew they weren't a good fit,

he couldn't help but want her. He couldn't help but want to rip out the throat of any man who so much as looked at her.

He'd never felt that way about any woman. Ever. It scared him a little that he did now, that she stripped away his carefully cultivated civility.

"What will you do if I kiss you again?" he asked, his tone a challenge, his chin thrust out in defiance.

Her eyes roamed his face as if searching for the right answer—the one that would hold him at bay. What she didn't know was she'd never find that answer in him. He couldn't think of a single thing she could do or say that would keep him from her. Let her threaten him all she wanted. As long as she continued looking at him the way she did now—like she wanted to eat him for dessert—he wasn't going to let any silly rules stop him from having her.

Maybe once he got enough of her, he'd work her out of his system. He'd go on with his regularly scheduled life. So would she. They just had to get past this inconvenient sexual attraction, and the only way he could think to do that was to barrel right through it.

He felt a grin tug at his mouth. That was his answer: Stop fighting it. Take her. Let her take him. Once they scratched the itch, they could move on. Get back on track to their respective futures.

He ducked his head and kissed her again, softly this time. Somehow that allowed him to feel the smooth, hot contours of her mouth more keenly. A few more seconds of this, and they were going to be right back where they'd been a second ago, panting and desperate for more.

The beat of a chopper's blades in the distance told him there wasn't time for such things. They had several unconscious men to gather and take in for medical treatment.

When he pulled away, her eyes were still closed, her

lips still parted. He wanted to devour her. Instead, he adjusted his pants over his erection and stepped back. "You should think of an answer, because I'm going to kiss you again, Bella. Soon."

She blinked slowly a few times as if she hadn't quite understood his words.

"A man should know the consequences of his actions," he said, stroking her bottom lip with the tip of his finger. "I'd like to know what all those kisses are going to cost me."

He watched as she tried to shed her lust and shift back into boss mode. Her spine straightened, her mouth tightened, and she closed her eyes. When she opened them again, the haze of desire had faded. "More than you can afford."

His grin widened at the thought of stripping away all that rigidity and making her limp and spent. No way would she be able to find boss mode after he'd made her come a few times. She'd be lucky if she could even stand. He could hardly wait to see if his hunch was true.

Victor bent his head as if he was going to kiss her again, but stopped short. He watched her pupils flare in eagerness and knew she was right there with him, twisting in need. "I have a feeling you're going to be worth it. Whatever the cost."

Chapter Fifteen

Jordyn waited until the guards changed shifts before she snuck into Gage's room. She'd disabled the audio feed from his microphone, but there was no way she could cut the video feed without alerting security. With Gage asleep, they wouldn't be expecting any sound to be coming from his room. A blank video screen would definitely be a red flag for them to come looking to see what was wrong.

There was only one blind spot in his room, and by the time the new shift of guards was in place, checking the video feed, both she and Gage needed to be in it.

She used a key card she'd programmed to open his door, held her breath, and slipped inside. A dim light set in the ceiling over his bed put off just enough of a glow to monitor his nighttime activities. The guards didn't put much effort into watching the test subjects sleep since they were all dosed at night with a sedative gas that kept them asleep and contained.

If Gage hadn't plugged the tube under his bed as she'd told him to do, his room would be filled with the gas and she'd pass out within a few seconds of entering. The staff bringing his breakfast tray would find her and she'd be in serious trouble.

The door shut behind her. Gage didn't so much as twitch in his bed.

A little wave of panic churned in her gut. Had he not seen her note? Had he ignored her instructions?

This was a horrible idea. What was she thinking coming here like this? She had nothing to gain by helping this man, and so very much to lose.

If Mother found out Jordyn was here, her punishment could kill her.

She turned to flee. Nothing was worth another trip to the White Room. Not even a man as compelling as Gage.

"I'm awake," he whispered, the sound so faint she could hardly hear it over her panicked heartbeat.

Jordyn froze. It wasn't too late to turn back. The door was only a few feet away from where she hid in the blind corner. She could slip out and never be discovered.

But what would happen to Gage? What if Mother began subjecting him to her experiments? If he stayed here he would die.

Jordyn had given up her freedom so that she could mitigate the damage Mother caused. What good was she if she didn't act?

"We don't have much time before the next shift starts monitoring the cameras. I need you to shove this under your blankets so it looks like you're in bed. Then come join me." She tossed a wad of rolled-up blankets across the room.

He caught it midair, did as she asked, and within a few seconds, he was on his feet and sliding silently her way into the darkened corner.

"They can't hear us right now," she told him. "And they can't see us as long as we stay in the shadows of this corner. Blind spot."

He glanced at the floor where the round pool of light from overhead hit the tile. There was less than two feet of clearance. "Not much room."

"We'll have to make it work. Just for a few minutes."

He moved into the shadow. The angular planes of his face and jaw darkened, but his faded blue eyes still caught and held the light. "I'll have to touch you."

She knew that. Part of her had known that from the second she'd devised her plan to come see him. The thought of having a stranger within striking distance should have scared her, but it didn't. Not with Gage. He'd showed no signs of aggression since his arrival, nor had he mistreated the staff in any way.

Maybe that meant he was a good guy, unwilling to hurt anyone, or maybe it meant he was biding his time, waiting for the right moment to strike. Either way, it was too late to turn back now. The shift change would have the guards walking down this hall sometime during the next fifteen minutes. She was trapped here until they passed.

Jordyn took a deep breath and nodded. "It's okay. I won't freak out and scream for help." If she did the guards would find her and she'd be in the White Room by morning. Nothing Gage did to her could be half as bad as what Mother would do.

He moved without a sound, entering the depths of the shadow where she stood. There was a scant inch between them, but it was still too much. His heels were in the light, which meant he could be seen.

"Closer," she said, making herself as small as possible so there was more room for his big body.

He slid one foot between hers, widening her stance. His calf grazed hers as he eased forward. Her knees parted to make room for his. By the time he was done moving, his thigh was between hers. His chest was pressed against her breasts. She was wedged in the corner, her nose at the same height as his throat, only two inches away.

The smell of his skin overcame her for a moment. He hadn't stepped one foot outside in weeks, but he still smelled like fresh air and freedom. She had the wildest urge to bury her nose in the crook of his neck and just breathe.

Hard, masculine curves fit against her softer ones. Her breasts flattened, except for her rebellious nipples, which hardened until they ached and tried to poke through her lab coat.

He tilted his head down to look her in the eyes. His pupils were huge, and there was something wild in his gaze she'd never seen before. It wasn't the kind of out-of-control anger or fear that so many of her mother's test subjects showed. It was quieter than that. Controlled. But no less powerful.

She wondered what it might mean as she stared up at him.

"Okay?" he asked.

She was better than okay with so much powerful male flesh plastered against her, but that only proved she was an idiot.

"Why did you come?" he asked.

"I needed to talk to you. Privately."

"About?"

"Jake Staite. I tried to send his friend Roxanne a drug protocol that I designed to help reduce the effects of what was done to him. Do you know if it reached him? If it worked?"

Gage was silent for so long she wasn't sure he was going to answer. Finally he said, "He got it."

Relief weakened her knees. She had to lock them to stay upright. She'd spent nearly a week in the White Room for bribing one of the lab techs to send that package for her. And while she'd prayed for death for days, what she'd endured was still better than her accomplice's punishment. His body would never be found. Mother made sure of that.

"Did it work?" she asked, trying to hide her desperation. "Were there any signs of his aggression and rage fading?"

"I don't know."

Disappointment weighed her down. She'd had such high hopes for that serum. She'd spent every waking minute working on it for months. She'd gone over her research several times, praying that her work was clean and complete. She hadn't dared test the drug on anyone here for fear that Mother would learn what she'd done. It was bad enough that she thought Jordyn had mailed a letter. If she'd known what was really in that package, there was no telling what kind of damage she'd do in her desire to retain control over everything that happened in her underground labs.

"Do you at least know if he was still alive before you came here?" Jordyn asked. If her work had killed Jake, she knew she'd never forgive herself.

"He was."

That was something at least. Not enough to help her sleep all night, but at least it might keep the nightmares at bay—the ones where she turned into her mother, experimenting on people like rats, not caring how much damage she did along the way, or how many lives she ruined.

Jordyn had to find a way to move on. There were more important tasks at hand now that Gage was here.

She refocused her attention, hoping she wasn't wrong about him. The risks were so high, she had to be sure he was as he seemed. "Everyone says you came here of your own free will, even though you knew it was dangerous. Is that true?"

"Does it matter?"

It did to her. If she was going to put her life on the line for a man, she wanted to know what kind of man he was. "Yes."

He gave her a tiny nod of acceptance. "I came for Adam."

"Your brother?" So the rumors were true. "Didn't you know what might happen to you if you came?"

He nodded again, never once taking his eyes off hers.

"Then why? Why come here at all?"

"Adam is happy."

The simplicity of Gage's statement spoke volumes. His brother was happy, and he didn't want to ruin that, so he volunteered to take his place.

The kind of man who would do something like that was definitely worth whatever risk Jordyn might take.

She made her mind up right then and there. She was going to help free Gage, and this time, she was going to free herself as well.

"I'm going to help you escape," she said.

"No."

Of all the responses she'd imagined, that was not one that had ever come up.

"No? What do you mean? Don't you want to get out of here?"

"I go alone."

"Why not let me help?"

"The risk. Stynger is a monster."

Jordyn flinched. She knew his words were true, but that didn't make them hurt any less. She hated that she came from such a twisted, selfish creature. Maybe Mother hadn't always been as willing to hurt people as she was now, but the path she was on was so dark, Jordyn could hardly stand to think about it.

She lifted her chin. "I'm aware of the risk. Even coming here tonight meant taking my life into my own hands. If Mother finds out I was here—"

"Mother?" His expression darkened as dangerous intent clouded his eyes.

Jordyn wanted to bite her own tongue off. "Unfortunately, yes. Does that mean you don't trust me now?"

"Never did."

"Then why risk putting yourself so close to me? For all you know, I could have a deadly dose of poison tucked in the syringe in my pocket."

The tiny muscles around his eyes tightened at her comment. That was all that changed, but she could feel the shift in his demeanor from relaxed to vigilant.

"Reach for it," he ordered.

Whether his command was a dare or a test, Jordyn wasn't sure, but something in his steady gaze told her she'd better do as he said. If she didn't, he'd take her for a coward—someone incapable of planning and executing a complicated escape.

Her hand lifted from her side toward her lab coat pocket.

His movement was fast and fluid. Before she'd shifted her hand more than an inch, his long fingers closed around her wrist, holding it in place with an unbreakable grip.

She should have been alarmed that she was no longer in control of her own hand, but instead all she could think about was the heat and strength of his grip. His palm was against her bare wrist, leaving no barrier between their skin. She could feel rougher patches along his fingers, the way they shackled her completely.

The strangest feeling swept up from some deep place she didn't even realize she had. It was like her whole body woke up and began to buzz with awareness. Her breathing sped. Her skin heated as it pulled warmth from his. She saw every little detail, from the rough shadow of his incoming beard, to the tiny scar on his chin, to the way his black eyelashes were so long they tangled.

There was something about this man that compelled her. Spoke to her. As if some part of him was all hers, just waiting for her to claim it as her own.

Her mouth was dry from nervousness and the strange power he had over her. She licked her lips to ease the dryness and his gaze tracked the sweep of her tongue.

His jaw clenched. "Go," he ordered, his tone hard and final.

Had she done something wrong? Could he see her strange reaction to his proximity in her face? Whatever the case, it didn't matter. "I can't. Not until the shift change is finished. I'll be seen."

He leaned into her, bracing one hand on the wall behind her. The other still held her wrist, making his next command impossible. "Go. Don't come back."

She wasn't going to let him intimidate her. If she ran away like a frightened child, he'd never see her as a useful ally. "You'll never make it out of here without me."

"I will."

"No, you won't. Our security is too tight. You don't even know which way to go. You need me."

"I'm smart."

"Not as smart as I am. And even if you are, you won't be given an opportunity to escape. Mother knows your value. That has to be why she hasn't started altering you yet. No conditioning, no drugs, no implants."

"Value?"

"She wants you for some reason I can't figure out."

He stared at her for a long time, as if trying to decide what to say. Or perhaps whether to say anything. "I was already altered. Before birth. That's why she wants me."

Jordyn suddenly recalled some files she'd read years ago about a pair of siblings that had their genetic codes tweaked. At the time she'd just learned that Mother had done the same to her before birth. Jordyn had wanted to know who her father was, but none of the research had given her a name. All she knew was she was different. The changes Mother had made to her were part of her genetic code. Unlike all the other subjects, she could pass her anomalies on to her offspring.

As far as she knew, there were only three genetically altered subjects who had survived.

"Do you know what she's going to do to you?" Jordyn asked.

"No idea. You?"

She shook her head. "I've searched your files. There's nothing in there about her plans. She's barely even touched you. Just taken some blood and that one DNA swab."

"Swab?"

"You don't remember?"

He shook his head. "Must have been asleep. Thanks for the gum."

"If they check your room they'll find it."

"I won't say it was from you."

"I'm not worried about that," she lied. If that gum was found, chances were Jordyn would spend some serious time in the White Room. Still, she wasn't going to show fear to this man—not when she was trying to convince him she'd be a good partner. "But we do need to make our move soon. The longer we go before getting out of here, the greater the risk of discovery." And of him having something horrible done to him.

"No. You've done enough."

"I'm not going to fight with you about this. Our time is better spent planning our escape."

"There is no *our*. I go. You stay."

"I can't stay. When Mother finds out what I've done— and she will—she'll put me in the White Room."

"What's that?"

"It's her version of a torture chamber. No blood or bodily damage. Just pain."

"I can take pain."

"Not like this. The last time she sent me there, I nearly died."

"You're her *child*," he said, his tone horrified.

"I'm her *experiment*. And I don't think she counts me as a successful one, either. Some days I wonder why she even cares that I stay here."

"You want to leave," he said.

"Wouldn't you?"

He stared at her for a moment as if searching for a lie. "Where are we?"

"If I tell you that, will you promise to take me with you?"

"No. Tell me."

"Why? So I can wait for the next test subject skilled enough to help me get away for good? I don't think so."

"You don't know my skills."

"I've looked you up. Read the reports. Mother has been keeping an eye on all of you at the Edge. She says that's where several of the people on the List have been hiding."

Jordyn had only recently learned about the List—a string of names listing those who had been subjected to the experiments of Mother and the other scientists working for the Threshold Project years ago. Most of them had been small children at the time—young enough to be altered by various drugs and procedures. Too young to be reliable witnesses.

Those children had since grown up, and Mother was determined to find as many of them as she could. She claimed they were the key to recovering the research that had been destroyed in the fire that had nearly killed her.

If there was one thing Jordyn knew as the absolute truth, it was that Mother would never stop until she had everything she wanted. It didn't matter how many people had to get hurt or killed. It didn't matter how many lives she destroyed along the way. Mother got what she wanted. Always.

Gage fell silent as he studied her face. Jordyn didn't know if he was searching for a lie or trying to figure out how to convince her to stay here. Maybe a little of both.

"You've been here for weeks," she said. "You haven't

figured out how to escape yet. Who's to say you don't stay here for years longer? Is that what you want? And what about me? I won't survive here much longer. Every trip I take to the White Room is worse than the last." She shuddered at the thought, but refused to look away from his steady gaze. "The next one could kill me. I *need* to get out of here."

His mouth tightened and his eyes closed for a moment. He let out a resigned breath. "What's your plan?"

"I get the new security codes for the external doors, come back here, take you with me. You'll have to be ready to run. We'll only have about three minutes to get out before the alarm resets."

"Weapons?"

"I don't have any."

"Can you get one?"

She thought through the process it would take to acquire one of the guard's guns. The armory worked on a completely separate security system. Breaking into that would not only be difficult, but it would also most certainly get her discovered before she had time to reach Gage.

Jordyn shook her head. "I can't reach the guns. It's too risky."

"Knife?"

"They're all implanted with microchips. If anyone tries to take one from the kitchen, it sets off an alarm. I might be able to hack the system, but I've never tried."

"Don't. Not worth the risk. What's your exit strategy?"

"I can cut off one of the elevators from the main control system, hijacking it. Once we reach the surface, we'll take one of the trucks. I should be able to get keys."

"Should?"

"I've done it before."

He nodded. "Where are we?"

"I won't give you specifics, because if I do, you'll think you don't need my help. But I will tell you that we're belowground. The nearest town is miles away. All that's nearby is grazing land filled with cows. Lots and lots of cows."

"How far to Dallas?"

"Hours. That's all I'll say."

Frustration lined his brow. He pressed his weight more fully against her, but instead of her body interpreting it as some kind of threat, that strange, deep part of her perked up in excitement. A quivering kind of energy spread down her limbs, making her shake. The oxygen in the room seemed to thin, forcing her to breathe faster to compensate.

She had the strangest urge to press her mouth against his. She was looking at it, trying to figure out why she'd want to kiss him when he tilted her chin up with one finger.

"Eyes up here," he said in a rough, quiet voice.

She did as he asked only to find that his pupils were huge. His skin was flushed. A line of sweat had formed along his brow.

His thumb stroked her chin. The caress sent all kinds of tingling sensations winging down her spine.

Whatever effect this man was having on her, she was certain it wasn't the kind of thing that was going to help her concentrate on escape.

Or anything else.

"I should go," she said. Her voice was faint and weak.

His hand slid down to encircle her throat. Now he was the one staring at her mouth. "Is it safe?"

"As safe as it's going to get."

He jerked his gaze away from her and focused on the wall just past her left ear. His spine straightened, and whatever heat she thought she'd seen in his eyes was gone now. "When do we go?"

"Soon. A day or two. I need some time to put things in place. It'll be around this time when we make our move."

"I'll be ready," he said, completely confident.

Jordyn only wished she could share his confidence, because the truth was, they were both probably going to die trying to make their escape. She only hoped that if she did, her life was ended with a nice, fast bullet, rather than days of suffering in the White Room.

Gage waited for over an hour before he moved back into the camera's eye. He didn't want to do anything to risk getting Jordyn discovered.

She was his way out, his ticket to finding Stynger's location and taking her down for good. Using the daughter to destroy the mother was his only option, but it didn't sit well with him.

He didn't like the idea of using Jordyn at all, but it was his only choice. He had to find a way to get past his guilt. Even when she looked at him like she wanted to kiss him.

He shifted in his bed, his dick as hard as a rock.

The woman got to him. He didn't know what it was about her, but she got to him deep down, exciting his body in a way he'd never experienced before. He'd barely even touched her, and all he could think about was how soon it would be until he got his hands on her again.

The memory of her smooth, soft skin under his fingers made his balls ache. Her clean, sweet scent went to his head. Even the feel of her body tucked in that corner with only him between her and the evil going on around them made his protective instincts kick into overdrive.

How the hell was he going to drag her into the kind of danger escaping this place would heap on them? Then again, how the hell could he leave her down here with that viper of a mother?

He couldn't see the sun, but even so, he could feel dawn coming. It would be here in a few hours, and with it would come another chance to do what he'd come here to do. It was up to him to find a way to keep both himself and Jordyn alive long enough to walk out of this place and see the sun again. Whatever it took, that was exactly what he was going to do.

Chapter Sixteen

Randolph stood before Dr. Stynger, feeling like a child summoned to the principal's office.

She sat behind her giant desk in her white office, her bony hands steepled in front of her. "Is this what you call results?" she asked as she slid the report across her desk. "Five men captured. They're in enemy hands, undergoing surgery right now to remove my property from their skulls. I hired you to disable one single woman, not destroy my entire life's work by letting it fall into the wrong hands."

"I made the right call," Randolph said, refusing to cower. A woman like Stynger would eat him alive if he let her think he was easy prey.

"Failure is the right call?"

"The operation didn't fail. You wanted Bella afraid, paranoid. What better way to do that than to make her witness the death of a man she holds dear?"

"She knows now that it wasn't Gage you shot. Do I even want to know who died for this charade?"

"Probably not. And it doesn't matter that she knows now that it wasn't Gage. There was a period of time when she believed. You said that the drug we subjected her to would activate if she was in a heightened emotional state."

Some of the anger on Stynger's face faded, replaced by scientific curiosity. "Did it work? Has she shown any signs of reversion?"

"I'm working on finding out. My contacts are limited. It may take a few hours to get all the players where they need to be to gather intel."

"I'm not a patient woman. I have too many loose ends left before I leave the country."

"Bella won't be one of them. You have my word."

"Your word means nothing. I want results. You may need to administer another dose of the serum personally if your previous plan fails."

"It won't."

"That remains to be seen. While you're wasting your time waiting around to see if your plan worked, there are a few other loose ends I need you to tie up."

Randolph didn't bother pretending he didn't know what she meant. "Who do you want me to kill?"

Stynger wrote down three names and slid the paper across the desk toward him.

He read the names and let out a low whistle. "These aren't nobodies."

"If they were easy targets, I would have already taken care of them myself long ago."

"How do you want it done?"

"Quickly. Cleanly. With absolutely no ties to me. We're running out of time."

"Any specific order?" he asked.

"I don't care so long as it's all done soon. And while you're at it, stop by this address and finish cleaning up the mess you left." She wrote down the address and gave it to him.

"What's here?"

"It's a medical facility where they'll take any of my

men who survived. Bella and her merry band think I don't know it exists. Then again, she's never suffered from being overly bright. Once we rid her of that pesky aggression, she'll be no more threat than a scared puppy."

"What do you want me to do?"

"Kill the surgeons and staff. Rescue any of the men who are untouched by them. Burn any bodies you leave behind."

"I'll see to it," said Randolph as he turned to leave.

"You have three hours," she ordered.

"That's barely enough time to fly to Dallas."

"Then I suggest you get moving. You really don't want to know what's going to happen to you if you fail me."

No. No, he did not.

Bella was still shaking several hours later as she waited to see if any of the men they'd tranqued could be saved. She tried to tell herself that her body was responding to the intense emotional reaction she'd had at seeing a man she thought was her friend being murdered in cold blood.

That was a lie. Victor was the one who made her tremble.

He sat quietly a few feet away in the tiny waiting room of the private medical office outside of Dallas. No one would know it from the outside, but inside this building was a state-of-the-art facility filled with the latest technology in the field of neurosurgery. Two of the world's leading surgeons were in the back right now, trying to save the lives of the men Victor and Bella had tranquilized.

It was nearly dawn. Another night had gone by with little sleep. Fatigue grated against her eyelids and ached in her joints. Even so, she knew there was no sleeping now, not with the hum of sexual frustration vibrating through her body.

I have a feeling you're going to be worth it. Whatever the cost.

That's what Victor had told her. Too bad he didn't know just how fucked up she really was.

The door to the waiting room opened and a man with a surgical mask dangling around his neck came out to speak with them. "We lost one man on the table. A second came through the procedure well. He's not out of the woods, but I'm hopeful."

"What about the others?" asked Victor.

"We're working on them as fast as we can, but keeping them sedated in the meantime."

"How long until we can talk to the survivor?" asked Bella.

The surgeon frowned. "You can't. My orders were clear. I was only to inform you of the outcome. You're not allowed to see any of the patients."

"Whose orders? One of my men is being held captive. I need to question these men to see if they know anything about his location."

"I'm sorry, but I can't help you. I need to get back there. We still have a lot of work to do."

He turned to leave, but Victor grabbed his arm. "She asked you a question. Whose orders?"

The man stared pointedly at Victor's big hand. "Payton Bainbridge gave the orders. General Norwood said I should follow them. I work for him, so that's what I did. Now let me go."

"Payton doesn't give the orders. I do," Bella said, trying to keep her fury from her voice. How dare Payton interfere like that? He had no right to poke his nose in and control things.

"Sounds like the three of you have some things to work out. That falls squarely in the category of things that are *not* my problem. The man on the operating table with a deadly implant in his brain is. Excuse me."

The surgeon left. Bella sucked in a series of deep breaths and shoved them out hard trying to dissipate some of her anger. "How dare Payton go behind my back like that?"

"Payton and Norwood go way back. I'm sure he didn't mean to keep you out of the loop."

"Of course he did. He's been keeping secrets from me for years."

"You should get some sleep before you talk to him."

"I don't need sleep. I need Payton to butt the hell out of my life. He's done enough damage for one lifetime."

He took her hand in his. "Let me take you home. You'll be able to make a better case with him after a few hours of sleep."

"You say that like there are two sides to the story, like he has a point. He doesn't. The man let people do horrible things to children. He found parents that didn't give a fuck about their kids and then paid them off so people like Stynger could use those children to experiment on. He doesn't get to act like that was just some little mistake he can rectify if he tries hard enough. The man doesn't have a fucking leg to stand on. He's a monster."

A hint of motion caught her eye. She turned to see Payton standing in the doorway. The look on his face told her he'd heard the whole thing.

For an instant she felt bad for what he'd heard her say. It was a knee-jerk reaction to their years-long friendship. A few weeks ago she would have sooner shot herself in the leg than hurt his feelings. He was the closest thing she had to a real father. But that was before she'd learned that all the carnage she'd seen—all the tortured souls and damaged minds and bodies—were at least in part his fault. He'd destroyed the lives of children, stripped away their innocence and all hope they had for a normal and happy future.

He'd lied to her for years, working beside her every

day, not caring that she might have a ticking time bomb in her head.

"I just came to tell you that I had the post-op survivor transported to a more secure facility for his recovery," Payton said.

"It didn't even occur to you that you should ask me before you acted, did it?" she asked.

"You're exhausted. Injured. And you don't have access to the resources that I do. It seemed the logical choice. I didn't think you'd mind. Obviously I misjudged."

"Yes. You did. I don't care what resources you have. If there's something I need, I'll ask Norwood myself. I don't need you butting in."

"You're carrying too much of a burden, Bella. And I *need* to help."

"I don't care what you need, sweetheart. Every judgment call you've made since the first kid you bought is suspect."

"It wasn't like that and you know it. I thought I was helping them escape lives that were going nowhere. The research was so promising I thought that one day those kids would thank me."

"Have they?" she asked. "Has a single one of them had a better life because of what you did to them?"

His mouth went tight and pale. "I thought I was doing what was right. As soon as I realized how wrong I'd been, I started working to correct my mistakes. What else would you have me do?"

"Walk away. Stop making the cleanup efforts left from your mess harder. Accept the fact that *we don't need you.*"

Payton flinched. In the space of a breath, he deflated and looked ten years older. "I'm sorry I've caused you so much distress. If you ever do need me, you know how to find me." With that, he turned and left.

His retreat was exactly what Bella had asked for, but now that she had it, all she felt was a sad emptiness. He wasn't the man she wanted him to be. He wasn't even the man she thought he was. But he had still been a huge part of her life for years. He'd kept her out of prison for murder. He'd funded her business endeavors. He'd been there for her every day, listening and giving advice.

Most of it had been good. Smart. Loving.

She sank into a chair and covered her eyes with the heels of her hands. There was simply no reconciling the man she'd known for years with the man he'd been before they'd met. Those two people could not possibly inhabit the same body. How in the world could she ever forgive him for stealing her childhood and subjecting her to experiments that had fundamentally altered her personality? At the same time, how could she go on with her life without Payton constantly poking his nose in her office and scolding her for her recklessness, impatience, or for blowing up something expensive?

The warm weight of Victor's hand on her shoulder eased her nerves enough that she could pull in a full breath. He was his own set of problems, but she could deal with pushing only one person out of her life at a time.

"Let me take you home, Bella. It's been a long day."

"It's been a long couple of months."

"You're exhausted. You should sleep."

"Every time I close my eyes I see that man I thought was Gage die. I wonder where he is, if he's safe. If he's alive."

"I'm sure he is. We have to have faith that his training will hold him up until we can find him. Or until he can find us."

The image of the man who looked so much like Gage being shot in the head filled her mind. She'd been certain that she'd lost him, and the devastation she'd felt had been unbearable. Even through the insulation of denial she had been savaged by her grief.

She couldn't lose him for real. She wouldn't survive it. Neither would her team. They all loved him like family.

"Until then, how am I supposed to sleep?"

"If you don't, you'll be of no use to him. We all need to be at the top of our game, ready to jump into action if there's any sign of him."

"I know what I'll dream about the second I fall asleep."

"That wasn't Gage who died tonight. It was a stranger chosen to rattle you. You have to remember that."

She was so tired. Running on fumes. Emotionally drained.

Afraid.

She looked up at Victor, hoping to see answers in his perfect features. "I feel like I should be here for these men. The people who love them can't be."

"I understand. Let me stay here while you get some sleep."

"You've been up all night, too. And I don't want to leave."

"Then slip into one of the exam rooms and rest. I'll wake you if any decisions need to be made."

She didn't have many options. Her body was giving out. If she didn't rest soon, her judgment would follow. Her team depended on her to keep them safe. If that meant forcing herself to sleep, then that's what she'd do.

"Will you wake me when the next man gets out of surgery?" she asked.

He nodded. "If that's what you want."

What she really wanted was a long, hot shower and her own bed, but that wasn't what she was going to get. At least not right now. "It is."

He held out his hand. "Give me your phone."

"Why?"

"Because business hours start soon and you'll be getting calls from people who don't realize how exhausted you are."

"What if Gage calls?"

"I'll answer."

She removed the password lock from her phone and handed it to him. "Promise you'll wake me if anything important comes up."

He slid a finger across his chest in an X. "Cross my heart."

Bella wanted to drag her own finger over his chest so bad it made her fingers clench.

Maybe what she really needed was to get his mouth back on hers for a while, maybe fuck his brains loose. Or hers. She hadn't been thinking about Gage or Payton or any of her other problems when he'd been kissing her. He'd been too much of a distraction, absorbing her complete attention.

She really could use a little of that right now.

Why not? Everything else was going to hell. Why not send her rules against employees dating right along with it? Use his body. Make herself feel good. Get off. Get some sleep. She'd make sure he enjoyed the fun, too.

"I figured it out," she said.

"Figured out what?"

"What I'm going to do to you the next time you kiss me."

His dark brows lifted. "Oh? And what's that?"

"I'm going to strip that glorious body of yours naked, climb on board, ride you and come until I can't stand even the thought of one more orgasm."

His gaze darkened. The clean-cut wholesome vibe he put off shifted into gritty, raw sex appeal. This was no boy standing before her. This was a real man—one who'd leave a mark if she let him.

She wasn't entirely convinced she didn't want that.

He wrapped his arms around her body and backed her up until she was pressed against the door. She could feel his erection growing between their bodies, jerking in an effort to get closer to her. His hold was solid enough she knew she'd have to break a sweat if she wanted to get free.

She didn't.

"Playing with me isn't the smartest thing you could do, Bella. I'm not like those boy toys you normally date."

She opened her mouth to tell him she didn't date boys, but the words were too thick and false to make their way up her throat. Compared to him, most men seemed like boys. They didn't have his strength, cunning or stamina. They didn't have his determination or dedication, either. And they sure as hell didn't have his mouth and skilled tongue.

Her toes curled up just thinking about what a man like him could do with a tongue like his.

"I'm not playing," she said. "I want you."

"What about your rule against fraternization?"

"It's my rule. I'm suspending it just this once. Extenuating circumstances."

"And what circumstances are those?"

"I'm horny and need to sleep. You're the only thing powerful enough to take my mind off my problems."

His arms went still around her. Small creases formed between his perfect eyebrows as he frowned. "You want to use me?"

"Is that a problem?"

He looked confused as he stared at her. Maybe even a little shocked. He pushed away and to his own bafflement said, "Yes. It is."

Bella leaned against the wall trying to catch up with what had just happened. "I thought you wanted to fuck me."

"I did. I do. But not like this."

"Not like what?"

He waved his hand toward the operating room behind the wall. "With the lives of men hanging in the balance. With death only a few feet away. With you using me to stop thinking about the other men in your life."

"It's not like I'm romantically involved with them."

"Apparently that doesn't matter to me."

She glanced down at his crotch. There was no mistaking that he wanted her. He was thick and swollen, the outline of his cock easily visible beneath his pants. "Are you saying you don't want me? This is a onetime offer I'm making here."

"And I thought I was cold thinking we could work each other out of our systems if we slept together a few times."

"Works for me. I can't guarantee I'll want you after today, but—"

He lifted his hands. "Enough, Bella. It's not going to happen. I have too much self-respect to be little more than a dildo for you. No matter how fun it might be."

She opened her mouth to respond, but before she could, she heard the sound of suppressed gunfire coming from the back of the building, followed closely by the unmistakable terror of a man's grating scream.

The building was under attack.

Chapter Seventeen

As soon as Victor heard gunfire, he knew the secret medical facility wasn't a secret anymore. Random punks looking to steal pain pills didn't use suppressors.

Bella had already pulled a gun and was headed for the door when he grabbed her arm.

"Body armor," he said, picking up her tactical vest from the chair where she'd laid it. "I'm not letting you walk into a gunfight naked."

"There's no time," she said, but shrugged into the vest faster than he'd ever seen anyone do before.

He slid his own over the scrub top he'd borrowed earlier. There were only two of them here to deal with this threat and no way of knowing how many bad guys they would face.

Another scream tore through the hallway. Victor blocked it out and focused on his training.

Bella started to barrel through the door, but he grabbed the handle and held on tight. "We go in organized."

"Fine. Me first."

He wasn't going to argue with her. She was already looking a bit wild-eyed and overeager. "On three."

"One, two, three," she said in rapid-fire succession, then pushed through the door.

Victor covered her and fell in line right behind.

The building was silent now. Doors lined the long, wide hallway. They were closed, but through a window at the far end of the hall, Victor could see orange, flickering light.

"They're torching the place," whispered Bella. "We have to save those men."

Victor doubted there was anyone left to save, but kept his fears silent. There was no way to know for sure until they got there and saw the situation for themselves.

Progress was slow down the hall. They checked each door as they went, ensuring that none of the bad guys were going to pop up behind them and trap them inside a burning building. Most of the doors were locked, but three were open. Each one took up precious seconds.

Smoke began to fill the hallway, curling along the ceiling.

"We're running out of time," said Bella. "Need to move faster."

She picked up the pace, moving fast enough to be on the verge of reckless. Victor pressed forward with her, choosing to back her up no matter how reckless she got. At least she wouldn't be facing armed men alone.

The operating room was at the end of the hall. One of the double doors was blocked from closing by someone's foot. It was covered with a blue fabric bootie—one of the doctors or staff. The room immediately to the left led to the recovery area. To the right was the back entrance to the building.

Victor poked his head around the corner for a split second, taking in everything he saw. There was a trail of blood leading out, but no bodies. No shooters. The door was closed. His guess was it was also wedged shut or barricaded.

Most of the flames seemed to be contained to the operating room. He could see them glowing through the open doorway.

"There are oxygen tanks in there," he said.

"There are also men in there. I'll take the operating room. You take recovery."

"No. We stay together."

She glared at him, then eased the swinging door to the recovery room open. There were two men in here hooked up to IVs. Both were covered in white sheets punched with bullet holes and drenched in blood.

The heart monitor hooked to one of them still beeped. He was alive.

The wall adjacent to the operating room—the one closest to the survivor—began to burn. The paint bubbled and blackened, spreading fast.

"I'll get him," said Victor. "Cover me."

He unhooked the man from the machines. He was still bleeding, so Victor folded a clean blanket he found and shoved that against the man's wounds. He draped him over one shoulder and did his best to balance the heavy load. The man was packed with dense muscle and bone, nearly too heavy to be real. If not for the faint groans of pain and sticky blood, Victor might have though him a fabricated distraction.

"Ready," he said.

Bella led the way out, but the flames in the operating room had spread too much now to even step foot inside. Smoke was pouring out through the opening created by the dead man's leg. It was down to their heads now and sinking lower with every second.

"We have to get out now," said Victor. "We've done all we can."

She nodded and ran to the rear exit but not before he saw a sheen of tears in her eyes. They could have been caused by the burning smoke, but something told him otherwise. There were at least five dead men in here, and neither he nor Bella had been able to do a thing to stop it. Chances were the man over his shoulder wouldn't survive either.

They'd deal with the emotional fallout of this later. For now, all they needed to concentrate on was getting out.

"It's stuck," she said, leaning all her weight against the door.

"I bet they've made sure it stays that way. Don't waste time trying to open it. Let's go out the front. They can't barricade a wall of windows. We can at least break our way out."

She turned and led them back the way they'd come.

The path to the front door seemed to take forever. Even without checking all the side rooms as they went, they were still forced to move slowly due to the weight over Victor's shoulder.

They veered past the waiting room and out into the reception area. The second they stepped foot into the space, he saw the pair of men with fully automatic assault rifles standing outside. He tried to shout a warning to Bella, but he was too slow.

The wall of windows along the front of the building erupted in shards of flying glass. Bella's body slammed back into the wall and slid down to the floor.

She'd been shot.

Chapter Eighteen

Victor's roar of fury kept Bella from passing out. She pulled herself together and dove blindly toward the sound of his voice.

One strong hand wrapped around her arm and pulled hard, dragging her across the floor out of the range of gunfire.

"How bad?" he asked.

"Hit the vest. I'm fine." It was one of the biggest lies she'd ever told, but that was just too damn bad. Her battered ribs and burning lungs were going to have to take a backseat to getting out of here alive.

Victor had dropped the unconscious man beside him. The blanket pressed against his chest fell away, showing far too much blood.

"He's not going to make it if we don't get out soon," she said.

"Neither are we if this smoke gets much thicker."

She looked up and sure enough, the smoke was right above their heads. If they hadn't been on the ground, it would have consumed them from the waist up. "Got any brilliant plans?"

"Not unless you've got a battering ram or tank in your pocket."

"I guess my equipment has been called worse things," he said. "What if I did?"

"I'd blast a hole through the wall. Make our own door."

"It's a prefab building. That could work."

"Except for the part where we don't have a battering ram."

"We might. Stay here. I'll be back in a second."

Before she could argue, he was gone, back down the hall. Anxiety bore down on her, making it hard to breathe. The walls seemed to close in on her. The man beside her opened his eyes, and when he did, flames poured from the openings. He smiled, showing multiple rows of jagged teeth like a shark. Smoke billowed from his nostrils as though he were burning from the inside out.

Bella knew it wasn't real. It couldn't be. Her mind was playing tricks on her. She'd hit her head when she'd been shot and all those things were just the concussion talking.

She breathed through the panic, wishing Victor would hurry the hell up. She didn't like being alone with a man who was probably going to die.

Just like all the others.

So many men had died because she hadn't stopped Stynger. Men had died helping her hunt the bitch down. No one could find her. No one could stop her.

By the time Victor came back, she was rocking on her heels, hugging herself and taking up the smallest space possible.

"You okay?" he asked.

She glanced at the dying man. No pointy teeth, no flames, no smoke. "I'm fine."

Victor nodded once, but looked unconvinced. He set down the oxygen tank he'd carried out here and propped it against an exterior wall. "We'll have to retreat down the hall when I set this off. The smoke is thick. We need to cover our mouths."

Bella ripped both her sleeves off and gave one to Victor. She grabbed the unconscious man by the arm and dragged him back down the hall to the first room. Each yard was hard won. She had to crawl under the smoke now, and the guy was so freaking heavy, he practically tore her shoulder from the socket with each tug.

She heard Victor move something heavy—a desk or bookcase, maybe. A few seconds later, he barreled into the room and dove for her, covering her body with his.

The explosion shook the walls. Nearby, several items rattled and fell from a desk. A chair danced across the floor.

"Move fast!" he shouted. "We can't let them block our exit."

He didn't have to tell her twice. She raced out the door, drawing two weapons to cover him as he hefted the man over his shoulder again.

She ran awkwardly, staying as low as she could, holding her breath until her lungs burned with the need for air. She ducked to suck in a few breaths and saw a pair of feet in the new opening Victor had blasted in the wall.

Bella aimed and fired at them. Her shots were off, but close enough to make the man outside dance like a monkey. He hopped around, then disappeared beyond her view.

Cool, fresh air rushed into the building. She hurried toward it, glancing back to make sure Victor was still right behind her.

The second she stepped through the ragged opening in the metal siding, she saw one of the bad guys steady his rifle.

Without a second thought, she aimed and fired, hitting him right above his body armor, squarely in the neck.

His weapon fired a couple of times as he fell, dead.

Tires squealed on the adjacent side of the building. Bella raced toward the noise, hoping to stop whoever was fleeing. By the time she cleared the corner, all she could see was a bloody haze of brake lights through the smoke of burning tires.

They were out of range—too far to risk a shot in an area this populated.

Sirens whined in the distance. She didn't want to be anywhere near this building when the authorities arrived—not when Victor had been taken into custody for shooting someone so recently. Such things were bound to look bad.

She sprinted for her truck. Victor was already halfway there, even with his heavy burden in tow. She opened the rear door of the crew cab for him and helped him push the bleeding man onto her leather seats.

Good thing she knew firsthand that blood washed off of her leather without too much fuss.

"Hospital?" Victor asked as he hopped up beside the bleeding man.

"Not with gunshot wounds. Leigh is a better option. She won't report the injuries to authorities."

"Dr. Vaughn is good, but she doesn't have the equipment to treat the kind of injuries this man has sustained. He needs surgery. You take him to her and he's as good as dead."

Bella let out a low curse as she flung her truck onto the highway, blasting past the speed limit and not letting up on the gas. "We can't risk his life. But you can't be attached to this mess, either. There's still the little matter of you killing a man in defense of another. A jury wouldn't look too kindly on two deaths attached to your name in the same week."

"I'd rather go to jail than see him die."

"Are you forgetting the part where he tried to kill you a few hours ago?"

"Not his fault. You know that as well as I do. Stynger is the one to blame. Not him."

Bella veered around some slow traffic, trying to still

her pounding heart. Her nerves were all over the place, making it hard to focus on the road as well as the bleeding man in her backseat and the equally distracting man keeping him from bleeding out everywhere. "A fact I keep repeating to myself about every five seconds."

"Hospital is the next exit."

"I know that. I'm going. But you're jumping out before I get there."

"But—"

"No arguments. Either you bail or I drive right past the ER."

"Okay. You win. I'll jump."

She slowed down the ramp, turning right down a residential street with a lower chance of traffic cameras to catch what was about to happen. "End of the block. Ready?"

"Yes."

Victor shifted the bleeding man so he could hop out. As soon as he did, the man let out a hiss of pain. His eyes flew open, revealing bloodshot hatred.

"Where is Gage Dallas?" demanded Victor.

Bella gripped the wheel and bit her cheek in an effort to stay silent and let Victor interrogate the only survivor. If she interfered, she'd only slow down the process, and there was no way to know if Gage had that kind of time left.

She split her attention between the road and the rearview mirror, hoping no one in the surrounding homes took note of them.

"You'll never find him," said the man, spittle flying in his rage. "He's ours now. One of us." He grabbed Victor by the throat and squeezed.

Panic jolted through Bella's system, clogging her brain for several seconds. She was usually cool in a fight, but she couldn't find any of her normal calm now—not when there was so much on the line.

Victor fought back, jabbing the man in the abdomen.

He let out a grunt, but that was all. Even wounded he was still strong enough to evade Victor's attempts to break free. He kept squeezing, blocking off Victor's air.

Bella slammed on the brakes and came to a skidding stop. She flung her seat belt off and pulled out the pistol she kept in a hidden compartment along the console. She turned in her seat so she could aim her weapon. What she really wanted to do was dive back there and shove her gun against the bleeding man's temple, but that was too much of a risk. She had to keep her weapon out of his reach.

The man still had Victor by the throat. It didn't seem to matter that he was taking a series of brutally hard blows from close range, or that each of them made him bleed more. All his focus was on choking the life out of Bella's man.

Strangely, Victor showed no sign of fear or panic. His blows were measured. Paced, as if he had all the time in the world.

"Let him go!" she ordered.

The man grinned and tightened his hold. "I'm going to kill him. Then you're next."

Bella's temper pounded at her, screaming at her to pull the trigger. Only the knowledge in this man's head kept him alive. "Where is Gage?"

"Safe. Hidden. He's Stynger's now."

Victor glanced her way. His face was red, and she could see from his expression that he'd had enough.

With a flick of his wrist, he jerked the blood-soaked blanket away and shoved his fingers into the bullet wounds lining the man's chest.

A scream of enraged pain echoed in the cab for a second before the man passed out.

Victor pried his hands away and leaned back, panting. His normal coloring returned quickly. "Sorry I couldn't let you question him longer. I was about to black out."

"You were letting him strangle you?"

Victor cut a length of seat belt with his pocket knife. "Thought it might be a useful distraction—that he might say something in his rage he otherwise wouldn't."

"Thanks for taking one for the team, but next time, try not to scare the hell out of me."

He used the length of seat belt to bind the man's hands behind his back. Muscles and tendons shifted under Victor's skin as he pulled the binding tight. "I'm on the side of hoping there is no next time."

"That works for me, too."

He leaned the man back and put the blanket back in place to slow the bleeding. After a few seconds, his movements stalled to a slow stop.

"What?" she asked.

He felt for a pulse. "He's gone. Dead."

The bottom fell out of Bella's stomach. She didn't even bother to hide her anger. "That fucking bitch! She's led enough men to their deaths. We end this. Now. We find her and take her out for good."

"We have another lead, but you know what you have to do to follow it."

She did, and the idea made her even more furious. "Payton can't keep me away."

"He's not going to want to give you access to his secret holding facility."

"I don't give a shit what he wants right now. Either he lets me talk to the one surviving man who might have an idea of where we find Gage, or I'm going to become unpleasant."

"Honey, you've been nothing but unpleasant with that man for weeks. It hasn't changed his mind about allowing you access."

"He's hiding something. Maybe if I shove enough C4 up his ass he'll tell me what it is." She put the truck in gear and drove.

"Where are you going?"

"To see Payton. We have a dead body to deal with. Since it's at least partially his fault the man is dead, it seems fair that he should have to clean up the mess. Just one little stop I need to make first."

"What could possibly be so important that you're willing to risk getting caught with a dead body in your truck?"

"I need to stop by my place and pick up some C4."

Chapter Nineteen

B ella had gone over the edge. There was no other possible explanation for her actions now. If Victor didn't do something fast, there were going to be two dead bodies to deal with instead of just one.

"You keep explosives at home?" he asked.

"Stable ones, yes. It's all perfectly safe and locked away behind a steel door."

"Explosives are only as stable as the hands of the person in which they rest. I'm not sure if you're aware or not, but you're a little . . . edgy right now."

"I'm a hell of a lot more than merely edgy. I'm pissed as hell and scared to death that a good man's life is on the line. Payton has been keeping too many secrets and holding too much control. That ends now."

"Okay. Fine. We put a stop to it, but perhaps not armed with explosives, toting a dead man who deserves to be treated with more respect than this. Someone loved him the way you love Gage."

The truck slowed as she eased off the accelerator. In her reflection in the rearview mirror, he could see her eyes glisten with tears. "What do you propose?"

"We take him to Dr. Leigh. She'll have connections to take care of his body properly. We'll demand that Payton pay for a burial and notify his family of his passing. I'm sure he'll be able to come up with some plausible cover story."

"More lies."

"Yes, but ones that will give a family comfort."

"And what about Gage's family?" she asked. "What about us?"

Victor ached to comfort her—to touch her shoulder and let her know that she wasn't completely alone—but his hands were covered in blood and he couldn't bring himself to let that reach her. "We'll find him. Things have changed. Payton will give in to our demands."

"And if he doesn't?"

"I'll hold him still while you insert the C4. I'll even bring the lube."

She let out a long breath and caught his gaze in the mirror. She was calmer now. Her hands were steadier. He even saw a hint of humor brighten her gray eyes. "Payton doesn't deserve lube."

"Probably not. But give him a chance to do the right thing."

"He's had so many chances, Victor. How many more should he get?"

"How many would you want if you were him?"

She let out a long breath that made her shoulders droop. "Fine. We'll go see Leigh. Then Payton. But if things don't go well, she's going to have more than one body to explain to the authorities."

"You're not going to kill Payton."

"You don't know that."

"I do. I've worked with you long enough to know that, while you may struggle with self-control, you always do the right thing in the end."

She pulled into Leigh's office and shoved the gearshift into park. Dawn was just beginning to break, and the streets were still quiet. The office was at the edge of a residential area, only a few blocks from where Leigh lived with her husband Clay.

"Always is a strong word," she said.

"And you're not a strong woman? I thought you were."

"Enough with the flattery. You're covered in blood and we're far too exposed here to suit me. Run inside and ask Leigh to come out with a wheelchair or something. I'm sure she'll let you wash up."

Before he could get out of the truck, Leigh hurried down the ramp leading to her office. Her husband pushed a gurney in her wake. He worked at the Edge too, and had proved to be a formidable ally in the couple of jobs Victor had done with him.

Right now he was hovering at his wife's side, his gaze watchful over the surrounding area. "One of Stynger's?" he asked.

"Yeah," Bella said.

To her credit, Dr. Vaughn didn't ask a single question about what had happened to the man once she felt for his pulse and found it missing. It hardly mattered now how he'd gotten this way. There was nothing she could do.

"Let's get him out of sight," said Clay. "I've background checked all the neighbors, but I still don't like the idea of a bunch of busybodies causing Leigh trouble."

They all funneled inside. The place smelled like a mix of scented candles and disinfectant. Soft, neutral colors warmed the space and almost made a person forget that it was chilly in here. Beyond the waiting area, which was more for appearances than function, was a series of rooms on one side of a hallway. They went past a couple of examination rooms, past what looked like a small operating room, and all the way to the end of the hall.

Leigh opened the door and a blast of cold air spilled out. "I'll keep him in here until it's time to move him."

"What are you going to do with the body?" asked Bella.

"Payton always makes sure that the victims of the Threshold Project get a proper burial. We've been through this before. Too many times."

"You smell like smoke and are covered in soot. Was there a fire?" asked Clay.

"There was," Victor said. "We couldn't get all the men out."

Leigh gasped. "They died in a fire?"

"They were shot. The fire was just the cleanup crew," Bella said.

Leigh glanced at Victor, then Bella. "You're both a mess. There's a shower in the bathroom behind reception you can use. There are scrubs in the cabinet you can change into."

"You go first," Bella said. "Blood will raise more questions than soot if someone happens to come for a visit."

"Are you expecting company?" asked Clay, reaching to the small of his back for his weapon.

"No. But that doesn't mean we won't have any. It's been a hell of a night."

"There's a couch in the waiting area and a bed in the recovery room," Leigh said. "You can stay here as long as you like. Or you could come back to the house with us."

"Thanks," Bella said, "but I don't want to impose. As soon as we get cleaned up, we'll get out of your hair."

"How are your wounds?" Leigh asked. "That surgical glue won't hold up if you keep going at this pace."

"I'm fine," Bella said, giving her standard answer.

"You won't be if you break those cuts open. You've got to take it easy."

"I will."

"Liar," Victor said, earning himself a warning glare.

"I'm being as careful as I can be under the circumstances."

"Your truck is covered in blood," Clay said. "I'll take it home and detail it in the garage, out of sight. You can use my wheels until it's done."

Bella nodded and sagged with fatigue. "Thanks. That would be a big help. As soon as I get cleaned up, I have things to do."

Clay frowned as he tossed her his keys. "It's barely dawn. What could you possibly have to do right now?"

"Stynger is still out there. Gage is still missing. Until that changes, I need to stay busy and keep looking. This attack tonight might generate some leads."

Clay nodded in understanding. "I'm close if you need help."

Bella offered him a halfhearted smile. "Thanks, hon. That means a lot."

"You two stay as long as you like," Leigh said. "I'll close the office until the body is delivered to the family. We don't need any pesky questions."

"Thank you," Victor said as he followed them out and locked the office door.

The space was quiet and dim. He was acutely aware of being alone in the same room with a woman who claimed his attention like no one else ever had. It didn't matter that they'd fought for their lives only a short time ago, or that he was covered in blood and soot. It didn't matter that she was strung so tight she looked like she might break. He still couldn't take his eyes off of her.

She stood near a window, peering through the blinds. The muted sound of two car doors shutting seeped in from the parking lot. He could hear Bella's truck start and the engine noise fade as Clay and Leigh drove away.

Still, Bella didn't move. Her gaze was watchful, her

body language tight and rigid. If he hadn't known better, he would have said she was afraid.

"Do you think we were followed?" he asked.

She didn't look his way as she responded. "Someone killed those men and set fire to the place. We didn't take them all down before they could escape. At least one of them got away. It would be stupid to assume no one followed us."

"I was looking for a tail when we left and didn't see one."

"Doesn't mean they're not there. Go clean up. I'll keep watch."

He almost balked at the order, preferring instead to stay and seek some way to calm her nerves. But the only thing he could think of to relax her was not something he'd do while covered in blood.

"I'll be quick so you can shower, too," he said.

She gave an absent nod as she took up a position watching the street. "No rush," she said, but her gun was in her hand and it was shaking.

He'd never seen her like this before. She was always calm under stress, or more accurately, reveled in it. This frenetic kind of energy she was putting off wasn't like her at all.

He took one of the fastest showers of his life, scrubbing away all the grim reminders of the night. When he came out, Bella was exactly where he'd left her, monitoring the entrance.

"Your turn," he said.

She jumped at the sound of his voice and whirled around, aiming her weapon at him. The barrel lifted an instant after she realized who he was. "Not healthy to sneak up on an armed woman like that."

"I wasn't sneaking. You're just on edge. Want to talk about it?"

She ran her fingers through her glossy black hair, smoothing away some of the tangles tonight's chaos had left behind. "What's there to say? We had several men alive and able to give us information only a few hours ago. They're all dead now."

"Except for the man Payton transported," he reminded her.

She flinched at the mention of Payton's name. "If you think he's going to let us talk to the guy, you're insane. He's going to do what he always does and keep me in the dark for as long as possible. I swear it gives him some kind of high to be such a control freak."

"A man who spends his life keeping big secrets can't afford *not* to be a control freak."

"Maybe so, but that doesn't mean I have to like it. Or play along. He's going to give us full access to that man or I'm going to take down his precious secret holding facility. The place is little more than a prison, anyway."

"We need some place to put the people who were too damaged by Stynger's experiments to live in the outside world."

Her lips went tight and she scowled at him with so much force, he was sure he felt a hot wind coming off of her. "You're taking his side? How could you?"

"I'm not picking sides at all. I'm simply pointing out the fact that we can't have deranged madmen roaming about freely, even if we all wish they hadn't been made that way on purpose."

Bella shook her head. "You know we're going to have to pull out the big guns to get Payton to cooperate, right?"

"How can you know that? You haven't even asked him to speak to the man yet."

"I know Payton. You'll see. He'll feed us a line of bullshit about protecting innocents and not risking compromising the facility's location, but what he really means is that he likes pulling all the strings. My guess is that it'll take a battering ram to get through the front door."

"You've got to find some calm, Bella. Control yourself."

"You think I lack self-control?" she asked. "If that's the case, then why didn't I blow that man's brains all over my back window? I knew the information in his head was important, so I didn't shoot him when he was choking you to death."

"I had it under control."

"Of course you did. You always do. Mr. Calm, Cool and Collected. Never raising your voice or misbehaving. There's no way all that restraint is healthy for a man. Your blood pressure must be off the charts."

"There are other ways of coping with stress that don't involve high explosives, weapons or a sparring ring."

"Name one."

"There are several, but since I don't think healthy adult conversation will count as a valid answer for a woman like you, I'll move straight to sex as a means to cope with stress."

"Okay. You have me there. Sex works. But that whole adult conversation thing? Total waste of time."

"You don't know until you try. Perhaps you should practice with Payton by asking him nicely to visit the prisoner."

She shot Victor a scathing look. "You think you're funny, don't you?"

"No, I'm trying to be serious. I can tell how on edge you've been these past few weeks. Tonight it's worse than I've ever seen. If you don't do something to control it, it's going to control you."

"I'm dealing. That's what adults do. We suck it up and deal and don't waste time discussing all the touchy-feely crap that really doesn't matter in the end. It makes no difference how I feel, only that I do the right thing, whether or not I feel like doing it. It's not like I take pleasure in the idea of hurting a man who I once thought of as a father figure. But I will if that's what it takes to get a lead on Gage so we can bring him home."

"You're too wound up, Bella. You're going to break."

"Leave it alone, Temple. I mean it."

He knew from experience that she called him by his last name only when she was at her limit. The only thing that would work now was a strategic retreat. Back off. Let her cool down. Once the steam stopped pouring from her ears, maybe then she'd see that he had a valid argument.

Then again, maybe what she really needed was for him to take her back to the sparring ring and work out her aggression in sweat and bruises. If not for her injuries, he would have done just that.

"You should go get a shower," he said. "The last thing we need is to be found wearing the soot and ash from tonight's version of fun with arson."

"You'll watch our backs?" she asked. "I still feel like we're being followed. I'm not sure Leigh would ever forgive me if her shiny new office went down in flames."

"Don't worry. I'll keep watch."

She turned to go down the hall, but stopped in the doorway. Without turning around, she said, "Thanks, Victor. For sticking by my side tonight. I know I have a tendency to give you shit, but I do feel better knowing you've got my back."

"Always, Bella," he said. "I'll always have your back."

He couldn't see her face, but he did hear tears thicken her voice. "That's what Payton used to say, too. I hope you're not as good a liar as he is. I really can't handle the idea of doing this all alone."

Victor was so surprised by her admission of weakness, she was already gone and behind a closed door before he found his tongue. "You won't have to," he said, even though he knew she couldn't hear. "I swear."

In that moment he realized that no matter what happened, until Gage was home, Stynger was behind bars or dead, and Bella was safe, he wasn't leaving her side. He was right where he belonged.

Chapter Twenty

Bella felt more solid after her shower. So much so that it made her realize just how unsteady she'd been feeling before. The lack of sleep and stress were getting to her much more than usual. Those freaky visions she'd had before they'd escaped the fire were proof of that.

It was more than the fact that Gage was missing. She'd worried about her men before and it hadn't affected her like this. There was something else going on—something that scared the hell out of her.

She was cracking. Just like the others. She could feel it seeping along the inside of her brain, worming its way through, destroying her.

If she went to the secret holding facility where Payton held the others who'd cracked, they might see just how bad she was and never let her leave.

How would she find Gage then? How would she kill Stynger?

She had to hold it together—at least long enough to finish her work. Maybe then she'd take some time off and regroup. Heal.

If healing was even possible.

She had blocked Payton's number on her cell, but she no longer had the luxury of being so petty. He'd hurt her.

Lied to her. She'd never trust him again. But she needed him now.

More important, Gage needed him.

She dialed the number and held her breath.

"Is everything okay?" answered Payton, his voice ruffled with panic.

"No worse than before."

"Then why did you call?"

"I need access to the man who survived."

Payton didn't respond for a second too long. "It's not a good idea, Bella."

"I need to question him."

"Let me do it. Just tell me what you want to know."

She bit her tongue to keep the sharp words inside her mouth. "I'd rather do it myself."

"You don't trust me to deliver the information, do you?"

"Why would I? I know you have no trouble lying."

"I'd be honest with you. I swear it."

She bowed her head. "I'm sorry, but your promises are worthless. Are you going to let me question him or not?"

"If I refuse?"

"Then it will be obvious to me that you don't give a shit about what happens to Gage. I'll no longer have need of you and I'll spend the rest of my life hoping we never speak again."

He let out a long sigh. "It's not safe, Bella. The people that come here . . . they're dangerous."

"You think I can't handle myself?"

"Against physical harm? Certainly. It's the emotional toll they take on a person that worries me. I don't want you to see the worst-case scenario and think that's where you're headed."

"We both know it could be. For all we know I could be inside one of those cells before the month is out." Just the thought was enough to make her break out in a cold sweat. It took all her willpower to keep the tremor from her voice as she said it.

"I won't let that happen."

"There's not a damn thing you can do to stop it. We both know that. All you can do now is help me find Gage. Help me find Stynger. To do that I need access to the only man alive in our custody who might know where they are."

"It's risky, but if you're sure . . ."

"I'm sure."

"I'll text you a meeting location. You'll be drugged for the flight so you don't know where the facility is."

"No. No drugs."

"You can't have knowledge of where the facility is if you get captured."

"You think I'd talk? I thought you knew me better than that, Payton."

"I don't think you'd intentionally tell anyone anything, but Stynger has ways of getting into people's heads. She can twist your mind around and make you think she's your friend. Our friend. You'll do whatever she wants. The only way to keep those poor souls safe is to make sure you have nothing to tell her."

"Then blindfold me, but no drugs. I have to stay sharp and alert."

"You could use the sleep. You sound exhausted."

"I'm fine," she lied. "No drugs. Period."

"It's against my rules."

"Fuck your rules, Payton. Your rules are what got us all into this mess to begin with. Maybe it's time you started using a different set."

He went quiet again—a sure sign she'd hit a nerve. "Are you able to go soon?"

"Yes, but you need to know that I'm telling Victor where I'm headed. If it's all the same to you, I'd rather have someone know whether or not I make it out of there."

"You think I'm planning to hold you against your will?"

"I wouldn't be the first person you've done that to, would I?"

It was anger that came through in his tone now. "I'll make arrangements with the pilot and contact you in a couple of hours. Once you have the coordinates, you'll have twenty minutes to make it to the rendezvous. If you're not there, the pilot will leave without you. Understood?"

"Yes. Make sure your pilot understands that if he even thinks about trying to drug me, the next time he flies, he'll whistle from all the holes I put in him."

"There's no need for violence, Bella."

"For your sake I hope not." She hung up and went to find Victor to tell him about her field trip.

She had her mouth open to start talking when she entered the reception area where he stood, but as soon as she saw him, all the words fell out of her brain.

The borrowed shirt he wore was far too small for his broad shoulders. The fabric pulled tight, showing off an array of muscles that made Bella's mouth water.

His stance was firm, his feet braced. His whole demeanor was one of vigilance. The butt of his gun peeking out from the back of his borrowed clothes was a reminder of the danger they were in, but only added to his appeal.

She knew she could take care of herself if things got ugly, but knowing she was backed up by a strong, capable man was more than a little reassuring.

The tendons in his forearms flexed as he parted the horizontal blinds. Streetlights silhouetted his body, draping deep shadows over the lean contours of his neck and jawline. A faint shadow of stubble graced his jaw, making him look less like a picture of military perfection and more real. More attainable.

He was just a man—flesh and blood like every other one—but there was something about him that called to her. She couldn't put her finger on what it was, why he got under her skin in a way no other man ever had.

As she watched him, her skin began to heat and some of the tension riding between her shoulder blades loosened. A sweet tingling nestled at the base of her spine and curled through her blood.

"Are you going to stare at me all night?" he asked.

She felt her cheeks burn with embarrassment. He hadn't turned to see her or even moved an inch, but he'd known she was there. As vigilant as he was, she should have realized that spying on him was a ridiculous notion.

Rather than answer his question, she changed subjects. "I spoke to Payton. He's going to let me into the facility to question the survivor."

"You mean he's going to let *us* in."

"No, but I do want you to know when I'm going and when I should be back so you can raise holy hell if Payton decides to kidnap me."

Victor turned around slowly. By the time he was facing her she could see just how pissed he was. "If you think I'm letting you walk into a meeting with a brainwashed soldier at a secret facility with no idea of where you are, you're insane."

"Letting me?" she asked, unable to get past the implication that he had a right to do such a thing.

"Damn right." His voice was calm, but she could feel his fury gaining steam as each second ticked by. "I was charged with making sure your operation got the job done. If you go down, there will be no one left to make your people stay on task. There's no chance in hell they'll listen to Payton. You made sure of that."

"He's not trustworthy. I wouldn't want them to listen to him."

Victor crossed the space between them, getting so close she had to tip her head up a little to keep looking him in the eye. "That's another reason not to let you go in there alone. He controls that facility. Once you're inside, he can keep you there for as long as he wants. You disappear, your business will fold. Your employees will scatter to find new work. The best hope we have of finding Stynger will be lost." He pulled in a long breath that made his chest expand to epic proportions. He was so close that the move pressed him against her breasts, causing her nipples to go instantly hard. "I won't let that happen. So unless you want to sign your company over to me, I'm going with you into the lion's den."

She didn't dare breathe. Pressing her nipples more firmly against his chest wasn't an option, not if she wanted to continue to be able to speak. All she could think about now was how much she wanted to strip that too-tight shirt from his body and rub her naked breasts against that glorious chest of his. If they both worked up a good sweat, the glide would be amazing.

"My company is mine," she said with less force than she'd intended. "I can handle myself fine while I'm at the facility."

"How in the world are you going to watch your back when you're barely even alert enough to pay attention to what I'm saying?"

That was true only because she was distracted by the scent of his skin and the feel of his chest against her straining nipples. When he was no longer around, her focus would return as good as ever. "I'm going alone. I don't want both of us to get stuck behind bars with no one on the outside to fight for our freedom."

He shook his head. "No. It's too dangerous. By the time I know you're in trouble, it will already be too late to help you. We'll make sure someone on the outside knows what we're doing, but either you let me go with you, or I tie you to a damn chair and keep you there until Gage is home and Stynger is neutralized."

"You wouldn't," she said, not even bothering to keep the venom from her voice.

He grabbed her around the waist, hooked a rolling office chair with his foot and pushed her down into it. His body caged her in. His big hot hands pinned her wrists to the armrests of the chair. His face was close to hers, giving her a direct view of his clear blue eyes. "I do what's best for the mission. If that means pissing you off, so be it. I'd rather have you angry and safe than dead or detained against your will."

"And you don't think tying me to a chair would be detaining me against my will? What do you think it would be? Fun?"

A flicker of a smile crossed his lips. "Depends on how many clothes you're wearing at the time. If I stripped you bare and tied your legs over the arms of this chair, I think we'd both be having fun once I got my mouth on your sweet pussy."

All thoughts of missions and danger trickled out of her ears, leaving a buzzing sound behind. Sexual awareness prickled across her skin until she had to shiver to shed its hold on her.

Victor's grip on her arms tightened. He leaned a little closer until his lips were only an inch from hers. His pupils were huge now, making his eyes appear darker. There was hunger there—a kind she'd never seen before. The man wasn't hiding a thing from her, as if he had no fear of her knowing just how much he wanted her.

"I'm your boss. You can't talk to me like that," she said. There was no bite of reprimand in her tone, only breathless anticipation.

"Sorry, Bella. I really don't give a shit what you are

right now. Boss, general—none of that matters, though I wish it did. Wanting you isn't easy."

She knew exactly what he meant. She wanted him just as bad, and it made each mission with him both more exciting and more difficult. If it weren't for the fact that they worked so well together, the distraction he caused would have been too much of a liability. But they did work well together. They fought well together. She was absolutely certain they'd fuck well together.

Just like that, she could see the two of them going at it, tearing each other's clothes off, battling for dominance. In the end it wouldn't matter who ended up on top. She knew it would be good.

His gaze fell to her mouth before coming back to her eyes. "I don't know what you're thinking right now, but whatever it is, it's hot as hell."

"I'm thinking that you should let me up before I head butt that perfect nose of yours and break it. Maybe you'll worry more about having better manners if you aren't so pretty."

He didn't even bother to shift away in the face of her threat. He stayed right in reach, showing no sign of fear. "No, honey. You're not going to do that."

"I'm not?"

"No." Absolute confidence.

"Why not?"

"Because you like the way I look. And because if you break my nose, it's going to be really hard for me to breathe when I go down on you."

A shiver coursed through her. Her knees tried to squeeze together to ease the sudden ache between her thighs, but he was standing too close, his body keeping her legs spread.

He saw her shiver and a knowing grin stretched his lips.

Her mouth watered for another taste of him. The

brief kiss they'd shared before wasn't enough. Not even close. She needed more.

Bella licked her lips and strained to close the distance between them. Victor's nostrils flared as he sucked in a deep breath. "You smell so damn good." He tucked his nose in the crook of her neck and breathed her in. "I know it's not perfume. You didn't have any of that here after your shower. What the hell is it?"

His lips found the side of her neck and grazed across the sensitive skin.

She stifled a groan and rolled her hips to ward off a sudden flare of need. Her voice lacked all traces of command, leaving behind only a wavering thread of sound. "I don't know what you're talking about."

His tongue flicked out just below her ear. "You taste so damn good, too. I want to eat you all up."

The image that presented was more than she could stand. A groan of raw, visceral want fell out of her and she felt her pussy heat and grow wet.

"Mmm. I like that sound, baby. It's so much better than all of that talk about putting yourself in danger alone."

She tried to form a coherent sentence about how her job was dangerous, he knew that, and that he was just going to have to get over his sudden case of overprotectiveness. Instead, his teeth raked lightly across her skin and all that came out was an incoherent whimper.

Women like Bella didn't whimper. They bellowed. They roared. They tore bad guys apart with their bare hands and a scream of triumph on their lips. And yet, after a few seconds of Victor's mouth on her neck, she was reduced to a mewling simpleton, incapable of speech. If he ever did get his mouth between her legs, she'd probably melt into a puddle of vapid mush.

His fingers trailed up her arm to circle the base of her throat. Her hand was free now. It wouldn't have taken much to grab his balls and twist, forcing him to set her free. But the idea of harming him in such a way was unthinkable.

She didn't want to damage what lay between his legs. She wanted to fondle and kiss and suck. She wanted to run her tongue over him and see how long it took him to lose control.

A man with an iron will like Victor's was going to be a fun challenge. Even thinking about it made her heart pound and her blood heat.

She so loved a good challenge.

She started to reach for his groin to see if he was as aroused as she was. Before she'd moved an inch, he grabbed her wrist and held on tight.

"I'm not letting you fight dirty," he said. "I know your tricks, and I'm not going to end up with my balls in a knot just so you can run off and leave me curled up in agony."

It hurt her that he thought that's what she would do, but his conclusion wasn't unfair. She *had* just been thinking about inflicting pain on him, if only for a brief second.

Still, the fact that he predicted her actions was enough to irritate her. "You don't know me as well as you think."

"No? Then look me in the eye and tell me you weren't thinking about giving the boys a hard twist."

Her gaze slipped away from his.

"That's what I thought. Your violent streak is a mile wide, Bella. It's going to be your undoing if you don't learn to control it."

"I control it just fine."

"Liar."

The insult pushed her over the edge. She braced her feet and shoved up hard with her legs, breaking his hold. She threw her weight at him and pushed him back while sweeping his legs. He tilted sideways and landed on the floor next to the receptionist's desk. Bella tried to disengage before he fell, but he tightened his hold on her and pulled her down on top of him.

She landed on his chest, one thigh between his, the other knee on the ground. He took control of her arms and held her in place so she couldn't stand up.

"See?" he said. "No control over your violent tendencies. Look where it got you."

"Maybe this was exactly where I wanted you. Did you ever think about that? Maybe I exerted just enough violence to get you here."

A look of pure lust claimed his expression, so hot it scalded her. "I want to believe you. But I don't."

With one powerful move, he rolled her over and pinned her to the floor. His thick thigh pressed deep between her legs, rubbing against her mound. She wasn't sure if the stroke had been intentional, but it sent a jolt of sensation winging through her all the same.

She lay beneath him and closed her eyes, feeling her body yield and melt. His weight was a delicious blanket draped over her, blocking out the rest of the world. Her submission was completely involuntary, sapping her strength and leaving her shaking and weak. There was no fear or panic under him. No freaky flashbacks to days long past. All that stood between them now was an inferno of need and way too many clothes.

"Bella," he said, her name a plea for strength. "You are so damn sexy I walk around half hard all the time. But like this—all soft and hot beneath me—you destroy my self-control. If you don't tell me to stop, I'm going to fuck you right here on the floor."

She opened her eyes and saw the raw need painting his face. Gone was the civilized mask of a gentleman he usually wore. She hadn't realized until this very moment that he'd been hiding the real him behind a thin facade.

There was a wildness in his eyes, a kind of feral energy

pouring from him. Restraint quivered in his hold, telling her he was skirting the edge of control.

And she loved it.

"What about the part where you don't want to be reduced to a handy dildo? I wanted you before and you turned me away. What's different now?"

"You push me past rational thought. I don't give a shit right now why you want me. All I care about is that you take what I have to give. Every inch, nice and deep, so I can finally get you out of my system."

"You think one fuck will be enough?" she asked, secretly hoping it wouldn't. They both needed to be able to concentrate on their work, but she didn't know if one night with him would ever be enough.

"Only one way to find out," he said. Then he kissed her.

It was no ordinary kiss. There were lips and tongues like every time before, but this kiss was different. Sharper. Sweeter. More urgent. His mouth covered hers, and it felt like he'd just slid a missing part back into place. The sensation was so shocking, she let out a small gasp. He swallowed it down and let out a low growl.

The sound slid over her tongue and sizzled through her body. Rough, hard hands grasped her, holding on to her like he was afraid to ever let go.

The taste of him went to her head. She wanted to consume him, devour him, make him hers for all time.

Stupidest idea ever.

This was just a meeting of the flesh, nothing more. They were both strung tight, both needing release. There was nothing more to it than the growing pressure of a biological need. She couldn't let there be more to it than that.

But if that was all this was going to be, then she was going to make the most of it.

Bella freed her hands enough to shove his shirt up over

his ribs. Her fingers slid beneath the tight fabric to splay across the hard male flesh of his back. Each of his hurried breaths expanded her hold. She could feel the power of his body flowing through him easily, without thought or effort. His heart pounded fast, telling her without words just how much their kiss was affecting him.

It rocked her just as hard, stealing her breath and making her dizzy. She needed more of him—all he had to give.

His knee forced her legs wider. His rock-hard thigh rubbed right against her clit, coaxing a gasp from her. The thin pants she wore were no protection from his strength and heat. Still, she needed to shed them and get as much of her skin against his as she could.

She pulled up on his shirt. The sound of seams ripping filled the quiet space, fitting perfectly between their labored breathing.

Victor moved just enough to pull the shirt over his head, giving Bella a clear view of his magnificent chest. She'd seen a lot of half-naked men in her life, but not one of them shook her the way he did.

Lean, sculpted muscles were shadowed by the growing dawn flowing in through the office windows. A light dusting of blond hair warmed his skin and made him look more real. Perfection like his could have easily appeared plastic and fake, but the man hovering over her now was all taut flesh and hot blood.

He reached for the vee of her scrub top, took hold and tore it open down the front.

Bella gasped in surprise. Her bare breasts jiggled with the force of his act. His eyes fixed on her nipples, and they tightened in response to his scorching gaze.

The slick heat of excitement eased from her pussy. She loved his lack of reserve, his desire, his strength. There wasn't a single worry that he'd use it to give her anything but pleasure.

"Leigh isn't going to be happy that you're tearing up her scrubs," Bella said.

"Don't fucking care," he growled. A dark stain of lust streaked across his cheeks. Those clear blue eyes of his were nearly black with want.

His hands covered her breasts, palming them. She wasn't overly busty, but they fit together so well, his hands seemed to be made for this task alone. Her nipples beaded up against his taut skin. His fingers dragged over the curve of her breasts until he was able to pluck at her nipples.

Lightning bolts of sensation streaked down to her core, making her hips buck beneath him. She thought it couldn't feel any better until he covered one nipple with his mouth. Hot, wet suction became the center of her world. Her whole body lit up until she was certain her skin was glowing.

Victor lifted his head. His jaw clenched twice before he spoke. "Take off the pants, or they're next."

"You first," she shot back. "I want to see you naked. All of you."

"I warned you," he said, then took the waistband in his hands and pulled hard.

The front of the scrub pants split open. She didn't have any clean panties with her, so she'd gone commando. Now that the pants were torn, there was nothing to cover her but the slick proof of her lust for him.

Victor's nostrils flared as he saw it. He grabbed both of her thighs right behind her knees and shoved them up, high and wide. A second later, his mouth was on her, licking and sucking. His tongue grazed her clit, and her whole body arched under the force of the pleasure he created.

A low male groan of satisfaction rumbled between her legs as he slid his tongue inside her.

Bella nearly came unglued. Her body zoomed straight

to the edge of orgasm and stayed there. He kissed and licked and sucked on her sensitive flesh until each breath was a ragged plea for release.

His hot hands gripped her hips and flipped her over onto her stomach. Long, thick fingers slid inside her.

"I love how wet you are for me, Bella. I'll be able to fuck you as fast and hard as I like, sliding in nice and smooth."

The picture his words painted made her tremble. The tips of his fingers hit a particularly sensitive spot that jerked a gasp from her.

He worked that spot as he pressed on the small of her back, forcing her to arch more for him.

"So pretty like this, on your knees."

The submissive posture should have bothered her, but she couldn't bring herself to think about anything other than what his skilled fingers were doing inside of her. So good. Just a few strokes more and she was sure she could come.

But he didn't let her. He stopped before she reached that point and pulled his fingers away. The heat of his body disappeared, leaving her chilled. She pushed to her knees and looked over her shoulder to see where he'd gone. She found him standing behind her naked, opening a condom.

The sight of his cock made her want to weep for joy. No way was he going to resist taking her with an erection like that. He was thick and hard, the veins bulging in time with his racing heart. She wasn't going to have to wait to be filled up much longer.

"Why didn't you let me come?" she asked.

"Because the first time I make you come, it's going to be around my cock. I want to feel that tight little pussy quiver around me while I drive deep."

He certainly had the right equipment for that kind of

operation. She'd had plenty of men in her life, but never one built like Victor. She was certain he could reach places no other man had ever gone before. She couldn't wait to see what that was going to feel like.

"Lie down," she ordered. "I'm going to ride you until I get off."

"You don't get to give the orders in this, honey. You'll ride me if and only if I let you."

"You think you're in charge?" she asked.

"I think that if you want me to take you, you'll lie down, spread your legs and ask nicely."

"Fuck you, Victor."

He stroked his erection. The open condom package sat on the desk next to him. He hadn't rolled it on yet, and she could see the gleam of precome sliding along his length. "I will if you ask nicely."

"And if I don't?"

He shrugged. "I can get off just like this, enjoying the sight of your naked body and the sweet taste of your pussy on my tongue." His fist stopped moving. "Or I can fuck you until you get off a few times. Let your pussy make me come rather than my own hand. It's your call."

"Is this some kind of game?" she asked.

"No game. I just want to make sure you understand that while you may be my boss, your authority over me ends once the clothes come off."

"I'm not some kind of submissive weakling you can push around."

"I know. If you were, my dick wouldn't be hard right now. I like you just as you are. Claws, teeth and all. Now lie down, Bella. Show me you want my cock."

She'd never had anyone talk to her like that, and the things it made her feel were both potent and shameful. She liked the way he took charge, the way he didn't back down, even if it meant sex was off the table. But mostly she liked the way he looked at her while he stroked his cock—like she was already his and was just waiting for her to realize it.

Still, if she gave him too much control, he might think it would carry over into their working relationship, and that was something she couldn't afford. No one could ever know about what they did here tonight, and if he treated her differently, everyone would know. Her employees were far too astute not to see it.

She lowered her gaze and tried to look like she'd succumbed to his demands. She closed the space between them and slid her hand down his body until her fingers covered his. Each tight stroke moved her hand until she couldn't stand not feeling his flesh against hers.

Her grip slid over him, pushing until he let go. The steely heat of his cock nearly took her breath away. Even the soft, smooth skin covering him couldn't diminish the power she held in the palm of her hand.

The stuff of female fantasies everywhere.

Victor's head fell back. His throat moved to make room for a blissful groan to escape his chest. His thighs were braced as he leaned his weight against the receptionist's desk.

If only the woman who sat here knew just how fine an ass was perched on her desk, she'd never get any work done again for all the daydreaming she'd do.

Bella kissed his chest as she worked him, each press of her lips drifting lower as she went. Finally, she made her way to the prize, bending over at the waist to take him into her mouth.

Victor grabbed her hair and held her close, breathing hard as if to regain control over himself. She tasted a salty drop of precome and reveled in the fact that she'd pulled it from him.

After a few seconds, his grip in her hair loosened, giving her free rein to do as she pleased. His fingers never strayed from her head, making her wonder if he was worried about losing control again.

The taste of him went to her head. The smooth glide of slick, hot flesh on her tongue and lips was an erotic thrill she'd never experienced quite like this before. Her mouth watered for more until she was lost in the act, moving on him with abandon.

His body tensed. She knew he was close to letting go and reveled in the knowledge that she'd brought him to that point.

Just as she was sure he was going to come, he jerked her head away and took her to the floor in one smooth maneuver. His body was between her knees, holding them open. Cool air swirled over the wet skin between her thighs, accentuating the ache of need he'd created in her.

The open condom went on in less than a second, and his cock surged inside of her, plunging all the way in a single, powerful stroke.

Bella's vision wavered in the midst of the acute pleasure and satisfaction he gave her. The emptiness was gone, and every nerve ending she had was cheering at the sensations rioting through her. So full. So good.

Once he hit bottom he went still. They were joined more deeply than she'd ever been with anyone before, and while it was intense and thrilling, it wasn't entirely comfortable. Her body wasn't used to his length, but it sure as hell wanted to be.

He kissed her face, returning every few second to her lips. "You hurt?"

"Not even close. But if you don't fuck me, I might hurt you."

His grin broke the tension riding his features. "I'm definitely going to do that. Once I can last more than three strokes."

"Have some control issues, do we?" she teased.

"Not usually. But with you . . . it might be a problem."

"You should have made me come with your fingers."

"And you should have spread your legs and asked nicely for my cock. Guess we're both going to be disappointed."

His erection jerked inside of her, and she nearly came right there. If not for the several deep breaths she took, she would have. "I kinda don't think that's going to be a problem."

"Good thing I'm on top," he said.

"Why's that?"

"Because if you were riding me, those sweet tits swaying, those curvy hips moving with every stroke, I would already be spent."

"You like being on top, don't you?"

"I like you knowing that this is separate from work. You can boss me around there all you like, issue me order after order, but when it comes to my cock inside you"—he slid out and right back in, seating himself to the hilt in a way that made Bella see stars—"I get to call the shots."

"If you think I'm going to lie back all passive and let you do what you want, you're—" She didn't have the chance to finish her sentence before he started to move. Once that happened, words no longer mattered. Whatever she'd been about to say was irrelevant. The only important thing going on was the way he stroked her, the way he filled her, stretched her, while grazing across her clit with each penetrating glide.

After only a minute, she was already careening toward the edge. He rode her all the way to the shimmering precipice, then stopped.

She stumbled back from the brink of orgasm, frustrated and dazed. "What the hell, Temple?" Her words lacked heat because she had to pant between every one of them.

"You'll come when I let you."

She wasn't sure what kind of mind games he was playing, but there wasn't enough brainpower left in her for her to figure it out or even question him further. As soon as she was safely away from her near orgasm experience, he began moving again.

Each slow, measured movement made her want. Need. She could tell she wasn't the only one riding that fine line. He was getting close, too. And each time he did, he froze until the tension passed and he was once again in control.

She'd never seen anything like it. Never felt anything like it. Over and over he pulled her back from the edge until she was no longer sure he'd ever let her fall.

He must have sensed her acceptance, because the moment she gave in to what he was doing, the very second she stopped trying to force his hand, everything changed.

Victor shifted his position slightly, coming down so that her breasts were flat against his chest. His soft hairs tickled her nipples, adding yet another layer onto the web of intense sensations he spread over her.

With each powerful move of his hips, her whole body shook. His mouth found hers, licking and sucking her lips between deep, scorching kisses.

She wrapped her legs around him and held on for dear life. There was so much strength and grace to his movements, so much determination, she could hardly believe he was real.

He kissed the edge of her ear, sucked the lobe into his mouth. When he spoke, his breath stroked her skin like a caress. "Are you ready to come now?" he asked.

"Yes."

"Say it."

"I'm ready to come."

"Not good enough, Bella. Ask me. Nicely."

She no longer cared about her role as his boss or

whatever pride she might have to swallow later. Right now, her body was on fire and only he could free her from the exquisite torment. "Let me come, Victor. I need it. Please."

It was her plea that won him over. He let out a low growl of victory, then slid his arm beneath her hips and tilted them so every deep plunge of his cock hit that sweet spot. Her clit was swollen and throbbing—an easy target for a man as skilled as he was.

Within seconds she was speeding back to the brink, only this time, he didn't pull her back. He shoved her over, driving her right into the most powerful orgasm of her life. She was consumed by it, surrounded by it, filled by it. Her whole body was aflame, soaring out of control as he rode her right through the storm. She heard the sound of her own screams of completion, but didn't care. The deep bellow of Victor's pleasure joined the noise, melding perfectly.

By the time it was over, she was blind, starved for oxygen and shaking uncontrollably. Her body was covered in sweat. Copious amounts of her own natural lube were spilling from her. Every muscle in her body shimmered with a kind of electric heat she'd never felt before. Even her brain felt different. Lighter. Singing with energy.

She lay there on the floor with Victor's body draped over her. He was shaking as hard as she was, panting like he'd just sprinted up a mountainside. Every few seconds his erection jerked inside of her, sending little frissons of orgasmic aftermath spinning through her.

"Did I survive?" he asked against her neck. Her hair muffled his voice, but she heard him just fine.

"Think so," she said. "Unless we both died."

"Hell of a way to go." He shifted just enough to pull out of her before the condom started to leak. Once that was done, he moved right back where he'd been, draped over her, pinning her down.

"I should kick your ass, you know," she said.

"For what?"

"Making me beg."

"You didn't beg. Besides, you can't tell me you didn't enjoy that. You left a puddle on the carpet under your lovely ass."

She slapped his shoulder, but the blow lacked any force. She was too weak for that. Too shaken.

He lifted his head, but she could tell it was a monumental effort. His eyes were still dark, but the ring of clear blue she was used to seeing was making its way home. "What? Not enough for you? Give me a second and I'll make you come a few more times."

Her womb clenched at the idea, but the rest of her was still vibrating from his previous efforts. "I'm good. Except for the fact that you fucked my brains loose. It's the only explanation for why I begged."

He laughed and rolled onto his back beside her. His hand splayed across her ribs, just below her breast, as if he couldn't stand the idea of not being in contact with her.

"You didn't beg, Bella. Maybe I'll make you beg next time, though, just so you can see the difference."

Reality intruded with bruising force, chilling her skin. "There's not going to be a next time, honey. We can't go making a habit of this."

"Twice is a habit?"

"No, but three times is, and twice is way too close to three for my tastes."

He propped himself up on his elbow. "I don't know about you, but I've never come that hard before. I'm going to want it again. So are you."

"You certainly don't lack any confidence, do you?"

"Your loose brains speak eloquently on my behalf."

He leaned over to kiss her, but she put up a hand and stopped him cold.

"Don't," was all she said.

"So, that's it? We're done?"

"No, *we* have a mission to complete. The fucking is done."

His mouth went tight with anger, but he nodded. "Fine. Whatever you have to tell yourself. But when you wake up in the night, aching and wet, needing what I just gave you, don't think I'll be waiting around."

"I do own a vibrator, you know." She almost laughed at how ridiculous and lame her self-inflicted orgasms seemed compared to what he'd just given her.

He stood and shed the condom. "Apparently I'm easy to replace then. Excellent to know."

She'd hurt him, which had been the last thing she'd wanted to do. "It's not like that."

He held up his hand for her to stop talking. "It's fine. I get it. You've been clear from the beginning that this thing between us could never be more than fucking. If that's the way you want it, then that's the way it'll be. You're the boss."

She flinched at the chill in his tone. Things had been so good just a minute ago, then she had to go and mess it up by opening her big mouth.

He picked up his clothes and stalked down the hall to the bathroom. She didn't follow. Not only was she worried she'd make it worse, she wasn't entirely sure her legs could support her weight right now.

She stripped out of the tattered clothes he'd ripped open, and eased into an upright position. The world was still spinning from the epic orgasm he'd given her.

She really wasn't sure how she was going to go through the rest of her life without feeling that again, but she needed to find a way. Fast. Pleasure like that could easily be addicting, and she needed to stop now, before she no longer could.

Victor came back, completely dressed, tidy and looking unfazed by the rocking he'd just given her world. The only sign of emotion she got from him was the heat in his eyes as his gaze slid along her naked body. "Your turn. There are still more scrubs in the cabinet for you to wear."

"I think we should talk."

"Nothing to talk about. Your position is clear—something I always appreciate in a manager."

"We can't let things get weird between us."

"Then perhaps you should clean up and put on some clothes. The wet gleam between your thighs is a bit of a distraction for me. It reminds me I haven't eaten in far too long."

She used the shreds of fabric to cover herself and scurried to the bathroom. One hit of an addictive man like Victor was bad enough. Two would hook her for life.

For the first time in years, she actually considered whether or not life with a man would be such a bad thing.

Chapter Twenty-one

"Where is she?" Randolph asked the second Lila answered her phone.

"What?" she asked, sounding confused.

"Where is Bella? You were supposed to be keeping tabs on her."

"I tried. I told you she doesn't tell me where she goes. It's early. She's probably home asleep."

"Wrong. I checked. There's a man in her house, but she's not there."

"Oh, right," said Lila. "I heard something about a rotating detail to watch her house. I guess someone broke in while she was gone."

That someone had been him, but he saw no reason to enlighten the woman. "Does she have a boyfriend? A lover?"

"Bella? Not that I know of. She doesn't have time for a social life."

"Then where the hell is she?"

"I'm trying to do what you want. I really am, but my hands are tied. There's a system that tracks the locations of everyone who works at the Edge, but I don't have access to it."

"Who does?"

"Bella does. So does Mira Sage. Maybe one or two others, but I don't know who they are."

Mira was the brains that ran the tech at the Edge. From what Randolph had heard she wasn't much use in a fight, but put her at a keyboard and she was a devastating force. "I want you to steal Mira's access information. Codes, passwords—whatever it takes to break into that tracking system."

"I can't do that without getting caught."

"Your son needs you. Find a way, Lila."

A sob tightened her voice. "I swear I would do it if I could, but there's no way. Mira is always in her office. Whenever Adam Brink isn't looking for his brother, he's with her. Even if Mira doesn't see what I'm doing, he will. That man misses nothing."

"There's got to be some way to break into her office when she's away."

"Even if I did, how would I find what you need? I doubt she has all of her passwords written down on a Post-it note by her keyboard. And even if she did, I wouldn't know how to use the system. It's a live tracking system, which means that I'd have to have constant access to it. I know Mira would be able to see that I was logged in as her."

Randolph couldn't risk losing an asset like Lila, not until she'd come to the end of her usefulness. But it had been too many hours since Bella had last been dosed with the drug that would be her undoing—the one Stynger had developed all those years ago to subdue Bella's aggression, making her obedient and afraid. It was supposed to be absorbed through the skin, activated through heightened emotional states. She needed only three or four doses to do the job. That's why he'd put it in her hot water tank. Was it too much to ask a woman to shower at home every day? He didn't think so.

Frustration rode hard on Randolph's heels, making his words clipped. "I need to find her."

"I can call around and see if anyone's seen her, tell them she has an urgent call. It might get back to her that I was snooping around, but I could probably come up with a cover story by then."

"Do it. Find her, bring her back into the office and when she's there, you're going to do something for me."

Fear made Lila's voice shake. "What?"

"I'll drop off a vial of medicine in your car tonight. Tomorrow, you will find Bella and make sure she takes it."

"Please don't ask me to poison her. I can't do that."

"It's not going to hurt her. She won't feel a thing."

"I don't care. I can't hurt Bella like that. She's my friend."

"I thought you wanted your son back."

"I do."

"Then do this one last job."

"If I do, you'll bring my baby back home?"

"You have my word. Now, follow my instructions exactly, or I'll be reporting back to Dr. Stynger that you've lost interest in getting your son home safely."

"Please, no. I'll do what you say. You promise it won't hurt her?"

"Just think of it as medicine she needs to remember who she really is."

"I don't understand."

"You don't need to. All you need to do is follow orders. Once I know you've done the job, you'll get your baby back safe and sound. But if you fuck this up, Lila, you will be sorry."

She started to cry. He hung up the phone so he wouldn't have to listen to her irritating sobbing. There was too much for him to do to waste time on her nonsense. Not only did he have to drop off Stynger's cocktail for Bella at Lila's apartment, he also had a man to kill. He probably should make it look like an accident, but in the mood he was in right now, there was bound to be bloodshed.

Payton was still wide awake when his phone rang. He hadn't slept at all last night and was starting to wonder if he ever would again. Every time he closed his eyes, all he could see was the faces of the kids he'd hurt, including Bella's.

She, the woman he loved like the daughter he never had, hated him. With good reason. The things he'd allowed to happen to her and countless others were not the sort of things worthy of forgiveness.

He'd been trying to make up for his crimes for decades and he still hadn't found a path to forgiveness. Maybe there was none.

He answered the call from General Norwood, bracing himself for whatever bad news was waiting for him this time.

"Good morning, General."

Norwood didn't waste time with pleasantries. "Kerrington was murdered less than an hour ago."

Shock ricocheted through Payton's system for a moment before settling through his body in a wave of grief and regret. There was no love lost between them, but he had a family, friends—people who loved him and would grieve deeply for him. "How?"

"Gunshot to the head. Stab wounds to the body. Lots of them. There was a lot of blood splatter, Payton—too much for the head shot to have come first. Someone was pissed."

"Were there defensive wounds?" asked Payton, hoping the man had been asleep when the attack had happened.

"He was bound."

Kerrington had been alive while the killer had worked on him, a notion that turned Payton's stomach. The senator hadn't been a great man. Most of the time he'd hardly been a good one. But no one deserved to die like that, not even after the things he'd done.

At least that's what Payton wanted to believe, because if Kerrington deserved a gruesome death like that, Payton deserved much, much worse.

"His wife?" he asked.

"Out of town visiting relatives. She's safe."

Payton let out a long breath. "Thank God."

"She's on her way back now. Local law enforcement assured me that they won't let her see him like that."

"Any idea who did it?"

Norwood paused for too long. "There was a note."

"What did it say?"

"Loose end number one. Two more to go."

Payton's breath caught in his chest. He knew that he was a walking target, that sooner or later Stynger would get tired of him nipping at her heels. But knowing that someone wanted him dead and knowing she was coming after him now were two different things entirely.

"Are you two or three?" he asked Norwood.

"No clue. But I'm protected. As long as I stay where I am, she'll need a bunker buster to reach me. You're the one who's vulnerable."

"Nothing new there. I can handle it."

"That's what Kerrington said, too."

"Yes, but he didn't have my skills, did he?"

"You're not as young as you used to be."

"I'm young enough to do what needs to be done." At least Payton hoped that was the case. And if not, if his crimes caught up with him, so be it. As long as he took the killer down with him so Norwood would survive to continue their work, he would be content. "What about the note? Why is she suddenly so interested in tying up loose ends?"

Norwood pulled in a long breath. "I'm not at liberty to tell you everything I know."

Payton shoved down his immediate surge of anger. He knew Norwood was in a tenuous position, and that every bit of information he divulged was a calculated risk. The fact that he told Payton anything at all was a blessing.

"I understand," said Payton, modulating his voice so none of his anger came through. "I can figure it out on my own."

"Just ask yourself, why would you want to tie up loose ends?"

"Because I got tired of having them hanging over me. Because I found an effective means to deal with them. Because something changed and I had to do it now before it was too late."

"Bingo. I think that's the winner. I think she's getting ready to make a big move."

"That's nothing new. She moves around all the time. That's why we have such trouble finding her."

"That's just her flitting around the States. We have reason to believe she's thinking bigger."

The pieces fell together in Payton's head. Stynger had been working to gain funding for her research—the kind of funding only larger governments could afford. There was no way the US would back her work. That meant she'd found help beyond the border.

"She found a backer," said Payton.

"I can't tell you that, but if she did, it would probably be one that really doesn't like us very much. Once she makes this move, she'll be out of our reach forever. Unless, of course, we want to start an international incident to take her down."

"You think she's worried that you and I have the clout to make that happen? Certainly she knows that's not true."

"She doesn't think like we do. She doesn't think about rules and laws, only what she wants. If she had the kind of connections we do, do you think we'd still be alive?"

Not a chance. "How much time do we have before she's out of reach?"

"I have no clue. My hands are tied. I've done all I could by giving you Victor and what few resources I've been approved to put at your disposal. The rest is up to you and your crew."

"You mean Bella's crew."

"She's still pissed, I take it."

"Understatement of the decade. But she's working on it. I'm letting her have access to the holding facility to question the one man we managed to save."

Norwood let out a soft whistle. "You really are desperate to make up with her if you're letting her in that place."

"We're running out of time. If she thinks she can get this man to talk, more power to her."

"And if she can't?"

"I'll keep him safe and comfortable, just like all of the rest."

"See that you do, Payton. Because if I find out that you've mistreated even one of those men, I'm taking it out on you, personally."

"It's no less than I'd expect."

"Watch your back, old friend. I'd hate to have to pretend to cry at your funeral."

"You be careful, too. I know you have all kinds of thick walls and skilled sharpshooters between you and the world, but that doesn't mean you're immortal."

"Don't worry about me. I'm holding out for grandbabies."

Payton laughed, letting go of some of his growing tension. "You may have one hell of a wait. Sloane loves her job at the Edge too much to be letting the mommy bug bite her."

"Guess she should have told that husband of hers. Too late now."

"Sloane is pregnant?"

"She doesn't want anyone to know yet, so don't be a jackass and ruin the surprise, okay?"

"That's shocking enough I'll probably still have my mouth hanging open when she does get around to sharing."

"I told her she can't take long to start her maternity leave. That damn job of hers is way too stressful and dangerous. Especially now. Will you see that she doesn't take any risks?"

"I'm not exactly in the popular crowd right now at work, but I'll do what I can. I have a friend who's spending a few months on the beach in Costa Rica. I bet I can convince her she needs a couple of bodyguards, especially if I foot the bill. Sloane and her husband would be a perfect choice."

"Thanks, Payton. I owe you."

"I stopped keeping track a couple of decades ago."

"Well, I didn't. You need to live long enough for me to wipe the red from my ledger, so stay safe."

"I will," said Payton, hoping it wasn't a lie.

Chapter Twenty-two

Jordyn was so nervous she puked three times before she was able to leave her quarters. The shift change was almost over, and her window was closing quickly.

She hurried along the halls as fast as she dared, knowing every camera she passed was recording her movements. She couldn't give anyone who might be watching any indication that she was about to free Mother's prisoner.

It was hard not to break into a dead run. Only the sure knowledge that the motion would be seen held her in check.

She entered Gage's cell as she had before, with a key card attached to an employee that didn't exist. As compartmentalized as things were down here, it would take security weeks to realize that the person was a fake.

Gage lay in his bed, unmoving. For a second, she worried that the sleeping gas Mother used had filled the space. She'd already pulled in a breath, so if the room was drugged, she'd be sprawled on the floor in seconds.

"I'm awake," he said, dispelling her fears.

Relief dragged at her weary limbs. She hadn't been sleeping well. She was exhausted all the time. Her nerves were getting the best of her, causing her to throw up nearly everything she ate. If this went on much longer, she wasn't going to be strong enough to escape Mother's clutches, much less help Gage to do the same.

She stepped in and shut the door silently. "I cut the camera to your cell. They can't see us for the next three minutes. It's time to go."

He sat up, tossing the blanket aside. He was fully clothed, shoes on, as if he'd been expecting her arrival.

A surge of suspicion swept through her. She gripped the spare lab coat she carried hard enough to wrinkle it. "Did someone tell you I was coming?"

"No." He crossed the space toward her, all smooth strength and flowing muscle.

Jordyn stepped to the side, out of his reach. "How did you know?"

"I didn't. I hoped." He tilted his head to the side, studying her. "You look sick."

She straightened her spine in an effort to hide her weakness. "I'm fine. Are you ready?"

He nodded. "The plan?"

"I've cleared us a timed path through the halls. We have to walk at exactly the right pace so that each camera deactivates as we enter the zone and reactivates as we pass. No hurrying. No running. Act like you're supposed to be there." She handed him the lab coat. "Can you do that?"

"Yes."

She checked her watch. "Two minutes left before it's time to leave the room."

"You're nervous," he said.

"Aren't you?"

His faded blue eyes twinkled with excitement. "Been caged too long."

"I couldn't get you a weapon. I'm sorry. It would have drawn too much attention."

He reached for her, his wide hand moving slowly as if

to avoid scaring her. He plucked the pen holding up her hair in a bun. "This will work."

Her hair slid over her shoulders and down her back. "You're going to use a pen as a weapon?"

"If necessary."

"Let's hope it's not necessary. Most of the people down here are innocent. Many of them are here against their will. I'd prefer it if you wouldn't hurt anyone."

"No promises."

She understood. She really did. The people down here would kill him if he didn't defend himself, but that didn't mean the thought of violence didn't upset her.

Her stomach churned dangerously, and she had to swallow hard several times to keep from throwing up again.

Gage pressed his hand to her forehead. "No fever."

"I'm not sick. I just know what will happen if we're caught. I promise, if you'd been to the White Room, you'd be a little queasy right now, too."

His fingers cupped her shoulder, giving her a reassuring squeeze.

His touch eased some of her anxiety and calmed her down. She took a few deep breaths, feeling better after each one. She was steady and centered now, but his hand remained in place, connecting them.

"We're heading to the elevators," she said, "then to the surface. Once we get there, go right. I've acquired keys to one of the employee's vehicles."

"Acquired?"

"Stole. From the employee locker room."

His eyebrows lifted.

"Don't judge. I know it's wrong. But after the last car I stole, Mother had devices fitted in all the vehicles to stop the engine if they're stolen. This was the best I could do."

"Not judging. Impressed. You're resourceful."

"I'm determined. I will make it out this time. And

when I do, I'm going to help take Mother's operation down for good."

He glanced at her watch. "Ready?"

She nodded and started to leave, but he pulled her back from the door.

"I go first. Catch any stray bullets."

She would have thought he was joking, but there was no hint of humor in his eyes. His game facc was firmly in place as he opened the door and led the way out.

Jordyn gave him quiet directions as they went. A couple of times her nerves got the best of her and she started to hurry. Gage grabbed her hand each time, slowing her pace to match his own.

They had just reached the elevators when one of the guards came around the corner and saw them.

"No one is authorized to leave this floor at this time of night. What are you doing?" he asked.

"We were headed up to the lab to check on some test results. Mother is waiting for our report."

The guard frowned as he studied Gage. "I don't know you."

"He's new," she said. "Just started this week."

"No one is scheduled to start until we move. I need to call this in and check his status." He held his hand out to Gage. "Badge?"

"I lost it," he said, his tone embarrassed and apologetic.

"I was planning to help him get a new one in the morning," said Jordyn.

The guard wasn't buying their story. He reached for his radio.

Gage was faster. He kicked the radio from the man's belt and spun around to land a second blow square in the center of his chest.

The guard let out a whoosh of air and flew back down the hall, sliding on his ass. He was shaken, but not so rattled that he didn't have the presence of mind to pull his weapon.

Gage grabbed Jordyn just as the gun went off, covering her with his body as he flung them around the corner.

He shoved her low to the ground and gave her a hard look. "Stay." Then he took off.

She had no idea where he was going, but that pen was in his fist and a look of pure killing intent was on his face. He flew down the hallway toward the armed guard.

The guard fired again. A second later, she heard a heavy grunt of pain. A quick glance around the corner showed her that the guard's hand was bleeding. Pieces of gunmetal littered the hallway. The remains of the pen still protruded from the barrel.

Gage had the guard by the neck, strangling him from behind. After a few seconds, he went limp as he passed out.

The elevator doors slid open with a cheerful chime.

"Get in!" she shouted. "Before they lock us down."

Only a few seconds had passed since the gun went off, but it was merely a matter of time before one of the guards reported the noise to the main office and they shut down the entire facility.

Gage sprinted for the elevator doors. Jordyn stepped inside and pushed the button to lift them to the ground floor.

He held the guard's radio in his hand. It let out a burst of static before a voice was clear. "Shots fired. Security breach. Initiating lockdown procedures."

Jordyn pushed the ground-floor button over and over, silently willing the car to move faster. The last thing they needed was to be stuck in here, trapped and waiting for Mother to find them.

No way could she explain what she was doing in here with Gage in the middle of the night. There were no plausible explanations that wouldn't land both of them in the White Room by morning.

Her whole body broke out in a cold sweat. The need to puke surged in the back of her throat.

"Easy," said Gage, his tone a low, crooning sound. "Almost there." His wide hand slid down her spine, over and over, giving her the reassurance of physical touch.

"There is always at least one guard topside. I cut the security feed to the elevators, but they might still know we're coming."

He took her by the shoulders and pressed her back into the corner. "I go first. You're too pretty for holes."

"I don't want you blown full of holes, either."

He shot her a cocky smile. "I got this."

The elevator doors opened. He poked his head around for a quick look. The guard stationed there opened fire.

Chapter Twenty-three

Gage used his bulk to cover Jordyn, pressing her hard into the elevator car wall. When the bullets stopped, he stuck out his hand, drawing another round of fire. He did it twice more, using different body parts each time.

She wasn't sure what he was waiting on, or what his strategy was until she realized that the walls were shiny. He could see the single guard drawing closer—almost within arm's reach.

The second the guard got close, Gage ducked under his aim and charged. He barreled into the guard's gut, taking control of the weapon in one hand as he went.

The elevator doors started to close. Jordyn shoved them back open and slipped out. As she ran toward their getaway vehicle, she saw the fight from the corner of her eye. Gage was taking a beating to his ribs as the guard tried to pummel him off. What he didn't realize was that he was being backed up into a wall with Gage serving as a human battering ram.

She didn't take the time to watch more. Instead she jumped in the car she'd stolen and tore out of the parking spot toward Gage. By the time she reached him, the guard was on the ground, unmoving.

Gage slid in the passenger side, holding his ribs.

"You're hurt," she said.

"It's nothing. Drive."

She did. She sped away from the only life she'd ever known. There weren't many signs that there was a large facility below ground. Just a tiny building big enough to house the elevators and a guard shack. There weren't even many cars here—not like there used to be when Mother had kept a full contingent of researchers on board. She'd pared way down for the big move, killing most of them so they couldn't talk.

Jordyn preferred to pretend that her friends were still alive, even though she knew it was a lie.

As the building became a speck in her rearview mirror, she knew she'd never again step foot underground. That was her old life. She had no idea what her new one would look like, but whatever its shape, it had to be better than what she'd always known.

At least she hoped so.

"What's the plan?" asked Gage.

She glanced at him. He was sweating and pale. Whatever had happened to him back there, he was still in pain. "Plan? We're out. What else matters?"

"I need to contact my people. Fast."

Jordyn hadn't thought that far ahead. "I don't have a phone. We'll have to find one, but the nearest town is over an hour away." After her last incident with making contact with locals, Mother had made sure that there were no locals around to offer help, support or protection.

It was dark out here. There were no streetlights or signs of inhabitants. It struck her just how alone she was with a man she barely knew.

"We'll stop first chance. Change vehicles."

"You mean steal another one?"

He shrugged. The motion made him wince. "Desperate times."

"How bad is it?" she asked. "Did you get shot?"

"A little."

"How is any gunshot wound little?"

"I'm still walking."

Her stomach swooped and spiraled at the thought of his pain. "Is there anything I can do?"

"Keep driving toward a phone."

She kept looking out her rearview mirror, worried that Mother's goons would be on her tail. So far, so good.

Jordyn was so worried about what was behind them that she didn't see what was headed toward them until it was too late.

A truck cleared the top of the hill, barreling toward them, headlights off.

"Look out!" shouted Gage as he grabbed for the steering wheel.

Jordyn tried to turn the car out of harm's way. Gage did, too. There was simply no time to correct their course.

The truck slammed into them head-on and the whole world went dark.

Chapter Twenty-four

Victor wasn't sure whether to be relieved or worried that he'd forced Bella to let him tag along with her to Payton's secret holding facility. His presence hadn't been part of the plan, but when he'd insisted and reminded her that she might need backup to get out of that place, she'd been more than willing to let him escort her.

He hadn't seen anything before landing—both he and Bella had been blindfolded for the trip. After nearly an hour in the air—likely with some creative flying to mask the location—it was hard to tell where they were in the world.

The chopper landed. They were escorted into a building before their blindfolds were removed. The place was large, windowless. The metal and concrete walls rose up over twenty feet in the air. There were overhead doors large enough for any vehicle allowed on the highways and a few that weren't. Several armed guards stood alert, watching them.

Bella shook her head as the blindfold came off. Her dark hair was a mess from the trip, but she was still so damn beautiful it made his stomach ache to think he'd never have her again.

Don't go there. Not now.

With an effort of will, he redirected his attention away from her to his surroundings.

A single desk stood in a small room on the other side of a glass door. Behind the desk was Payton, suit pressed, hair perfect, looking for all the world as if he didn't have a single worry or care.

"He's waiting for you," said the young man who removed their blindfolds. He couldn't have been more than twenty-five, but there was something about his eyes that made him seem much, much older. Victor had seen that look before.

The kid had been through hell at least twice. Maybe more.

He escorted them to the door and pressed a button. A light turned green and the glass shivered a little as the lock was released.

Bella walked through first. Victor followed, feeling naked without his weapons. They'd all been removed before he'd climbed on the chopper. He was capable in unarmed combat, but all the men here were armed, skewing the odds a bit too much for his peace of mind.

"What the hell are you doing here?" she asked Payton the second the door closed.

"You think I'd let you have run of the place without my supervision?"

"I don't need a babysitter. I'm only going to ask a few questions."

"And I'm only going to be present when you do." His gaze flicked to Victor. "We didn't agree he could come along."

"And I didn't agree to letting you witness my interrogation," Bella said.

"It's not happening any other way. Deal with it or leave empty-handed."

She let out a low growl of frustration. "Where is he?"

"In the infirmary. He's was awake for a while, but refused to answer any of our questions."

"How persuasive were you?" Victor asked.

"Apparently not persuasive enough," Bella said.

Payton stood from his chair and buttoned his suit. "I won't let you hurt the man. The things he's done are not his fault."

"I know that," Bella said. "I also know that a lot of other people are going to get hurt if he doesn't talk."

"Do you think I don't realize the risk?" asked Payton.

"Either lead me to him or step out of the way."

Victor wasn't sure how much longer this tension could go on without erupting. "Why don't I escort Bella to the man's room, and you can wait outside. I won't let her do anything to hurt him. I swear it."

She narrowed her eyes at him. "I don't need you babysitting me, either. I have enough self-control to perform one simple interrogation without resorting to violence."

Payton let out an ugly bark of laughter. "Not likely. And the way you've been acting lately . . . let's just say that the last person I'd put this man alone in a room with is you."

Her hand strayed to where she usually kept her weapon. If she hadn't already been stripped of it, she would have pulled it on Payton.

Victor stepped between them. "Can we get this show on the road?"

Payton gave a sharp nod, then turned and walked out through another door. His back was straight, his movements stiff as he led the way through a series of halls. There were guards posted at several doorways, acutely alert and ready for action.

No way were they getting out of this place unless Payton allowed it.

Victor memorized their path, hoping that there would be no need for him to fight his way free. While he and Bella were a formidable team, they were unarmed, and these men were the good guys. Hurting them had to be a last resort, done only if Payton tried to imprison them, and then only if all the other options were completely exhausted.

Payton stopped in front of a locked door flanked by two guards. Victor didn't recognize the uniforms they wore here, but their bearing was military, through and through. He'd bet his fortune that Norwood had supplied this place with only the best, because if even one of the people held here escaped, there was no end to the harm they could do. Stynger had made sure of that.

At Payton's nod, one of the guards unlocked the infirmary door and let them pass. Inside was another hall lined with small rooms. Each door was wide enough for wheelchair access. At the end of the hall was a door labeled SURGERY. In the center of the hall was a room larger than the rest, with reinforced glass windows. Inside were several desks where he presumed the medical staff worked. No one was inside, but there were more armed guards posted along the hallway.

"He's in here," Payton said, pointing to room number three. He motioned to the nearest guard—a wiry man with dark skin and the kind of casual bearing that told Victor he had nothing to prove to anyone; he was a badass. "Please open the room."

The guard considered them both with careful scrutiny before he complied.

Payton held out his hand for Bella to lead the way. She did.

Victor was right on her heels, well within reach of whatever danger might come flying her way. Sure, she could take care of herself in a fight, but that didn't mean he was going to let it come to that. Sex may not have changed anything for her, but it did for him. Maybe it was his upbringing or some deeply buried set of caveman instincts, but whatever it was, he couldn't just sit back and let a woman walk into danger when he'd had his cock buried in her only hours earlier.

He used the excuse of parting a privacy curtain to get between her and the man inside. The scrape of metal curtain rings was loud in the small space.

There were no windows. A dim light glowed over a locked cabinet and sink. Other than that and a few lighted pieces of medical equipment, the room was dark.

A man lay on his side on the bed. The back of his head was covered with a thick pad of gauze to cover the incision they'd made to remove Stynger's device. Most of the men who'd undergone the procedure had died. The lucky few who lived were still controlled by whatever remnants of Stynger's brainwashing remained, but at least the poison housed in the device could no longer kill them.

Bella stepped closer, reaching out her hand to shake the man awake.

Victor grabbed her wrist. "He's already awake, waiting for you to get close."

The man's cheek lifted in a grin and he rolled onto his back. "I almost had her."

Bella's expression changed from one of sympathy to a cold, hard mask. "You should thank him for stopping me. Trying to catch me off guard wouldn't have ended well for you."

Payton stepped up behind them. "This is Aaron," he said, as if making introductions at some charity gala. "Aaron, these two have some questions for you. It would be in your best interests to answer them." He looked at Victor. "I'll be right outside the door if you need me."

Payton left.

Aaron looked to be in his late twenties, with a heavy, muscular build and a body covered in thick black hair.

His head had been recently shaved, leaving only the shadow of stubble beneath his olive skin. Dark brown eyes stayed fixed on Bella, completely ignoring Victor. A metal handcuff kept one of Aaron's wrists chained to the bed. He patted the mattress beside him with his free hand. "Have a seat, sugar."

"No, thanks, pumpkin," she replied. "I'll stand."

He shrugged. "Suit yourself, but it's been a long time since I've seen a woman as pretty as you. I could show you a really good time."

Bella's body went fluid, moving with sinuous sex appeal. She leaned down close enough for Aaron to feel the warmth of her breath against his temple as she spoke. "Honey, with that hole in the back of your skull, your brains would come shooting out if I got my hands on you. We wouldn't want that now, would we?"

He reached for her in a move so fast there was no way he was still suffering from the effects of anesthesia. His fingers closed around her wrist in a brutal grip. In a move just as fast, she slammed the heel of her other hand into his nose, breaking it with a snap.

Aaron instantly let go, covering his nose while he gurgled in pain.

Bella grabbed a few paper towels from the sink and tossed them at him. "Clean up. You're leaking blood and tears everywhere."

He held the paper to his nose and gave her a look that promised revenge.

"Now that I have your attention," she said, "let's start with a few simple questions. Where is Dr. Stynger?"

Aaron stared straight ahead, silent.

"Don't know that one? Gage Dallas seemed to think you'd know. And that you'd rat her out."

"That asshole doesn't know a damn thing. He was kept in isolation."

Victor was impressed at the clever way she got him to

answer. He'd always known she was smart, but interrogations were a fine art, and he'd always seen her as more of a force of nature than an artist.

There was a flicker of excitement in Bella's eyes before she covered it. At least now they knew that Gage was alive the last time this man saw him. And that he was a prisoner. That alone was more information than they'd found in the weeks since he'd gone missing.

"Not anymore," she said. "He's ours now. Just like you are."

"I won't be here long," Aaron said.

"No?" she asked. "Why's that?"

"Because she'll come for me. I'm too important for her to not take me with her."

"She's not taking you anywhere. We found out all about her plan. She's on the run now, and there's no way in hell she's worried about a peon like you."

"I'm no fucking peon. I'm one of her generals. She needs me."

"For what? Cleaning toilets? She has other men far more skilled than you, *general*."

"You're wrong. I've been specially selected. She told me so herself."

"To do what?" asked Bella, disbelief hanging on every word.

"I'm in charge of upkeep at the new facility."

Victor chimed in. "It's just like you thought. Upkeep is a fancy name for cleaning toilets."

Aaron's face turned red. "Her new facility won't run without me. She knows that. And when she comes here to rescue me, every one of you is going to be mowed down like weeds."

Bella ignored him and turned to Victor. "There's no way she's going to the new facility now. Everything will fall apart without General Plunger here. If we kill him, her whole operation will fail."

Aaron wadded the bloody paper towels in his fist. "You're not going to kill me. That's not the way you people work. I know the rules. You'll hold me here until I die of old age or until I'm rescued, whichever comes first."

Bella crossed her arms over her chest. "That's for people the world knows exist. You, pumpkin, are a ghost. No one knows where you are. I could strangle you with my bare hands and no one would ever know or care. We'll incinerate your body and throw the ashes out with the rest of the trash."

"You won't," he said, but his tone screamed that he no longer believed his original stance quite so deeply.

She shrugged. "We might. We *have* kept a few helpful resources alive here. The stubborn ones end up in the landfill, but you could get lucky. You might know enough for us to keep you alive for a while."

He shook his head. "Interrogation techniques. You're lying."

"Maybe. Maybe not. The question is, do you want to risk finding out which it is?"

Aaron stared at the wall, looking past her. "I'll take my chances. Stynger is far more dangerous than you could ever hope to be. My money's on her."

"We're done here," Victor said, taking Bella's arm. "Either he doesn't know enough to be useful, or he does and he won't tell us. Either way this is a waste of time. We have others to question."

She played along, following his lead. "If you think of anything you want to tell us, let the guards know. We'll be here for another hour. After that, you're on your own."

They left the room to find Payton waiting in the hall. "What he said confirms my suspicions. Stynger is getting ready to make a move—one that will put her out of our reach."

"You heard?" Bella asked.

"Of course," Payton said. "You think I'd let you go in there without monitoring what was going on? You should know better."

She let out a sound of frustration worthy of any enraged teenage girl. "I can't believe you were spying on us."

"I can't believe you'd think I wouldn't."

Before this got out of hand, Victor stepped between them. "We give Aaron a few minutes to digest what we said, then we go in and try again."

"It won't work," Payton said. "Believe me, I've tried. You can't force these men to say a word. The best you can do is trick them into saying something they don't realize is important, just like you did."

"Is his implant removed?" Victor asked.

"It is."

"Then you don't know he won't talk."

"You've seen the video recordings of Jake Staite, haven't you?" Bella asked.

Victor suppressed a shiver at the memory. That poor man, once a proud soldier, was now a raving maniac, determined to kill his best friend Roxanne—or Razor as she was called—in the most brutal ways imaginable. He'd been implanted with one of Stynger's devices and given orders to kill. The implant was gone, but the compulsion to kill was still there, as strong as ever. Because of that, Jake had been detained against his will for months.

"I have seen the tapes," he said.

"Then you know it's no use. Whatever Stynger put in that poor man's head will be there until the day he dies. It doesn't matter if the implant was successfully removed or not," she said.

"That's not necessarily true," Payton said.

"What do you mean?" Bella asked. "I've seen the recordings. He still dreams about killing Razor."

Payton let out a long breath and stepped down the hall,

out of earshot of any of the guards. "Razor got a package a few weeks ago. It was from Jordyn Stynger, Norma's daughter."

"And you're just now telling me this?" Bella demanded.

"You can beat the hell out of him for that later. Now isn't the time," Victor said. He turned to Payton. "What was in it?"

Payton kept his voice quiet. "It was an experimental treatment—one designed to reverse the mental conditioning done to Jake."

"Please tell me you didn't give it to him," Victor said.

"We did. With his agreement. We waited until he had a lucid period, then made sure he accepted the risks."

Bella's voice shook with quiet rage. "The daughter of a monster sends you experimental drugs to give to a helpless man held in your custody against his will, and you use him like a lab rat? How could you? Did you not learn your lesson after what you did to all the kids like me?"

"We took every precaution," Payton said.

"What does that mean?"

"We analyzed the drug and tried to re-create it so that we'd have enough to use on lab animals for testing purposes. To make sure it was safe."

There was something he wasn't saying. Victor could tell by the man's tone and the way his gaze slid to the wall. "But?"

Payton took a long breath—one of surrender. "But it was too complex. We couldn't replicate it. She'd included two doses on the off chance that it worked on Jake and could be used on someone else, but we burned through one of them with testing."

Bella's eyes turned a stormy gray color Victor knew meant she was furious. "So you decided to assuage your guilt at drugging a helpless captive with an unknown substance by having him take the responsibility for whatever happened? I suppose you also asked him to sign a waiver, too, didn't you?"

"It's standard procedure—"

"I can *not* fucking believe you, Payton! How could you do that? After all these years of pretending you were seeking forgiveness, you turned around and did the same thing all over—"

Payton grabbed Bella by the arms, shutting her up. "It worked. Jake has been himself since the day after the drug was introduced into his system. No bouts of rage, no outbursts, no desire to kill Razor. We even showed him her picture. This time, instead of ripping it to shreds with his hands and teeth, the man wept and hugged the photo, begging for forgiveness."

Bella jerked out of Payton's grasp. "Just because it worked doesn't mean you did the right thing."

"Maybe we got lucky, but the fact is that the choice I made gave one man back his life. If you don't like it, then that's your problem. Not mine, and sure as hell not Jake's."

"You should have told me," Bella said.

Payton shook his head. "You just don't get it, do you?"

"Get what?"

"If I'd told you that Jordyn Stynger had sent a package to Roxanne containing a possible way to reverse the damage done to all those men, what would you have done?"

"I would have hunted Jordyn down and made her take the drug herself, just to be sure she wasn't trying to kill anyone."

"Exactly my point," Payton said. "Jordyn's not the enemy, but you would have killed her because you're too narrow-sighted."

"What the hell is that supposed to mean? If Jordyn wasn't trying to screw us, then no harm would come to her."

"You don't think so? Think again. Her mother is a jealous bitch who stakes a claim on everyone she touches. Do you think she'd just let us take her daughter into custody without consequences?"

"What consequences?"

"If Jordyn was working against us, then her mother would stop at nothing to get her back. If she's turned on her mother, then her mother would stop at nothing to destroy her before she could offer us too much assistance."

"Either way, Dr. Stynger comes out of hiding and we get her."

"Except she wouldn't come out of hiding. She'd send men to do her dirty work—men we'd either have to kill or subdue, assuming we were lucky enough to do either."

"So, just because you're worried about protecting Jordyn, you're willing to let Jake assume all the risk in taking the drug she sent?"

"No," Victor chimed in, hoping he wasn't going to get his head chewed off by either of them. "That's not it at all. We have to protect our asset by keeping her in play. If Jordyn is on our side, she's exactly where we need her to be—inside Stynger's lab. If she's not on our side, then we certainly don't want her where she can find our soft spot."

"So you agree with him?" Bella asked. "He should have let Jake take experimental drugs?"

"I think that the only way to know whether or not Payton made the right call is to ask Jake. See if he's lucid, if he agreed to take the drug while he was in his right mind."

"I can't believe you two. There's no way in hell the man in those videos was capable of making up his mind about anything more complicated than what he wanted for lunch."

Payton shot Bella a hard stare. "Just ask yourself this:

If I'd come to you when we first met and told you that I could undo the damage done to you with a drug, but that it might kill you, what would you have done?"

Victor could see the answer plain on her face. She would have taken it.

Payton gave a slow nod. "Now maybe you can understand how Jake felt. I offered him hope. He took it knowing the risks. Just as you would have." He turned and stalked off with a curt "Watch them" to the nearest guard.

The guard did as he was told, turning his complete attention on them.

Bella fell to a crouch, hugging her knees. A series of ragged, angry breaths fell from her lips. Victor knelt beside her, hating to see her in such distress.

He put his hand on her shoulder. "Easy, Bella. Just breathe."

She took several deep breaths. He saw her relax, but only a little. She was still brittle with tension.

"How can he do this?" she asked. "How can he pretend to want forgiveness for experimenting on people all those years ago when he's still doing the same thing now?"

He kept his tone gentle. "What would you have done differently?"

"I wouldn't have given an unknown drug to a captive man, that's for damn sure."

"Even if he wanted it?"

"He's not in his right mind. How can he even know what he wants?"

"You haven't watched all the videos of Jake, have you?"

She looked at him, fury still shining in her eyes. "What's that supposed to mean? Are you telling me that you agree with Payton?"

"Jake isn't always deranged. Sometimes he's perfectly calm, completely sane."

"How do you know?"

"Because he begs for us to kill him before he can hurt anyone else. Especially Razor."

Bella fell silent. Victor could feel the guard lurking nearby, but decided not to let that stop him from offering her what comfort he could.

He wrapped his arms around her and hugged her against his chest. She curled into him for a brief, beautiful second before pulling herself together and drawing away, back under her own strength.

"I don't know how to do this," she whispered.

"Do what?"

"Forgive Payton for playing with the lives of others—risking their safety—when I do the same thing all the time."

"What do you mean?"

"If not for me, Gage would be safe right now, rather than the captive of a maniac. I made him go. It's my job to bring him home."

"You didn't make him do anything. He volunteered, remember?"

"I could have said no."

"To Gage? Have you met him? Come on, Bella. You know you can't control other people. All you can do is help them when they step into trouble."

She pushed to her feet, straightened her clothes with purpose. "I'm going back in to talk to Aaron. He's going to give me the answers I want about where to find Gage."

"No, he's not. Not when you're so all over the place. You need to calm down. Control yourself. Be smart. It's the only way we're ever going to get anything out of him."

Victor addressed the guard. "Is there a place we can get some coffee?"

The guard nodded. "Break room is this way."

Victor took Bella's elbow, nudging her into motion.

What she really needed was a good night's sleep, but not in this place. A lot of people came to this facility and never walked out again. He didn't want himself and Bella upping that number by two.

The sooner they got out of here, the better.

A few minutes after they sat down with their coffee, some kind of alarm went off, accompanied by flashing lights. Guards rushed past, but the one assigned to them stayed nearby, shifting anxiously from one foot to the other.

"What happened?" Victor asked.

"No idea, sir," the guard said. "Please stay seated."

Bella straightened in her chair. "We need to know what's going on. Fire? Attack? Escape?"

The guard didn't sway from his assignment. "You'll be told what you need to know, ma'am. Until then, please stay calm and stay seated."

"I'll show you calm," she said, rising to her feet.

Victor grabbed her arm and pulled her back down. "That's not going to win you any favors. He's just doing his job. He's been with us the whole time. Chances are he knows no more than we do."

"We can't just sit around like this, waiting for them to lock this place down, pretending there's some kind of emergency. There's no telling how long we'll have to stay here. I can't be locked away—not when Gage is still out there, missing."

"I understand your concerns, but there's no way they're going to deal with us right now. Let the incident pass, then we'll find Payton and figure out our next move."

The sirens and flashing lights stopped.

Bella still looked more nervous than he'd ever seen her. "I wish I was armed."

"So do I, but we're not. Warm up your coffee?"

She looked down at her full cup and frowned. He saw

the moment it dawned on her what he meant. A steaming cup of coffee could be a useful improvised weapon if things got ugly.

"Yes. Thank you," she said.

Victor got them both fresh cups of coffee and sat back down under the watchful gaze of the guard.

Her anxiety was clear in the tension around her eyes and the way she held her cup so tightly that dark rings shimmered in the surface of the steaming liquid. She was an intense woman, brimming with power and energy, but this was different. Darker.

She was afraid.

He wanted to pull her against him and offer her what comfort he could, but not only was this not the time or place, what had happened between them complicated things. She'd been clear that sex had been a onetime deal. Trying to force physical contact now was only going to make him look desperate—something a woman like Bella would never appreciate. Not in an employee, and sure as hell not in a boyfriend.

Victor's thoughts stilled as that concept entered his mind. Did he really want his relationship with her to deepen like that? To what end? A few good times?

Truth was, he loved this job. He loved working with the people at the Edge. Sleeping with her once had jeopardized that. Trying to have a relationship with her would almost certainly ruin any chance he had at maintaining his position as her employee.

Once General Norwood found out that he was sleeping with her, he was going to throw a fit. And the only hope Victor had of the general not finding out was if he kept his pants firmly zipped for the duration of the mission.

Easier said than done around a woman who called to him on such a deep level. It was more than just her beauty that drew him in. If it had just been that, he would have passed on her as he had countless other beautiful women. But none of them had her spirit, her fire. He had no desire for a woman who didn't know how to grab life by the horns and enjoy the ride. Though even he had to admit that she was more the type to grab life's balls than its horns.

She watched the guard, eyeing the room and the visible cameras. He could see the wheels turning in her head as she planned an exit strategy and contingencies. He'd been through too many scrapes with her not to know how her mind worked.

And right now, she was about two minutes away from jumping the guard and busting through this place like some kind of human tornado.

The door to the break room opened. Payton walked in, his face grim.

He found them pretending to sip bad coffee at a quiet table in the corner. Bella looked at him once, then went back to her drink, dismissing his presence.

"Aaron is dead," he said. "He killed a nurse, an orderly and one guard trying to escape, but not before the guard managed to get in a kill shot."

Stunned silence filled the space for a moment as they absorbed the news.

Aaron was dead, taking with him everything he knew. No more interrogation. No more chance to pull from him Gage's location.

"We did this, didn't we?" Bella asked. "We pushed him too far. *I* pushed him too far. That's why he tried to escape."

Victor found her hand and gave it a squeeze. "This wasn't your fault."

"No," Payton said, his face grim. "It was mine. I know how strong these men are from what Stynger does to them. I shouldn't have let his injuries lull me into a sense of false confidence."

"If anyone is to blame," Victor said, "It's Stynger."

Bella's jaw bulged with anger. "We're leaving," she told Payton. "I'm done playing games with that bitch. She's going down, no matter what I have to do to make it happen."

"Do you have a new idea of how we find her?" Payton asked.

"Yes," she said. "Bait. If I dangle myself out there far enough, she'll have no choice but to take a nibble. And when she does, she's dead."

No way was Victor going to let that happen. Bella might not know it yet, but she was no longer running the mission. As of right now, he was taking over.

Chapter Twenty-five

Gage wasn't sure how much farther he could carry Jordyn's limp body. He'd already lost a lot of blood from his gunshot wound. He could feel his heart fluttering, struggling to keep up with the demands he placed on it.

Still, there was no other choice. She was unconscious from a blow to the head, and if they stayed in that wrecked car, it was only a matter of time before Stynger's men found them.

At least the man who'd crashed into them wasn't a threat. There was no way he was ever walking again—not with his legs pinned the way they'd been.

Walking away from a man in need had been one of the harder things Gage had ever done, but he was short on options. He couldn't carry two people, and even if he could, the scar at the base of the man's skull said he'd be toting around one of Stynger's puppets—a move far too dangerous with Jordyn in tow.

Gage shifted her weight on his shoulder and forced himself to take one step after another. The creek he trudged through made walking harder, but he had no doubt that the people searching for them would set dogs on their trail. His only hope was to mask his scent the best he could in the running water.

He had no idea how far he'd hiked when a giant wave of dizziness drove him to his knees.

Rocks bit into his skin. The sudden shift of Jordyn's weight tore at his wound. He felt a fresh trickle of blood glide down his abdomen.

Weakness bore down on him, holding him in place in the cold water. He was losing heat fast, but didn't have the strength to regain his footing.

He didn't know how long he stayed there, shivering and panting. Every second he delayed was a risk — a risk they'd be found, a risk he'd pass out from blood loss.

He had to keep moving. Find a place to hide until his strength returned.

Gage surveyed the area. He couldn't see much from the wooded ravine he'd been traveling through. He needed higher ground.

It took far too long for him to gather enough energy to climb the creek bank. In the end, he had to set Jordyn down on a grassy spot so he could finish the climb.

There was nothing around but rocky countryside. No people, no structures, just pasture and scrub in the low-lying areas.

This was the kind of land that could go on for miles without anything more than cattle. He'd come across a ranch or farm eventually, but it could take days at this pace.

Jordyn didn't have that kind of time. Neither did he.

Gage looked back down the bank to where she lay. She was still and so incredibly pale he wondered if her skin had ever seen the sun.

Had she spent her whole life underground in her mother's labs?

Just the thought was enough to give him the strength to carry on. He couldn't let her be found. He had to get her far enough away from her mother to give her a chance at a normal life.

She'd risked everything helping him escape. It was his job to make sure her efforts were not in vain.

Gage eased her limp body into his arms, ignoring the pain pounding through his system. All he had to do was put one foot in front of the other for just a few more miles.

He pulled her hard against him, hoping the pressure would slow his bleeding. But once he got her there, a strange sense of peace consumed him. He'd never felt anything like it before. Whatever it was, he welcomed the sensation, letting it ease his pain and wash away his weakness.

He didn't know what it was about this woman that compelled him, but he knew that one way or another, without a single doubt, that he would find a way to see her to safety.

Or die trying.

Chapter Twenty-six

As soon as there was no more reason for Bella and Victor to remain at the holding facility, he grabbed her hand and hauled ass out of there. Not even Payton had a chance of slowing him down.

Bella stayed quiet on the way out, knowing that Victor never did anything without a good reason. She'd been in too many tough situations with him for her not to know his patterns.

And right now, he was following the bat-out-of-hell pattern.

The second they were out of the helicopter and back in their own ride, away from Payton's men, she popped the cork from her mouth.

"What the hell was that about?" she asked. "I haven't seen you move that fast since we were taking enemy fire down south."

He started the engine and left rubber on the pavement as he sped away from the parking lot at the Edge. "I didn't like being in that place. I liked you being there even less."

"Why?"

"Because you're on the List. The way some of the

guards were eyeing you, I wonder if they weren't told about that little fact before we arrived."

"You think they were worried I'd break down and turn on them?"

He spared her a quick glance. "Wouldn't you be if you were them?"

As points went, that was a sharp one. She had to clamp her lips shut to keep the grunt of pain from leaking out. The last thing she wanted was for a bunch of people to know her past and think she was teetering on the edge. Sure, they'd all seen what that looked like, but she was solid. Stable.

Wasn't she?

"I'd know if I was about to go sideways, wouldn't I?" she asked.

He didn't look at her. "You're surrounded by people who care about you. Nothing bad is going to happen, but if it did, one of us would make sure you didn't hurt any-one. Including yourself."

"So you've thought about it."

"Would you have hired a man who hadn't thought through the possible outcomes? Worst-case scenarios are what we face every day, Bella. As close as you and I work together, I'd be an idiot not to consider yours."

She stared out the side window. The streets became more familiar as they neared her neighborhood. "I don't like you thinking about me like that."

"Too bad. It's reality, and wishing it away isn't going to change that."

"Once people at the Edge find out that I'm on the List, they'll worry about me. Maybe even lose respect and trust for me."

"How are they going to find out? Are you planning to tell them?"

"I've considered it. I know how pissed I'd be if one of them didn't tell me."

"Do you feel out of control? Having strange thoughts? Want to commit violence?"

She ignored the time she'd freaked out at the gym. That was just stress. And the strange hallucination she'd had at the surgical facility had merely been something she'd inhaled—some medicine that had burned and was lingering in the smoke from the fire. Nothing more. "I feel fine, and the only violence I condone is the kind that's well deserved. Some of the people we face won't respond to anything but violence. And I'm fine sending them a message."

"That's not what I mean and you know it. Do you want to hurt people you know don't deserve it?"

She shook her head. "I save my ire for the scumbags who have it coming."

"Then we're fine. I've got your back, Bella. If you start to do anything you shouldn't, I'll call you on it. Or stop you."

He would, too. She could see his resolve shining in his eyes.

"And if you're not around?" she asked.

"I will be." He pulled into her driveway, next to Franklin's car. The engine fell silent. He turned to her. "And this is the part where you accept that. From now until this whole mess with Stynger is over, I'm living in your hip pocket. And I'm calling the shots. Just in case you aren't thinking clearly."

Calling the shots?

A swirl of outrage started at the base of her skull and exploded behind her eyes. She kept her voice quiet, knowing those wing-nut ears of Franklin's would pick up any raised voices, even behind closed doors. "You're not the one who gives orders here. I am. And if you think I'm going to step aside and let you take over the mission, you're the one who needs a rubber room."

Victor unbuckled his seat belt and leaned over the

console, crowding her space. He got right in her face, his clear blue eyes showing no signs of backing down. "You're compromised. Your friend is missing. A crazy bitch of a scientist is on the loose. Countless lives are on the line. There are more important things in the world than your ego. I don't give a shit if you're the boss. You could be the damn president for all I care. My job is to see Stynger's reign of crazy come to an end, and neither you nor Payton nor Norwood nor anyone else is going to stand in my way. If that means locking you in a closet until this whole thing is over, then so be it. Your only choice now is whether you fight me, or come along quietly so that I can at least take your opinion into consideration."

She grabbed his shirt and pulled him closer. The scent of his skin invaded her, dulling her anger for a split second. "No one takes away what's mine. I'll always choose to fight. You should know that by now."

He pulled in a breath so deep it strained the seams of his shirt. When he let it back out again, he was completely calm. "Okay, then. You've made your choice. So have I."

He got out of the car and came around to her side. She had no idea what to expect from him. When he opened her door and held out his hand for her to take it, she was confused. This was the move of a chivalrous date, not an angry employee trying to usurp her authority.

The second her fingers touched his, he closed his grip, pulled hard, ducked low and tossed her over his shoulder.

She was too stunned for a moment to do more than hang there. He carried her up the steps to her front door with his hot hand splayed across her ass.

All sorts of nerve endings fired off in glee at his touch. They had no idea they should have been outraged on her behalf.

"Open the door, Franklin," he said, not raising his voice.

Bella's shock wore off in a heartbeat. Seconds from now, Franklin was going to see her in this state, tossed over Victor's shoulder like a duffel bag. Minutes from now, everyone at the Edge was going to know about it, too.

She started to move in an effort to get down. Maybe she hadn't even gotten that far—maybe she'd only thought about fighting her way free. Whatever it was, Victor swatted her ass and whispered, "Settle down or I won't cover for you."

Cover for her?

The door opened. Her time was up. She went still as embarrassment swept over her.

Franklin's worried voice hit her hard. "Whoa. Dude. Is she okay?"

"Fine. She's punishing my insolence by making me do practice drills," explained Victor. "Fireman's carry for the next hour. If you don't want a piece of this, then you'd better go. She's in a hell of a mood."

As pissed as she was, she still had to hand it to Victor for thinking fast on his feet. He had her at his mercy. He didn't have to save her pride. If not for the fact that it was his fault her pride needed saving, she would have thanked him for the thoughtful gesture.

"Less talking, more lifting," snapped Bella. "Or you can carry Franklin next."

"No, thanks," said Franklin. "I'd puke down his back."

"Is the house clear?" asked Victor.

"Someone's been here the whole time she was gone. Call if you want me to come back." The young man scurried off.

Victor carried her into her house and locked the door behind them. "If I set you down are you going to attack me?"

"No," she lied.

He leaned forward and eased her onto her feet. The second the blood rush to her head cleared and she had her balance, she swung for his pretty-boy eye, fist balled for a hard strike.

He caught her fist in his hand before she'd had time to build up any momentum, killing the power of her swing.

With a shake of his head and a tsking sound, he spun her around and levered her arm behind her back.

Bella went up on tiptoe to ease the strain in her shoulder. He wasn't pushing hard enough to damage her, but after all the beatings she'd been through lately, she still felt her body bitch and moan.

"You really are predictable," he said. "I don't mind sparring with you if that's what you need, but I'd really rather not have you damage my face. The ladies like my face."

That shoved a surge of jealousy through her system. "It's not your face they like, sweetheart. It's that fat wallet you carry around."

She felt him flinch and knew she'd hit a nerve.

"You think I have nothing to offer a woman but money?" he asked, his voice silky smooth. "Have you ever come as hard in your life as you did with me?"

"Fine, so you have a nice cock, too."

"Damn right. And I'm good in a fight, too. Admit it."

"Bite me, sweetheart."

His teeth closed against the tender skin where her neck and shoulder joined. Hot streamers of sensation jolted down her spine, melting low in her belly. Against her will, a low whimper of need slipped out of her.

Victor's tongue swiped across the sweet sting his teeth had left behind. "Admit it, Bella. You and I make a good team. You've put your life in my hands when bullets were flying. You've put your body in my hands and I've sent you flying. Trust me to give you what you need now. Trust me to do what's right."

His lips opened against her neck, sucking lightly on her skin. Whatever she'd been about to say was lost in the sweep of pleasure that passed through her.

His arms wrapped around her from behind, pulling her up against his chest. Her hand was free. She could have fought him now, flipping him to the ground. She could see the move in her mind, feel what it would be like for her body to flow through the motions. He was easy prey. Distracted.

She couldn't do it. Hurting him was unthinkable. If she did, his mouth would stop weaving pure, blissful sensations over her skin.

One big hand splayed across her abdomen, while the other cupped her breast. Suddenly, anger evaporated into hot, steamy need, and there were far too many clothes between them.

She would deal with his insubordination later, but right now, running her company was the farthest thing from her mind.

Bella stripped her shirt off, baring herself to his touch. The raspy heat of his fingers slid over her, lighting up nerve endings that had lain dormant until he'd walked into her life. She didn't understand what it was about him that made her glow, made her burn, but Victor held the key to unlocking some kind of magic inside of her — a kind of magic she desperately needed to free.

"A bed this time," he said. "I'm going to take you on a proper bed."

Before she had time to tell him the way to her room, he was already tugging on her hand, leading her there. Gone were any thoughts of whether or not she'd let him have her. She was his now, and there wasn't a thing in the world she wanted more than to feel him stake that claim.

The moment they were in her room, he fell to his knees. He kissed and nibbled her abdomen as he jerked her pants open and down her thighs. Within seconds, she was bared to him, shackled only by the fabric binding her ankles together.

"I'm going to lick that sweet pussy of yours until you come, Bella. There's not going to be any waiting for your orgasm this time. I'm going to wring as many from you as you have to give me."

Her knees wobbled at his words. Standing was starting to be a problem, but before she could topple over, he picked her up around the waist and lifted her onto the edge of the bed. Her knees hit the mattress. She fell forward, catching herself on her hands. The move put her ass in the air and coaxed a groan of need from Victor's lips.

"So fucking sexy. Stay just like that, baby."

Normally she would have balked at his command, but the way he said it, with such demanding heat and desire, forced her compliance.

Her shoes hit the floor one at a time. Victor stripped her pants from her ankles. The ceiling fan overhead sent a wash of cool air over her labia, chilling the damp flesh. A second later, his hot tongue glided across her lips, bathing them in scalding heat. His fingers pulled her open, exposing her core. His mouth covered her, licking and sucking like he was starving for her taste.

He moaned into her, the deep sound vibrating her clit as it passed through. One big hand pressed between her shoulder blades, urging her head to the mattress.

She complied with his silent demand, and her reward was the deep plunge of his tongue.

There was nothing she could have done to stop the high, desperate sound that fell out of her. Her whole body was melting, succumbing to his skill.

Adept fingers slid over her clit, rubbing the hard little nub until she was squirming, trying to get him to give her more pressure. All her efforts gained her was a light smack on her ass and a rough, "Hold still, baby. Or I'm going to stop."

Bella went still, panicked that he might not finish what he'd started. Instead she felt the long, slow glide of three fingers inside her pussy. She was slick enough to take him, but the stretch had her panting, and her toes curling as she struggled to accept what he wanted to give her.

"Mmm. What a pretty sight that is. I love seeing you open up for me."

He twisted his fingers, rubbing up against a spot that came to life at his touch. She felt her body tense. Sweat beaded up along her spine. She tried to hold back for as long as she could, taking a page from their last session, but he was relentless. His fingers kept stroking inside while his other hand went to work on her clit, sliding across it in her own slick juices.

There was no more maintaining control. Her body took off like a rocket, sending her crashing into her orgasm. Every muscle in her body constricted as it bore down on her, stealing her breath while simultaneously making her soar.

The shimmering pleasure of it went on and on, but just as she was starting to come back down, Victor increased the pressure on her clit, holding her high for a while longer.

She went limp, smashing her face into her comforter. Her legs were shaking in an effort to keep her ass in the air. She wanted to collapse onto her side, but his fingers were still inside her, pinning her in place.

"I love hearing you scream like that," he said.

Her words were muffled by the mattress. "I don't scream."

"You do. Franklin probably heard it miles away."

She reached back to swat him playfully, but her aim was off. He grabbed her wrist, and she could feel his fingers were hot and slick against her skin. He'd done that to her—made her melt.

His voice was pure sin. "I can hardly wait to hear you scream for me again, Bella."

"No, thanks. I'm good. Just let me rest."

"Not yet, baby. Not until you've given me what I want."

Her brain was too starved for oxygen to figure out what he meant, right up to the point where she felt the head of his erection press against her opening.

Instantly, her body was no longer quite so sated. She needed him inside her again, just like she'd had him before.

She tried to roll onto her back, but he grabbed her hips and held them in place.

"I'm going to take you like this for a while. Keep that curvy ass in the air for me, sweetheart. I like you on your knees."

That comment alone should have earned him castration, but she just couldn't bear the thought of hurting his manly parts when he was about to use them on her in such a delightful manner. "Don't get used to it."

He surged forward, sliding all the way in. Instantly, Bella regretted every single one of her words. He could do this to her all he wanted, as often as he liked. The man was built to hit all the right spots when he took her like this.

His fingers gripped her tighter with every thrust. She could hear the deep ebb and flow of his breathing speed. Never before had she had a man inside her so deep, filling her so completely. Maybe it was the position, or maybe Victor was just born to please her. Whatever the case, she knew two things: First, when it was over, she was going to regret every second she spent on her knees. Second, there was no way in hell she could find it in her to care about the consequences of her actions right now. She was all his to do with as he pleased, and she both loved and hated it.

He leaned over her, covering her body with his bigger, hotter one. One hand stroked along her spine, soothing her, while the other grabbed a fistful of her hair and held on tight, inflaming her deeper.

Each move pushed her closer to another release. The man knew exactly what he was doing. Each swivel and grind of his hips was a carefully executed plot to destroy her resolve. The soft, sweet, naughty words he murmured in her ear made her flinch with acute arousal.

"I could fuck you like this for days, baby. Your pussy was made for me. Just me. No other woman will ever do to me what you do."

She knew they were just words—words he'd probably said to a hundred women before her. But she found herself giving in to the picture he painted, letting it fill her with the pretty lights and colors of impossible dreams.

"You're so damn beautiful. I can't stop thinking about you. Can't stop wanting you."

She had to touch him, so she leaned up and reached over her head to wrap her arms around his neck. Instantly, his hands covered her breasts, pinching and tugging at her nipples while he held her upright against him.

"I could take you every way known to man and still need more of you, Bella."

His fingers trailed down over her stomach, sliding between her legs to find her clit. He'd somehow learned just how she liked to be touched and displayed his newfound skills with eager excitement.

She felt surrounded by him, filled with him. Every breath she drew was scented by his skin and the smell of sex growing between them. Every inch of her skin tingled and shimmered from his touch. Every move he made coiled her tighter.

Bella couldn't stand it. She couldn't last under his onslaught. And he knew it. She could hear the pleased smile in his voice.

"That's it, baby. Give me what I want. Come all over my cock."

His words lit a spark in her mind, which set off the keg of gunpowder her body had become. She exploded in ecstasy so intense, every splinter of it seemed to slice her open.

This time she heard herself scream.

Victor rode her through it, but gave her no respite. He flipped her onto her back, pushed her ankles up over his shoulders and shoved his throbbing cock right back inside of her.

"I can't," she panted. "Too much."

"I'm not done with you yet, baby. You've got more to give me. I know you do."

She didn't think it was possible, but the man knew what he was doing. Each stroke of his erection slid across a secret button that turned her blood to electricity. He drove deep, to places no other man had ever found in her before. Within minutes, she was drenched in sweat, shaking and struggling to breathe as yet another climax came for her.

The next two after that nearly killed her, but Victor refused to relent. He kept driving her to new heights, demanding she go where he led.

Finally, when there was no strength left in her to fight, she let go, surrendering to him completely.

His words were nearly a growl of sound. "That's what I was waiting for, Bella. That's what I needed. You're mine now."

Words were beyond her now. All she knew was that her body was his, just as he'd said. He was going to make it do whatever he pleased, and all she could do was let him.

His body tightened, curling around her. "One more time, baby. Come for me one more time and I'll let you rest."

He shifted slightly, hitting yet another spot created just for him. Her whole world burst into light and flame. It licked over her mind, surged across her skin, and filled her until she could hold no more. Pleasure became her existence, and surrender her only option.

Victor roared in triumph. His cock swelled and throbbed inside her as he came. Her pussy quivered around him, grasping tight to hold him in place.

The storm passed and everything went quiet. Calm. Dark. The only sound she heard was their heavy breathing and the pounding of her pulse in her ears. The air turned cold as her sweaty skin cooled. Every muscle in her body became a useless mass of flesh. Had Stynger herself walked into the room, there wouldn't have been a thing Bella could have done about it. She was drained. Spent. Weak.

That thought gave her pause, but then the sound of Victor's voice drowned it out. "Sleep now, Bella. I'll take care of everything else. Your only job right now is to rest. I'm not going anywhere."

If anyone was tough enough and capable enough to keep track of things while she took a quick nap, it was Victor. The fact that he was on the job gave her that tiny push she needed to drift off. When she woke, she was going to have to beat his ass for taking liberties, but that could wait. He'd still be here. He'd promised.

Victor had fucked up. Not some little mistake, some tiny whoopsie he could use a do-over to correct. This one was big. Monumental.

He'd fallen for his boss. His dick had led the way, but his heart hadn't just been along for the ride. It had been right there, laying down cover fire and making sure nothing got in the way of their goal. They both wanted Bella to be theirs. In a forever kind of way.

Now what the hell was he going to do?

Denial wasn't going to work. He'd already admitted his feelings to himself, though how anyone could pretend not to feel what he did was a mystery. She consumed his every thought, both waking and asleep.

Not that he'd spent much time sleeping lately. Neither of them had.

He looked down at Bella. She was naked on top of the covers, still glowing with sweat. Every few seconds her body twitched, quivering the way it always did after she came. Her breathing had evened out, and the deep flush of lust had started fading from her face and chest. Her dark hair was a tangled, glossy mess across her pillows. The skin between her thighs was shiny and slick, her labia puffy and pink from his attention.

She was so fucking beautiful he wasn't sure how he would ever stop staring at her.

She was going to hate him when she woke up. There was no doubt in his mind about that. She was going to sit up, start lashing out at him for manhandling her the way he did, and probably never stop.

How in the world was he going to survive her anger? Not kissing her? Not touching her? Not feeling the slick clenching of her sweet pussy?

Victor had accomplished some nearly inhuman feats of strength and stamina over the years, but not even he was that strong of a man.

The only thing he could think of that might have even a slight chance of winning her over was if he found Gage. She loved that man—enough that it made Victor's throat tighten with jealousy just to think about it. If he could find her missing friend, maybe she'd speak to him again with something other than hate in her voice.

Big maybe.

Victor forced his legs to hold him up long enough to get rid of the condom. He briefly thought about crawling in bed with her, but knew he wouldn't last ten minutes before he fell asleep. That simply wasn't acceptable. He'd told her he'd watch over her, and that was exactly what he was going to do.

With a silent scolding for what he was about to do, he covered up her gorgeous, naked body and stalked out of the room. He had some calls to make to some very powerful people—favors to pull in. Every one of them was a long shot, or he'd have contacted them weeks ago, but they'd run out of all other options.

Victor loved Bella, and because of that, he was going to find some way to bring Gage home to her.

Chapter Twenty-seven

Jordyn woke up inside a small, dark space. She was sitting on a cold floor. Something hard and hot was at her back, but the rest of her was chilled to the bone. Her head throbbed so bad she almost thought she was in the White Room again. If not for the soothing darkness of this place, she would have panicked.

She shifted to stand, but a pair of arms tightened around her.

"Easy," said a low voice.

Gage. He was behind her, holding her.

Why?

She tried to recall the last thing she could remember. They'd tried to escape. Been caught. Ran. Gage was shot.

She gasped and lifted her weight from his body so she wouldn't hurt him. "Are you okay?" she asked.

"Fine. How's your head?"

"I've had worse headaches." But not many. As it was, she was fighting the urge to vomit all over the concrete floor.

She eased off of him, turning enough to see his face. Pain scrunched the skin around his eyes and bleached his lips. There was a dark stain of blood across his white lab coat.

"Tough girl," he said. "Sexy."

She scoffed at that while she opened up the lapels of his coat. More blood soaked the shirt beneath. Too much. "How's your breathing?"

"Trying not to."

"Don't do that," she advised. "Tell me what happened. How did we get here?" She picked up the flashlight and angled it to shine on his injury.

"Remember the crash?" he asked.

"Unfortunately. Was the person in the truck hurt?"

"Yes." Something about the tone he used told her there was more to his answer than a simple word.

"Is he alive?"

"No."

Again, there was more he wasn't saying. "Are my brains scrambled, or did he come at us with the intent to crash into us?"

"Your brains are fine."

So it hadn't been an accident. The man in the truck must have been one of Mother's, ordered to stop them by any means necessary. Which raised one more question.

"Was he alive after the crash?"

"Briefly," was all Gage said, leaving her to wonder if the man's death had been intentional or accidental.

Either way she mourned another life wasted, thanks to her mother.

Jordyn eased his bloody shirt up and eyed the wound. There was a single bullet hole drilled through his skin, right along his ribs. His flesh was red and hot. In fact his whole body felt overly warm. Fever? Infection? Probably, and there wasn't a single thing she could do about it out here, wherever they were.

"Where are we?"

"Storm cellar. Abandoned ranch house."

She knew the place. It was only five or six miles from

the labs. If they didn't get out of here soon, they were going to be found.

She reached around to feel for an exit wound, but the move put her face close to his, distracting her from what she was doing for a moment.

He was such an alluring man. Even injured, he still had a kind of power about him. She didn't understand what it was. The only power she'd ever experienced in her life was the overt kind Mother exerted on the people around her, controlling them through pain, fear, drugs and surgical implants.

Jordyn realized she'd been staring at Gage for too long—a socially awkward length of time. She hadn't been raised with other children, but knew from watching videos online that some of her habits weren't socially acceptable. Still, Gage didn't shy away from her or give her that look that told her she was doing something bizarre. Instead, he let her stare, leaning back, relaxed and calm.

Even though he had to be in a lot of pain, he wore a little half smile on his face, as if she amused him. As soon as she saw it, his mouth drew her in until she was studying the shape of his lips and the way there was less tension in them now than there'd been a minute ago.

Jordyn finally gathered her wits enough to lean back so that she wasn't thinking about kissing him. "No exit wound."

"No? Maybe you should pet me more to be sure."

Pet him?

Suddenly she realized that she was stroking his skin with her fingers, running them over the smooth, hard planes of his back. She'd touched every inch already, so there was no reason for her to caress him like this unless she simply enjoyed the feel of him.

A blush heated her cheeks. As pale as she was, there was no chance she could cover her embarrassment. "Sorry. I wasn't thinking."

"Don't be. I liked it."

Oh, my. A little thrill went singing through her at the thought, but as soon as she realized she had no right to touch him, that thrill died a sudden death.

She scooted away from his body enough that they were no longer touching. His long legs were splayed, making a space for her between them. His pants were wet from the knees down. There were small puddles under his shoes.

She'd been leaning against his chest while she slept, using a poor, injured man as a chair. "We need to get you medical attention."

"Soon. I'm resting."

"Resting? There's no time for that. Mother's men will be looking for us. And the longer that bullet is in you, the worse for you it will be."

"We're hidden."

"We were too close to the compound when we crashed. She has dogs. They'll find us. She'll put us in the White Room." Panic started closing in around her, pitching her voice higher and higher with every word. "With your injuries, you'll never survive—"

He cradled her face in his hands and captured her full attention. "I was careful. Hid our tracks. We're safe."

The meaning of his wet pants kicked in. He'd walked through water, masking his scent.

But her pants were dry. Which meant . . . "You carried me."

He nodded once.

"With a bullet wound. After a crash."

"Yes."

"You could have made the bullet shift. You could have bled to death. You could have killed yourself."

"I didn't." He was so casual about it, as if he rescued people every day.

A man like him might do just that, for all she knew.

He was far too good a man to die here, inside some dingy concrete closet. "I'm going for help."

She pushed herself up, but before she made it all the way to her feet, his hand closed around her arm. "No."

"But you need medical attention."

"So do you, concussion girl."

"I'm fine now. I've felt much worse than this and still functioned. This little headache is nothing."

His fingers trailed over her wrist. "We go together."

As much as she liked that idea, she knew he needed help sooner rather than later. "I'll be fast, and I promise to come back for you. I'd never leave you."

"Then don't. Stay." His eyes were drooping, fatigue riding him hard. "Promise."

How could she not? The man had helped free her. He'd taken a bullet getting her out of that place. He'd carried her for who knew how long to get her to safety. How could she not give him whatever he wanted?

"Okay," she finally said. "We'll stay for a little while so you can rest. Then we go wherever we're going to go together."

He closed his eyes and nodded. "I like that."

Chapter Twenty-eight

Bella woke almost exactly eight hours after Victor had fucked her unconscious. Her body still buzzed with the aftereffects of such mind-blowing orgasms. She was deliciously sore, starving and mad as hell.

She took a quick shower, and then found the focus of that anger sitting in her favorite chair. As soon as he saw her coming, he held her gaze while deftly ending in a matter of seconds a phone conversation he'd been having.

"Sleep well?" he asked.

"You know damn well I did. That was your plan all along, wasn't it? Make me come until I was too exhausted to see straight?"

"There were other reasons, but, yes, that was among them."

"I don't like being manipulated."

"And I don't like having to manipulate you. Next time, perhaps you should take a nap without having to be coaxed into it."

"What you did wasn't coaxing. Not even close."

He rose from the chair, all masculine grace and power. "Tell me you didn't like it. Go ahead. Lie to my face."

She couldn't. Not after the way he'd made her feel.

Subterfuge aside, forcefulness aside, anyone who lit her up like that deserved at least a little attaboy for his efforts. "Fine. It was good. Better than good. That doesn't change the fact that there's a little matter we have to discuss about you thinking you're in charge now."

"You liked me being in charge a few hours ago. You might like it now. Why not give it a try?"

"That was just fucking. This is business. *This* is important."

He flinched at her words, but for the life of her, she couldn't figure out why.

"Our fucking seemed fairly important to you at the time. Maybe next time I'll stop in the middle and you can let me know how high it rates on your priority scale."

"There's not going to be a next time, Temple. I'm cutting you off."

He closed the distance between them. She refused to back up a single inch. Let him crowd her space. Let him do his worst. She'd come so hard so many times, she was sure she could go another year without needing to scratch the itch.

The second he reached for her, she knew she had been mistaken. Men like Victor and the pleasure they brought were not so easily dismissed. Her body knew a good thing when it found one, and he was definitely good.

His fingers slid into the hair at the nape of her neck. His hand tightened into a fist, pulling the strands taut. Then he kissed her like the world was screaming to an end right here and now. He kissed her like it was the last kiss humanity would ever have.

He kissed her like he loved her.

Bella panicked. She lashed out blindly, shoving hard against his chest.

Victor landed on his ass five feet away, looking up at her with such keen betrayal on his face she knew she'd hurt him.

"I'm sorry," she said. She should have said more. Wanted to. But the tears were coming now, and all she could think about was fleeing before they started to fall.

What the hell was wrong with her? She never cried, and yet her whole system seemed to be straining with the need to let out about a gallon of tears.

She made it halfway to the bathroom before he jerked her to a stop and pinned her against the wall of her hallway.

"What the hell, Bella?" Fury rode his features, painting them a vivid red.

She tried to turn her head away, but it was too late. Her eyes were prickling. Burning. The wetness pooled along her lashes, spilling out to glide unchecked down her cheeks. *Fuck.*

Victor's rage melted into instant concern. "Whoa. Are you hurt?" He ran his hands over her body as if checking for broken limbs.

She tried to tell him she was fine, but a lie that big wouldn't fit out of her mouth. Instead, all she could manage was a soggy plea. "Don't you dare fucking fall in love with me, Temple. I mean it."

He stepped back fast, like he just found out she had the plague. "What makes you think I will?"

"I know how it goes." She was quivering. Out of control. Her skin burned and itched, making her wish she could shed it like a snake.

"How what goes?"

She didn't know how to answer his question. All she could do was fight the words trying to spill from her mouth. "You seduce me. Make me care for you. Make me think you love me. Then the insults start. The pain."

"What the hell are you talking about?"

"I won't let you lock me away. I won't let you pretend you love me while you make me drink out of the toilet and beg you for food."

"Did someone do that to you?" he asked, his tone moving from confused to gentle.

Despite her shame, the tears wouldn't stop. They flowed faster. Harder. She had to struggle to catch her breath. "Love isn't an excuse to do whatever the hell you want to me. I don't care how powerful you or your friends are."

He took her by the arms. She tried to jerk away, but he was too strong. "Honey, tell me what you're talking about."

What was the use of hiding her past from him now? He'd already made her surrender to him. He'd already told her he wanted to take over her mission—that she was too compromised to risk leading the people she cared about.

Maybe he was right. Maybe she had no business playing boss when so many lives were on the line. She couldn't even stop the damn tears falling down her face.

She wasn't herself anymore. Pretending otherwise was only going to get people she cared about killed.

Victor stroked her hair. "Tell me, baby. Tell me why you're crying. I swear to God I'll try to fix it."

There was no fixing this. It was ancient history. Scars.

She had nothing to lose. She was already as low as she could go. Broken. Damaged. Beaten. Her shame couldn't make it any worse.

"When I was a kid, Dad was a shitfaced drunk and Mom couldn't take it anymore. She left. He took it out on me."

"Oh, honey." The pity in his tone nearly stopped her cold, but she forced herself to keep going. Pity was exactly what a life like hers deserved. It was a sad, sorry thing she couldn't seem to escape.

"It wasn't that bad." A lie, but a necessary one. "I was a fighter. Got bigger. Smarter. Found some guys willing to teach me how to defend myself. I was almost big enough to take the fucker down." She pulled in a deep breath. "That's when Stynger found me. She had her men bring me in. She ... did things to me. I still don't know exactly what. I guess I'd blocked most of it out. All I remember was crying every time her goon came to get me for a 'doctor's visit.' I'd come home and be sick for days. Delirious. Dehydrated. Dad barely gave a shit if I lived or died, except if I died, he'd have to take care of his own laundry and cook his own meals."

"Sounds like a candidate for father of the year."

She stared at the far wall, noticing a chip in the paint for the first time. She focused on it so she wouldn't have to think about what she was going to say next. "The last time I came home from one of those trips to Stynger's lab, I woke up ... different."

"Different how?"

"I didn't feel like fighting anymore. I stopped learning self-defense. Stopped doing my homework. I was scared all the time. Timid. Whatever Dad said, I did. No more rebellion."

"That doesn't sound like you at all."

"Because it's not me. It's what Stynger *did* to me. Aggression reduction was what they called it. Basically, they removed my spine, killed my courage and nearly stripped me of the will to live."

"I don't understand. Why would anyone do something like that?"

"I destroyed every file I came across out of sheer spite, but from what I read, she was working on a way to remove the desire to fight from enemy forces. Spray them with some kind of toxin and they start looking around for a white flag to wave. Easy victory."

His arm tightened around her. "And you were one of her test subjects."

Bella nodded. "Whatever she did to me stuck. I got used to it. Learned to cope with the fear. Learned to obey and please everyone around me so no one would get upset. I avoided conflict at all costs and tried to make the most of my crappy life."

"I can't even imagine what that must have been like."

"It was like walking in a fog all the time. The real me was still inside, but she was locked up, beyond reach."

"And because of that, your dad knocked you around more," he guessed.

"No. I still played punching bag once in a while, but when I stopped trying to defy him at every turn, he stopped getting pissed at me quite so often."

"So what happened?"

"I married young," she said. "We were madly in love the way only kids can be. He was my hero, my savior. He got me out of a crappy home and into a life I could be proud of. The wife of a cop. Protected. Safe."

She felt Victor tense and knew he'd started putting the pieces together.

"Dan picked me because he liked his women docile. He got off on control. I realize now he had his own issues, and an itty bitty penis to live down, but at the time I had no clue. He was my first . . . everything."

"So, if you were perfect for him, then what happened?"

"Perfect was never perfect enough. He blamed me for everything. It was my fault he didn't get a promotion. My fault his hair started falling out. My fault the IRS was breathing down his neck for unpaid taxes, even though I was never once allowed to know how much money we had in the bank, much less control any of it. I got just enough cash to buy groceries and whatever else he thought I needed." She could still see him now, his forehead streaked red because of something he'd perceived was her fault. "I tried to get him help. Counseling. I even talked to his friends when I managed to get them alone. Not one of them believed me. Dan was smart. He made sure what he did never left a mark. He hid his temper from the world—it was only for me. And cops stick together."

She remembered those days of terror, when one of his buddies would come into the kitchen while she was in there fixing snacks for some game or whatnot. It took everything she had to open her mouth and ask for help. The last time, Dan had walked in on it. He joked and laughed the rest of the day with his friends, but once they were gone, she paid the price for her bravery.

"Did you ever try to leave him?" Victor asked.

"I thought about it, but I didn't know where to go. He cut me off from the few friends I had. I didn't have any family. And, much to my shame, I loved him. He didn't deserve it, but I couldn't see that at the time. All I wanted was for him to love me back, for us to be happy. I didn't realize it was impossible for him to love someone the way I wanted. The only person he knew how to love was himself."

Victor's hand swept over her arm, soothing her with a light touch. "When did you realize he wouldn't change?"

"I didn't. I changed."

"How?"

"One day, I was in the kitchen fixing dinner. I wasn't fast enough. He came in there, bellowing at me, telling me how slow and lazy I was. I guess I didn't turn around fast enough to face his ire, because I remember him grabbing my arm and spinning me around." Her hand clenched involuntarily. "I was holding a knife, chopping vegetables. The blade cut through his shirt and nicked his skin. The second the blood started soaking through, all I saw was red. I snapped, and all that fog burned off. I was myself again. A fighter."

"What happened?"

"To this day, I'm still not entirely sure. He was strong, tough, trained. He should have been able to fend me off. I didn't have the muscle mass I do now. I was puny and weak. But I stabbed him to death. Got in a lucky hit, I guess. All I remember was waking up, straddling him, both of us covered in blood. The knife was in both of my hands, and it was buried in his chest." She could still see the pattern of blood splatter all over the kitchen floor she'd just mopped. All over the cabinets. "Dan died before the ambulance got there. Since that day, whatever Stynger did to me disappeared. I wake up every day glad I'm me again. Whole."

She fell silent. She hadn't told a single person that story since her trial. Payton had encouraged her not to mention the part about her doctor's visits as a kid—said it would weaken her case. She'd been so grateful for his help, she hadn't questioned him. She'd followed her attorney's advice and said only what they thought would clear her name. It had worked. She was a free woman, the charges of murder dropped.

Victor was still by her side, seemingly not scared off by her tale. "Do you worry that whatever she did to you will come back?"

She nodded. The wet streaks on her face were a terrifying development. "It's the only thing that really scares me. I can handle everything else but being that weakling again."

"That's why you're so afraid for Gage, isn't it?" he asked.

"I can't let her do something like that to him. He's a good man. One of the best." Like Victor.

It struck her then just how much she respected the man holding her. He was confident without being cocky. Competent. Skilled. Fantastic under pressure and even better in bed.

Bella turned her head enough to stare into his clear blue eyes. There was compassion there, but any pity he'd had for her was gone. He looked at her no differently now than he had before hearing her sad story.

In that instant she knew that if she wasn't careful, she could fall for him. Hard.

She scrambled to her feet, needing to put some distance between them. There was no time for emotional roller coasters right now. There was way too much to do. Now that she'd gotten some sleep, she was ready to tackle the world and take Stynger down.

Victor wanted nothing more than to hold Bella while he sorted through the emotions her past evoked in him. Of all the things he thought he'd hear, a story about a timid, weak Bella was nowhere on the list.

But rather than keep her by his side, he let her go. She needed her space, so that's what he'd give her.

At least for now.

She might not know it yet, but she was falling for him. And as inconvenient as it was going to be to have an armed hellion for a girlfriend, wife, and mother of his children, that's the only thing he wanted. A weaker woman simply wouldn't do. He wanted Bella.

Too bad she wasn't on the same page with him. Hell, she wasn't even in the same library.

Good thing he loved a challenge.

Chapter Twenty-nine

Gage was dying. Jordyn knew death well enough to see the signs hovering around him.

She patted his arm, too afraid to shake him. "Open your eyes. Look at me."

His faded blue eyes fluttered open for a second before closing again.

Jordyn lifted his shirt and moved the makeshift bandage she'd managed to fabricate from her clothes. He wasn't bleeding like before, but there were angry red streaks of infection leading out from his wound. His skin was burning up, and there was no longer that keen sense of awareness in his gaze.

She was losing him.

Death had been a constant at the labs. She'd grown up with it. Been surrounded by it. But for some reason, facing Gage's death was simply too much to ask of her.

He had to survive. No matter what.

Jordyn left the little storm cellar where they were hidden and found her way outside. She was right where she thought, in the middle of nowhere, miles from the nearest town. This ranch might have been filled with people fifty years ago, but it was little more than wood, metal and cobwebs now. All the people who had run the ranch had long since moved on, leaving nothing behind but vacant, crumbling buildings.

The nearest road with any kind of traffic was over a mile away—too far for her to move Gage. And even if she did go out there, most of the cars she'd encounter would be on their way to or from the labs. She would have to follow that road for thirty miles or more before she reached a place with any kind of safety. And that was assuming that Mother didn't have her men posted around the town, looking for them.

No way was Mother going to miss such an important detail.

Jordyn went back to Gage's side. His breathing was shallow, his pulse weak. Sweat covered his skin, and he shifted in his sleep, moaning quietly from the pain.

He wasn't going to survive for much longer.

Unless she took him back to Mother.

She had a use for Gage, and even if Jordyn didn't understand it, Mother wouldn't let him die if he had a purpose for her research.

Jordyn sat for several minutes, searching for other options.

In the end, there was no other choice. She couldn't let an innocent man die, no matter the consequences to herself.

"I'll be right back," she told him, smoothing his hair away from his sweaty forehead. "Don't worry."

Before she could change her mind, she went back outside toward the road, knowing every step she took was one step closer to the White Room.

Chapter Thirty

Bella sat in the conference room at the Edge, going through every piece of information they had on Stynger, searching for some pattern to her movements. There had to be something here in all these seemingly unconnected actions. Some glimmer of hope.

Mira walked in and stopped when she saw the array of chaos in paper form.

"Whoa. Dead tree alert," Mira said, cradling a plastic box in her hands.

"What's up?" Bella asked. "I'm busy."

"Not too busy for this. Check it out." Mira set the box on top of a stack of photos and opened the lid. Inside was a spindly device with several thin wires connected to a series of circuits. In her hand was what looked like a radio handset.

"What is it?"

"An edge, I hope." She pointed to the handset. "This is like a remote, sending out a blocking signal."

"What's the other thing?"

"One of the implants Stynger puts in people's brains."

Bella put the pieces together. "You found a way to block Stynger's device?"

Mira grinned. "I call it a screamer. Payton tested it on

one of the guys the surgeons couldn't fix. He said the man was himself for as long as the signal was active. In a bit of pain—well, a lot of pain—but no longer Stynger's brain puppet."

"What's the range? How many implants will it block? How many of these things can you make?"

"Jeez, Bella. Slow down. How about a little pat on the back before you start slapping me with questions."

"Sorry, honey. I'm just a bit tense. This is fantastic work. You are so getting a raise."

Mira beamed. "Thank you. Fifty feet, I don't know, and about one an hour. More if I have help."

"What?"

"Your questions. The effective range is about fifty feet. Past that the signal degrades significantly. There shouldn't be a top capacity for the number of implants it blocks, but I haven't done that kind of testing, so I don't know. And if I get some help from some people who know their way around circuitry, we should be able to knock out a dozen by the end of the day. I don't have parts for more than that."

"Get on that," Bella said.

"Yes, ma'am."

"Start issuing them to the employees as fast as you can. Make sure they get whatever training they need. There's no way of knowing who's going to run into one of Stynger's puppets while they're out in the world. Having those on hand might save a lot of lives."

Mira's grin widened with pride. "I've still got all my normal work to do, so if there are fires to put out, things might get delayed."

Bella waved. "Nothing is more important than this. Keep the screamers priority number one."

"You got it. I'll be in my office if you need me."

Mira left. A few minutes later, Lila came in carrying a steaming cup of coffee. "I thought you might need a pick-me-up," she said. Her drab clothes and mousy hair seemed even duller today than usual. Her eyes and nose were red from crying. Again.

Bella really wanted to find a way to make Lila come out of her shell and learn to live again, but she'd been working with the woman for months with no progress. Lila seemed disinclined to do anything to improve herself. All she did was work and go home. She never hung out with anyone or went on dates. She never even accepted invitations to go to lunch with her coworkers. It was like she didn't want to make friends.

"Thanks, Lila," Bella said. "That was thoughtful of you."

"Can I get you anything else? Do anything for you? You're probably going somewhere again soon. I could make arrangements for you if you like. Just tell me where you're going."

"Right now all I'm doing is sorting through this mess."

"Can I help?"

"The coffee was help enough. Why don't you go spend some time in the gym or at the firing range? A little stress relief could do you some good."

Lila nodded, but said nothing. Bella doubted the woman would leave her desk. She was glued to the thing, even when she didn't have to be.

Bella shoved her worry for Lila aside for now. She still had three more boxes of papers, files and photos to sort through.

At least she had caffeine to keep her sharp.

Lila dialed Randolph.

"Yes?" he answered.

"I did what you asked."

"How did you administer the drug?

"In her coffee."

"That will work well. Faster than the dose she got from her water heater at home, no doubt."

It was evil that Lila had done, but she couldn't think about that right now. Her hands were tied. Even Bella would understand her choices. Lila hoped. "Can I speak to my son now?"

"I'm not with him right now, but you'll see him tonight, just like I promised. I'll tell him how brave his mommy is and how much she wants him to come home."

Lila didn't even try not to beg. "I need to see him now. I need to know he's safe."

"He'll stay safe for as long as you do what you're told. We'll meet tonight after you get off work."

"And I'll get my baby back?"

"You think I'm lying?"

She wasn't sure what to think anymore. There was no one else she could talk to. No one she could trust.

What she did know was she had to play along and not piss off the man who could bring back her son.

"I'm just making sure. That's all."

"Relax, Lila. Everything is going to be fine as long as you do what you're told. Now go on about your work as if nothing has happened. In about twenty minutes, you're in for a show."

Randolph hung up.

Lila sat there for a moment, unable to accept what she'd just done. The woman who'd taken her in and given her a job when she had nowhere else to go was sitting down the hall, within arm's reach of a toxic substance that would do God-knew-what to her.

And Lila had handed it to her.

She couldn't go through with it. She couldn't turn on Bella like that. She had to come clean. Confess everything. Beg Bella to rescue her baby boy. If anyone had the power to find and save him, it was Bella.

Lila rushed down the hall to the conference room, her

mouth open in anticipation of the confession she was ready to give. The room was empty. So was the coffee cup.

It was too late. The damage had been done.

Bella walked in behind her, opening a new box of thumbtacks. "Did you need something?" she asked.

The words caught in Lila's throat. What could she say now? *I poisoned you. I have no idea what's going to happen to you now. Sorry, but a man on the phone made me do it.*

None of that would help. But there was someone who could—someone who knew the score.

Lila shook her head and rushed past Bella into the hall. What she was about to do was even more unforgivable than poisoning Bella, but it was the woman's only hope.

Chapter Thirty-one

Victor found Bella in the conference room. Papers were scattered everywhere, taped to the walls and laid out on the table and floor. Red string wrapped around thumbtacks connected several photos and papers to a map, as if she were following some train of thought.

"I figured you might want some food by now," he said as he walked in.

She turned to him with a pair of scissors in her hand. The woman who stared at him looked like Bella, but it wasn't her.

"Dan?" she whispered, her face going pale with fear. "It can't be you. I killed you."

Victor had no idea what was going on, but he knew it wasn't good. He held up his hands and stopped dead in his tracks. "Honey, I'm not Dan. I'm Victor."

Her hand started shaking, making the blade of the scissors tremble. Her knuckles were white, her tendons straining to tighten her grip. "You're dead. You can't hurt me anymore."

Holy hell. This was not the woman he knew. Whatever had happened to Bella was bad—the kind of bad that scared him shitless. "I'm not going to hurt you, sweetheart. I'm going to stay right here and we're going to talk." Maybe then he could figure out what the hell had been done to her.

She shook her head. "Killing you was the best thing I ever did. It freed me. I won't let you cage me again."

"I'm not going to—"

Bella charged.

Victor had no choice but to defend himself or take the shears she wielded in his heart. He was as careful as he knew to be, but Bella was fast. Strong. Trained. She came at him like she meant it, and when his muscle memory took over, and his body flew into action, he knew there was no way he hadn't hurt her.

She landed on her back, pinned under him. The scissors were still in her hand, but he was controlling them now, holding them out to her side. The bones in her forearm shifted under his brutal grip, but it was either that or let her stab him.

"I'm not Dan," he growled at her. "Snap out of it!"

She didn't. She thrashed under him, screaming and kicking and struggling to get free. Her hips bucked, nearly tossing him off before he managed to pin her back down.

Payton rushed into the conference room. "What the hell is going on here?"

"Bella flipped out," Victor said as he struggled to hold her in place. "Call an ambulance."

"Get the fuck off me!" she shouted. "I killed you once, I'll kill you again."

Payton shouted down the hall for Lila to call Dr. Vaughn. Then he came over and pried the scissors from her hand.

Her eyes went wide with fear the second she saw him. "I won't let you take me back there. I'll kill you, too."

"What's she talking about?" Victor asked.

"The labs. She's delirious. Lila poisoned her."

"Lila?" Well, that was a *what the fuck* moment if Victor had ever heard one.

Lila hovered in the doorway. "Is she going to be okay? Please tell me she's going to be okay."

Bella snarled and tried to bite Victor. Tears were rolling from her eyes now, and the wild panic coursing through her made her whole body shake.

"Does she look okay?" he snapped.

"We need to sedate her," Payton said. "Fast."

Bella screamed and redoubled her efforts to break free. Victor had to hold her so tightly, he was sure he was going to leave bruises or break open her cuts.

"I don't happen to have any sedatives in my pocket," Victor snarled. "You?"

Payton stepped up, covered her nose and mouth with his hand and held on tight.

Victor couldn't believe his eyes. The man was suffocating her right here in front of witnesses. "What are you doing?"

"Saving her life." Payton was calm, determined.

Bella fought harder to free herself, getting in a good hit to Victor's balls. He saw stars for a second, and when they wore off, she was unconscious.

He stayed where he was, wondering if she was playing possum. When she didn't move, when he realized just how still and relaxed she was, he knew it was no act.

"I can't believe you did that," Victor said.

"I had no choice." When Payton pulled his hand back, it was bloody from where she'd bitten him. He held it away from his designer suit, letting it drip onto the carpet. "How far out is Leigh?" he asked Lila.

The mousy receptionist stared at them in shock. "She said she was ten minutes away."

"Let's get Bella to medical," Payton said. "If Leigh can't purge the drug from her system, we're going to have to take her to a hospital. They'll have no clue how to treat her there without me revealing far too much secret information—the kind that gets innocent people killed."

Victor rose over Bella's body to keep everyone else away, and turned to Lila. "Why did you do this to her?"

Tears began streaming down her face. "I didn't want to."

"We'll deal with her later," Payton said. "Right now Bella is our priority."

Victor picked her limp body up off the floor and carried her toward the door. On the way out he stopped next to Lila. "We will have words. If you so much as leave my sight, I'll hunt you down, assuming you meant to kill Bella. My response to you running will not be kind. Do you understand?"

Lila nodded and stepped out of the way so he could pass.

"I hope so, because I'd really rather not have to kill someone else this week."

Chapter Thirty-two

Victor paced as Leigh worked to clear the toxin from Bella's system.

As small as the medical facilities were at the Edge, they were stocked with enough supplies to take care of everything from splinters to patching up bullet wounds. Pumping stomachs wasn't standard fare in their line of work, but Leigh seemed to know what she was doing. Apparently guarding VIPs meant the company was prepared for a dose of poison or two.

The job was messy. The convulsive choking sounds Bella made were enough to break his heart and enrage him to the point of losing control. He breathed through his nose, keeping his fingers clenched so that he wouldn't wrap them around Lila's neck.

She sat in a locked examination room—one that served as her prison cell for now. He wanted to question her, but he was far too furious for such delicate work.

Payton stepped up beside him. "It's not as bad as it looks."

"No? And how would you know?"

"I've been poisoned a time or two. It's not fun, but she's barely aware of what's going on. Chances are she won't even remember it."

"Why do I have the feeling you're lying?"

Payton sidestepped the question. "Lila doesn't know what the drug is. All she knows is that it was given to her by a man who used to work for Bella."

"Who?"

"He was from before your time. Let's just say that he excelled at violence. She fired him after only a few weeks, but he is the kind of man who knows how to hold a grudge."

"Was the poison meant to kill her?"

Payton shook his head. "I don't think so, or she'd be dead."

"Was he just trying to mess with her head? Whatever he gave her made her think I was her late husband."

Payton frowned as if remembering something. "Are you sure?"

"Positive. She thought I was Dan."

"Hang on."

Payton went into the room where Lila sat crying. Victor watched through the glass as she spoke to him. The floodgates of tears broke open until she was sobbing inconsolably. She uttered a few words with each sobbing breath.

Finally, Payton had heard what he wanted to, because he came back out. His face was grim.

"What?" Victor asked.

"Stynger is behind this. She's got Lila's son and is holding him to ensure Lila's cooperation."

Violent urges swelled in Victor's gut. He tended to be a methodical man, thinking things through before acting, but he was on edge, terrified for Bella and furious at Lila for what she'd been forced to do. "She has to pay for her actions."

"I know," Payton said.

"But we're still going after her son."

"That's my inclination as well, but until we find Stynger, there's not much hope for the boy, either."

Leigh stepped out of the room, giving Victor a brief glimpse through the doorway. Bella lay still on the bed and was far too pale.

For a long, excruciating moment, he was sure they'd lost her. And in that moment, his world started to crumble. She meant far more to him than he'd let himself acknowledge. She'd become part of his foundation, and the thought of her gone from this world left him shaky and weak.

He slumped to the floor, sliding down the wall for support.

"Whoa," said Leigh, rushing to his side. "She's going to be okay. I had to sedate her so she wouldn't fight the tube down her throat, but I think we pumped out most of the toxin."

Victor let the words settle in, filling the cracks that had started to form under his feet. He pulled in one deep breath after another, replaying Leigh's words in his mind over and over. *She's going to be okay. She's going to be okay....*

"How long until she wakes up?" Payton asked. He was looking a little shaky himself, but far steadier than Victor.

Leigh shrugged. "At least another hour or two. She was fighting the sedatives pretty hard, so I couldn't go easy with the dosage. But she metabolizes sedatives fast, so it shouldn't be long. Just know that if you hit her with a hundred problems the second she wakes up, I won't be pleased. And, as a general rule, you really don't want to piss off the woman who sews you back together."

"We'll be gentle with her," Victor promised. As far as he was concerned, he'd protect her from every little problem that came her way for the rest of her life if she'd let him. Seeing her out of her mind like that had left a scar on him he knew would not soon fade.

Leigh eyed Payton. "Come on. We'll get your hand

patched up. I saw the blood on her teeth. That can't feel good."

"I'll be along shortly."

"You have until I'm done setting up the room. After that I'm coming for you. Be ready."

Payton nodded. "I will. Victor and I need a minute."

Leigh went into the room where Lila was sobbing and went to work soothing the distraught woman.

As soon as Leigh was out of earshot, Payton said, "We need to plan our next move. I assume you have an idea."

Victor pushed to his feet. He couldn't plan an attack slumped on his ass. Bella was safe. He had to find the strength to lead the team until she was well enough to do the job herself. "I do. You said a man gave Lila the drug?"

"Yes."

"Then we use him. Lure him out of hiding and follow the drone back to the queen bee. Once we take her out, the rest will fall into place. We'll cure her victims, find Gage and Lila's son, and make sure Stynger is never again able to hurt another living soul." Especially Bella.

"It won't be that easy. Randolph is smart. He's going to expect a trap if Bella survives."

"She's going to survive." Victor simply couldn't let himself imagine another possible outcome. He needed her alive and well, bossing him around and making his whole world a brighter place.

"You and I know that, but that doesn't mean the world has to know."

Pieces began shifting in Victor's head. "You want us to pretend she died?"

"It's the only way to make sure Stynger doesn't keep coming after her. It gives Bella a layer of security she'll get no other way."

He was right. No one would bother wasting time coming after a corpse. Unless they wanted to perform an autopsy, which was always a possibility with someone as deranged as Stynger.

Victor shook his head. "Bella is not going to like sitting back and hiding while the rest of us move in for the kill."

"She doesn't have to like it. All she has to do is accept it. That's where you come in."

"You think I can talk her into handing over the reins?"

"I sure as hell can't," Payton said. "She'd be convinced that was my plan all along—that I poisoned her to make it happen."

The man was right. Everything Payton did or said was suspect. If anyone was going to have a chance at getting Bella to play along, it was Victor.

Now all he had to do was fundamentally alter Bella's DNA so that she would willingly sit back and play dead.

He let out a long breath. "You know we're going to need a plan B, right?"

"There is no plan B. Make it work, Victor. It's our only shot at keeping her alive."

And because of that, because it was true, he was going to make Bella acquiesce, no matter what it took or how hard he had to push to make it stick. In this, she would submit.

Chapter Thirty-three

Gage woke up handcuffed to a hospital bed, staring up in to the face of Satan.

Stynger's bloodred mouth stretched into a gruesome smile. "Glad to see you survived. It was a close call there for a while."

He tried to move, but the pain riding his ribs took him off guard. He collapsed back to the bed, panting and weak.

"None of that now," Stynger said. Her spindly body moved around to the far side of the bed to push a button on his IV pump. "Your fever finally broke. We can't have you pulling out the stitches my surgeon put in. That bullet did plenty of damage, thanks to your little escape attempt."

He could already feel the numbing weight of painkillers flooding his system. "Where's Jordyn?"

"She found one of my men and got you the care you needed. She, of course, had to come back home. I'm not done with the girl yet, despite her rebellious nature."

"If you hurt her—"

Stynger laughed. "You're barely able to hold up your own head. What on earth do you think you could do to me?"

Gage refused to rise to her taunt. Better to save his strength so he could show her what a man like him could do to a bitch like her when the time came.

"That's better. I've always liked the strong, silent type." She patted his arm. "Get some rest. I have plans for you."

His eyelids grew heavy, and he had to fight off his lethargy. "I want to see Jordyn."

"She's . . . indisposed."

Thoughts of that horrible White Room that terrified Jordyn so much sprang to his mind. He had no idea what the place was or what had happened to her while she was in there, but the fear he'd seen in her eyes had been real enough for him to know she wasn't making it up. "Let. Me. See. Her."

"So cute. Truly, you amuse me more than any of the other subjects I've had over the years. I'm glad, since I'll be keeping you around for a while."

"Why?"

"I have need of your unique genetics." Her bony fingers trailed down his thigh and back up over his groin. His balls tried to crawl up into his abdomen in order to get away from her touch. "You're a lovely creature. If I were younger, I'd make use of your sperm myself. But I guess I'll just have to be satisfied with living vicariously through Jordyn."

Gage laid there in shock for a full ten seconds before the meaning of her words finally sank in. "You think I'm going to fuck your daughter?"

Stynger frowned. "Why in the world would I want you to do that? It serves only to allow the two of you to create unnecessary emotional attachments. I took care of the insemination myself, rather than leaving such a thing to chance. Everything went beautifully. Jordyn doesn't know she's expecting yet, of course, but she's smart. She'll figure out something is going on when I don't send her to the White Room for her latest escapades. Can't risk the embryo now, can we? Your offspring is an important piece of genetic history in the making."

He couldn't quite get his head around what the woman was saying. The words were clear, but their meaning escaped him completely. "Offspring?"

Stynger patted his arm like he was a slow child. "Yes, dear. Jordyn is pregnant with your child, and my newest test subject. She has been for weeks now. The first of many offspring, I hope. Congratulations, *son*." She left his side and went to the door. "Get some rest now. I think it's best if the news comes from you. Jordyn seems fond of you, and we wouldn't want to do anything to upset her in her condition now, would we?"

Stynger closed the door behind herself, leaving Gage to his stunned silence. Jordyn was pregnant. With his child. He'd barely touched her, leaving him with no way to predict this kind of consequence. He sure as hell couldn't have guessed such an outcome. He hadn't even known they'd taken his semen. They must have done it while he was in a drugged sleep somehow.

What the hell?

In the weeks he'd been here, he'd thought of a lot of reasons why Stynger had been keeping him locked up, but never once had he considered it would be to use him as a sperm donor.

What the motherfucking hell?

Poor Jordyn. Her own mother had done this to her. Impregnated her without her consent or knowledge. That kind of violation wasn't going to be easy for her to swallow. She was already dealing with so much—she was nervous and frail. He couldn't imagine how it was going to feel for her to know what her own mother had done to her.

Then it hit him. Some of the shock and drugged lethargy cleared and he realized the monument of all of this. Jordyn was carrying his child—a child who was going to be the victim of whatever twisted experiments Stynger wanted to run on him or her if Gage didn't get Jordyn out of this place.

He thought he'd wanted to escape before, but that desire paled in comparison to the furious need that possessed him now. He hadn't asked for this child. He hadn't even participated in its conception. But he'd be damned if he was going to sit back and let his child and its mother suffer.

One way or another, he was getting Jordyn out of here. Before it was too late.

When Jordyn was dropped off at her quarters instead of in the White Room, she knew something wasn't right. Mother didn't do lenience. She didn't understand forgiveness. Punishment for Jordyn's actions should have been swift and severe.

Why then was she sitting on her bed, safe and sound, rather than strapped to a gurney, screaming for mercy?

Something was terribly wrong.

Jordyn's stomach did a low, swooping dive. She lurched for the toilet in time to distract herself with a painful bout of vomiting. As soon as the worst of it passed, she cleaned up and tried to still her nerves enough to think.

Mother always did things for a reason. Was she postponing the torture in order to give Jordyn time to dread it more? Or was she simply dealing with more important matters before getting to the job of making her daughter pray for death?

And what about Gage? He was too valuable to let die, but what if Jordyn had acted too late? What if she hadn't realized how bad his wounds were in time for the medical staff to save him?

Anxiety over his health outweighed her desire to stay hidden. She left her room and hurried down the halls to the infirmary. Guards watched her as she passed, but none of them moved to stop her. It was almost as if her escape attempt had never happened.

She made it all the way to Gage's room on shaky legs. A guard stood outside, but rather than block her path, he opened the door to let her in.

Gage was chained to the bed with a pair of handcuffs around one wrist. Thick layers of bandages swaddled his chest and abdomen. His skin was pale, and there was a heavy kind of listlessness to his posture.

As she came in, his eyelids fluttered slightly under the weight of the drugs being pumped into his system. A flare of recognition lit his features, and he reached for her.

"Don't move," she said as she rushed to him. "Just lie still."

"You're safe?"

"I'm fine. How are you?"

She could see him trying to shed the effects of the drugs through sheer force of will. "Need to wake up."

"No, you don't. Just sleep for now. Everything's fine."

His words slurred together. "Have to go. Baby."

His endearment warmed her heart and made her even more determined to see him recover. "We'll go as soon as you're well. I promise."

"No. Baby." He grabbed her hand as if trying to make her understand. His eyes shut under the weight of the medication he was on, but he was still shifting as if trying to get out of bed.

Jordyn didn't know how else to ease him, so she climbed in bed beside him and held him down. "Lie still. I'll stay with you." For as long as Mother allowed. "Everything will be fine once you sleep."

He grabbed her like he was afraid she'd float away. The chains on his handcuffs rattled. The hot strength of his arms felt good. She hadn't realized just how worried she'd been until seeing he was alive with her own eyes. The exhaustion of their ordeal sank in, and she let her eyes shut. There was no way of knowing how many precious minutes they'd get together like this. She was going to soak him up for as long as she could. As soon as she woke, she knew she'd be headed for the White Room.

When she went, she wanted to take this memory with her to keep her strong and help her live through the pain.

Chapter Thirty-four

Bella felt like she'd been turned inside out and used to clean a hot charcoal grill. Her whole body ached, and someone must have shoved a dirty toilet brush down her throat a few times to make it so raw and swollen.

She shifted in her bed just enough to wish she hadn't.

"Easy," came Victor's low voice.

She opened her eyes. He was right beside her, standing over her bed. Light from above glowed around his head like a halo. "Pretty as an angel," she croaked.

His hand pinned her shoulder to the bed so she couldn't sit up. "You're still very much of the living, sweetheart. And I'm no angel."

"Need to sit up."

Rather than move his hand so she could, he did something to make the head of the bed rise up slowly. "Water?"

She nodded, and was blessed with a cool cup of liquid pressed to her lips. It slid down her throat, easing the burn.

"That's enough for now. Doc said not to push it."

Doc? "What happened?"

He paused for so long she forced herself to look back up at him, squinting at the light.

"We'll get to that in a minute. How do you feel?"

"Shitty."

"Are you in a lot of pain?" he asked.

"Not enough for drugs, if that's what you mean. Now tell me what happened."

"What do you remember?"

"I was working on sorting through files we've collected on Stynger. After that, things went a little sideways with a visit from my dead husband and a few of his crooked cop buddies. I'm guessing that didn't actually happen."

"Fortunately, no. You did, however, get a not-so-healthy dose of something Stynger cooked up."

"Drugs?"

Victor nodded as he stroked the back of her hand. "Everything seem clear now?"

"I could use a nap or three, but yeah, no more ghosts."

He was pondering something. She could see it in his clear blue eyes.

"Want to tell me what's going on?" she asked. "Any idea who tried to kill me?"

He pulled up a chair and sat down close enough he could still touch her. She knew they were in one of the medical rooms at the Edge, and that anyone could walk in at any time, but damn it, his touch felt good. After the day she'd had, she deserved a little something nice.

Victor took her hand in his and held it tight. He looked right in her eyes with an expression of apology so thick, she could almost feel the bad news before it reached her. "We don't think anyone was trying to kill you. We think the drug you were given was meant to screw with your head. Leigh is having a friend of hers analyze a sample, but the effects were pretty . . . convincing."

"It was Stynger, wasn't it? Anyone else would just kill me and get it over with. That crazy bitch likes fucking with people's brains way too much to let her keep breathing free air."

"About that we agree. But there's something else you need to know. And it's not going to be easy to hear."

"What?"

"You were drugged by one of our own, Bella."

"Payton. That bastard! I'll—" She threw off the covers so she could go find him and confront him, but Victor stopped her cold.

"No, Bella. It wasn't Payton. It was Lila," he said. "She was the one who drugged you."

Lila? No way. Bella had taken her in. Bought her clothes. Found her an apartment and helped her furnish it. Given her a job. She'd picked the woman up from the depths of her despair and made sure she was on the path to a new life. There was no way Lila would do that to her. Was there?

"I'm sorry, honey." Victor stroked her arm, staving off some of the chill her shock had brought down on her.

"Are you sure it was Lila?" Bella asked, her voice small and weak.

He nodded, sorrow drawing his mouth down. "She confessed. Stynger has her son. She felt she had no choice. It doesn't excuse what she did, but it does explain it."

"Lila has a son?" How could Bella not have known? How could Lila not have so much as mentioned him in all the months they'd worked together?

"Apparently so."

"I didn't know."

"None of us knew. Stynger has had him all this time, using him as a lever to gain Lila's cooperation. It's why Lila applied for the job—Stynger forced her to find a way into your life."

Pieces clicked together in Bella's head. "She was the one who drugged Sophie, too, wasn't she?"

Victor nodded. "She's done a lot more than that, but we'll worry about that later. You need to rest now."

"Fuck rest. Tell me. You have interrogated her, haven't you? We need to know what she's done."

"Payton and I both questioned her. And if it's any consolation, she never wanted to hurt anyone. I believe that."

"Tell me what she's done."

He sighed, but didn't try to dodge her question. "She planted bugs in your office. She fed information about our efforts to find Stynger to her allies. She planted misleading information in our files to throw us off Stynger's scent. She let that man who attacked you into your office the other day without a background check. And she gave someone else a key to your house so he could plant that bomb. He also put a drug in your hot water tank so you got a dose of it every time you took a shower."

The pain of Lila's betrayal nearly drove the breath from Bella's body. She still couldn't wrap her mind around how blind she'd been. How foolish she'd been to trust someone she barely knew. It shouldn't have mattered that Lila tugged at Bella's heartstrings. She should have questioned her more carefully, screened her better—something to uncover the truth.

"Stynger knew your history, Bella. She knew you'd be drawn to Lila's story of abuse—that your shared past would connect you and make you sympathetic. Stynger threw Lila in front of you so she could get someone in the door here."

"It was all lies?"

Victor shook his head. "Not all of it. Lila was running from a nasty ex. Stynger used that weakness to gain Lila's trust and steal her baby away. I know she did bad things, but I can't honestly say I would have done anything differently if it had been my son at stake. Can you?"

Fury blazed through Bella's system, helping her shed every last bit of remaining lethargy. "I would have killed Stynger."

"Can you really see that as an option open to Lila? She's not as strong as you—either physically or mentally."

"Stop making excuses for her. I know she was up against a wall, but she could have come to me and told me the truth. I would have moved heaven and earth to find her baby and take him back."

"Lila has seen the kind of destruction you leave in your wake. It's not fair of you to ask a distraught woman to put her child at risk like that."

"I never would have let anything happen to him."

Victor got right in her face, forcing her to look him in the eye. "You can't make guarantees like that. You know as well as I do that bad shit happens. Even to babies. It doesn't matter what Lila should have done at this point. All we should worry about is where we go from here."

"You say that like you already have a plan."

"We do."

"We?"

"Payton and I have discussed our options. We need an edge, Bella, and you're not going to like where we get it."

"What's that supposed to mean?"

He took her hands in his and held them tight. She wasn't sure if it was for comfort, or if he was trying to keep her from striking out at him.

"We need you to play dead," he said. "Let Payton take over the operation. And the company."

"Not only no, but *hell* no. You can't ask that of me."

"We have no choice. If Stynger is to believe you're dead, it has to look real."

"I'm not going to sit on my hands while everyone else is out there working. Have you forgotten that one of my best friends is still a prisoner of that psychotic bitch?"

"You have to let us handle it. We can consult with you in secret, keep you hidden, but nothing we do can have your signature on it."

"My plans are solid, Temple. They've gotten you out of more than one messy situation alive."

"I'm not questioning your ability to lead, Bella."

"Then what? Why do I have to play dead?"

"Because it's the only way you're going to survive this mission. Stynger wants you out of her way, and if we're spending precious resources watching your back, then we're not using them to take her down."

Bella let her head fall back against the pillows. She'd never considered she might be slowing them down, making it harder to find Gage. But now that she saw it from Victor's viewpoint, she could see just how much effort was going into keeping her sorry ass alive. All the manpower to keep her house safe. All of Leigh's efforts to patch up Bella after she was injured.

"You're right," she said. "There's far too much manpower going into guarding my back. If I'm out of the way, you'll be able to work faster." She pulled in a long breath, hating what she was about to do next. "But I'll chop off my own hands before I'll give my share of the Edge to Payton."

"Now, Bella, you need to look at this—"

She cut him off before he could piss her off more. "I will, however, give it to you. Draw up the papers if you want. I'll sign them before I 'die.'"

Victor rocked back on his heels. "Are you sure? Payton's a better choice."

"Payton is not an option. Anyone who knows me would see right through that. And when you have the papers drawn up, you'd better make sure they're legit. Stynger probably has an army of lawyers working for her. She'll spot a scam in five seconds flat."

"You realize that if something really does happen to you, the deal will be binding."

"I'm aware, Temple. Now go and get your fancy lawyers to work their magic before I change my mind."

He leaned down and kissed her forehead with such tender sweetness it made her eyes prickle with tears. "I know how hard this is for you. The only consolation I can give you is that it will all be over soon and you'll be back behind the wheel, steering the ship."

She grabbed his shirt and held him close. "Just be sure you don't crash it on the rocks, honey. I need her back in one piece."

"I swear on my life that I won't betray you."

She almost laughed at the ridiculous nature of his vow. She apparently invited betrayal. Her father betrayed her. Her husband. Payton. Even sweet Lila. Trusting that Victor would be different was simply asking for pain. "I'm satisfied with you knowing my true nature. You've seen what I'm capable of. That should be motivation enough to be smart about how you behave. I still have that C4, you know."

He grinned. "Such a violent creature."

"Aww, sweetie. You say the nicest things. Now go and take Stynger down like a good boy."

He winked at her and hurried out the door to take away the thing she'd worked for her whole adult life. All her blood, sweat and tears were in this company, and she was about to sign it over to a man who might betray her as easily as Lila did.

At least with Lila, Bella only got her feelings hurt. With Victor the stakes were much, much higher. The man had the power to break her heart in a way she wasn't sure she'd survive. She'd promised herself she'd never again give a man that kind of power over her, but as she listened to Victor's heavy steps echo down the hall, she knew that was one promise completely shattered.

She'd gone and fallen for the man, and there wasn't a damn thing she could do to catch herself.

Chapter Thirty-five

Norma Stynger watched her daughter snuggle up against Gage Dallas. It was strange that she'd created such a close bond with the man in the little time they'd had together.

As Norma made notes in her journal about the odd observation, she wondered if there was some instinct that drove Jordyn to bond with the man whose offspring she was carrying. It was an interesting question—one that bore further research.

Next time Norma bred her daughter, perhaps she'd pick a different man to lend his DNA, just to see if the effect moved from one man to the next. Of course there was only one more man alive that Norma knew had the right genetics to be worth nine months of waiting: Gage's brother Adam.

Once Bella was out of the way and the Edge crumbled, perhaps Adam would reconsider his employment with Norma. She'd be safely out of the country by then and able to spend less time and money on evading notice and more on actual research. A man as skilled as Adam could come in handy.

"Do you want me to separate them?" asked the guard on duty.

"No, my daughter needs to rest before we relocate. I don't want her falling ill."

The guard looked at Norma like he didn't recognize her. "Yes, ma'am."

"Don't let him leave this room," she ordered.

"No, ma'am."

"And when Jordyn wakes, let me know. We still have to discuss her punishment."

The beefy guard paled and swallowed hard. "Yes, ma'am. Would you like me to escort her to the White Room?"

"That won't be necessary. I have something else in mind." Something far worse than the physical pain of the White Room—a punishment her tenderhearted daughter would never forget.

Payton had lied to a lot of people over the years, but this lie was going to be hard. There was no telling how many people Stynger had working for her. Or where. Lila was proof of that. The fact that Payton hadn't seen through the lies and known what she was proved he was rusty, because a sobbing mess like Lila simply wasn't that skilled.

She was, however, highly motivated.

Norwood picked up the phone after about ten rings. "Norwood here."

"Bella is dead," Payton said, letting his voice catch with emotion.

Silence echoed on the other end of the line for a long minute. "Confirm that. Bella Bayne is dead?"

"Yes."

"When? How?"

"A few minutes ago. She was poisoned. We tried to save her, but . . ." He trailed off, remembering how she'd looked in that bed, pale and lifeless. It wasn't much of a stretch for him to get choked up.

"I'm sorry, Payton. I know she was like a daughter to you."

Payton cleared his throat. "We're postponing the funeral for a few days so her employees have time to complete their jobs and come back to the States."

"I'll be there," promised Norwood.

"No. It's too dangerous. Stynger could use it as an opportunity to reach you. We can't forget that both of us are high-risk targets right now."

"I don't care. I'll still be there. But I'll be careful. Tell me you will, too."

"I will. But there's so much to do. No one knows yet."

"Are you keeping it under wraps?"

"You can tell your staff, but let's not spread the news too far until I have time to let our people here all know. I want them to hear it from me." Which, while true, was not what would happen. Word would spread fast. Payton was counting on it.

"Understood."

Payton didn't have to lie about this next part. "I don't know what to do now. We still can't find Stynger. Gage is still missing."

"Do you have any leads?"

"Bella was working on something when this all happened. I'm going to sort through her work and see if it sparks anything."

"What about the person who poisoned her?"

Payton hesitated. He really didn't want anyone to know that they were still holding Lila in a locked room at the Edge. Once she was toted away to the secure facility, then it would be safe to mention her name. Until then, it was better to keep that part to himself. "We're working on it."

"Let me know if I can help, okay?"

"This doesn't change anything with Temple's assignment, does it?"

"It will, but I can hold off on that for now. With Bella

gone, there's no one there leading the charge except you. And unfortunately, the higher-ups here don't trust you."

Payton grunted in mock amusement. "I can't say I blame them."

"My suggestion is to do what you can as fast as you can. I know it's hard to carry on with a man down, but you've got to try. We're both running out of time and options, old friend."

"What have you heard?"

"Nothing directly. But we both know how it works around here. Results speak loudly, and right now, you guys are barely a whisper. That needs to change. Fast."

They were going to lose their funding and support. That's what Norwood was trying to warn him about without saying it directly. "How fast?"

"Red tape is thick, but someone's got a machete."

"Stynger's influence?"

"Suggesting something like that could get a man like me in hot water up to my neck."

That wasn't a no. "I see. I'll stop trying to scald you, then."

"Let me know about the funeral arrangements as soon as they're made. I will be there."

"Will do. Until then, watch out for yourself. You don't want to be the next victim of poison."

"Neither do you. Seems like a good time to go on a diet to me."

"I was just thinking I needed to lose a few pounds myself. Talk soon."

Norwood hung up, leaving Payton feeling queasy. He hated lying to his oldest friend, but he knew there was no other choice. Bella's life depended on them selling this lie, so Payton would use every ounce of experience he had to make sure everyone he knew believed it. Even if they never forgave him.

After everything he'd done to Bella, it was the least he owed her.

Chapter Thirty-six

Bella waited until she was sure Victor and Payton were both occupied before she left her room. Leigh had said Lila was nearby, and there was something Bella needed to do before that changed.

She pulled her IV stand along, not even caring that her ass was hanging out the back of her hospital gown.

The small office across the hall—the one Leigh used when she was here—was serving as Lila's holding cell. Clay stood outside, visibly armed.

He held up his hand. "Payton said no one was allowed inside. He's arranging for her to be moved to a secure facility."

"I don't give a shit what Payton said. Move aside."

"I can't let you hurt her."

"I have no intention of hurting her."

"Right now," he finished. "Ten minutes from now you might feel very differently."

Bella got up close to Clay. "Please don't make me get ugly. I'm too tired for ugly. All I want to do is talk to her."

He let out a heavy sigh. "You and I have been through hell together at least three times. I love you like a sister, but I know you. You're not so good with talk. You prefer action."

"I'm sick. Weak. Hell, as far as the world is concerned, I'm already dead. There's really not much I could do to her before you could stop me. Unless you've gotten soft since hooking up with Leigh."

He lifted a brow in amusement. "Does that kind of obvious baiting normally work for you on fully grown men?"

"You'd be surprised how often, honey. Now step aside and let me have a chat with my secretary."

"I'm going to regret this, aren't I?" he asked.

"You're going to regret trying to stop me more. I know you've got a great health plan, with your own personal doctor, but that doesn't mean you should take chances."

Clay shook his head and stepped aside. "Go for it. But if I so much as hear you raise your voice at that woman, you're out of there. You're supposed to be playing dead, anyway."

"I'll play dead when I'm done. Once Payton trucks her off, we'll never hear from her again. I have a right to ask the woman why she tried to kill me."

Clay opened the door. Bella stepped inside and closed it behind herself, turning the lock.

"That won't stop me from coming through the glass," promised Clay from the other side of the door.

Bella ignored him and faced the woman she had thought was her friend.

"I'm so sorry," Lila said, breaking down into tears again. Her nose and eyes were already red and swollen from the sobfest she'd been having. There was a mostly empty box of tissues beside her and a trash can full of the refuse.

Bella felt a moment of pity for the woman. Like Victor had said, what person wouldn't do just about anything to protect their child? Bella could only imagine the havoc she'd wreak if someone tried to hurt her baby.

"I'm not here for apologies. I don't care why you did it. I need answers."

"What answers?"

"I want you to tell me every encounter you had with anyone associated to Stynger. Start with the latest one and work your way back."

Lila wiped her eyes and sniffed. "His name is Randolph."

"I know him. He used to work here. Did you meet him?"

"Not this time. He called me. They gave me a special phone to use—one that couldn't be used to trace back to them."

"So there was more than one person you took orders from?"

"Yes. Whoever called, I did what they said."

"Stick with Randolph. When was the last time you saw him?"

"In person?"

"Yes."

"A few weeks ago. He wanted the key to your house. I knew you kept one in your desk. I made a copy for him."

The idea of that man roaming around her house was almost enough to set her off, but she held it together and focused on the task at hand. "Where did you meet?"

"A grocery store."

"Which one."

"The one down the block. I was on my lunch break. We met at the salad bar. He was in line behind me. I set the key down. He picked it up. We never spoke."

"Did you see what kind of car he drives?"

"A black truck."

Probably the same one he'd had when he worked at the Edge. "Have you ever seen Norma Stynger in person?"

"No."

"Spoken to her on the phone?"

"No."

"Do you know where they're keeping Gage?"

Her face crumpled and tears streamed off her chin. "No. But I know they have him at the same place they have my baby."

"Why do you say that?"

"Because of something Randolph said."

"What?"

"He was upset that they were stuck in one spot now, getting ready for some big move. He said there was barely room to keep my son and that if I didn't cooperate, they'd get rid of him to save space." She sucked in a huge breath of air to steady her voice. "This was right after Gage went missing. I kept thinking that if Gage saw him, my baby would be safe. Gage would protect him."

She was right about that. Assuming Gage was able to do anything at all. As long as there was fight left in that man, her child would be safe.

"Did you ever get a feel for how far away it was from here to wherever they're holed up?"

She thought about it for a minute. Then her eyes widened. "Yes. He called me once. Stynger interrupted him, so he was with her. We met a few hours later."

"How many?"

"Five or six. I saw his truck. It was covered in dust like he'd been out on gravel roads. It had rained the day before, so it had to have been fresh."

That was something, though it left a hell of a lot of ground to cover. There were miles of dusty gravel roads within five or six hours of Dallas. "What else? Did you hear anything else when he was with Stynger?"

She frowned, thinking. "That's all I can think of."

"When were you supposed to contact him next?"

"I wasn't. We were going to meet tonight. He promised he'd bring back my baby if I gave you that drug."

"Where?" demanded Bella.

Lila blinked. "What?"

"Where were you supposed to meet him?"

"There's a park a few miles from here. I was supposed to go there on my way home."

Bella didn't have much time until then.

She took Lila's hand. From the corner of her eye, she could see Clay watching them. If she made any sudden moves, he'd be in here before she could blink.

"Have you told anyone else this?"

"That I was going to meet Randolph?"

"Yes."

Lila frowned and sniffed. "I think I told Victor. I don't know. Maybe it was Payton. They were both flinging questions at me like crazy."

"Do me a favor and don't tell anyone that you told me, okay?"

"Why? What are you going to do?"

"I'm not going to do anything," she said. "I'm a dead woman."

Chapter Thirty-seven

Victor didn't understand why Bella was so quick to sign the legal documents he brought her until he saw her sitting across the park. She didn't look anything like herself, dressed like an old woman the way she was, but Victor had spent way too much time looking into her beautiful gray eyes not to recognize them when he saw them. It didn't matter that she was wearing tons of makeup to age her, or that her baggy clothes hid her figure. She was his woman and he'd know her anywhere, if only by the way his cock woke up and took notice.

He stayed hidden behind the tinted windows of the van, watching her through binoculars.

She sat on a bench, working diligently on a crossword puzzle book. There was an air of watchfulness about her, but her gaze stayed fixed on the page. His guess was she was making use of at least one hidden camera and the screen was tucked inside the covers of her book.

His first instinct was to rush over and shut her down, toss her over his shoulder and dump her in the back of the van. Once he got her there, he wasn't entirely sure what he'd do with her, but it would likely involve some way to restrain her, spanking her ass for scaring him, and a whole lot of licking, kissing and teasing her until she promised never to put herself in harm's way again.

As if any of that would work on Bella.

He sighed in frustration, forcing his line of sight to extend beyond her and the immediate surrounding area. He was here to find Randolph and follow him back to wherever it was he called home. With any luck at all, the man would lead him to Stynger.

And if not, at least they'd have a nice, private place for the conversation that was headed his way.

There was too much at stake not to force Randolph to talk. Gage. Lila's baby. All those innocent souls tortured by Stynger.

Victor wasn't a fan of torture, but he knew the instant he heard about the child that things had changed. Either Randolph was working for Stynger willingly, which meant he deserved what he got, or he was a puppet and might still be able to help Victor take down the woman responsible for pulling the strings so he could be free. A good man would thank him for doing what was necessary to stop her, even if he had to endure a little torture to make it happen.

At least that was what Victor was telling himself.

That thought was better left for another time, so he set it aside and activated his comms. "Do you see her?" he asked Payton, who was in his own vehicle on the far side of the park. He didn't use Bella's name for fear that someone might be eavesdropping, but there was no doubt that Payton would figure it out.

"Someone needs to rein that girl in."

"Easier said than done."

The sun was below the horizon now, the sky darkening fast. It was warm enough for there to be a few people enjoying the park, but many of them began heading home in search of dinner and family time. A few joggers set out for some postwork exercise, but as the light failed, even their numbers grew thin.

Bella pushed to her feet slowly, displaying a convincing show of geriatric stiffness. Then again, after what she'd been through over the past few days, maybe it wasn't much of an act.

She settled on another bench a few yards away, doubtlessly seeking a different vantage point.

"What do you want to do?" Payton asked.

It was just the two of them here. Victor was afraid that if they pulled in any more people, the chances of being made would go way up. They couldn't afford that kind of mistake, even if it meant limiting their reach.

And if Victor was being entirely honest, he wondered if someone else at the Edge might be compromised the same way Lila was. Anyone willing to use a child as leverage had an unfair advantage when it came to turncoats. Only a fool would think otherwise. The fewer people involved in this delicate task, the better.

"Stick with the plan. We watch, look for a chance to plant trackers, and then follow. With any luck at all, he'll lead us closer to the prize."

"Our girl doesn't know the plan," Payton reminded him. "She's flying solo."

"I realize that, but if either one of us steps out there, we're made. He knows your face for sure, and I'm not about to risk him recognizing me. We sit tight."

"If something happens to her—"

"I know," Victor said. "Believe me. I'll be the first one sprinting that way, guns blazing. But for now we have to let this play out. It's what she'd want us to do." He knew it was, because he absolutely hated the idea of letting her sit out there in the open, an easy rifle shot from far too many hiding places. "I hope she has the good sense to at least have some body armor on."

"And a helmet under that wig," Payton added.

It wasn't possible, but Victor still let himself believe.

As the shadows lengthened across the grass, movement on his left caught his eye. A man on foot walked along a sidewalk that wound through the trees, snaking back and forth between park benches. A couple of joggers passed him by without a second glance, but there was something about him that piqued Victor's interest.

"See the man in the hoodie?" he asked Payton.

"Could be our man. He's heavier than I remember, but it could be something under his sweatshirt."

Victor had seen photos of Randolph from the employee records. The man was average height with dark, deeply recessed eyes. His dirty blond hair had been buzzed close to his skin, showing off several old scars along his scalp. He was built like a bull, with a thick neck and broad shoulders. The man walking across the park was covered enough that it was hard to tell if he matched that description, but the height was right. So was his walk. He moved like a man comfortable in his own skin, like a man with no fear of what might be heading his way.

"You have a better angle than I do," Victor said. "Can you see his face?"

"Not enough to be sure."

"He doesn't have Lila's son."

"Did you really think he would?" Payton asked. "No way would they give up an advantage like that. Lila was a fool to believe they would."

Old lady Bella never once looked up from her crossword puzzle book as the man neared, but there was a change in her demeanor, a subtle shift from vigilant to alert. "I think she recognizes him."

"She's going to go after him," Payton said. "Ruin the whole thing."

"She's smarter than that. He's not her target. The queen bee is. We've got to let this play out."

What choice did he have? If they rushed in to stop her from making contact, Randolph would know he'd been spotted. Their best bet was to tag his car and let him go on his merry way. Taking him into custody and questioning him was the backup plan—done only if plan A went to hell.

"I'm in the parking lot," Payton said, "putting trackers on every vehicle here."

"How many?"

"Six."

They could manage that many. The tracking equipment was in the back of Victor's van. If they kept eyes on Randolph, they'd be able to narrow down which signal was his without trouble.

"I've got an issue," Payton said.

"What?"

"Police just pulled in. I was only able to tag half the cars."

Shit. "Do you need a distraction? I could call in a burglary nearby."

"Hang on. Incoming." Payton's tone lightened and took on a nonthreatening lilt as he engaged in conversation with the police.

Victor kept tabs on it, but was far more concerned about the shortening distance between Bella and Randolph.

She shifted on the bench and reached into the huge handbag sitting next to her. A ball of yarn rolled out just as Randolph crossed her path. Bella stood to go after it. Before she could reach it, he stopped to pick it up. The second his attention was diverted on the yarn, she grabbed his arm as if she had lost her balance.

There was no doubt in Victor's mind that she'd just tagged him with a tracker. Now all she had to do was back off before she was recognized.

Victor's hands tightened around the binoculars. Bella was not the kind of woman who backed off from anything. She charged forward, roaring into battle against whatever foe stood in her way.

Randolph handed her the ball of yarn. She took it. Thanked him, keeping her head down. Shuffled back to her bench.

He kept walking to the place where he was supposed to meet Lila.

It had worked. Bella kept her cool. Victor held himself back from rushing in to save her when she didn't need it. Randolph was tagged and none the wiser.

Payton's voice rattled in Victor's comms, still dealing with the police. He was weaving some story about a lost coin that had rolled out of his hand and under the row of cars. The coin had been handed down to him by his grandfather, and had so much sentimental value that Payton simply couldn't walk away from it.

The officer was now helping him look for the coin while Payton tagged the rest of the cars in the lot with trackers.

Bella sat back down on the bench and went back to her crossword puzzle book. She'd angled it differently, so that it was facing Randolph, who was now several yards away.

He glanced over his shoulder at her. His pace slowed until he came to a stop.

Warning bells went off in Victor's head. This wasn't good. Randolph should have kept walking.

"We have a problem," Victor said. "Get the cop out of here."

"I found it!" shouted Payton with obvious relief. Under his breath, he said, "Status?"

Randolph turned around and looked at Bella. To her credit, she didn't once break character. She sat still and relaxed, a woman completely at ease.

He tilted his head, studying her. Turned around.

"Bella's been made," Victor said. "I'm going in."

Chapter Thirty-eight

Even on the tiny surveillance screen affixed to her crossword puzzle book, Bella could still see that Randolph had figured out she wasn't what she seemed.

Interacting with him had been a risk. She knew that, but it had been the best option she could think of with the limited time she'd had.

She sat still, hoping his suspicion would fade if she looked innocent. Just a little old lady enjoying some fresh air. Nothing to see. Just keep moving with that tracker in tow, asshole.

But he didn't keep moving. He studied her for what seemed like an hour, but was probably only a few seconds. His posture shifted slightly as he put his hands in the pockets of his hoodie.

Randolph was reaching for a weapon.

Bella was torn between staying in character and grabbing her own gun. If she shot him, he'd never carry that tracker anywhere near Stynger. If he shot her, she wouldn't be able to follow his movements. The only hope she had of finding Gage and Lila's baby was to sit completely still and pretend she wasn't bursting with the need for action.

Two seconds later, she knew her decision had been made for her.

The dark shadow of a matte black gun appeared in Randolph's hand. She was just about to jump over the bench and behind the nearby decorative rock wall she'd scouted earlier when a flash of movement caught her eye.

Victor was racing toward her, down the hill leading to their location. He lifted a silenced weapon and fired it at Randolph.

She was so stunned to see Victor that she hesitated. If she moved now, he would be the only available target. As the only good guy currently armed, her best chance was to make sure Victor stayed standing.

Randolph turned his attention on Victor. Bella charged Randolph, going in low to barrel into his gut. He fired off a shot before she made contact. There wasn't time to see if it had hit before she tackled him.

He went flying back, landing on his ass a few feet away. She took control of his weapon arm, using every bit of strength she had in both hands just to keep him pinned.

It wasn't enough. Randolph was stronger than she remembered. He flung her off with as little effort as it would have taken to move a small child. She slammed into the ground like some kind of floppy cartoon character. Her head hit hard, making her world erupt into screaming pain.

A pitiful, agonizing sound ripped free of her against her will. Bright blobs of color swam through her field of vision, shimmering as they went.

He picked her up and pinned her to his front like a living shield. Bella tried to fight him, but she couldn't quite remember where she'd left her hands. Wherever they were, she couldn't feel them.

Victor lifted his weapon slightly, but his finger moved from the trigger. "Let her go, Randolph."

"Yeah. I'll get right on that. Right after you drop the weapon and kick it my way."

"I don't have to drop anything. There are cops down in the parking lot. All I have to do is wait right here for them to arrest all of us and sort it out. I'm pretty sure I'll be free in a couple of hours. How about you?"

Tension vibrated through Randolph's hold on her. She couldn't see any cops, but there were about three parking lots stacked on top of one another from what she could tell, and every one of them was a wild blur.

"You're lying," Randolph said.

Victor shrugged. He was so damn handsome it made her heart lurch toward him. Even now, with a pissed-off ex-employee holding a gun to her head, she still couldn't get over just how much she loved him.

Love?

Now she knew she was concussed. She wasn't loving any man ever again. Doing so once had nearly killed her. "I'm not going to love you," she shouted at Victor, just so he'd know where she stood. "I don't care how many assholes put guns to my head."

Victor's voice was gentle, concerned. "Bella, you hit your head. You're bleeding. We need to get you to a hospital. Can you get free?"

Of course she could get free. All she had to do is figure out how to stand up without Randolph's help.

"Sorry I scrambled your girlfriend's brains," Randolph said. "She's hot, but then the crazy ones usually are. Too bad she's also got a raging case of controlling bitch to go along with that hard body."

That pissed her off. Her swing was awkward, but she managed to land a blow along the underside of his chin.

The barrel of the gun left her head for a split second— just long enough for him to slam the butt of it into her temple.

She felt herself slip away as unconsciousness took her.

The last thing she saw was Victor's too-perfect face twisted by his horrified expression. After that, there was nothing.

Victor nearly lost it when Randolph knocked Bella out cold. She was already bleeding badly from where her head had been slammed into a rock earlier. He'd tossed her around like a rag doll, displaying the kind of inhuman strength Victor had seen only in other men altered by Stynger's research.

It wouldn't have taken much effort at all for Randolph to rip her apart, killing her with his bare hands.

The comms unit came to life in Victor's ear. "Cops heard the shot. They've called for backup and are moving in. Clear out."

Victor debated his options. Bella had planted the tracker. Her stuff was still sitting on the park bench. It wouldn't take much to find the signal and trace where it led. But in order to do that, he was going to have to let Randolph go. With Bella.

Another option was to kill the man where he stood. But if he did that, no one would ever follow him again.

The last option was to stand here until the cops arrived. Everyone would be taken in and Randolph would likely never walk free again. If he did, it wouldn't be with a tracker in place.

Gage would stay missing, as would Lila's boy.

"Let Bella go and you can walk away," Victor said.

Randolph laughed as he backed up. "The second I drop her, I'm a dead man."

"Cops are headed this way. If you don't drop the gun, you're going to be taken down, anyway."

He frowned, turning his head slightly as if he heard something. "I thought you were lying about the cops."

"They can't see us from the other side of the hill, but

they're not far. You've got a few seconds at most. Drop her and you might have time to get away."

Randolph lifted her over his shoulder. She was pale and limp, blood dripping from her head, wetting the gray wig she wore.

Victor tried not to let the sight cloud his thinking, but it was impossible. The woman he loved was in the hands of an enraged man who was likely under the control of a lunatic scientist. Once Bella was out of his sight, there was no way he could protect her. For all he knew Randolph would let her bleed out or toss her out of his car as he sped down the highway.

"Let the woman go," he warned.

"I like my chances better with her in tow. Tell the cops I said hi." Randolph turned and sprinted for the strip of woods at the back of the park.

Victor lifted his weapon, but he had no clear shot. Bella's head was swaying across Randolph's spine with each step, making any shot too much of a risk.

Instead, he holstered his weapon and set out at a dead sprint after him. He'd gone no more than ten paces when an artificially amplified voice boomed across the park. "Stop and drop your weapon!"

The police had arrived, and if Victor didn't do as they ordered, he was risking being shot. If he ended up dead, he wasn't going to be able to go after Bella. The thought of letting her rot in some lab of Stynger's while they did God knew what to the woman Victor loved stopped him cold.

All he had to do was survive long enough to follow Randolph and save Bella. Nothing else mattered.

Victor put his hands in the air and waited for the police to come for him. "Payton, Randolph has Bella. She's unconscious. She planted a tracker on him. Her gear is probably in her bag on the park bench. You need to get it and follow them."

"I'm sorry, but I'm currently being detained."

"Get on the ground," came the next authoritative command from the police.

Victor turned around to see what kind of odds he faced. There were four uniformed officers here, and every one of them had a gun trained on him. Their pistols weren't accurate at this range. Neither was his. He'd never even consider shooting one of them—these were good men doing their jobs—but that didn't mean he was going to stand around and take orders when Bella's life hung in the balance.

Someone had to be free to go on a rescue mission. If Payton couldn't do it, then Victor would.

"Can you give me a distraction?" Victor asked, moving his lips as little as possible.

"Are you sure?" Payton asked.

"She's hurt. Unconscious."

A roar of fury erupted in Victor's ear as Payton went berserk. Two of the officers here became distracted with what was going on at the bottom of the hill.

Victor wasn't going to get better odds than these, so he sprinted for the trees, following the path that Randolph had taken.

Weapons discharged behind him, but he wasn't hit. He kept running, praying their aim wouldn't improve.

Chapter Thirty-nine

Jordyn answered her mother's summons with fear twisting in her gut.

She'd been expecting her punishment, but knowing that it was here, and that she had no choice but to endure it was enough to make her shake and sweat.

She'd showered, put on comfortable clothes, and pulled her hair back in a braid so that she wouldn't get vomit in it when the drugs took effect. As sensitive as her stomach had been lately, there was no doubt in her mind that she'd get sick in the White Room.

Still, no matter what Mother did to Jordyn there, Gage was alive and well. Whatever suffering she had to go through to pay for that was worth the price.

At least she thought so now. Once the pain started, it would be a lot harder to remember that.

With shaking hands, she opened the door to the White Room. As its name implied, everything inside was glaringly bright. Sterile walls were broken up only by a window leading to a soundproof observation room. The floor was shiny white tile with a drain in the center to wash down the mess left behind. The ceiling was an array of lights so bright it hurt to look up at them. In the center of the space was a stainless table complete with straps to hold down whoever was unlucky enough to be restrained here.

Right now that table housed a small boy young enough to still be in diapers. He was sobbing, fighting against the restraints caging his little body. An IV fed into his arm. It was attached to a pump stocked with three different colored liquids.

Jordyn knew from experience that when injected, each one of them created a new definition of pain.

Behind the glass, in the soundproof room, stood Mother. A tech sat at the control panel, looking a little queasy himself. Jordyn had never spoken to the man, but she recognized him from all the times she'd been the one strapped to the table. She'd always thought that he seemed to enjoy his job. Until now.

Outrage slapped her hard, driving away the worst of her fear. What possible gain could Mother get from punishing a child like this? He was too little to have information she wanted. He was too young to remember whatever lesson she thought to teach him. All she was going to do was cause him pain.

"What is this?" Jordyn asked, her voice shaking more with anger than fear.

"You defied me," Mother said. "I've tried over and over again to rid you of your rebellious streak, and yet you continue to do what you know will displease me. I thought a different sort of lesson was in order—one that would teach you that your actions have consequences for others, not just yourself."

Jordyn's blood began to chill as the meaning became clear. "You would torture a child to teach me a lesson?"

"If that's what it takes, yes."

"You could kill him."

"I'm aware. But don't worry. He bears no scientific importance. He's just a normal child."

"You think *that's* what worries me? Do you have no soul at all?"

Mother frowned in displeasure. "Souls are fantasies conjured up by religious zealots. I raised you to know better than to buy into such myths."

"That answers my question. Of course the woman with no soul would think they didn't exist."

"Don't you get lippy with me, girl. I can make this experience far worse for the child if that's what it takes to reestablish your respect."

Jordyn began unhooking the little boy's IV. "There's not a damn thing you could ever do that would make me respect you. Torture me, torture my friends, torture innocent children . . . all it does is prove my point that you're not worthy of respect from anyone."

"My scientific accomplishments are groundbreaking."

"If you call manipulation and brute force groundbreaking, perhaps. Me? I tend to think of it more as excessive bullying."

"How dare you? I bore you, raised you, taught you everything you know."

"Not everything. Somewhere along the way I learned compassion—something you wouldn't recognize if you sat on it. Face it, Mother, I'm a better woman than you will ever be."

"Weaker."

"Kinder."

"Less dedicated."

"More caring."

Mother's face darkened to an angry shade of red that nearly matched her lipstick. "Naive."

Jordyn cradled the child and kept her voice calm in an effort to soothe him. "Sympathetic."

"None of that will serve you well where we're going."

"I hate to break this to you, but I'm not going any-

where. I'm an adult now. You can't force me to go with
you like you could when I was a child."

"You're *my* daughter. You'll go where I tell you."

"You know what, Mother? There's something I've
been meaning to say to you—something long overdue."
Jordyn pulled in a deep breath to steady her nerves and
make sure she was clearly heard. "Fuck you, you heart-
less bitch."

She didn't stop to think about what she'd done. She
simply turned and walked out of the room with the toddler, ignoring Mother's screaming through the speakers
behind her.

Such defiance was likely going to come back to haunt
her, but for now it felt really good.

Now all she had to do was keep the little boy safe
until she could find a way out.

Fortunately, she knew exactly where to take him.

Chapter Forty

Victor met Adam in the back booth of a small diner outside of town. "Were you able to get it?"

Adam pushed a padded envelope across the table. "I had to break about ten laws, but yes. I got it. If you'd called any later, it would have been in the evidence locker and completely out of reach."

Victor looked inside the envelope and saw the tracking signal receiver matching the device Bella had planted on Randolph.

"Stynger had protocols for checking for tracking devices. There's no way that made it past her security."

"Maybe not, but it was live when Bella tagged him. If it gets us closer, then it's better than what we have now."

"I want my brother back as badly as you want Bella. I've been calling in every favor I have, using every resource at my disposal. I'm desperate to get him out of Stynger's hands, but we have to be careful. If any of this looks too easy, it's because Stynger is luring us in. It would be just like her to make us think we have a shot so she can be there waiting, goons armed and ready to mow us down."

"I'll be careful. We know she'll move soon. If we get close, then maybe we have a chance to see the activity on satellite. It's got to be quite an endeavor to move that many people and that much equipment."

"She always did it in stages. Moved slowly over time, at night. She employed various types of trucks, following different paths. Believe me, if we've thought of using it against her, she's already covered it. The woman is smart. Cunning."

"You probably know her better than anyone. She's got to have a weakness."

Adam shook his head. "She has a tendency to be a bit overconfident, but not often. There's a reason we haven't caught her yet, and it's not for lack of trying."

"I have to try. Even if Bella would normally be able to fight her way free, she's injured. I could see in her eyes that she wasn't thinking clearly. She looked confused and disoriented."

"I'll back your play. Payton should be able to join us soon."

"I figured he'd be detained for a while," Victor said.

"That man has more favors saved up than anyone alive. When I was at the precinct, he was cashing all of them in to get out of there."

"Did you bring the gear I asked for?"

Adam nodded. "I did. Mira's in, too, but she's doing it from a distance. I'm not risking her life ever again. I still have nightmares about what she went through with her father."

"I understand. Mira's more use in front of a keyboard, anyway."

"She already did a scan for all of Bella's personal trackers. The ones in her keys, her purse, her dog tags, her car ... they're all dead. If she was wearing one, Stynger found it."

"Could there be any others we don't know about?"

Adam shook his head. "Mira knows them all. I'm sorry."

"At least she tried."

"What's your plan?" asked Adam.

"We go to the place where the tracker Bella planted on Randolph was last detected and see what's there."

"Mira did that."

"And?"

"There was nothing. It was in the middle of nowhere, miles from any paved roads."

"Just the kind of place Stynger likes, away from prying eyes," Victor said.

"That's what I thought, too."

"Care to join me?"

Adam grinned. "I was hoping you'd ask."

Jordyn went straight to Gage's room, toddler in tow. She didn't dare let the boy out of her sight for fear of what Mother might do.

Jordyn had riled the beast. It was only a matter of time before it came back to bite her.

The boy fell asleep in her arms within minutes, exhausted from crying. His fingers were in his mouth, drool painting his chin. She walked with purpose, head high and forcing herself to look each guard in the eye as she passed so they wouldn't question her presence with the child.

When she came to Gage's door, she shot the guard an expectant look, then glanced pointedly at the knob. "My hands are full," she said with curt impatience.

The guard hurried to let her in, shutting and locking the door behind her.

Gage woke immediately as she walked in. She could see a haze of drugs clouding his eyes, but she didn't doubt for a second that he was alert enough to do whatever needed to be done.

His gaze moved to the child. Something in his face

shifted, softening his expression. He nodded once as if resolved to something, then eased himself upright. "Friend of yours?"

"Mother was going to torture him. I decided not to let it happen."

"Good choice."

She kissed the top of the boy's head, marveling in the softness of his skin. "One I'll pay for later, no doubt. Which is why I intend to be gone from here soon. How are you feeling?"

"Depends."

"On what?"

"Are we walking out or running?"

"Mother won't let us leave. We're going to have to fight our way free."

"Weapons?" he asked.

She didn't know if she could get her hands on anything conventional, but there was a chance she could come up with something. There were some tranquilizer guns they used on lab animals. One of them might go a long way toward getting free. "I'll see what I can do. But I can't take him with me and I don't dare leave him alone."

Gage scooted over on the bed, wincing as he moved. "There's room here."

"You'll guard him?"

He nodded slowly, giving her the oddest stare, like he was making plans that involved her somehow. "With my life."

"You should get all the sleep you can. You're going to need your strength."

He grinned. "Yes, ma'am."

She settled the boy on the bed next to him. His thick arm cradled the child, keeping him from rolling onto the floor. In that moment she knew she'd made the right choice. Gage wouldn't let anything happen to the toddler. Not even Mother.

"I'll be back as soon as I can. If you don't see me in one hour, find a way out without me."

"Not going to happen," he said.

She nodded toward the boy. "He needs you to make it happen."

Gage was silent for a long time, simply staring at her like he was coming to some kind of decision. She was just about to say something when he broke his gaze and looked at her lab coat pocket. "I need your pen."

She handed it to him without question. If he wanted to write a note for a loved one, or pen some kind of hate letter to Mother, that was fine with her. Whatever got him ready to move when the time came. "Anything else?"

"There's something you should know."

"What? There's not a lot of time to do what I need to do. There are no guarantees Mother won't come for me to punish me before we get free. If she does, it will be days before I can walk again. I need all the time I can get to find weapons and clear our path."

He hesitated for a second, then shook his head. "It can wait. Stay sharp."

She nodded. "One hour, Gage. No longer."

"I'll be here."

Chapter Forty-one

Bella woke up with her head splitting into fragments of pain. She tried to reach for her skull to hold the pieces together, but her arms wouldn't move. Panic cleared away a bit of the fog and forced her to open her eyes.

Light drilled through her eyeballs and into her skull. The pounding increased until she was barely staving off the urge to puke.

"I'd rather you not choke on your own vomit," said a woman. "You have far too much potential to die like that."

The whole surface under Bella spun until she was upright, suspended by a series of wide straps. A pair of black high heels on the ends of scrawny legs came into her field of view. She followed those legs upward, recognizing the sticklike figure of a woman Bella knew all too well.

Dr. Norma Stynger's bright red mouth curved in a smile. "Better?" she asked with mock concern.

"Where am I? How did I get here?"

"Randolph brought you here as a courtesy. I heard you were dead, but I can see that report was premature."

"Why am I here?"

"I understand you've been looking for me. I've been hoping we might have the chance to meet."

Cold dread settled over Bella's skin. "Where is Gage?"

Stynger ignored the question. "How's your head? You took a nasty blow. I stitched you up, but I'm afraid you've sustained a concussion. It's a shame, really. I'd hoped to give you the best odds."

"Odds of what?"

"Surviving the surgery, of course."

Bella didn't need to hear more to understand exactly what the woman was going to do to her. She'd seen it too many times in others—the scar at the base of the skull. The implants that were driven into people's brains, turning them into little more than mindless puppets. "I'll die before I let you do that to me."

Stynger continued as if Bella hadn't spoken a word. "I'd like to wait until the swelling goes down, but there just isn't time. I need you ready for transport too soon. And the first twenty-four hours are . . . precarious."

Bella strained against the straps holding her in place. Not only were they too secure for her to break, the effort made her head throb.

"You really should rest while you can. I'll be back in a few hours to check on you. I have a couple of arrangements to finish for our relocation, but I should be able to start the surgery tonight. Most of my female subjects didn't survive, but you're stronger than they were. I'm sure of it." She patted Bella's arm. "You're going to wake up tomorrow feeling like a new woman. Assuming you wake up at all."

There was no way in hell Gage was leaving Jordyn behind. Not only was she carrying his child, she was far too kind to deal with the level of psychotic violence Stynger could dish out.

The little boy snoozing beside him proved just how low the bitch would go.

Rage tried to gain a foothold in Gage's chest, but he took deep breaths, staving it off as much as he could. Jordyn wasn't the only one who needed to stay sharp and focused. He did as well.

He'd almost told her about the baby. She had a right to know. But he didn't dare take the chance that the shock would slow her down or distract her. She was determined to do what needed to be done to free them. For now that had to be enough.

As soon as they were out of here he'd tell her. He didn't know her well enough to have a clue how she'd react, but whatever her reaction, he'd deal with it then.

He had to admit that she looked comfortable holding the little boy. There was no awkwardness or hesitance. Her instincts to protect him had taken hold and compelled her to act. It was the kind of thing any good mother would do.

That reassured Gage on a level so deep he hadn't even realized how worried he'd been.

He pulled the sheet up over his lap to hide his actions from the cameras he was certain had to be watching. He unscrewed the pen and used the clip to make quick work of picking the lock on his handcuffs. Once that was done, he screwed it back together and readied it to be used as a stabbing weapon if the shit hit the fan.

An hour was a long wait—more than enough time for excrement to start flying.

Chapter Forty-two

Bella was sweating and panting from her efforts to get free when the door opened and Randolph walked in.

"Didn't think I'd see you again," she said. "Figured you'd be slinking off with your reward by now."

"Stynger and I don't see eye to eye on my pay for the job of bringing you in. I decided to take my own benefits where I could find them."

There had been a time when Bella had liked this man. He'd been easy to laugh, good at his job and even better with a rifle. If not for his overconfidence and a morally gray streak that made him genetically incapable of following the rules even when he had no reason not to, he would have been an asset to the company. He'd fooled her for a while, covering up his mistakes with grand, nearly heroic stories. But eventually she'd figured it out. He was just one more cocky asshole with a gun and a desire to pull the trigger as often as possible.

"Here for a little slap and tickle, heavy on the slap?" she asked.

He snorted. "Don't flatter yourself. I prefer my women a little softer than rawhide."

"At least now I know you like women. I always wondered." The straps holding her to the steel table cut into her skin. It took all her willpower not to keep working to loosen them.

A rolling table draped with a blue cloth sat in one corner of the room. He pulled the cloth away to reveal an array of surgical instruments.

Bella's blood froze solid, stopping her heart for a few painful seconds. She had to take several breaths before she could find enough air to speak. When she did, she tried not to sound as terrified as she was. "So, is this the part where you exact your pound of flesh, then?"

He ran his finger over the instruments as if trying to decide which one to use first. "You know what your problem is?"

"I'm strapped to this fucking table?" she asked. "You could fix that, you know. Let me free. We could sit down and discuss your grievances. If it will make you feel better, I could go back and redo your performance evaluations. Add team player to the list of your attributes."

"You never think things through," he said, as if she hadn't spoken. "That's your problem. You charge in, certain you know exactly what's going on when you really only have half of the story."

"Are you saying I only know half of your story? And that if I'd known the whole thing I wouldn't have fired you? Feel free to enlighten me."

He picked up a scalpel and tested its edge on his forearm, cleanly slicing away the hair there. "I was finally getting my shit together when I came to work for you. My parents were proud. My ex stopped bitching that I never paid her child support. Hell, even my bookie was smiling."

"If you liked your job so much, then why did you kill that kid?"

"You say I don't follow orders, but that's exactly what I was doing at the time. You said to take out the hostiles. They were shooting at our principal's motorcade. We had every right to defend him and ourselves."

"You had no right to shoot a child."

"She had no right to be in the way. They were using her as a fucking human shield."

"I don't care!" Bella shouted, making her head pound. "You find another way. You don't mow through innocents."

"It's not like her life would have been worth living. Poverty, squalor, life as some man's property. I was doing her a favor."

"Yeah? Maybe someone should have done you that favor when you were a kid and saved us all the trouble of locking you up now."

He balled up his fist and hit her. She didn't even see it coming. Her already concussed head screamed in agony, and her vision dimmed for a few seconds.

When her bell stopped ringing, he had her hair in his fist and his face only inches from hers. "See what I mean? You never think."

"Kinda hard to think when you're scrambling my brains like that. How about you let a girl free and we'll fight it out like men."

Randolph laughed. "I just bet you would have liked to have been born with a dick."

"I bet you would have, too."

His expression tightened into a snarl. She was sure he was going to hit her again, but instead he backed away and went to the little table of instruments. "I'm done letting you get under my skin, because in a few hours, Stynger is going to get under yours. She's going to shove one of her toys in your brain, and you'll know exactly what it's like to have someone boss you around."

"No, thanks. I'll pass, honey."

He picked up an electric razor. "No more passes, *honey*. Time to prep you for surgery."

Chapter Forty-three

It had taken Jordyn nearly an hour to do what she needed to do. The wheeled cart stocked with instruments and boxes helped give her an air of legitimacy. Her rushed demeanor and a healthy dose of fear did the rest.

Every tech she passed gave her that sympathetic look that told her they knew what it was like to be on an errand for Dr. Norma Stynger.

All around the labs, techs were packing up equipment and files. Jordyn hadn't been notified of the exact time of the move, but it had to be happening soon. The groups were intentionally compartmentalized to keep socializing to a minimum, but each group would be moved as a unit.

The blue unit was apparently the next one on the truck to wherever it was they were going this time.

A group of guards oversaw the whole process, but she doubted that a single one of them would know what any of the equipment being packed was for. All they were probably worried about was making sure it all got packed on time so there were no delays.

Jordyn was counting on it.

She pilfered what she needed, tucking it all inside boxes, out of sight. The red unit next door was asleep, giving her plenty of room to work. She did everything she could think to do, including a little bit of hacking into the security system. The delays she set were already counting down when she made it back to Gage's room.

This time she didn't have to be let in. The door was wide open and filled with a pair of burly guards.

Jordyn shoved her way between them with one of her boxes of contingency plans. Inside the room, Gage was holding off another pair of guards with her ballpoint pen. The little boy was screaming in fear, dangling from Gage's arm. Another guard was on the floor, blood pooling under his head. There was a ragged hole where his eye had once been. The other eye stared sightlessly in death.

One of the guards leveled a weapon at Gage's head. "Let go of the kid," he demanded.

Gage said nothing, but the look he gave the man was sharp enough to cut glass.

"This isn't going to end well for you. You're already bleeding all over the place."

And he was. A trickle of blood was seeping out from under his bandages, which were soaked through bright red.

"What's going on here?" Jordyn asked, working hard to sound like she had every right to know.

"Doc sent us for the kid," said the nearest guard.

"I don't care who sent you. I put that child here myself. Now go find someone else to bother."

"Can't do that, ma'am. We have orders."

They also had implants driven into their brains that made them incapable of defying those orders.

Jordyn had no choice but to use up one of her tricks now.

She caught Gage's eye. "Remember the gum?"

He nodded.

"Deep breath."

She wasn't sure if he understood what she was going to do or not, but there was no more time to explain. She used one hand to strap a mask on over her nose and mouth while opening the valve on the pressurized container with the other. The gas they pumped into rooms at night to keep people asleep flooded the space with a fine mist. She grabbed up the second mask she'd brought with her and tossed it toward Gage. "Heads up!"

She couldn't see if he caught it or not. The air was too thick. She did, however, hear several heavy bodies hit the ground. The little boy's screams cut off, leaving the room blissfully quiet. Only the faint hiss of the emptying can of sedative remained.

Jordyn stumbled over one of the guards toward Gage. She was close enough now to see he was still on his feet, mask in place.

She took the child from his hands and hurried him out of the room before he could breathe in too much of the gas.

Gage was right on her heels.

As soon as they were in the hall, she grabbed the wheeled cart with one hand and pulled. "We have about a minute before every lock in this place opens and every alarm goes off."

He took the cart from her hands, freeing her to maneuver the child easier. She wasn't sure if he was trying to help, or if he needed to lean on something. From the look of the blood seeping into his pajama pants, his surgical wound had reopened.

"How are you doing?" she asked.

"Keep moving."

"There's a tranquilizer gun on the bottom shelf of the cart. It's only got three shots in it before you have to reload."

"Range?"

"None. You have to touch them with it to trigger it."

They were almost out of the medical wing when there was an audible click of every electronic lock opening at once. A heartbeat later, sirens began to blare and lights started flashing.

The little boy didn't even stir. If not for the strong pounding of his pulse under her hands, she would have worried he'd been hurt.

"Will the elevators lock down?" he asked.

"No. I overrode that part of the code." She hoped. Otherwise, they were trapped down here. There were no stairs leading up, no other way out.

Jordyn turned the corner, but Gage was no longer with her. She backtracked to see where he'd gone and found him disappearing into one of the surgical rooms.

The second she looked through the glass window, she knew their escape had just gotten a lot harder.

There was a tall, dark-haired woman strapped face-down on one of the surgical tables. The back of her head had been shaved, and whoever had done it hadn't been careful. Her skin was bleeding in several places, matting what little hair was left. Her arms were bruised and bloody from where she'd been fighting to escape.

As still as she was now, there seemed to be no fight left in her.

"Bella?" Gage said, leaning down to see her face through the horseshoe headrest.

She let out a rough moan and started thrashing.

He put his hand on her arm. "Easy."

"Gage?" Her voice was thick and muffled.

He began to undo the straps holding her down. "Hang on."

She was barely free when she burst off the table like she was spring-loaded. Her face was bruised and covered in drying blood. Her bangs were matted with more blood. Both lips were swollen as if she'd taken a couple of hard hits.

She swayed on her feet. Gage grabbed her arm to steady her. As soon as her eyes focused on him, she launched herself at him, grabbing him in a hard hug. "You're alive!" She let out a sob of relief before catching herself and regaining control.

Jordyn watched the display, marveling over it. She'd never seen people hug like that before in person. She'd seen it on the Internet, but never in real life. It was so . . . intimate.

A spike of jealousy caught her off guard. She knew better than to think she had any right to mind if the two of them stripped down and had sex right here on the floor, but that didn't stop her from wanting to finish ripping the woman's hair out.

He hugged her back, but not nearly as hard. Fresh blood oozed from his bandage. After a couple of seconds, he pulled away, allowing Jordyn room to breathe again.

"You good to go?" he asked Bella, holding her face between his hands so she had no choice but to look him in the eye.

She gave a weak nod. "Always. But they dosed me with something. If I start acting screwy, don't hesitate to knock me out."

"Screwy?" Gage asked.

"You'll know it if you see it."

He nodded.

"I'm Jordyn." She shifted the boy's weight to offer her hand.

Bella didn't take it. She looked at Jordyn with suspicion. "Stynger's daughter?"

"Unfortunately."

"She saved my life," Gage said.

Bella nodded, seemingly satisfied with his reference, then turned to Gage. "What's the plan?"

"Follow Jordyn."

Bella picked up a scalpel from the instrument table. "Lead on. If you see that asshole Randolph, he's mine."

Jordyn knew the man and wanted nothing to do with him. He was selfish in a way that suited Mother well. As long as she had something he wanted, he was her pawn.

"This way," Jordyn said as she led them down the hall. "The elevators aren't far."

Gage was right on her heels, sticking close. Every few seconds his hand would brush against her arm so she'd know he was still there. If not for the reassurance of his presence, she would have been terrified right now. As it was, she was merely scared.

Jordyn turned the last corner before the elevators. A pair of guards were waiting for them no more than fifty feet away.

They opened fire.

Chapter Forty-four

Gage jerked Jordyn back before she could take a hit. In the split second that passed between when he saw the threat and reacted to it, he realized just how much she meant to him. How much their child meant to him.

He hadn't asked to be tied to her in this way. Neither had she. But they were tied, and unless and until that changed, he would protect his family with his life.

She looked up at him, pale and shaking, her pretty eyes filled with fear as she cradled the little boy against her chest. "They're blocking the exit. What do we do now?"

"Make a hole," Gage said.

Bullets ripped into the nearby wall. Splinters of concrete showered over them.

"Easier said than done without any real weapons," Bella said.

"There's another pressurized can of sedative on the cart," Jordyn said. "But I only brought two masks. I wasn't expecting company."

"Stay here. I'll go back for it," Bella said. She was gone before anyone could argue.

If he didn't make it out of here, there would be no one

outside of the labs who could explain to Jordyn what had been done to her—that she'd been impregnated with a virtual stranger's baby without her knowledge or consent. She was smart and would figure it out eventually, but it was dangerous for her not to know she was pregnant. Even that sedative that she had been toting around could be harmful.

"Your mother did something to you," he said, wondering how one eased into such a subject.

"She did a lot of things to me. I've never been anything more to her than an interesting experiment."

"No, she—" His words were cut off by another volley of gunfire. The men's voices were closer now as they coordinated their attack.

Gage was running out of time. They all were.

He gripped the tranquilizer gun tighter, readying it to strike whoever came around the corner first.

Blood dripped along his ribs. The top of his pants were wet and cold with it, making him wonder just how much he could bleed before his strength failed him completely.

"She what?" Jordyn asked. "If you know that Mother did something to me, you have to tell me."

There was no easy way to say it, so he just set the words loose. "You're pregnant with my baby."

He saw shock ricochet through her system, rocking her visibly. She blinked a couple of times, her jaw slack. The little boy began slipping from her grip before she shifted him back against her chest. "You had sex with me while I was unconscious?"

"No. I never touched you. I was asleep, too."

"How . . . ?" Her eyes widened with understanding. "That was the DNA sample she took, the one in your file. She . . . violated you."

"Not as much as she violated you. I'm sorry, Jordyn. I would have stopped it if I'd known."

She shook her head. "There's nothing you could have done. Mother always gets what she wants. Our child is just one more experiment to her." She went still, then looked him in the eye. "Our child. The concept seems impossible."

He'd had more time to digest it than she had, but even he still had trouble wrapping his head around it. The only thing he knew for sure was that he had to see Jordyn safely out of this place so that she could start making decisions for herself for the first time in her life.

One way or another, he would free her from Stynger's grasp.

Another burst of gunfire cut off whatever he might have said. Not that he had any clue what to say in a situation like this. There were no words. All he could do was shield Jordyn, the boy and their unborn child with his body and pray for a miracle.

Bella came around the corner, hands full. She slid to a stop, holding out her findings.

Gage picked up a mask and fit it over Jordyn's head. He opened the canister of sedative and tossed it around the corner.

More shots went off before falling silent.

Footsteps and voices sounded behind them.

"We have company," Bella said. She pulled on a mask and darted out of sight toward the elevators. A second later, she came back with a pair of ARs taken off of fallen guards. "I'll cover your exit," she told Gage. "Take them and run."

Gage knew that if he did that, Bella would die down here. He loved her too much to let it happen.

He picked up one of the ARs, using his free hand to push Jordyn toward the elevators. "Go. I'll be on the next ride up."

"You heard her. Come with me."

"Not yet. Now go. I need you to live—both of you."

The tears in her eyes told him that she understood what he meant—that he needed her to get their child to safety.

She nodded and kissed his cheek. "I'll be waiting for you topside."

"No. Go to the road. Hide. I'll find you."

Before she could hesitate more, he pushed her gently toward the elevators.

She cleared the corner just as a horde of Stynger's soldiers came charging down the hall.

"There's nothing here," Victor said, scouring the landscape for some sign of an entrance to Stynger's labs.

Mira sat in the back of the mobile command center—MCC—surrounded by computers and gadgets. "This is where the tracker on Randolph stopped dead. The trail is cold."

Adam pulled the RV-turned-MCC over to the side of the road. It was loaded with instruments and weapons, along with a decent array of first aid supplies and tactical gear. If they could find where Randolph had gone, this vehicle had the resources to support a small war.

Payton was riding shotgun, talking quietly on a satellite phone to General Norwood. "We're visible on satellite," he said to the group, "but there's nothing nearby to indicate where Randolph might have gone."

Mira typed furiously on a keyboard, doing who-knew-what. Adam got out from behind the wheel and joined Victor in back. "We could set out on foot. Things look different from the ground than they do from above. Stynger is smart enough to hide her facility from the eyes in the sky."

Victor shook his head. "We don't have that kind of time. If we pick the wrong direction, Bella is as good as dead."

"Not necessarily," said Mira. "Stynger is far more

likely to experiment on her for a while than she is to kill her outright. That would be wasteful."

The idea made Victor's heart lurch into his throat.

Adam patted Mira's shoulder. "Not helpful, love."

She looked up from her computer screen. "Maybe it's not a warm, fuzzy thought, but I'd far rather find Bella alive and part cyborg than find her dead. We can fix cyborg."

Payton rose from the front seat. "We have a live feed. Someone is on foot nearby."

Mira switched computers and pulled up the image of someone headed their way with a large bundle held against their chest.

"Can you zoom in?" Victor asked.

She did, revealing a woman with long dark hair on the screen. She looked around like she was afraid of what might be on her heels.

"That's Jordyn Stynger," Payton said.

"What's she carrying?" Mira asked.

"Who cares?" Victor said, who was already strapping on equipment. "She knows the way in. She can lead us to Bella."

"You don't know what's going on," Payton said. "We need a plan."

Victor picked up several spare magazines of ammunition and headed for the door. "I make her lead me to Bella. That's my plan."

Before anyone else could argue, he was gone, jogging toward the woman.

He found her a few hundred yards away, stumbling toward the road. It wasn't a bundle she carried, but a small child. Her pale face was streaked with tears, and some sort of gas mask dangled from her neck.

As soon as she saw him, she came to a dead stop. He could see a decision warring in her mind. Did she stand her ground or flee?

Victor really didn't feel like chasing her. "I'm not going to hurt you," he said. "All I need to know is how to get inside the labs."

She cradled the child closer. "Who are you?"

"I'm looking for Bella Bayne. That's all you need to know."

"Are you going to hurt her?"

"No. I'm going to get her out of that place and bring her home."

The woman nodded. Swallowed. "Is there a safe place I can leave him?"

"I have friends nearby."

"They won't hurt him?"

"They'll keep him safe. I promise."

"Okay, then. Show me your friends and I'll show you the way in and give you the codes you need to get through the doors. Just promise me that you'll get Gage out, too."

"He's one of ours. Of course I will."

"Then we'd better hurry. He and Bella were taking fire when I left."

Bella was alive. That was his first thought. But before any kind of relief could set in, he realized the rest of what she'd said.

Victor took the child from her arms and sprinted for the MCC. The woman he loved was under attack, and everything in him demanded that he save her. She might not like his old-fashioned sentiment, but that was just too damn bad. If she didn't want to be saved, then she could just get a safer job. A man could only take so much.

Bella and Gage were pinned down. They couldn't make it to the elevators, and they couldn't move away from the doorway they currently used for cover.

She was trying to conserve ammunition, but they were still running out. Even worse, Gage's bleeding hadn't stopped, even after he'd put pressure on the wound. His skin was ashen, he was sweating, and she could see his pulse fluttering in his throat.

The man didn't have much time.

The need to find the closest closet to burrow in nearly overwhelmed her. She was tired. Weak. All she wanted to do was hide until the danger went away, just like she used to do with Dan.

No! She wasn't that person anymore. That was just Stynger's fucked-up drugs talking. She was strong. She was a fighter. She didn't need any damn closets.

"I'm not letting you die," she told Gage, "so don't even think about it. I've spent weeks looking for you. We are making it out of here."

"Yes, ma'am," was all he said, and even that sounded weak.

Randolph's voice echoed down the long hallway. "You can't make it out of here, Bella. You might as well give up before we have to kill you."

Her voice shook, and she hoped it sounded more like fury than fear coming through. "I'd rather die than let you cut into my skull."

"I can arrange that, but the good doctor has her heart set on playing with you for a while before she opens you up to see what makes you tick."

"You want to know what makes me tick?" she shouted. "Beating the hell out of you. That's what's keeping me going, you fucking asshole."

"Go for the exit," Gage said, his voice quiet. "I'll cover you."

She wanted to run. Hide. She wanted it so bad her muscles began tensing in an effort to move her body in that direction. She had to fight the urge and stand her ground. "You can barely hold your own head up, much less a weapon. We go together or we don't go at all."

His head slumped back against the wall and he swallowed weakly. "Can't walk."

"Then I'll carry you. Now stand up. That's an order."

She helped him to his feet, feeling just how much effort the move cost him. Gage was no lightweight, and between his blood loss and her own recent visit to concussionville, she wasn't sure either one of them was going to be very steady on their feet.

"It's ten yards to the end of the hall and the elevators," Bella said. "Randolph has a handful of guys at the other end, another twenty yards away. If we can make it to the corner before his men blow holes in us, then we have a fighting chance at living until the elevator doors open."

Gage lifted an eyebrow in disbelief. "Really? That's your plan?"

"Do you have a better one?"

He shook his head and his eyes fluttered shut.

He was dying. She was too late. Too weak to save him.

No! She shook her head to ward off those negative thoughts and patted his cheek roughly. "None of that. You have to stay awake. You're too damn heavy to carry."

Gage opened his eyes wide, but she could see he was losing the battle fast. If she didn't do something, he wasn't going to make it out of here alive.

She eased him into a rolling office chair and peeked down the hallway toward Randolph and his men. "Stynger wants me alive, right?" she yelled.

"Those are my orders."

"You let me put Gage on that elevator and she can have me. I won't resist."

"No!" Gage shouted. He tried to stand, but his feet fell out from under him and he sloshed back in the chair.

"Do we have a deal?" she asked Randolph.

"Sure. Why the hell not? He's probably not going to

survive anyway. And if he does, we'll just collect him later."

"No. You promise to leave him alone."

He let out an exasperated sigh. "Fine. I promise. I'll give you thirty seconds to load him up. After that, I'm having the men open fire. And if you try to go with him, I'll kill you myself."

Bella didn't hesitate. She grabbed Gage's chair and hauled ass for the elevators. With every step she half expected to have a hole blown in her back, but the bullet never came for her.

The elevator doors seemed to take forever to open. When they did, she could crawl inside the small space and hide.

Not going to happen, she reminded herself. If she tried to run, she was sure Randolph would make good on his threat to kill her.

"Ten more seconds," he called, sounding more than ready to pounce.

Finally, the bell dinged and the doors slid open. Gage tried to stop her from rolling him inside, but he was far too weak to fight her. She pushed the button for the surface, and prayed that Jordyn was still up there, close enough to wheel him to safety.

As the doors slid shut, Randolph stepped out, rifle pointed right at her. "Drop the weapon."

Fear scorched her veins, burning away all her oxygen. Gage wasn't free yet. He hadn't even had time to get more than a few yards away. She had to buy him more time.

With slow, methodical movements, she pulled the rifle strap over her head and laid the weapon on the ground.

"Kick it this way," Randolph ordered.

She did as he said, obeying quickly, as she always had with Dan. One of the guards nearby picked it up.

Randolph motioned to the pair of men standing behind her at the elevator doors. "Go after him. Bring him and the others back."

Fear blasted out of Bella. "You promised to leave him alone."

"I lied, you idiot. Now let's go. Stynger's waiting to open that pretty head of yours."

Chapter Forty-five

Victor, Payton and Adam took cover while they waited for the elevator doors to open. The code Jordyn had given them seemed to work, but there was no way to know if armed men might be waiting inside to ambush them.

The doors opened with a chime, revealing a bloody, limp Gage slumped on the floor in front of an office chair. His arm was extended as if he had been reaching for the control panel. Blood was smeared all over the stainless steel wall, indicating where his hand had slid down.

Victor rushed forward. Adam was at his side. They eased the man into the chair and rolled him outside.

The elevator doors started to close, but Payton's heavy bag of gear caught them before they did. "We can't wait. We have to go now, before they know we're here."

Bella was still down there. The fact that she hadn't been the one to bring Gage to the surface meant she was incapable of it. For all Victor knew, some of the blood in the elevator was hers.

For all he knew, she could already be dead.

Before that kind of thought could take hold, he shoved it aside and looked at Adam. "Take him back to the MCC. Call for a medic. Catch up with us if you can."

Adam picked up his brother and started to run. Victor stepped into the elevator car with Payton and let the doors close behind them as they descended into the belly of the beast.

If Randolph chose not to keep his word, that freed Bella of any guilt over breaking hers. She was no longer a willing captive; she was now a hostile. Very hostile.

Fear had carved out a summer home in her chest, settling in for a long stay. It didn't matter that she knew the drugs were the cause, she still felt every quivering second of the terror that radiated out of her.

She wanted to be strong again. Brave. She wanted the real Bella to come and save her from this phantom creature that had taken over her body.

"The doc said you'd be scared, but I didn't think the drugs would work this well. Poor little girl is about to piss her pants, isn't she?"

She ignored his jab and took a deep breath. Two. Finally some of the panic receded enough that she could control her trembling limbs.

Before she lost her nerve again, she grabbed the weapon out of Randolph's hands and opened fire in a wide arc. He was so surprised by her move, he was unable to stop her. He took a hit to his thigh and went down, screaming in rage and pain. Men dove for cover, scrambling to fire back.

She kept them pinned down with a steady stream of fire, while inching closer to Randolph.

He reached for his sidearm.

She moved behind him and settled the hot muzzle of her rifle against the back of his skull. "I will kill you," she promised, her voice vibrating with more fear than confidence.

"Hold your fire!" he shouted.

"Hands in the air," she ordered.

Randolph did as she asked. She bent down to relieve him of his pistol, but the move put her too close. She didn't see the danger until it was too late.

He grabbed her head and arm and used them to flip her. Her finger squeezed the trigger unintentionally, firing off a round into his neck.

She landed on her back, half in his lap. He screamed and held his throat, but she could tell by the power of the blood spray that it was too late. The bullet had severed some major blood vessel, and he was only seconds from bleeding out.

He knew it too.

With one of the last breaths he'd ever take, he yelled to the surrounding men, "Kill the bitch!"

Chapter Forty-six

Victor heard gunfire on the opposite side of the elevator doors. Part of him was elated, because if someone was shooting, that meant Bella was still alive enough to piss them off. The other part of him was terrified, because she might even now be taking the bullet that ended her life.

Payton hit a button on the screamer riding his belt. A high-pitched whine revved up until it was no longer audible.

The elevator doors slid open. Bella was covered in blood, tucked into a low crouch against a narrow indentation in the wall. Bullets dug chips out of the concrete near her head, coming from a horde of guards stationed at the end of the hall. She looked terrified and vulnerable—two things that didn't fit her well at all.

After less than a second, the gunfire stopped and men everywhere started to scream. Except the one lying in a pool of blood right outside the elevator doors. Randolph.

His scream had dimmed until it was only a weak puff of air. He struggled to regain his footing, but it was no use. The blood made everything slick, and he was too weak to support his own weight. He collapsed onto his side and went still, staring blindly in death.

Bella looked up in surprise. She saw Victor and Payton standing there, then pushed to her feet. She swayed, caught herself, but her balance was obviously precarious.

Someone had beaten her. Her face was a swollen, purple mass of bruises. Much of her long hair had been chopped off in back. What was left was caked with dried blood. Her entire body shook as though she was running on willpower alone. "I killed him. He's dead. But there's more. They're coming for us. We have to hide."

Victor rushed toward her and gathered her in his arms. "Let's get you out of here."

The armed guards at the end of the hall were still holding their heads, screaming. Some of them had passed out. Not one of them had the ability to hold a weapon anymore.

"Mira's gadgets work," Payton said.

A bald man in a lab coat scurried down the hall toward them, hands raised. "Don't shoot!"

"There are innocents down here," Payton said. "People Stynger is using to do her research."

"The screamer isn't working on him," Victor said, "so either he's immune, or he's not implanted."

"Not implanted," the man hurried to say. "I just want out, like all of you. Dr. Stynger is holding my family hostage. All I want is their safe return."

Victor kept an eye on him while Payton triggered the elevator doors to open. The second he did, a siren blared and the arrows over the doors began blinking red.

"She locked us down here," the man said. "But I know another way out."

Victor patted the man down, finding no weapons. He carried nothing bigger than a ballpoint pen in his pocket.

"This way."

Victor motioned for him to lead on. They passed through the now-unconscious mass of guards, moving south through the sterile hallways. Bella was unsteady on her feet, but gathered two weapons and extra ammo as she went. She was shaking so hard, he wasn't sure how she was going to use them.

"In here," said the bald man, holding the door open for them to pass.

Payton went in first. Victor brought up the rear, watching Bella for signs that she might topple. He took one more glance down the hallway before entering.

The room was large and empty. It had once been filled with tables and chairs, based on the marks on the tile. Wires hung from conduits overhead to bring power to whatever had once been here. Bright fluorescent lighting made the open, sterile surfaces glow with a yellow cast. There was a bank of file cabinets across the back wall, and behind that was a series of doors that appeared to lead to offices or storage of some kind.

"What was this room?" Victor asked.

"One of the labs. I used to work in here before Dr. Stynger started relocating everything. There's an emergency exit leading to the surface. We'll have to take about a million stairs, but we'll be able to get out this way."

Payton studied the bald man. "None of the other facilities we found had a secondary exit. Stynger likes to control people. Her MO is to have only one way in or out."

The man's bald head started to sweat. "I don't know anything about that. I started working for her about a year ago. This is the only place I've ever been. I've heard the others talk about the other labs, but never seen them myself." He pointed toward the leftmost door at the back of the room. "That's the stairway."

There was a faint buzz of a camera rotating overhead. Victor couldn't quite see it through the dark plastic covering, but there was no mistaking the sound. "We're being watched."

"We should go," Bella said, moving toward the exit. "I

don't like being down here. It's too open. We need to find a place to hide."

Payton frowned. "Something isn't right."

The bald man shifted nervously from one foot to the next. "You guys can stay down here if you want, but I'm leaving." He headed for the door he'd pointed out, following close on Bella's heels.

As soon as he was too far away for Victor to reach, every door at the back of the lab burst open. Half a dozen children filed out, followed closely by several armed men. At least three of them aimed their weapons at Bella.

She squeaked in fear and froze.

Victor didn't dare shoot—not with so many children to serve as accidental targets. He was certain that was exactly what the bad guys had counted on when sending the kids out first.

Stynger stepped out, holding the hand of a little girl. "Excellent work," she said to the bald man. "You may have your daughter back. I have what I want." She looked at Bella. "Set your weapons down and come with me, or I order these men to kill your friends."

Chapter Forty-seven

Bella froze in place. She'd been fighting the growing weight of fear for hours now. Ever since Randolph had gotten his hands on her, every second had been a battle not to curl up into a ball and hide until all the bad stuff went away. She'd stayed strong because Gage had needed her. She'd held it together because now Victor and Payton were trapped down here if they didn't find a way out. So were all those kids.

But the pressure was growing within her, pounding at her to just let go. Give up. If she stopped fighting, the fear would recede and she would be able to breathe again.

She knew it was the drugs talking, but that didn't make the frantic emotions any less real.

Bella glanced at Victor. He stood there, so strong and solid, as if nothing could so much as make him sway. He wasn't worried. He wasn't afraid. When she looked at him, she could almost remember what that felt like—to be completely confident and certain of victory.

The little girl Stynger had been holding hostage raced across the space to her father, hugging his leg.

"Are you okay?" the bald man asked her, stroking her fine blond hair.

She nodded her head and clung more tightly to him.

Victor took a step toward the pair. Every gun the bad guys held shifted its aim to him.

Payton turned up a dial on the screamer, but not a single man was fazed.

Stynger's bloodred mouth curled. "You think that technology is the only way I control my men?" she asked Payton. "While that's quick and easy for the muscle, there are far less invasive ways to keep the scientists in line. I wouldn't want my toys damaging those valuable brains, now would I?"

Now that Bella was looking past the weapons, she could see that not one of the men with the rifles seemed comfortable. They were shaking, sweating and swaying on their feet. Several of them kept their eyes on the kids, rather than on their targets.

Not one of them wanted to hurt anyone. Except, possibly, Stynger.

"Now, all of you are going to set your weapons down," Stynger said.

The compulsion to obey was so strong, Bella's fingers twitched to let go of her rifle. She had to grit her teeth and remember that she didn't have to do what this woman said. Did she?

"If you think we're going to just roll over," Payton said, "you're more of a crazy bitch than I remember."

Stynger dragged a tall boy in front of her, pulled a pistol from her lab coat pocket and shot Payton in the arm. He gasped in pain, but refused to lower his weapon.

"Put down your guns," she repeated with growing impatience.

Bella had never wanted to run and hide more in her life than she did right now. But the boy in front of Stynger needed her to stay here. Stay strong.

When no one did as Stynger ordered, she leveled the pistol at the kid's head.

One man let out a whimper of fear. "Please don't hurt him."

Stynger gripped the boy's neck tighter. "I won't if our guests here will lay down their weapons."

"You don't have to do this," Bella told the armed men. "I know what it's like to be afraid, to stand there shaking and immobile with fear. I know what it's like to feel helpless. Trapped. Alone." She caught each man's eye, praying they'd listen. "You're not alone. All of you want the same thing: Stynger defeated. Powerless. I can give that to you. Put down your weapons."

"She has my son," said a dark-haired man with trembling hands and tears in his eyes.

Another man spoke. "My whole family is being held by one of her goons. If she doesn't call him every day and tell him I'm cooperating, he'll kill them."

"My family, too," another man said.

"We can help," Victor said. "We have resources. We can find your families and protect them."

"We don't know where they are."

"Enough of this talk!" Stynger shouted. "Everyone here is smart enough to know that if I die, lots of other people die with me. Your only option is to do what you're told. Protect your families." She swung her furious gaze toward Bella. "You, put your weapons down."

Bella took the rifle sling from over her head before she realized she was blindly obeying. "Fuck you."

"You were trained to obey. Submit. You know you'll be happier if you do. It's so much easier if you simply do as you're told."

Bella panted through the urge to comply with the woman's command. Those feelings were just the drugs pumping through her system. Nothing more.

"She'll never stop," Bella said. "She tortured me when I was a child. She tried to destroy me. Even now, all these years later, she's still trying to destroy me. Once she gets her claws into your children, she'll never let go. None of them will truly be safe until she's dead."

"Kill me, and fifty people die before sunrise," Stynger warned.

Bella lifted her rifle, aiming for the small section of Stynger's head visible behind the kid's skull. "If you live, a lot more than fifty will die. Countless more will suffer. The world is a better place without you. And I'm going to make it happen."

She wanted to end this woman's life, to snuff it out. She wanted to try to steal back some of the years she'd lost. She wanted to find a way to make up for all those nights spent terrified and suffering.

"Don't, Bella." Victor's voice. Calm. Certain. "We need her alive."

Payton's warning from years ago rang in her ears. *You're never going to escape the person you were. You'll carry her with you for the rest of your days. Acceptance is your only option.*

She shook her head. She would not accept her weakness and fear. She would fight it every step of the way. "The world needs her dead. All I need is one clean shot."

Her hands trembled so hard, she wasn't sure she could make it.

"We need the knowledge that's in her head," Victor said. "Once we have her in custody, she'll tell us what we want to know. She'll tell us what she did so we can fix the people she hurt."

"I'll never tell you a thing," Stynger said. "I'll sit in your prison for the rest of my life, amused by the knowledge that you're all scrambling to undo a decades-long legacy. The people who work for me will continue their efforts. My work will live on long after I'm gone."

Bella looked at the men holding the weapons, surrounded by their kids. "Is that what you want? Is that the legacy you offer your children? Blind service to a heart-less bitch?"

Two of the men wavered. The muzzle of their rifles dropped in indecision.

The man whose son stood as a human shield in front of Stynger took a half step forward, solidifying his aim on Bella. "I can't let you take that shot—not while my son's life is at stake."

"She's right," another man said. "The only way Stynger will ever stop is if she's dead."

The man on the end spoke up. "You say that because your child is right here. My daughter is locked away somewhere in another state. I won't let her die just so these people can have their revenge."

Stynger looked at Bella. "This is what real power looks like. Not one of these people has as little to lose as you do. They have families, children. All you have is a company filled with people who only pretend to respect you. Now. Drop your weapon."

Her hand shook as she fought the urge to obey. It was so much easier to give in. Stop fighting.

"Steady, Bella," came Victor's calm voice, pulling her back from the edge.

She caught the boy's gaze. He was crying silently, as terrified as she was. "Tilt your head to the right just a little," she told him. "This will all be over soon."

Stynger grabbed him tighter, locking his body against her spindly one. "Do what she says and I'll shoot you myself."

Victor had been inching across the floor for a while. Bella saw now that he was slowly angling himself for a better shot.

The idea that he'd be the one to kill Stynger made her furious. This woman had ruined Bella's life. If anyone got to kill her, she did.

"On three," she told the kid.

"Bella," Victor said in a warning tone. "You don't have the shot."

"I do." She had to have it. She had to kill Stynger once and for all. That was the only way to escape all the fear and pain the bitch had caused.

"Stop him," Stynger said as soon as she saw that Victor was getting too close.

The father of the kid was no longer sure where to aim.

"One," Bella said, steadying her aim. She could be afraid all she wanted to later, but for right now, she needed to be solid. Strong. Brave.

"Don't!" shouted the father, aiming at her.

"Shoot her," Stynger ordered as she pressed her gun against the kid's head.

If Bella shot now, reflexes might squeeze Stynger's trigger finger and kill the boy.

"Bella," Payton said. "It's too risky."

"If she lives, that kid is as good as dead, anyway. He'll grow up in places like this, working for her against his will. Helping her do evil. He'll be afraid all the time, constantly fighting the need to cower."

The kid flinched and more tears streamed down his cheeks. She knew her words were cruel, but that didn't make them any less true. His father needed to understand that. Find another way to free his son rather than giving in.

"Two," Bella said.

Stynger shot the father a hard glare. "I will kill him while you watch."

"No, she won't," Bella said. "She's bluffing."

"I can't take that chance," the father said.

Bella made eye contact with the kid. "Move your head. I won't miss."

"I can't," the kid sobbed.

"You can. You will," Bella said. "The only choice Stynger has now is to shoot me or die."

Stynger did exactly what Bella was hoping she'd do:

She moved the weapon from the boy's temple back to Bella, freeing her to fire.

Bella pulled in a deep breath and let it out. Her hands were completely steady. There was no more fear. No more question.

She'd won. Beaten whatever drug Stynger had put in her system. She was herself again, strong and fearless the way she'd been born.

That's when she knew that she couldn't kill Stynger. If she did, she'd destroy every chance they had at learning the woman's secrets to undoing the damage she'd done.

Bella lowered her weapon.

Everything happened at once. Stynger aimed the gun at Bella and began to squeeze the trigger. The kid screamed and shoved himself away from Stynger wind-milling his scrawny arms in an effort to catch himself.

Victor charged in, plowing into Bella just as Stynger's gun went off. A series of bullets sprayed out from the weapon as she fired repeatedly. One grazed Bella's arm, but the rest hit Victor square in the back.

A wave of panic crashed against Bella, sucking her under the surface of it. She couldn't breathe. Couldn't think. Victor was hurt. Maybe dead.

All she could do was scream and cling to him.

Stynger kept firing as people everywhere ducked and cowered. Payton charged and grabbed her by the throat. More shots were fired, but Bella couldn't figure out where they'd gone.

There were more armed men in the room, but none of that mattered. She heard kids crying, men sobbing, but it was all irrelevant. The focus of her whole world was Victor and his breath wheezing in her ear.

She rolled him over in her arms, cradling him in her lap. His arm was bleeding badly. He was gasping for air. His clear eyes were wide, and she could see pain burning in them.

"You're okay," she chanted, over and over. "You have to be okay."

Blood began to slicken her hold on him. So much blood.

One of the men who'd been present came over. "I'm a doctor. Let me look at him."

She didn't want to let him go, but she didn't know what else to do.

The man stripped open Victor's vest. There was blood everywhere, but she couldn't tell if it was from his arm or something else. He felt around his back just as Victor sucked in a shallow, pained breath.

"His armor took the worst of it, but at least two of the shots got through."

"You okay?" Victor asked in a pained whisper.

"Save your breath," she told him. "I'm fine. So are you."

He had to be. She couldn't stand the idea of losing the man she loved.

As that thought settled in, driving away some of her panic, all hell broke loose. The doors to the lab opened, and about fifty armed soldiers poured in.

Norwood's men.

Things went fast after that. Bella sat back and let them take over. It was the quickest way to get Victor the medical care he needed.

She tried to go with him, but they said there were more serious casualties that needed transport first. She'd have to wait her turn.

She thought they were talking about Gage's condition until she realized that there was a congregation of men around the place she'd last seen Payton.

She shoved her way through the crowd to see several medics working on him. He was pale and bleeding profusely from a hit to his thigh and another to his shoulder. Stynger was lying beside him, her spindly neck bruised and obviously broken. Her head lay on her own shoulder, leaving her grotesquely deformed.

Behind an oxygen mask, Payton said, "You were right. The world is better off now. I should have done that years ago. I'm sorry."

Bella looked at the man she'd once thought of as a father. He seemed different now in his weakness.

Human.

She realized then that she'd held him to a higher standard. She'd expected him to be perfect. Infallible. Now, seeing him lying there, a broken man, she knew she was just as imperfect. Maybe worse.

She believed him when he said that he'd gotten involved with the Threshold Project in order to make the world a better place. Making kids faster, stronger, smarter ... those were all good things. She could see how someone like Stynger could convince others that science was a magic bullet curing all the world's ills. Someone like Payton could take children from sad, desperate lives and give them a fighting chance.

She knew that everything he'd done since abandoning the project had been done with the aim of fixing his mistakes, as well as those of others. But there were too many to fix. The ripples of their actions were far greater than one man could ever hope to calm. It was unfair of her to think he could work magic, just because he'd always seemed like such a magician to her. He'd swooped in and fixed all of her problems, saving her from a life behind bars for murder, giving her a career and a thriving business.

Bella took his hand in hers. "You did the best you could. That's all any of us can do."

And just like that, she forgave him for what he'd done to her all those years ago, just as she forgave Lila for the things she did in order to save her son.

With those burdens gone, Bella felt light. Strong. Ready to clean up the mess Stynger had left behind and start restoring broken lives.

If anyone knew how to make that happen, it was Bella.

"We have to move you now, sir," said one of the medics.

"Victor first," Payton croaked.

"He's already gone, sir, just like you said. The next chopper is yours."

Payton had insisted that Victor leave first? That was one more debt of gratitude she had to pay.

"Let's get you out of here and all sewed up," she said. "You and I have a lot of work to do to clean up the mess Stynger left behind."

"I promised you my resignation."

"You can shove that up your ass, mister. You're too young to retire and leave me to do all the work. I need you."

Payton squeezed her hand and nodded. "Yes, ma'am."

Chapter Forty-eight

Mother was dead.

Jordyn should have felt some kind of grief or loss at the news, but all she could find inside herself was a kind of numb sense of relief. There would be no more experiments. No more suffering. No more White Room.

Jordyn had never been a free woman before. She had no clue what to do first. The only thing she knew was she needed to see Gage and thank him for helping her escape.

He was sitting up in his hospital bed, looking far healthier than the last time she'd seen him. There was color to his complexion, and a brightness in his eyes that hadn't been there before.

He saw her hovering in the doorway and welcomed her in with a twitch of his fingers. "You're okay?" he asked.

"You're the one who got hurt. Not me. How are you?"

"Recovering." His eyes slid over her frame, resting for a second on her stomach. "You?"

"I'm healthy." She paused, uncertain of how to proceed. "We both are."

He nodded slowly. Some of the tension riding along his shoulders sloughed off. "What now?"

"I guess I'm going to find an apartment. Get a job. I've never had those things before. I'm not entirely sure if I have the proper credentials to do much of anything. Mother taught me everything I know, which makes it suspect."

"What do you want to do?"

"Help the people Mother hurt. I know her work. With the right facilities and supplies, I think I could develop a protocol to undo the damage she did."

"A cure?"

"It won't be as simple as a pill or anything, but yes. I think I can help cure them."

"That gives you clout."

She laughed at the thought of having any kind of power. "I've already had several offers of *help* from various authorities, and while I'm inclined to listen to their advice, I really don't want a bunch of people telling me what do to. I've had enough of that to last a lifetime."

"I understand." He sounded sad, almost dejected.

"You want me to get involved with them?" she asked, genuinely confused.

"Not them. Me."

She paused, trying to make sense of his words. It sounded like he wanted some kind of relationship with her, but that couldn't possibly be true. Not after what Mother did to him—basically raping him. "What do you mean?"

His mouth tightened for a second. His eyes closed. He looked like he was revving himself up for something, but she had no idea what it might be.

"I want to be there for you. And the baby. If you're keeping it."

She'd spent all of ten seconds considering her options, and there was only one possible path for her. "I am. But that in no way obligates you. I know this wasn't your idea. You didn't even get to have any fun making the child. I have no expectations around your involvement."

"Then you should start. Because I'm going to be involved."

She nodded, accepting his decision. A huge sense of relief fell over her, weakening her knees. "I don't know how to be a good mother," she admitted. "It'll be helpful for our child to have at least one parent who knows what he's doing."

"You could come live with me. Let me take care of you two."

The idea of being with this man thrilled her, but she knew better than to give in. "I need some time to live on my own. To be independent."

"Will you see me?" he asked.

"I don't know where you live or if my apartment will be close enough to see you."

He grinned. "No. Will you spend time with me? Date me?"

A thrill fluttered through her. "Oh. Yes. But just because I'm pregnant with your offspring doesn't mean we have to become romantically involved."

"You don't want that?" he asked, sounding hurt.

Jordyn didn't understand relationships with men beyond work. She knew that women sometimes played games and were secretive and coy, but she had no idea how to manage those things, so she settled for the truth. "I want that more than just about anything."

"Then it's settled. We'll date. See how it goes."

"What if you hate me?"

"I won't."

"What if I hate you?"

"I'll try harder. For our kid. He deserves two parents." He held out his hand to her.

She took it, letting him tug her close to the bed.

"Not close enough," he said, pulling harder on her hand until she had no choice but to climb up beside him.

He slid his arm around her and held her close against

his side. The warmth of his body sank into her, easing some of the fear she hadn't even realized she'd been carrying. Her whole life was ahead of her—this bright, shiny, terrifying new world. And it thrilled her.

His fingers stroked her arm, soothing her as if he knew how much she needed his touch. "Everything will be fine," he promised.

"How do you know?"

"Because we'll make it that way. Together."

That was the moment when Jordyn knew that he was right. Everything was going to be fine. There was no doubt in her mind that she could grow to love a man like Gage. She had no delusions that their road would be smooth or straight, but they were inextricably bound now, and while it wasn't her choice, she was glad that if she was bound to anyone, it was a man as honorable and good as Gage.

She had a family now—a real one. Maybe it didn't look like a normal one, but she, Gage and their child would make this bright, shiny, terrifying new world their own.

She squeezed his hand. "If you keep saying things like that, I'm going to fall in love with you."

He grinned and kissed the top of her head. "Good."

Chapter Forty-nine

Bella had been scared before, but never had the stakes been so high.

Victor's surgery had saved his life, but the bullets he'd taken for her had done a lot of damage. If not for his body armor, he would have been dead. She'd been wearing none, which meant that he'd saved her life yet again.

He'd been under anesthesia for hours, and had slipped into a coma shortly after they'd closed him up. He'd lost too much blood on the way to the hospital. If Payton hadn't given up his seat on the chopper, Victor wouldn't have made it this far.

It was one more debt she owed Payton.

The hospital staff had tried to shoo her away, but she refused to budge. She'd gone as far as showering and changing her bloody clothes, but those were all the concessions they had. She wasn't leaving until he was awake and asked her to leave.

His parents had rushed here, flying home early from a European vacation. They had stayed by his side for more than a day before leaving to find a hotel room so they could get a nap.

A flood of people called until she finally shut her phone off completely. More people sent flowers and cards. A few tried to stop by, but there was a contingent of Edge employees stationed outside the doors that kept them and their germs away.

Bella wasn't taking any more risks with Victor's life. He was far too precious for that.

She held his limp hand, wondering how she'd ever gotten by without him. She couldn't even picture her life without him now. When she tried, it was a bleak, desolate place where nothing made any sense. He was the first thing she thought about in the morning and the last thing she thought about when she closed her eyes. Her dreams were filled with him in between.

"It's time to wake up now," she told him for the hundredth time. "We have a mission to complete. All of Stynger's files were there in the lab. We know the names of everyone she's ever hurt. We have to find them now. Help them."

As usual, he lay still and unresponsive.

"She's dead, Victor. She's never going to hurt anyone ever again." She stroked his hand. "Everyone is really worried about you. They need you to wake up now." She felt her eyes sting with tears and had to bite her lip to fight them off. "I need you to wake up. What we had . . . it was more than just sex. More than being good partners at work. I think we'd make good partners, period." She stroked his hair away from his face. "I need you in my life. I *want* you there. No more fighting it. I love you, Victor."

His eyelids fluttered. His fingers tightened around hers.

Excitement rolled through her, driving her from her chair. "Victor? Can you hear me?"

He nodded, and moved his mouth like he was trying to speak. Nothing came out, so she poured him some water and lifted it to his lips.

He drank a few sips before letting his head fall back to the pillow.

"About damn time," he whispered.

"Time for what?"

"That you admit you love me." He pinned her with a clear blue gaze, and she could see her love returned. He loved her too. "Say it again."

"I love you," she admitted, letting the power of those words strengthen her resolve. She'd been afraid of those words for far too long. Saying them now set her free. They made her whole again.

"In that case, I quit," he said.

She eased back, hurt trickling in. "What? Why does everyone suddenly want to quit?"

"Your strict no-fraternization policy is a problem. So I quit. Because I plan on fraternizing with you a lot. As often as possible. For as long as you'll have me."

She grinned. "You're on. Once the stitches are out, we'll fraternize like bunnies. But I reject your resignation outright."

"What about your policy?"

"I'm changing it. Everyone breaks the fucking rule anyway. Might as well give up and do what all the cool kids are doing."

He pulled her down to sit on the edge of the bed. "My parents are going to hate you," he said with a grin.

"I've already met them. And for the record, they love me."

"Do they know you're always armed?"

"I already promised to show your dad my gun collection. He's going to be so jealous. Your mom said I could teach her how to shoot."

"You're lying," he said in disbelief.

"I am not. They'll be back in a few minutes and you can ask them yourself."

He let out a small laugh, shaking his head. "Of course you won them over. You win at everything you do."

"I do. And my sights are turned on you, Temple. I love you and plan to keep you, so get used to the idea."

"I'll consider myself warned. And for the record, I loved you first."

Bella laughed and snuggled up beside him, being careful of his wounds. She was sure now that he would recover fully. He was far too strong a man to do anything else. Especially with her taking care of him.

She didn't know where they were going from here or how they'd get there, but she knew without a doubt that they'd do it together. Forever.